THE DIXIE DUGAN TRILOGY

Books by J. P. McEvoy

Novels
Show Girl
Hollywood Girl
Denny and the Dumb Cluck
Mister Noodle
Society
Are You Listening?

Poetry
Slams of Life
The Sweet Dry and Dry

Nonfiction
Father Meets Son
Charlie Would Have Loved This

Children's Books
The Bam Bam Clock

J. P. McEvoy

THE DIXIE DUGAN TRILOGY

Show Girl • Hollywood Girl • Society

Edited and with an Introduction by
Steven Moore

TOUGH POETS PRESS
ARLINGTON, MASSACHUSETTS

Show Girl copyright © 1928; © renewed 1955 by J. P. McEvoy

Hollywood Girl copyright © 1929; © renewed 1956 by J. P. McEvoy

Society copyright © 1931; © renewed 1958 by J. P. McEvoy

The Dixie Dugan Trilogy copyright © 2024 by the Estate of J. P. McEvoy

Introduction copyright © 2024 by Steven Moore, abridged from "The Avant-Pop Novels of J. P. McEvoy," *Número Cinq* 8.3 (March 2017)

Cover art by John Streibel (1928)

ISBN 979-8-218-35367-4

Tough Poets Press
Arlington, Massachusetts 02476
U.S.A.

toughpoets.com

INTRODUCTION

The 1920s saw a surge in experimentation with the form of the novel. In *Ulysses* (1922), James Joyce used a different style for each chapter, including the play format for the notorious Nighttown episode. Jean Toomer's "composite novel" *Cane* (1923) consists of numerous vignettes alternating between prose, poetry, and drama. John Dos Passos in *Manhattan Transfer* (1925) abandoned traditional narrative for a collage of individual stories, newspaper clippings, song lyrics, and prose poems. Taking his cue from European Surrealists, Robert M. Coates likewise deployed newspaper clippings, along with footnotes, diagrams, and unusual typography, in *The Eater of Darkness* (1926). Djuna Barnes's novel *Ryder* (1929) includes a variety of genres—poems, plays, parables—and is written in a pastiche of antique prose styles. William Faulkner scrambled chronology and used four distinct narrative voices in *The Sound and the Fury* (1929), and later even added a narrative appendix. These were all serious novelists who disrupted nineteenth-century narrative form to reflect the discontinuities, upheavals, and fragmentation of the early twentieth century, a time when many new media emerged that would rival and in some quarters supplant the novel in cultural importance and popularity.

But literary historians have overlooked a novelist from the same decade who deployed these same formal innovations largely for comic rather than serious effect, adapting avant-garde techniques for mainstream readers instead of the literati. Between 1928 and 1932, J. P. McEvoy published six ingenious novels that unfold solely by way of letters, telegrams, newspaper articles, ads, telephone transcriptions, scripts, playbills, greeting card verses, interoffice memos, legal documents, monologues, song lyrics, and radio broadcasts. Ted Gioia described *Manhattan Transfer* as a scrapbook, which could describe McEvoy's novels as well, and in fact a reviewer of his first novel used that very term.[1] Given their concern with a variety of mostly new media (vaudeville, musicals, movies, newspapers, greeting cards, comic strips, radio) and their replication of the print forms of those media, they might better be described as multimedia novels. But perhaps the best, if anachronistic, category for McEvoy's novels is "avant-pop," that postmodern movement of the late 1980s/early 1990s which (per Brian McHale, quoting Larry McCaffery) "appropriates, recycles and repurposes the materials of popular mass-media culture, 'combin[ing] Pop Art's focus on consumer goods and mass media with the avant-garde's spirit of subversion and emphasis on radical formal innovation.'"[2]

Since McEvoy is all but unknown, a brief biographical sketch follows.

An orphan, Joseph Patrick McEvoy told the *Rockford Morning Star* later in life that he didn't "remember where he was born—but he has been told that it was New York City and that the year was 1894." Newspaper comic historian Alex Jay, who records that remark in a well-researched profile,[3] gives a number of possible birthdates ranging from 1894 to 1897, but McEvoy's birth certificate reads 21 December 1894 and confirms New York City as his place of birth. Possibly born Joseph Hilliek or Hillick, the boy was adopted by Patrick and Mary Anne McEvoy of New Burnside, Illinois. The same *Rockford Morning Star* piece reports him as saying "he didn't go to school—he was dragged. This went on for a number of years, during which time McEvoy grew stronger and stronger—until finally he couldn't be dragged any more. This was officially called the end of his education." In the contributors' notes to a 1937 periodical, he wrote (in third person): "While he was still a guest in his mother's house,

J. P. McEvoy started his writing career at the age of fifteen as Sporting editor of the *South Bend Sporting-Times*.[4] He later admitted (in first person), "I remember my first assignment as sports editor for the *News-Times* [sic] was to cover a baseball game. I was a descriptive writer. I became so interested in what was going on that I omitted the detail of scoring the game. I had to call *The Tribune* (a rival newspaper) to get the score."[5] In 1910 he enrolled at the University of Notre Dame, which he attended until 1912.

After graduating, he moved to Chicago and was hired as a cub reporter in the sports department of the *Record-Herald*. He began creating several comic strips there beginning in 1914, and moved on to the *Chicago Tribune* in 1916 for further strips before joining the P. F. Volland Company, which published books, postcards, and greeting cards. McEvoy published two illustrated books of sarcastic verse with Volland, both in 1919: *Slams of Life: With Malice for All, and Charity Toward None, Assembled in Rhyme*—with a postmodernish introduction in which McEvoy refers to himself in the third person as "his favorite author"—and *The Sweet Dry and Dry; or, See America Thirst!*, a mélange of poems and strips protesting the passing of the Eighteenth Amendment prohibiting the sale of alcohol. *Slams of Life* in particular trumpets the linguistic ingenuity that enlivens his later writings. The mostly comic poems are bursting with wordplay, slang, raffish rhymes, typographical tricks, and flamboyant diction. Many are quite literate, even erudite: "That's a Gift" namedrops the historians Taine, Gibbon, and Grote, while another ranges from "the Ghibelline and Guelph" to "Eddie Poe." The latter's "The Raven" is parodied in "A Chicago Night's Entertainment," and "Lines to a Cafeteria or Glom-Shop" is a takeoff on a canto from "Kid" Byron's *Don Juan*.[6] A poem with the baby-talk title "Bawp-Bawp-Bawp-Bawp-Pa!" acknowledges the ancient Greek orators "Who slung a mean syllable over the floor / Isaeus, Aeschines, Demosthenes, too," and McEvoy seems to have been au courant with the latest poetry and art as well, for another one is entitled "An Imagist Would Call This 'Pale Purple Question Descending a Staircase.'" He introduced Sinclair Lewis at a talk before the Booksellers' League in Chicago in 1921; reporting the event, *Publishers Weekly* identified McEvoy as the author of *Psalms of Life*, a sanctification of his *Slams* that probably amused him.[7]

McEvoy wasn't happy at Volland, despite his lavish General Manager's salary ($10,000 a year, equivalent to $175K today) and the prestige of being "the first writer of greeting-card sentiments to be admitted to the Author's League."[8] Until he resigned from there in 1922, McEvoy continued to write for the *Chicago Tribune*. It ran a serial of his called *The Potters* in 1921, illustrated by a friend he had made at Notre Dame named John H. Striebel (1891–1962), with whom he would later collaborate. *The Potters* was described as "a new weekly humorous satire in verse on married life in a big city" and was later turned into a successful play and published in book form in 1924.

By then McEvoy had left Chicago and was living in New York City, leaving behind both greeting cards and comic strips to write for the stage. First he wrote a revue called *The Comic Supplement* (1924), which was produced by Florenz Ziegfeld and starred W. C. Fields.[9] McEvoy wrote the original "Drug Store" sketch, one of Field's favorites and reprised in some of his later films. Ziegfeld forced unwanted changes on McEvoy's script, but later repented and invited him to begin writing for the Ziegfeld Follies. McEvoy co-wrote the 1925 production (with Fields, Will Rogers, Gus Weinberg, and Gene Buck), and continued to contribute skits and songs until 1926.

In 1926 he wrote a two-act revue entitled *Americana*,[10] a smart but zany show that Gershwin biographer Howard Pollack describes in terms that anticipate McEvoy's novels: "*Americana* . . . satirized American life, including an after-dinner speech at a Rotary Club and an awkward attempt by a father to talk to his son about sex; it also took aim at opera ('Cavalier Americana') as well as Shakespeare by way of [composer Sigmund] Romberg ('The Student Prince of Denmark'). Critics welcomed the show as refreshingly clever—a 'revue of ideas,' as the *Times* headline stated. . . ."[11] His other revues—*No Foolin'* (1926), *Allez Oop* (1927), and *New Americana* (1932)—were less successful but provided plenty of backstage material for his novels.

It was at the Ziegfeld Follies that McEvoy met the inspiration for his first novel. Louise Brooks (1906–1985) was a featured dancer in the 1925 edition, and caught the eye of Paramount Pictures producer Walter F. Wanger, who signed her to a five-year contract later that year. "Having watched Brooksie in the *Follies*," her biographer Barry Paris writes, "McEvoy was one of her ardent admirers, once describing her as looking 'like a naughty altar boy.'"[12] He thought the wild-living Brooks would make an attractive heroine for a comic novel, and after naming her "Dixie Dugan" began writing a fictional account of her madcap adventures in show biz. *Show Girl*—made up of letters, telegrams, newspaper clippings, and so forth—was serialized in *Liberty Magazine* from 14 January to 14 July 1928, illustrated by his Notre Dame classmate John Striebel, who modeled Dixie on Brooks, working from stills of the actress. It was published in book form by Simon & Schuster in July of the same year, and was an immediate success, going through six printings in three months for a total of 41,000 copies in print—not to mention hardcover reprints by two other U.S. publishers, two British editions, and a German translation (*Revue-Girl*, adapted by Arthur Rundt). *Show Girl* deals with Dixie's zigzagging path to success on Broadway; in its sequel, *Hollywood Girl*, Dixie travels out to Hollywood (as did Louise Brooks) for further risqué adventures. Like its predecessor, *Hollywood Girl* was first serialized in *Liberty* (22 June–28 September 1929), then published by Simon & Schuster in book form later in 1929. Both were quickly made into movies, *Show Girl* (1928) and *Show Girl in Hollywood* (1930); it was initially reported that Brooks would play Dixie, but she didn't get the part, possibly because she was under contract to another studio, though she had been loaned out before.[13] Both films starred Alice White instead, who resembled It girl Clara Bow rather than the vampy Brooks. Stills from the films were tipped into later printings of both novels, an early example of media synergy.

In 1929, McEvoy's former employer Florenz Ziegfeld, who appears as a character in *Show Girl*, produced a musical entitled *Glorifying the American Girl* with a script co-written by McEvoy, and then staged a musical version of the novel, on which Gershwin again collaborated.[14] The lamest but longest-lasting spin-off of *Show Girl* is the comic strip *Dixie Dugan*, which McEvoy and Striebel began in October 1929 and which ran until October 1966, long after both had died.[15] The show-biz premise was soon dropped for a series of light romantic adventures, and today the strip is held in low esteem by most comic book historians. As Jay notes, McEvoy appeared in the 17 October 1939 edition of the strip, metafictionally depicted arguing with Dixie over money made from the franchise. A forgotten movie version, also called *Dixie Dugan* and starring Lois Andrews, was released in 1943.

McEvoy followed *Hollywood Girl* with four more novels in the same multimedia format. *Denny and the Dumb Cluck* (Simon & Schuster, 1930) is about a greeting-card salesman named Denny Kerrigan, who was first introduced in *Show Girl* as a long-distance love interest of Dixie's. (The "dumb cluck" of the title is Denny's new girlfriend, Doris Miller.) His fourth novel, a satire of the comic-strip business entitled *Mister Noodle: An Extravaganza*, was serialized in the *Saturday Evening Post* from 15 November to 20 December 1930 (a little too elegantly illustrated by Arthur William Brown) and published in book form by Simon & Schuster in April 1931. In the fall of that year they also published *Society*—serialized as "Show Girl in Society" in *Liberty* between 30 May and 8 August, again illustrated by Striebel—which picks up the Dixie Dugan story where it left off at the end of *Hollywood Girl* and, after a satiric view of high society in both Europe and the U.S., brings her zany story to an end. McEvoy's final novel, *Are You Listening?*, was serialized in *Collier's Weekly* between 17 October and 12 December 1931 (illustrated by Harry L. Timmins) and quickly made into a movie with the same title before it was published in book form by Houghton Mifflin in August of 1932. McEvoy's last two novels apparently didn't sell well, for they are nearly impossible to find today.

He continued to work in movies and publishing throughout the 1930s and 1940s. He appears in the opening credits of the 1933 film *The Woman Accused* as one of the ten authors who wrote a chapter each of the serialized novella (in *Liberty*) from which the screenplay was adapted; he collaborated again with W. C. Fields on the latter's 1934 films *You're Telling Me!* and *It's a Gift*; wrote nonfiction accounts of his life in upper New York State; published a children's book called *The Bam Bam Clock* (Algonquin Publishing Co., illustrated by Johnny Gruelle); and he wrote a humorous advice column called "Father Meets Son" for the *Saturday Evening Post* (published in book form by Lippincott in 1937). He coauthored the screenplay for Shirley Temple's musical *Just around the Corner* (1938), along with an article on her ("Little Miss Miracle") in the 9 July 1938 issue of the *Saturday Evening Post*, which reproduces a photograph of the author sitting next to the ten-year-old actress. He wrote the book for *Stars in Your Eyes*, a 1939 Broadway revue starring Ethel Merman and Jimmy Durante (the latter had a cameo in McEvoy's first novel). Other notable magazine contributions include an interview with Clark Gable about *Gone with the Wind* in the 4 May 1940 issue of the *Saturday Evening Post* (there's a photo available of a tuxedoed McEvoy dancing with Gable's co-star Vivien Leigh), and a profile of Walter Howey, editor of William Randolph Hearst's *Boston American*, in the June 1948 issue of *Cosmopolitan*. He was famous enough to be featured in magazine ads for White Owl cigars, "just off the plane from Havana" (reproduced by Jay).

McEvoy spent the rest of his life contributing to *Reader's Digest* as a roving editor, travelling with his third wife, and entertaining a veritable who's who in America. Visitors to his large estate near Woodstock included members of the Algonquin Round Table, Frank Lloyd Wright, Clarence Darrow, Rube Goldberg, and avant-garde composer George Antheil. "One hectic weekend," a local newspaper reported (per Jay), "almost the entire membership of the American Society of Artists and Illustrators attended a fabulous weekend party." In 1956, McEvoy published his last book, *Charlie Would Have Loved This* (Duell, Sloan and Pearce), a collection of humorous articles. He died on 8 August 1958.

"Get hot!": The Dixie Dugan Trilogy
Warning: spoilers follow.

For most readers in 1928, *Show Girl* looked utterly unlike any novel they had ever seen. Preceding the title page is a teaser with some hype from the publisher's Inner Sanctum imprint,[16] and the title page itself is an elaborate cast list "In the order of their appearance," as in a theater program or the opening credits of a silent film. Each "performer" is followed by a saucy descriptive line, beginning with "Dixie Dugan: The hottest little wench that ever shook a scanty at a tired businessman." The novel proper begins with a dozen pages of letters—familiar enough from epistolary fiction—which are quickly followed by a cavalcade of telegrams, Western Union cablegrams, newspaper articles (in two columns and a different font) and letters to the editor, playlets in script form, police reports (IN SMALL CAPS), poems and greeting card verses, a detective agency log, various theater materials (ads, reviews, notices, house receipts), one-sided telephone conversations, a dramatization of a business convention, radiograms, even a House of Representatives session reprinted from the *Congressional Record*.

All of this narrative razzmatazz supports a screwball-comic Broadway success story that occurs over a six-month period in 1927. (Nearly every document is dated, from May 1st to October 22nd.) The first half of the novel tracks Dixie's hectic rise to notoriety. As this 18-year-old Brooklynite explains in a letter to her long-distance boyfriend Denny Kerrigan, she's hell-bent on joining the chorus line of the Ziegfeld Follies.[17] He, on the other hand, writes that he wants to "get married and get a little apartment in Chicago, and I'll come home to you every Saturday night after my week on the road selling mottoes and greeting cards in Indiana" (98).[18] Failing her Ziegfeld audition, Dixie instead becomes a specialty dancer at the Jollity Night Club, where she attracts the smoldering glances of "a tall, dark-haired, black-eyed tango dancer" named Alvarez Romano, who turns out to be the son of a Central American president. (She enjoys making out with him: "And when he kisses—well the kid goes sorta faint and dreamy and don't care-ish and can barely get through the front door and slam it shut.") She also attracts the attention of a 45-year-old Wall Street broker named Jack Milton,[19] who one night after the show invites Dixie and other dancers to a party with his Wall Street buddies. He gropes and mauls her, only to be interrupted by Romano, who stabs him.

The *New York Evening Tab* (i.e., the *New York Morning Telegraph*) turns it into a salacious scandal, and as a result Dixie is deluged with job offers, endorsement deals, and marriage proposals. The *Evening Tab* begins running Dixie's first-person life story, ghostwritten and completely fabricated by reporter Jimmy Doyle, whom Dixie describes as "cute as a little red wagon and writes beautiful and I think he's hot dog." Fairly literate (though he confuses Swinburne with Browning), he describes his "bogus autobiography" to a Hollywood friend as follows, in a representative example of McEvoy's jazzy style and his contempt for tabloid readers:

> Well, I'm still Dixie Dugan and my contribution to the Fine Arts is monastically entitled "Ten Thousand Sweet Legs." Boy, it's hot. With one hand I offer them sex and with the other I rap them smartly over the knuckles with a brass ruler and say "Mustn't touch. Burn-y, burn-y." Then I sling them a paragraph of old time religion and single standard and what will become of this young generation. (I hope nothing ever becomes of it. I like it just the way it is.) And then another paragraph like the proverbial flannel undershirt that is supposed to make you hot and drive you crazy, and presto! the uplifted forefinger, "But this is not what you should be interested in, children." And then a little Weltschmerz and then the old Sturm und Drang—a Sturm to the nose followed up with a Drang to the chin—the old one-two. So, as you may gather, this opus is the kind of love child that might result from an Atlantic City week-end party with the American Mercury and True Stories[20] occupying adjoining rooms. So much for literature!

Spying on Dixie one night outside the theatre of her new show, Jimmy sees Romano abduct Dixie (to take her back to "Costaragua" to marry her), abducts Dixie himself when their limousine crashes, and then convinces her to lay low while his newspaper milks her disappearance for weeks. The recovering Jack Milton hires detectives to find her, offers to underwrite a musical for Dixie, and enlists Jimmy to write the book and lyrics for it.

The second half of the novel documents the progress of the musical from its contentious beginning—Milton hires show-biz producers who rewrite Jimmy's script and bring in outside contributors[21]—to its disastrous out-of-town opening, to its eventual success after Jimmy takes charge and restores his original conception. Retitled *Get Your Girl*, the musical makes Dixie a star, and Jimmy realizes he loves Dixie as much as she does him: "Besides being cute and all that she's got a quick mind, a keen sense of humor and says just what she thinks," he writes to his Hollywood friend. "And she really thinks." Meanwhile, Dixie's three suitors come to different ends: she rejects the marriage proposal of her sugar daddy, Jack Milton. Denny Kerrigan, still pining for Dixie, makes a big splash at a greeting-card convention in Atlantic City (where he catches Dixie's show), and heads home with a promotion if not with the girl. On a darker note, Alvarez Romano returns to Costaragua to help his father lead a counterrevolution, is captured, and sentenced to death. He escapes, but all his fellow prisoners are slaughtered, as a two-page article from the *Evening Tab* reports in gruesome detail. McEvoy places that tragedy near but not at the conclusion of the novel in order not to spoil the happy ending: Dixie finds success and love, conveyed by some clever parodies of notable theater critics of the day (Percy Hammond, Alexander Woollcott, Alan Dale, Walter Winchell) and a flurry of giddy radiograms.

Aside from the novelty of its format, the most appealing aspect of *Show Girl* is its language. Often sounding like a risqué and snarky P. G. Wodehouse, McEvoy offers a fruity cocktail of slang and flapperspeak, most of it from Dixie herself. She slings words and phrases such as "into the merry-merry" (show biz), "a good skate" vs. "a wet smack" (a fun vs. dull person), "gazelles" and "gorillas" (young women and nightclub predators), "butter and eggers" (theater audiences), "ginny" (tipsy), "static" (unwanted advice), "goopher dust" (a legal loophole), "blue baby" (a dud play), "clucks" (dumb people), "crazy as a brass drummer," and exclamations like "Tie that one," "skillabootch," and "Get hot!" (encouragement shouted at a good dancer). Glib Jimmy Doyle has already been quoted, and throughout McEvoy inserts some clever song lyrics, parodies, and greeting-card verse; he even has Denny quote and praise a song from his own musical *Allez Oop*. There are times when the insider theater lingo becomes hermetic ("the old comedy mule stunt . . . an easy hit in the deuce spot . . . an unsubtle comedy team in 'one' with Yid humor and soprano straight . . . novelty perch turn in four . . . the choice groove next to shut"), but all the slang and shoptalk is a constant delight. One reviewer said "Five years from now *Show Girl* and *Hollywood Girl* will need a glossary."[22] Dixie agrees: she starts a diary in the latter for the benefit of her future biographers:

> I can refer them to you Diary and they can see for themselves I'm not handing them a lot of horsefeathers. I suppose too Diary we should keep posterity in mind because when they came across a word like horsefeathers and didn't know what it meant we should have it defined somewhere, so for the sake of posterity horsefeathers means a lot of cha-cha and cha-cha means what diaries are usually full of.

Dixie is the first of many independent, untraditional young women in McEvoy's novels. She is a self-proclaimed representative of "flaming youth" (a 1923 novel and silent movie), and in her declaration of independence to Jack Milton expresses, according to biographer Paris, "an underlying flapper philosophy that was never better articulated, in or out of Fitzgerald." At a time when most young woman wanted to get married as soon as possible, Dixie tells Denny, "I don't want to marry you or anybody else. . . . I'm young and full of the devil and want to stay that way for a while"—a sentiment that will be voiced by many of McEvoy's young heroines. Sometimes she sounds surprisingly 21st-century: "The real ambition of our young generation . . . is to be cool but look hot."

In *Show Girl* McEvoy introduces other themes that will run through all of his novels, dark undercurrents beneath their playful surfaces. His contempt for the general public has already been noted in Jimmy's condescending remarks on his newspaper readers, an attitude that McEvoy will later extend to theater audiences, greeting-card customers, comic-strip fans, and radio listeners. When

Jimmy meets with the Broadway producers who want to dumb down his play, we get this exchange:

> DOYLE (*bitterly*): I suppose if you got "Romeo and Juliet" you wouldn't produce it unless you could buy a balcony cheap.
> EPPUS: "Romeo and Juliet"? Pfui! I seen that once. There wasn't a hundred dollars in the house.
> KIBBITZER: That kind of play don't make money. You got to stick to things people understand.

Kibbitzer later makes a pass at Dixie, and sexual predation in show business is another recurring theme. Dixie breezily dismisses that incident—"Well, that's what a female gets for having Deese, Dem and Doze"—but along with her earlier sexual assault at Jack Milton's party and the lascivious advances of club "gorillas," McEvoy dramatizes how dangerous show biz is for "gazelles" like her.

The mendacity of the media is mostly played for laughs here, with the joke on the dumb clucks who take celebrity gossip as gospel and actually believe the "sediments" expressed in greeting cards, but corruption is handled more seriously. When the police arrive at Milton's wild party and arrest Alvarez, Dixie notes that one of the guests, "Wilkins his name was, a big politician I found out later—got the cops off to one corner and gave them some sort of song and dance" that keeps their names out of the papers the next day. Near the end, Alvarez's father travels to New York and promises Milton the oil concession in Costaragua in exchange for financing his revolt; Milton gets a few of his Wall Street pals together and decides "that would be the patriotic American thing to do. Our country may she always be right," Dixie remembers him saying, "but right or wrong we've got to have oil." Milton enlists an Alabama congressman named Fibbledibber to convince his fellow representatives via patriotic rhetoric that America's honor depends upon &c &c &c, and sure enough Congress authorizes the Marines to intervene in the Central

American country. These darker elements add depths to what would otherwise be a light entertainment—depths that were drained by the producers of the 1928 movie version (no doubt of the same mindset as Kibbitzer & Eppus), according to those who have seen it. The novel is dark and daring, like Louise Brooks; the movie is blonde and harmless, like Alice White.

Show Girl's reviews were as boffo as those for Dixie's performance in *Get Your Girl*. Marian Storm quite rightly praised it as "a show-case of language. Whirling, whizzing, dizzying—a bombardment upon eye and ear of monotonous, accurate, faithful ugliness, of snappy similes." Proposing a new criteria for judging literature, the *Springfield Republican* said, "If making 'whoopee' is one of the aims of literary art, Mr. McEvoy has scored a literary success." Ziegfeld himself called it "The Comedy Bible of the Follies" and reviewed it for the *Saturday Review of Literature*—despite appearing in *Show Girl* as a character!—and described it as "show business 'hoked up' to the saturation point.... The action races by and every typographical ingenuity is used to emphasize and amplify the 'punch stuff'"—slinging slang as deftly as Dixie, but perhaps not entirely comfortable with seeing his profession mocked.[23] Edward Hope's review in the *New York Herald-Tribune* was so rapturous that Simon & Schuster printed the entire thing on the dust-jacket flaps of later printings. The great cartoonist/inventor Rube Goldberg said, "*Show Girl* is a riot. Am getting to be a bore among my friends talking about it. Every once in a while I think of a passage from the book and burst out laughing right in the street." Walter Winchell described it as "incessantly hilarious," and the aforementioned Walter Wanger told McEvoy, "If Dreiser contributed *An American Tragedy*, you certainly have contributed the American Comedy. *Show Girl* is the first authentic record of life along the Main Stem. I am sure it will go down in history as such."[24]

Published a little over a year later, *Hollywood Girl* is one of the first and still best satires of Hollywood—a clichéd subject today but a novelty in 1929, when the industry was still young and making the transition from silent films to talkies. It begins seven months after the conclusion of *Show Girl*, and ends a year later (i.e., May 1928–April 1929), and features a similar story arc. *Get Your Girl* having run its course, Dixie is back in Brooklyn looking for work while Jimmy tries to write a new star vehicle for her, vowing to marry Dixie as soon as it is staged. When Dixie learns that flamboyant movie director Fritz Buelow[25] is in New York casting his next epic—*Sinning Lovers*, based on "The Charge of the Light Brigade"[26]—and is "hot for a jazz-mad baby that could make yip yip and faw down in a new squeakie," as Dixie puts it, she finagles an interview and passes a screen test, on the basis of which she's given a tentative contract and sent to Hollywood. She gets only bit parts at first, and then none at all, and learns the studio will not be renewing her contract.

At this low point, nearly halfway through the novel, Dixie delivers an emotional, 18-page interior monologue modeled on Molly Bloom's in *Ulysses*, at the end of which Jimmy calls her and vows to help. (He too is now in Hollywood as a screenwriter.) He feels a publicity party is what she needs to attract work, which results in a remarkable chapter entitled "Hollywood Party: *A Talking, Singing, Dancing Picture with Sound Effects*," another 18-page tour de force that ends with the suicide of an "aging" actress. ("I'm thirty two," she tells Dixie, "and in this business if you're [a woman] over thirty you're older than God.") While the party rages, Dixie goes off with Buelow to another party and is nearly raped. All this Sturm und Drang is heightened by troubling rumors that a Wall Street syndicate of bankers, including Dixie's old admirer Jack Milton, will be merging the major studios, eliminating jobs, and moving the whole business back east.

At about the same structural point in *Show Girl* where Jack regains control of his musical, Dixie learns she has been given the lead in *Sinning Lovers*, once again thanks to Jack Milton. (Ironically, the studio had decided to give the role to the aging actress the same night she committed suicide.) Dixie is tempted to accept Milton's marriage proposal after she and Jimmy have the last in a series of fights, but after the preview version of the movie flops, she drops him because he wants to give up on the film (and on her career). She is shocked at his philistine views: "Jack says so far as the bankers are concerned if it doesn't make money it's not a good picture and I says what about *Caligari*[27] and he says I never saw it and from all I've heard of it I never want to see it. . . ." Fortunately, another producer and director step in, save the film (retitled *Loving Sinners* under pressure from the censorious Hays office), and the movie makes Dixie a star, as attested by another raft of rave notices—more real-life reviewers, this time representing Los Angeles.

But this is where the novel takes a surprising turn. Unexpectedly, Jimmy Doyle is *not* called in to save the screenplay, make up with Dixie, and marry her at the end. Instead McEvoy lets fame and riches go to her head: Dixie starts hanging out with silly rich people, indulges in trivial pursuits, and only two weeks after meeting Teddy Page, a "New York millionaire sportsman and young society aviation enthusiast," she elopes with him in Las Vegas.[28] She's aware he's a binge-drinking, hell-raising skirt-chaser, but she's convinced she can change him. "It's only because he hasn't met the right kind of girl." (Cue reader's rolling eyes.) The penultimate page of the novel featured a tipped-in wedding photo of the couple (with a dead ringer for Louise Brooks as Dixie), followed by an announcement in the *New York Times* that Page's wealthy family has cut ties with him.[29] This unexpected ending is a daring subversion of the wedding bells convention typical of most romantic books and movies, but *Hollywood Girl* is not a typical novel.

In addition to all the narrative bells and whistles of *Show Girl*, the sequel sports a publicity release, cast lists and shooting schedules, the morality clause from an actor's contract, interoffice memos, six drafts of the opening sentences of a letter, screenplays (complete with camera directions), a full-page ad in *Variety*, and some unpunctuated, modernist-looking dialogue. Plus there's a parody of Edgar Guest (reminiscent of the poems in *The Sweet Dry and Dry*) and that Joycean monologue. Dixie starts and abandons a diary, which feels like a narrative crutch on McEvoy's part, but Dixie is so entertaining that it would be churlish to complain. There's another slew of slang: "maddizell," "laying down a few flat arches" (dancing), "belchers" (talking pictures), "dog house" (a bass violin), "sitzplatz" (sitting place=ass), and "Hot cat!" (expressing excitement). Jimmy is as glib as ever, as when he is asked by a reporter for his first impression of Hollywood: "Offhand, it looks a little bit like Keokuk [in Iowa] on a Sunday afternoon, except that the houses and vegetation seem to have been retouched by one of those disappointed virgins who go in for painting china." But he can't top Dixie on the difference between the Big Apple and the Windy City: "New York is a jazz-band playing diga-diga-doo but Chicago is just a big megaphone with an overgrown boy hollering through it: Look at me, ain't I big for my age."

Like the first novel, there are a few celebrity cameos, including Dixie's counterparts Louise Brooks and Alice White, aptly enough, and Aimee Semple McPherson via the radio airwaves. Von Stroheim is seen working with Gloria Swanson on *Queen Kelly*, a production as costly and strife-ridden as *Sinning Lovers*, and fans of pre-Code Hollywood will revel in all the namedropping, tech talk (UFA angles, lap dissolves), and insider dope.

Sexual predation is even more prominent here than in McEvoy's first novel, and creepier: *Show Girl* is PG-13, *Hollywood Girl* R-rated. Director Buelow is a letch who indulges in Trump/Bush "locker room banter" and seduces the *Evening Tab* reporter who interviews him near the beginning of the novel (and who begins dating Jimmy at the end, when he returns to his job there), and plans to do the same with Dixie. (First, she has to fend off his manager with a joke about pedophilia.) Warned by Jimmy that Buelow "was on the make for me," Dixie tells her diary "of course he's on the make and what of it, all men are, only some are sneaky and don't admit it. . . ." Jimmy tells her she will have to put out to be put in Buelow's movie, which causes their first spat, but Dixie sees plenty of that after she's been in Hollywood a few months. She keeps saying no to all the men who hit on her, including Jimmy's Hollywood correspondent, unlike those who say yes: "that's how you get along say yes talk about yes-men you never hear of the yes-girls but they're the ones with the Minerva cars and three kinds of fur coats I guess I could get there too if I said yes . . . ."[30] The novel is frank about the sex appeal of movies. The aging star says of the latest starlets,

> they've got one thing I haven't got—youth. They've got young necks and young legs and young eyes. And nice slim, soft young bodies. And you can't fool the camera when it comes to those things. And that's what they want out here in this business. Youth. Young flesh. And they feed it into the machine and out comes thousands of feet of young eyes and young legs and young bodies. Reels and reels of it. And that's what people want to see. Men go there and watch them hungrily all evening and then go home and close their eyes when they kiss their wives.

McEvoy would have used a different verb than "kiss" if he thought he could get away with it. A month later Dixie is almost raped by Buelow, and after her success she speaks of budding actresses in terms of prostitution:

> Hardfaced mothers from all over the country dragging their little girls around to studios ready to sell them out to anyone from an assistant director to a property man just to make a little money off them. Agents with young girls tied up under long term con-

tracts at a hundred a week leasing them to studios for ten times that and pocketing the difference. Hundreds of pretty kids from small towns, nice family girls, church girls, even society pets going broke and desperate, waiting tables, selling notions, peddling box lunches on the street corners—I could tell you stories that would curl your hair.

Passages like this are what make *Hollywood Girl* closer in tone and intent to *Caligari* than *Singin' in the Rain*.

These intimations on immorality in show biz perhaps account for the curious number of biblical allusions in the novel, beginning on the first page, when Dixie blithely answers an imaginary interlocutor: "Where've you been? On Broadway, sez I. Where on Broadway, sez you. Up and down, sez I—up and down, between Forty-eighth and Forty-second, looking for a job"—the final word punning on the source of Dixie's diction, Job 1:7: "And the Lord said unto Satan, Whence comest thou? Then Satan answered the Lord, and said, From going to and fro in the earth, and from walking up and down in it." Over the next few pages there are allusions to the twelve apostles, Jonah and the whale, the book of Genesis, Noah's ark, and the Four Horsemen of the Apocalypse. Though based on Tennyson's poem, *Sinning Lovers* inexplicably begins with the Garden of Eden (with Dixie in Eve's role), and when Dixie resignedly decides to marry Milton, she says, "sometimes I feel like that bimbo in the Bible who sold out for a mess of pottage" (cf. Gen. 25:29–34; "bimbo" is used of men and women in the novel). The most sustained biblical allusion is the radio broadcast Dixie and Jimmy endure while in a restaurant: from L.A.'s Angelus Temple Aimee Semple McPherson delivers a hokey sermon on Daniel in the lion's den, spread over four pages in small caps, exhorting her listeners to tune out "all the jazz bands and the frivolous things of this world" and to sing along with her (to the tune of "Yes Sir, She's My Baby"):

Yes sir here's salvation
No sir don't mean maybe
Yes sir here's salvation now
Goodbye sin and sorrow
Welcome bright tomorrow
For we've got salvation now

This is too ludicrous to take seriously, and though Dixie occasionally refers to herself in terms such as "a devil on wheels," she is hardly Satan, much less Eve, Esau, or Daniel, and her thoughtless elopement at the end makes a mockery of finding salvation. Nor is McEvoy calling for readers to renounce "the frivolous things of this world" like Broadway musicals and Hollywood epics; for his purposes, the Bible is no longer a moral guidebook but a source of wisecracks, but the recurring biblical references add one more unexpected level to the novel.

As with *Show Girl*, the reviewers ignored the dark depths and stayed at the bright surface of the novel, which they found a little dimmer than its predecessor. "The book is amusing, filled with Hollywood madness and Hollywood slang," said the *New York Times*, "but it lacks the easy, hilarious fun of 'Show Girl.'"[31] not considering the possibility that McEvoy was aiming at something more than "easy, hilarious fun."

Two years later, McEvoy concluded Dixie's sassy saga with *Society*, which picks up the same day *Hollywood Girl* left off.[32] The first half of the novel documents the first few months of Dixie and Teddy's impulsive marriage: honeymooning down in Mexico and then up in Monterey, Teddy continues drinking and chasing after women, which soon drives Dixie to Hollywood to resume her career. But they make up, and Dixie begins learning more of Teddy's rich family: his 18-year-old sister Serena, whom he calls "a wet smack and dumb as a duck," who is preparing to make her debutante debut that fall; his 16-year-old sister Patricia, a hellion already wearing heels who has seen Dixie's film and runs away from private school to pursue a similar career in Hollywood; and Teddy's predictably stuffy mother and father; in order to trace his daughter, the latter hires the same Open Eye Detective Agency that searched for Dixie in *Show Girl*. Mr. and Mrs. Teddy Page, as they are called—Dixie loses much of her independent identity after she marries: "Teddy is my career now"—then sail to France to continue their honeymoon, but during the crossing Teddy lusts after an Apache dancer called Le Megot—"cigarette butt or a snipe," as Dixie translates, and described as "one of the sexist little devils I ever saw with a wild shock of hair, a slim lazy body, big black eyes and a red mouth that must drive men crazy." Upon arrival in France, Dixie sends a telegram wittily announcing "LAFAYETTE I AM HERE," but no sooner is the honeymooning couple settled in Paris than Teddy sneaks off to London "on business" to catch Le Megot's act at the Kit Kat Club. Meanwhile, Dixie is escorted around Paris by an Italian gigolo who had tried to seduce her during the ocean crossing. After another big fight—Dixie throws "a complete set of Victor Hugo at [Teddy], all of which he managed to dodge with the exception of Volume II of 'Les Miserables'"—they make up and head down to the Riviera.

At that point, halfway through novel, the plot takes a metafictional turn: we learn that Jimmy Doyle is in Paris, working for Colossal Pictures again and "gathering material for a high society movie." Excited to learn that Dixie is also in France, he telegraphs his producer with a revised idea: "COULD COMBINE EUROPEAN ANGLE SOCIETY AND DIXIES POPULARITY" [sic]—which sounds like a note McEvoy made to himself after finishing *Hollywood Girl*. Dixie continues to party with the idle rich and tells Jimmy she's having fun, or "fun in a way. But it's no pleasure—if you know what I mean. We're all so bored—Teddy's friends and their friends—

and they work so hard to be amused—and nothing really makes 'em really laugh—only when they're full of champagne and are their real selves but don't know it." Dixie is excited to learn she's pregnant, but just then Teddy gets involved in a sex scandal and both have to sneak back to New York. As the Page family prepares for Serena's obscenely expensive coming out ball at the Ritz-Carleton on Thanksgiving Eve ($50K, nearly a million dollars today), Patricia reconnects with the young communist radical she had met while en route to Hollywood, and attends a rally in Bryant Park at which he speaks the night of Serena's ball. Learning the cost of the ball, her Red beloved leads a protest march to the Ritz, which is broken up by the police—or as the headline in the communist *Daily Worker* puts it:

TAMMANY COSSACKS DEFEND SACRED RITZ
FROM CONTAMINATION BY STARVING WORKERS
THOUSANDS OF DOLLARS FOR ORCHIDS
WHILE MILLIONS CRY FOR BREAD.

Early the next year, Jimmy returns from France, manuscript completed, and tracks Dixie down in Palm Beach, where she is drinking to excess, experiencing cramps, and having doubts about becoming a mother: "I'm so tired of this silly empty life and realize the baby is going to tie me down tighter than ever." On the next page we read a news account of an explosion on a yacht, in which Dixie was seriously injured. When she learns she has lost the fetus, she declares herself through with it all. Her decent father-in-law arranges a quickie Mexican divorce (and a generous stipend for life), and Dixie agrees to star in Jimmy's movie *Society Girl*, "A Sensational Expose of the Haut Monde At Play" as a full-page ad on the penultimate page describes it. The movie is a "smashing hit" (with more fake quotes from real reviewers of the time), and Dixie and Jimmy decide to rest by sailing together for France. Meanwhile, Teddy is already on to his next showgirl, who Walter Winchell informs us (in a tidbit from his column) is "the third gel from the left in Earl Carroll's Fannyties."[33]

Though *Society* lacks the hellzapoppin' energy and jazzy lingo of its predecessors—which in fact would be inappropriate for the leisurely pursuits of the rich and fatuous—the novel is more ingenious than the average satire of high society due, once again, to the novelty of its materials. The title page resembles a formal invitation, set in a Copperplate font and even blind-stamped. In addition to the usual letters, telegrams, playlets, and news clippings, we're treated to Dixie's ocean crossing diary, shipboard schedules and announcements, formal invitations and cards of introduction, menus, invoices, legal documents, a Junior League report by Serena on "A Trip through a Biscuit Factory," and best of all, several chapters from *The Memoirs of Patricia Page (To Be Opened Fifty Years After Her Decease)*, an amusingly self-dramatizing, misspelt account of the 16-year-old's runaway adventure. There are self-conscious narrative winks from McEvoy, as when the stage direction in one playlet describes the head of the Open Eye Detective Agency as "one of those fiction detectives who can only be found in real life," and when Jimmy remarks on the coincidence of booking a hotel room next to Dixie's: "If a fellow wrote that in a book they'd say he certainly had to reach for that one." As Jimmy adapts his film plans to fit Dixie's life, and even asks her to supply background material on debutantes (which she does in snarky fashion), it becomes obvious that his *Society Girl* is a metafictional mirror image of McEvoy's *Society*, a film of the novel/novel of the film.

The darker themes in the first two novels are lighter here: sexual predation takes the forms of handsy gigolos and rampant adultery. As early as the third page Dixie reports that one of Teddy's rich friends "went right on the make for me—didn't seem to mind I was on my honeymoon. Teddy didn't either. Seemed flattered if anything." A dozen pages later he shacks up with his ex-fiancée, and his tomcatting ways result in the suicide of one betrayed husband. Prostitution imagery is used both for debutantes—their coming out balls are sales displays for the marriage market—and for "society girls who are poor as church mice and yet have to keep up a swank front and be seen everywhere in the swellest clothes and what they won't do to get by would put a Follies girl's gold digging into the 'come into the drug store with me while I get some powder' class." Patricia's communist friend reprises Alvarez Romano's role in *Show Girl* to introduce political elements in the novel, railing against the decadence of capitalist society in America and aristocratic privilege abroad, which McEvoy records in garish detail.

He also slips homosexuality into the novel. In a brilliantly rendered playlet set in a Paris nightclub called Le Fétiche, two Harvard boys "doing post-graduate field work in abnormal psychology" marvel at the lesbians. "A rosy-cheeked, bright-eyed contralto in tweeds" sings three new stanzas of Cole Porter's "Let's Do It, Let's Fall in Love," another opportunity for McEvoy to show off his gift for parody. This scene is followed by a letter from a *Variety* reporter describing the sights to be seen on the way south to the Riviera, including "a little hideaway tucked between [San Rafael and Toulon], entirely populated by the most delightful pixies, male and female, but you'll never find it unless you meet one of three people, names enclosed here in sealed envelope. They'll take you there if they like you." In a trilogy about show business, it's about time McEvoy mentioned the gay element, though it was a daring move for a commercial novelist in 1931.

Though Dixie takes up with high society, she's never taken in by it. She mocks as she learns "society patter" and affected enunciation, yet can still deliver snappy similes such as "he closed up like Trenton on a Sunday night" (i.e., stopped talking). As she occasionally reminds people, she's still just an Irish "punk" from Brooklyn, and despite a number of poor choices throughout the novel, she retains her best qualities. Teddy's father praises her "spirit and independence in refusing alimony or settlement," and the news item that concludes the novel indicates she's single: she has reunited with the love of her life from *Show Girl*, but she hasn't married him. Perhaps McEvoy merely wanted to leave the door open for another sequel, but it's more likely that he intended Dixie to follow in the dance steps of his original model, Louise Brooks, who except for two very brief marriages spent most of her life single.[34] (We can only hope that Dixie didn't wind up like our Miss Brooks did.)

Society is blander than its predecessors, but together the Dixie Dugan trilogy is an endlessly inventive portrayal of female independence as well as a damning indictment of show business, politics, sexual attitudes, and society at large. "To those who have followed him since 'Show Girl,' Mr. McEvoy has always meant humor and bite," wrote the *Saturday Review of Literature of Society*. "The ridiculous and the sharply ironical were always blended," and though the reviewer felt "the irony has wilted and the humor become worn" in the third novel, it's that blend of humor and bite, of ridicule and irony—shaken and stirred with linguistic and formal ingenuity—that makes the trilogy as a whole a mordant, madcap masterpiece.

Notes:

1. "*Manhattan Transfer*: The American Novel as Scrapbook," http://www.fractiousfiction.com/manhattan_transfer.html. T. S. Matthews, *New Republic*, 25 July 1928, 259. The most famous predecessor for the "scrapbook" novel is Bram Stoker's *Dracula* (1897).

2. *The Cambridge Introduction to Postmodernism* (New York: Cambridge University Press, 2015), 83.

3. "Ink-Slinger Profiles: J. P. McEvoy," <http://strippersguide.blogspot.de/2015/06/ink-slinger-profiles-by-alex-jay-jp.html>, posted 8 June 2015. This treasure trove of research is the source for many of the biographical details that follow.

4. *North American Review* 244.1 (Autumn 1937): 206.

5. Quoted in Ray Banta, *Indiana's Laughmakers: The Story of over 400 Hoosiers* (Indianapolis: PennUltimate Press, 1990), 115.

6. *The Sweet Dry and Dry* includes a parody entitled "The Boobyiat of O Howdri Iam."

7. "Lewis Talks to Chicago League," *Publishers Weekly*, 19 March 1921, 914.

8. James Curtis, *W. C. Fields: A Biography* (New York: Knopf, 2003), 157.

9. For details, see Curtis (157–64) and especially chapter 23 of Simon Louvish's *Man on the Flying Trapeze: The Life and Times of W. C. Fields* (London: Faber and Faber, 1997). Louvish says they had a lot in common, physically and temperamentally, and concludes, "McEvoy's influence on Bill Fields was profound and long-lasting" (254). They appear together in a photograph on p. 255.

10. It was registered with the Library of Congress as *Americana: A Novel Revue*—an inadvertent (or not) pun setting the stage for the revue-like novels McEvoy would soon write.

11. *George Gershwin: His Life and Work* (Berkeley: University of California Press, 2006), 377. Gershwin wrote a song for the show ("That Lost Barber Shop Chord"). McEvoy was assisted by Morrie Ryskind and Phil Charig, and worked with composers Con Conrad and Henry Souvaine on the score. Conrad (1891–1938) writes the music for the musical in McEvoy's first novel.

12. *Louise Brooks* (New York: Knopf, 1989), 204.

13. Later in 1928, Ziegfeld invited her to play Dixie in a stage version of *Show Girl*, but she turned him down to play the immortal Lulu in *Pandora's Box*.

14. See Pollack 451–61 for a detailed account of the musical, who notes that the script "lost much of the charm of the original novel" (453). Ethan Mordden agrees: "Very little of McEvoy's satirical view of how scandal and crime sell fame came through" (*Ziegfeld: The Man Who Invented Show Business* [New York: St. Martin's Press, 2008], 268).

15. Jay records McEvoy's remark that he stopped writing the strip around 1936 and turned it over to his son Denny and Striebel. See the feature story on the origins of the strip in *Modern Mechanix*, April 1937, 57, 143–44.

16. "*Show Girl* was what *The Inner Sanctum* calls a Life Saver. Part of it showed up on a gray afternoon and promptly ran away with the working day of our staff. It was read and accepted in twenty-four hours. Laughter is an irresistible salesman. [¶] A number of other customers fell in line. *Liberty* laughed

and bought *Show Girl* for serial publication. First National is filming it and a musical comedy is in the offing."

17. Her age is given in the radio bulletin on page 84 of *Show Girl*, which also informs us she is five feet two inches tall and weighs 110 pounds—Louise Brooks's stats.

18. Barry Shank offers some informed observations on Denny and his profession in *A Token of My Affections: Greeting Cards and American Business Culture* (New York: Columbia University Press, 2004), 148–51, one of the only treatments of McEvoy in recent criticism (though he gets some plot details wrong). Of McEvoy's *Slams of Life*, Shank writes, "As an attempt at satire, the book fails to sustain a critical viewpoint. But it functions quite well as a document of the cheap cynicism that seemed to haunt those who produced culture on demand for commercial purposes in the first half of the twentieth century" (147).

19. His formal name John Milton is given a few times; apparently McEvoy liked the idea of naming a horny Wall Street broker after the Puritan poet.

20. *American Mercury* was the leading literary journal in the 1920s; *True Story* [sic] featured sleazy "sin-suffer-repent" confessions by women (often male ghostwriters).

21. Real-life Broadway veterans Con Conrad (music), Sammy Lee (choreography), Herman Rosse (scenic design), and Walter Donaldson and Gus Kahn (additional songs). Several celebrities make cameos in the novel, including Florenz Ziegfeld, Jimmy Durante, and evangelist Aimee Semple McPherson, and many others are namedropped.

22. *Saturday Review of Literature*, 30 November 1929, 491.

23. All quoted from the 1928 edition of *Book Review Digest*.

24. The last three quotations are from an undated newspaper ad, apparently from the *New York Times*.

25. He is called Fritz von Buelow only on the cast list in the front of the book, and is apparently based on McEvoy's friend Erich Von Stroheim, who also makes a few cameos in the novel under his real name.

26. In 1929, the idea of making a romantic movie out of Tennyson's 55-line poem was absurd, but in 1936 there appeared *The Charge of the Light Brigade*, starring Errol Flynn and Olivia de Havilland.

27. *The Cabinet of Dr. Caligari*, the 1919 German Expressionist masterpiece.

28. Paris notes Page is "a millionaire polo player much like the one Brooks soon married in real life" (205n).

29. The final page of the *Liberty* serialization (28 September 1929, 73) is much more elaborate: the *Times* announcement mimics the paper's actual display and text fonts, and the extended photo includes several wedding guests and a caption, not just the wedded couple as in the published book. See p. 419.

30. This occurs in Dixie's monologue, echoing the closing line of Molly Bloom's monologue in *Ulysses*: ". . . and yes I said yes I will Yes." Like alcohol, *Ulysses* was prohibited in America at this time, but McEvoy managed to obtain both.

31. Quoted in *Book Review Digest* for 1929.

32. However, there is an inexplicable dating discrepancy: *Hollywood Girl* ends in April 1929, but *Society* begins in April 1930. A few references in the past tense to the Crash of '29 indicate the novel is indeed set in 1930, the bulk of it from April to December, and concluding around the time of the book's publication in the fall of 1931.

33. A Joycean pun on Carroll's stage revue *Vanities*. Wikipedia: "Known as 'the troubadour of the nude,' Carroll was famous for his productions featuring the most lightly clad showgirls on Broadway."

34. Brooks first married director Eddie Sutherland, who is mentioned on p. 415 of *Hollywood Girl*.

A Note on the Text

This edition replicates the texts of the first editions, with one exception: at the end of *Hollywood Girl*, the cropped photo of the book version is followed by the uncropped, captioned photo as it appeared on page 73 of *Liberty*, 28 September 1929, with a different officiant and additional guests. (I believe "the peach on the right" is showgirl/actress Nancy Carroll, mentioned on pp. 318 and 497.) Errors and some inconsistencies have been corrected, others allowed to stand. In *Show Girl*, the real city of Managua (first edition) has been changed to the fictitious city of Sanaguay (later editions). In *Society*, McEvoy (or his publisher) dispensed with the telegram headings of the first two novels.

SHOW GIRL

By J. P. McEvoy

Author of The Potters, Americana, etc.

CAST

(In the order of their appearance)

Dixie Dugan:	"The hottest little wench that ever shook a scanties at a tired business man."
Denny Kerrigan:	Greeting Card Salesman, strewing cheer throughout the land.
Nita Dugan:	Dixie's sister—"Sees all—knows all."
Alvarez Romano:	A sun-kissed tango dancer from the coffee belt.
Jack Milton:	A rich Sugar Dixie leaves standing in the rain.
Sunshine:	A blonde hip-twister in the Scandals.
Jimmy Doyle:	A Ghost Writer on the Evening Tabloid—the lowest form of astral life.
Kibbitzer & Eppus:	Broadway Producers—"Par Nobile Fratrum."

Also Greeting Card Salesmen, Night Club Babies, Teddy Zest, the Heart-throb Poet, Detectives Who Never Sleep, A Publisher, His Daughter, and an Assortment of Playboys from Wall Street, Atlantic City Hot Dog Vendors, Herrera, the Butcher of the Costaraguan Revolution, and Congressman Fibbledibber from Alabama.

I

Brooklyn, N. Y.
May 1st.

Denny, My Love:

Your little brown-eyed playmate has went and done it. Left her happy home, flat as egg on a vest and gone into the merry-merry for better or worse, or what am I offered? Soon you will see this name which you are so set on changing, busting out all over Broadway in a rash of Mazdas and these round knees all sun-burnt now from night life, coyly crossed in all the Sunday rotogravure sections.

But if you think the folks took it lying down, you're crazy, my own sweet thing. It was a finish fight, starting out with gloves, referees and things and finishing on the floor, catch-as-catch-can no holds barred. Mother got in some nasty jolts but this flaming youth was still burning bright even after she asked a lot of those mother questions, for which there aren't any answers in the back of the book. I could always come back with "Well you was young once, wasn't you?" It seems she was, although she can't remember now what it was like. "I'd rather see you dead than in a show," she kept on saying. And I said "Maybe we'll both get our wish. I've seen a lot of acts die right on the stage."

I got permission yesterday from mother to go into the Follies. All I need now is Mr. Ziegfeld's, but persuading him should be easy compared to selling the folks. Pa is dubious which sounds like a rap but isn't. He says he can't keep me in nights and he doesn't think Ziegfeld can either. I wish Nita was here to back me up. She's such a good skate. Of course, she would have to go dashing over to Paris on one of her buying trips for Waffleheimers. They're showing their Fall collections now. I hope she collects some cute things for herself that I'll like. Every time I realize we're both the same size, it makes me religious. The big brother, Sam, doesn't know what to think about it yet. But then he isn't bright anyway. It has been so long since he has read anything except the Graphic that he can't even dial his own telephone numbers now. We're going to have to put little pictures there instead of figures.

I've got a date tomorrow to see Mr. Ziegfeld. I called up the office today and the girl said yes, he'd be there tomorrow and if I can see him, it's all right with her. So that's that.

Don't worry about me. This story going around about the show business being dangerous for young girls is propaganda from the employment agencies who are short of kitchen help. I've been in too many taxis not to know that a girl is lots safer with an orchestra between her and the tired business man, who don't act nearly as tired as you'd think. But then, I should tell you, a star travelling salesman, how the tired business man acts!

I wish you could sneak me some more of that swell imported Italian stationery. I think you should anyway. I am using it all up writing to you. "And who else," sez you. "Just you," sez I. "Whoops, tell me another," sez you.

Well, as you were, until I write again. I love you, I love you, I love you, I love you. That oughta hold you.

DIXIE.

P.S. Have you heard the Hurdle Song: "I Can't Get Over A Girl Like You Loving A Boy Like Me."

MUNCIE, IND.
May 4th.

DEAR DIXIE:

Well, I just got back from Minneapolis where the boss has had a convention of us salesmen which means he feeds us until we're groggy, and then shoots us full of hot air how great the home office is and what a lot of bums our salesmen are for not co-operating. You would think to hear him tell, we just saunter from town to town making life a pleasure for the lady buyers and always sweep our samples under the bed to get them out of the way. My God, I would like to see him carry these four hand trunks of valentines and mother mottoes and God bless our homes all over these United States. Here I have been hopping around from one hash town to another for years carrying things like—

Home is lovely
Home is sweet
Home is a pleasure
Home is a treat
Oh, how could anyone ever roam
Away from that dear old place called Home?

But we got a swell new line of Vals and Easters and for once the damn creative department, as it likes to call itself, has kicked in a good bunch of ten-cent religious sellers. My God, they have been yelling for those for years and all McNulty would ever make was rabbits, ducks and bunnies. But we got a new man there now called Levinson and he says if they want religious Easters, let's make them religious Easters. So Levinson came through with some swell ones. One is a pip showing angels rolling a big stone away and in old English it says—

> *Lo, He has risen*
> *He is not here*
> *But we wish you an Easter of love and cheer,*
> *Alleluia.*

Boy, that will kill them here in Indiana.

So, you think you are going into the Follies? Well, I wish you buck teeth and bow-legs. But what's the difference? Every dame that isn't forty years old and a menace in looks thinks she can get into the Follies by rolling her eyes at Ziegfeld's office boy. The day you go into the Follies I will buy control of the Standard Oil and give you a can for luck.

Well, I got to go out and pour a lot of banana oil into Miss Schwartz's ear. She is the buyer for Ye Quainte Lyttle Gifte Shoppe. The only way I can sell her anything is to get her all warm and confused. Lady buyers are like that, the country over. It rather taxes the energies of us good looking salesmen, but then I guess that's part of our jobs making life worth while for them.

I am tired of hash houses, lady buyers and selling home mottoes and not having any place of my own to hang them. Why don't you stop your kidding and let's get married and end it all? Huh, what do you say? As one of our best selling Vals says, No. 32V10

> *Cheer up, little girl*
> *You're a long time dead*
> *And besides when you cry*
> *Your nose gets red*

DENNY

BROOKLYN, N. Y.
May 8th.

DENNY DARLING:

Your pious prayer that I get buck teeth and bow-legs duly received and forwarded to Heavenly Headquarters. A lot of my own have gone up that way recently and judging from the results, God must be in conference and left word not to be disturbed. I can see a lot of these snooty angels sorting His mail and messages in the morning and coming across one of mine saying "Please help me to get a good job in the Follies." And then Private Secretary Angel Number One saying "The Follies? Why the Boss hasn't had anything to do with that for years. We've never had any one up here from the Follies." And then Angel Number Two "Oh yes, Bert Williams." And then Angel Number One "I mean the girls." And then Angel Number Two "I don't blame 'em. Kinda dull up here with these same old harp players doing the same old voh-doh-dee-o through all the ages. I'm for putting in a couple of good loud-speakers and getting Whiteman or Ben Bernie once in a while." "A fat chance" says the other Angel, "with all these old conservatives running things. What this place needs is some young blood!"

And so much for your prayers—you sweet thing—and now for the big news. I went up to see Ziggy yesterday—all us girls call him "Ziggy," including a lot of 'em who have never been able to get into his office. Well, anyway I went up to see him and the outer office was splashing over into the lobby with beautiful women who had got the same idea somehow. Tall blondes with complexions like fresh cream and hair like twenty dollar gold pieces and those yellow green eyes that tigers in the zoo have on Sunday when they don't feed 'em. And running all around under them little brunette dancers with legs like acrobats—and perched on a line of chairs against the wall, a lot of those slim, slender-legged young things looking boyish and silky at the same time. The real ambition of our young generation, Denny my darling, in case you don't know it, is to be cool but look hot. Well anyway, I tottered right through them on my high heels till I got to Alice who runs the telephone and lets the girls cry on her shoulder. "I want to see Mr. Ziegfeld," I says to her. And she says, "Darling, what I want to know is does he want to see you? And anyway he's not in. And if he is in, he doesn't want to be disturbed. And if he does, you have to have an appointment. If you have, you've got to make me believe it first. And if you can do that, you're a wonder." And I says to her "Honey, it's like this, Ziggy has been struggling along now for years, doing his best, but he has been considerably handicapped by not having me. I wanted to do something about it, but I was busy growing up and rounding into shape, so to speak, but now that I've got the job pretty well in hand, I don't think you're serving his best interests by not letting me add that touch of color and life and gladness to his chorus, which would be me." "How pleased he'll be to hear this" she says. And she says "Wait a minute" and gets busy with her switchboard saying "No, he's not in" to some and "Yes, he is, but doesn't want to be disturbed" to others and "Wait a minute, he'll talk to you." And "I'll call you later" and "No, he's gone for the day," after which she turns to me and I says "Lovey, how do you expect me to believe you after all that?" And just then, what do you think happened? Mr. Ziggy himself walked right through the office. And I got a great hunch. I says to myself "Who is the last person in the world he'd expect me to have a letter from?" And then myself says immediately "His wife, Billie Burke." So I says "Mr. Ziegfeld I have an important message for you from Miss Burke which I must deliver right away." And he looks surprised, as you can well imagine. And he says, "Oh, come right in." And I followed him into his private office but I turned around at the door to make a face at all the other girls, any one of whom could have gladly stabbed me to death right then with a lipstick.

But as soon as I got into his office, I was scared pink. It's all velvet and mahogany and a big gold piano and flowers all over the place and he says "Sit down, won't you?" And I think I fell down or something. But he looked at me very gentle-like and says "Did I look surprised when you told me you had a message from Miss Burke." And I said "Well yes, a little." "When did you see Miss Burke" he says, soft-like. I says "This morning." And he says "That's odd. Here I've been wasting time trying to sign Lindbergh. And you saw Miss Burke this morning?" Well I wasn't feeling so sure about it by this time but I figured that was my story and I had better stick to it and I says "Yes," and I added, "ten o'clock this morning," to make it good. He says "That's marvelous, because I got a cable from her from Paris last night and she didn't say anything about sending anyone over with a message this morning. Do you think she could have forgotten it?" And I says to myself "It's too late to lie out of it now so I might as well continue so I says to him earnest-like "Well, you know a woman has a lot of things on her mind when she's in Paris and she must have forgotten all about it." "What was the message?" he asked. And I says "I want to go into the new Follies." And he says "This is the message Miss Burke sent you across the ocean with overnight? You must really want to go in very badly." I says "Well I couldn't think of any other way to get to you. And I can dance and you can see for yourself how I look." He says "Well, your face is all right but then who is going to look at your face in the Follies?" And then he reached for a push button and my heart nearly stopped beating. "Here comes the gate" I thought, but then he smiled and said "Sammy Lee is trying out some dancing girls down on the stage now but I wouldn't have the heart to ask you to go down after your long journey from Europe. You must be very tired." And I says "Oh no." But he says "You can't go that way anyway. How do I know but you're knock-kneed." And I says "Well I could bring a letter from my mother." And he says "Leave your name and address with Alice and when she calls you report at the stage door of the New Amsterdam and bring a bathing suit and if Mr. Lee says you can dance, I'll look at you." And do you know, Denny darling, I can't remember now how I got out of that office. All I remember is when he said I could report tomorrow for a try-out, bells began to ring, whistles blew and the stars came out and I heard all kinds of sweet music and I just sorta floated right out of that office right through all those girls waiting outside trying to get in and even the B.M.T. to Brooklyn didn't wake me up. Just think—me in a bathing suit doing my stuff on the New Amsterdam stage, before Mr. Ziegfeld! I've got to keep my teeth clenched right now or my heart would jump right out here on this letter and wouldn't you be surprised when you opened the envelope and it fell out—beatin' like everything for you. And what would the beautiful Miss Schwartz of Ye Quainte Lyttle Gifte Shoppe say then?

It will be time enough to talk about settling down and building a home around one of your mottoes after I have made my name and fortune on Broadway. That may not be so long either, Big Boy.

Well the tub is running over, the telephone is ringing and I'm sitting here with practically nothing on. Adios—and a big kiss . . . hold on to it as long as you like. . . . Whoa! that's enough.

As ever yours,
only more so,
DIXIE.

~~~~~~~~~~~~~~~

<div style="text-align: right;">SOUTH BEND
May 15th.</div>

SWEET CHILD:

It's just like I told you. The ten-cent religious line is a wow! Wrote $150 Val and Easter order the other day for the Oliver Hotel Gift Shop and then went right around the corner to Ye Merrie Lyttle Nooke and took Miss Cassidy there for a big Val and Easter order and big Every Day order and a whole flock of mottoes. I had to take her out last night and hold her hands but you have to do everything in this business. And I didn't mind so much because she's not really so hard to look at—besides she's crazy about me. Of course that may sound like a boost for myself at first, but then you have to be in this town a while to see that it isn't. As soon as the boys make enough money to buy long pants they put them on and go to Chicago and all that's left is the Rah-Rah overflow from Notre Dame. It's kinda tough for the local gazelles because the boys out there are so busy learning to play football they have no time to perfect their petting technique and then there being no co-eds out there, the opportunities for additional work outside the curriculum are not so good.

I sent a good idea into the home office today but I guess that they just threw it into the waste basket as they always do. My God, you would think that us salesmen out in touch with the trade would be more likely to know what the people want than those goofs sitting up there in the creating department pulling them out of thin air. This is an idea for a card to be sent to a new father. It shows a picture of a stork and a man shooting at it saying "Take that, you big bum." Don't you think that's good? I think it is a wow! Well, you mark my words—that has just as much chance getting into the line as you have of getting into the Follies.

All joking aside, it looks like I am going to come East for the mid-summer convention in Atlantic City. Wouldn't it be hotsy-totsy if you could come over? Oh, boy!

Don't you think this is a good one? I think of you every time I read it to one of the dealers. It's a swell seller, too. No. 25M11.

> *All the world I've sorted out*
> *Into classes two—*
> *Folks that I could do without,*
> *And you.*

Gee, it's lonely in these hotel rooms. You know I could work twice as hard if I had someone like you to work for. Well, I bet if you come down to Atlantic City you will leave there one of two things—a lovely bride or a beautiful corpse.

Your own,
DENNY.

~~~~~~~~~~~~~~~~~~~~~~~~~~~

<div style="text-align: right">BROOKLYN, N. Y.
May 14th.</div>

DEAR NITA:

I suppose mother has already written and told you about your young cracked-brained sister kicking over the traces and making a dash for the Follies. Well, I did make the first lap all right—got in to see Ziggy and even got as far as the New Amsterdam stage in my bathing suit—the one the moths wouldn't eat—but Sammy Lee didn't think my hoofing was so hot. He said I had lots of action but needed more experience because I was little. If I was larger, I wouldn't need anything except what mother gave me—because then I could walk around with a lot of rhinestones on and look sneerful at all the big butter and eggers out front. But if you are little, the customers want to see you move lively. But he was so nice about it. When I asked him what I might to do, he said "Get more dancing experience with an orchestra under you. Go into a vaudeville tab or night club." Well, I was dashed, as we used to say in dear old London and I could see mother letting me go into a night club without a struggle. But one of the girls I met at the tryout (her name is Sunshine something-or-other) took a shine to me—no joke intended—and said she would get me in with her over at the Jollity. There was a vacancy there so I went over with her that same night and luck was with me for a change. I go on about four times and sing the same song and dance two choruses. The festivities start about midnight and I get away about a quarter of three. I don't know what mother is going to do for sleep. She's been sitting up now three nights running hoping the club will burn down or I'll break a leg. It isn't a bad job. I get $50 a week and bacon and eggs at two in the morning. When I finish my turn, I duck out of sight and stay there. The boss wanted me to join some friends of his at the table the first night but I says to him "There are no gorillas in my contract." Sunshine says you might just as well bang them on the nose with the truth at the start instead of breaking it to them gradually, because sometimes they outguess a poor girl, if she starts to play fox.

You can bet I haven't told Denny anything about it. Oh boy, the explosion in Chicago would sound like a new gang war.

What's the well dressed young woman wearing along the Roo de la Pooh? I wish you would send me the string of genuine imitation pearls you promised me before you left. You should know by this time I remember every word you say except what interferes with my pleasure.

Fred has called up three times a day since you left. Please write to him and save the wear and tear on our telephone. I told him the last time you wrote you told us you were out dancing that night with Georges Carpentier. I think he believes it. God help him! Of course, tastes in men differ and you are older than I and you ought to know more than I do, but I think you're a bum picker.

There's a tall, dark-haired, black-eyed tango dancer in the Jollity who has been throwing burning glances at me. I got a couple but have been letting most of them go by. I'm afraid I'm going to be afraid of him. Every time he comes around now, I shut my eyes and keep saying "Denny, Denny, Denny, Denny" as fast as I can. Some day I'm going to forget to shut my eyes. Well—here today and gone tomorrow. Lots of love.

Dixie.

P.S. Can I wear that evening shawl you left? I can't manage it very well in a taxi but I won't let any one burn cigarette holes in it, I promise you. No foolin' can I wear it—honest?

TELEGRAM

MAY 15 5 PM

NA 581 72
CHICAGO ILL 545 P
DIXIE DUGAN
        439 FLATBUSH AV BKLYN NY
GEORGE MORTON WRITES HE SAW YOU DANCING
IN JOLLITY NIGHT CLUB STOP WHAT DOES
THIS MEAN STOP WIRE AND TELL ME HE IS A
LIAR STOP LOVE
                               DENNY

TELEGRAM

MAY 16TH 12 NOON

RH 361 84
BKLYN NY 1235 P
DENNIS KERRIGAN
        TOWER BLDG CHICAGO ILL
WHAT OF IT?
                               DIXIE

```
                    POSTAL TELEGRAPH – COMMERCIAL CABLES
                                  TELEGRAM
```

                                                    MAY 16TH 4PM

16 NK 129
CHICAGO ILL 156 P
DIXIE DUGAN
            439 FLATBUSH AVE BKLYN NY
I DONT WANT YOU DANCING IN A NIGHT CLUB
I WONT HAVE IT
                                            DENNY

```
                    POSTAL TELEGRAPH – COMMERCIAL CABLES
                                  TELEGRAM
```

                                                    MAY 17TH 2PM

26 RG 421
CHICAGO ILL 531 X
DIXIE DUGAN
            439 FLATBUSH AVE BKLYN NY
WHY DONT YOU ANSWER MY WIRE STOP I
DEMAND A REPLY IMMEDIATELY
                                            DENNY

```
POSTAL TELEGRAPH – COMMERCIAL CABLES
TELEGRAM
```

                                         MAY 18TH 3 PM
NA 7272 7
BKLYN NY L7 618 Z
DENNIS KERRIGAN
              TOWER BLDG CHICAGO ILL
WHERES THE FIRE?
                                         DIXIE

```
POSTAL TELEGRAPH – COMMERCIAL CABLES
TELEGRAM
```

                                         MAY 18TH 5PM
NB 244 152 171
CHICAGO ILL 29
DIXIE DUGAN
              439 FLATBUSH AVE BKLYN NY
I WONT HAVE YOU DANCING IN A NIGHT CLUB
STOP AND THATS FINAL
                                         DENNY

```
                                                    MAY 20TH
LCO NITA DUGAN AMERICAN EXPRESS PARIS
NEW YORK 122 36 X
HIS NAME IS ALVAREZ ROMANO   WHAT SHALL
I DO  OH BOY
                                                       DIXIE
```

II

439 Flatbush Av.
Brooklyn, N. Y.
May 22nd.

Dear Nita:

Well, well big girl, you should see my handsome Alvarez, you should! Big brown eyes the boy has, like a St. Bernard, but he uses them like a vibrator. All over me—zoop! Sotch gooseflesh! And when he kisses—well the kid goes sorta faint and dreamy and don't care-ish and can barely get through the front door and slam it shut. Nothing like this ever happened to the baby sister before. So this is love! Stop it, I love it!

He isn't a Spaniard at all. He's an Argentine or something and when he tangoes the floor smokes and they have to throw water on the orchestra. His partner—Raquel Argentina she calls herself—is a wet smack. If she's a dancer, then Lon Chaney is America's sweetheart. Alvarez promised me last night to let me dance with him soon. That'll knock Raquel into a coma. Raquel! I bet her real name is Bessie Glutz and all her Argentine relatives live in South Bend back of Oliver Chilled Plow Works. Her tango is a glass crash. Means well, poor kid, but no starch in her spine and her wiggles lack authority. And her kicks! Some kind friend oughta take her out and have her knees lifted.

And what do you think has happened to my other ga-ga? Denny, no less. At first he burned up the wires telling me what I could and could not do. "I won't have you dancing in a night club" he telegraphs straight message, and I wires him, "Hooey," collect. And then he day-letters me: "Are you going to do what I say or not? Answer me at once. Important Rush." So I sends him a post card saying "Walk your horses." And then he calls me long distance from one of those little Indiana towns that the Century throws dust on and he feeds me a lot of static about how I'm breaking his heart and he has heard all about this rum hole I'm working in. "You'll have to get out of the Jollity" says he, "it's full of crime and corruption or sin and seduction" or something like that and I says "Aren't we all?" "There's another man in your life" he says, "but I love you and I'll not see you go to perdition in this way" and I says "I don't get this perdition gag, do you mean maybe I'm going to hell or something" and he says "You're going to hell in a hand basket and it's time some man took you in hand" and I says "Well, that's sweet of you but you'll have to get in line. You can't just step up to the head of the class like that. You'll have to work your way up to show you're worthy of this great honor. Applications will be acted upon in rotation as received. Write name and address plainly. Block letters please. Last name first, first name last and enclose certificate of good conduct from your parish priest. A few gold stars from your Sunday School teacher won't hurt. And meanwhile here is a kiss from my last batch. They're getting better. Youth isn't everything. Experience is now entering my life." And then poor Denny sorta moaned and since I just can't stand suffering I hung up. So I guess I'll hear from him again pretty soon.

Your loving sister,
Dixie.

P.S. Dick is going over on the Leviathan and will look you up. Will you steer him over to Coty's and sell him the idea of surprising me with some wicked perfume. No high pressure stuff, sis. Easy does it with Dick. The dear old boy loves finesse as much as though he really had a brain—God forbid!

Terre Haute, Ind.
May 25th.

Sweet thing:

After that long distance talk with you the other night, I decided I'd scratch you right off the list but then I thought it over and decided you're so young you don't know what it's all about anyway and you're kinda dizzy with your first job and everything and you don't know anything about men and you need a smart guy like me to steer you right, so you go right ahead giving me the air if you get a kick out of it but I'm going to hang right on just the same, that is unless you get too fresh, because if I ever do get off you, I can forget you so completely I'd have to be introduced all over again.

And now I've got some real news for you. We're getting out a new line of wall mottoes on velvet, stamped in gold and stencil printed in nine colors with a choice of gold frames or passe-partout to retail $2.50 or fifty off to the trade in gross lots of twelve titles assorted. Doesn't that sound like a wow! Oh boy! And the sentiments! There's one that I love because I always think of you when I read it over to the trade. It's No. 40XY10 and it goes—

> 'S'queer the way I miss you
> 'S'funny how I sigh
> When you ain't near I can't be glad
> No matter how I try,
> 'S'fierce to like you so darn much,
> 'S'awful, sure enough . . .
> Wherever I go I miss you so
> 'S'terrible . . . 'S'tough!

Last night was another one of those outings that drive good looking salesmen into monasteries. Leola Fitzgibbons, card buyer for Swartzenheimers, gave me a big repeat order on boxed Xmas assortments so it was up to me to take her out and give the Terre Haute night life a look. The picture wasn't so bad—John Barrymore in something romantic with tights which gave little Leola a chance to freeze onto my hands and look swoonful and after that one of those talking pictures which sound like the first phonographs when they used to have big tin horns and started every piece with "Columbi-yaah REC-corrrd." Well, after that spree, we went over to a chop suey and had chicken chow mein and a bunch of dances. The band was hot and Leola switches a mean skirt so that part of it wasn't the washout it might have been, but all the time I was wishing it was you I was cutting corners with. Leola says I'm a sweet dancer, but then all the lady buyers find that out sooner or later. What are you doing now this minute while I'm sitting up here in this lonesome hotel room thinking of you? Hoofing for a lot of plastered goofs in that bum night club.

I wish I could forget you, but I'm awful glad I can't. Say, that wouldn't make a bad motto. I'll have to send that hunch in to the office. And a heluva lot of attention they'll pay to it, or to any of my hunches. They think they know it all, the big stiffs!

Love,
DENNY.

~~~~~~~~~~~~~~~~~~

<div style="text-align: right;">439 FLATBUSH AV.
BROOKLYN, N. Y.
May 27th.</div>

SUNSHINE, DARLING:

You missed it when you left this menagerie for the Scandals. You should have stuck around if only for what happened last night. But I don't blame you for doing chorine police at fifty bucks with lots of spare time at home instead of this night club racket where you don't get out till three a. m. and then have to fight your way home. But last night was the cats. The club filled up early with a lot of customers who looked as though they came from the annual outing and fish fry of the Old Soaks Home. All the tables were having a contest to see who could get the most bottles underfoot and still leave room for the waiters to get around.

By two in the morning the air was so thick you could have bottled it, the floor was jammed, the band was trying to drown out the drummer and who should come in but Aimee Semple McPherson herself and a bunch of newspaper reporters. You know dear, she's that Los Angeles evangelist who was found by radio or something and she's been around taking big city night life apart to see what makes it click. Well, when Jimmy Durante tells me who she is you could have knocked me over with an elephant. And my turn next to go out there in shorts and sing "Fifty Million Frenchmen Can't Be Wrong." Well, I wangled through it and was hot footing it back to the dressing room when Larry—you know Short-Change Larry?—headed me off and said Miss MacPherson would like to have me come over to her table and talk to her. Feature that!

She was sitting there very calm and shook hands with me and introduced me around to the lady reporters who were bombarding her with questions. Well, I sits there with my ears nicely adjusted but saying nothing and taking it all in. Finally, she says "I'm surprised to see so little drinking" and I looks at her to see her laugh, but no, not a smile. And I says "What do you suppose those things are under the tables?" And she takes a good look and says "Why they're bottles" and I says "What did you think they were, ducks?" And just then a lady at the next table sings out to her gentleman friend that she'll be a such and such if any so and so can steal her drink while she's dancing and if she wasn't a lady she'd knock his you-know block off with a bottle. And Aimee took my hand and says softly "They're all little children in here tonight. Little children looking for the light." And I couldn't help saying they're not looking for any light—they're all lit, but she didn't seem to understand.

Just then Jimmy Durante got out on the floor and sang "If I Didn't Know Your Husband and You Didn't Know My Wife," which has some pretty swift ones in it, and what do you suppose Aimee says? "A hungry heart" she says, looking at Jimmy who has been in the night club racket since he was three years old down in the Bowery. "A hungry heart seeking God" says she. Tie that one!

Meanwhile what you told me about my Argentine ga-ga is all coming true. He's getting harder to handle all the time, and jealous! Wow! The other night I was sitting at a table with a couple of Harvard boys—sweet kids both of them—just college boys—not an ounce of harm in a ton of them—and Alvarez was just boiling over. When I went back to change he started to pop and the place was full of strange Spanish sounds there for a while before I could cool him off. After that he was so sweet and sorry and affectionate, it made me feel just terrible. I tell you, Sunshine, that boy makes me dizzy, the way he's raising the devil one minute and the next all sweet words and soft caresses. I don't know whether I'm afoot or horseback. He's got me all worn out just saying No-no-no-no-no-no. I didn't know what an easy time I had with a goof like Denny who sat right up and snapped sugar off his nose if I said "Boo." These Argentines think all they have to do is make a chest at a woman and she'll swoon mitt scrims frum delight.

Toodle-oo,
DIXIE.

439 Flatbush Av.
Brooklyn, N. Y.
June 1st.

Dear Nita:

Well sis, I guess now it can be told and you're the only one I can tell it to. If Ma ever heard the half of it, I wouldn't have any more home than a banshee. But I hardly know how to start—the whole thing is such a mad blur. If I had only known what I was yessing myself into! But how can a girl tell these days? Almost all parties look alike at the takeoff—a few high balls, a few dances, and the boys getting merry and making preliminary passes to sort of get their bearings generally. But this one turned out differently. And how!

To begin with, Jack Milton showed up at the Club with a birthday. He has already had more birthdays than Methuselah and every one is an excuse for a party. But this time he had a bunch of his tired Wall Street friends with him—all of them fifty or thereabouts and crawling with money. They've been to the Club any number of times since I've been working here and the boss told me before that Jack liked me, which meant nothing in my life, but this time he said Jack wouldn't be happy unless I came to his birthday party and I asked the boss "Where?" and the boss says "Up to his house" and I says "Nix, I'm too young to be going to rich bachelor's houses at three a. m. on parties." And the boss says "You're not going alone. Don't be silly. Some of the other girls are invited too and anyway Jack is A No. 1 and his friends are all as reliable as U.S. Steel—and besides if it gets too wild, you can always call Lenox 2300 and taxi yourself home." So you see, he talked me into it.

Well the men waited for us until we dressed and then we all piled into a couple of limousines and off we went. I wish you could have seen this house of Milton's—four or five stories high, rugs knee-deep, antique furniture all over the place, one of those private elevators that you get into and push buttons and it takes you everywhere, a real cellar with all the kinds of liquor that ever was invented and popping out from behind every door, Japanese spies with trays full of cocktails. . . . There were four other girls and myself, and mine host and his four substantial friends from down town. They seemed to be nice enough eggs—more like a bunch of school boys playing hookey than big financial wizards, or whatever they are in their working hours.

Well the party jumped right off the dock and lit running. I never said yes to so many different kinds of cocktails and highballs in my life. After an hour of this, I vaguely remember quantities of food appeared magically and then Jack began to pop out of the cellar at pleasant intervals toting real champagne which nobody had the heart to turn down. By this time we had all told all the stories we knew and were pretty well acquainted. The usual amount of dancing and petting but nothing to call out the reserves for, so the baby sister was feeling all set up about everything especially since Jack was making all kinds of fuss over me, telling me how sweet and young and pretty I was and could I learn to care for him, that he was crazy about me, and would do anything for me if I could learn to love him just a little, and me telling him not to be silly and keep his hands to himself and this must have been going on for some time 'cause when I looked around everybody had skipped into other parts of the house and there I was alone with this little prairie flower who was growing wilder every minute.

Well I thought I had learned something about maidenly jiu jitsu battling with Alvarez but this Jack Milton was something brand new. He was so ruthless and yet kept on talking so sweet to me all the time he had me panicked. I tried to get out of the room several times but he headed me off and finally I began to scream. And then what do you think this big bruiser did? He clapped his hand over my mouth, carried me over to the elevator, slammed the door shut and whisked us up to the next floor, paying as little attention to me as if I were a rag doll. He carried me into the library and dropped me on the divan, still holding his hand over my mouth. Then he started to talk but by this time I was so hysterical with real fear I didn't hear half of it. All I got was that he was sorry but he couldn't have me screaming because the police would come in and there'd be a scandal and he didn't want to hurt me and he loved me and would do anything for me and he was awfully sorry if he frightened me and would I give him just one kiss and be friends, and a lot more out of the same basket, and I thought I can't get anywhere fighting this big gorilla so I better try yessing him a little or anything to get me out of this mess so I relaxed a little and when he took his big paw off my mouth I sat up and started to cry. And then he apologized and let me go, you think? Well, think again. That seemed to start him all over again. He grabbed me and began to kiss me and I went right after him teeth and fingernails and there we were going for each other like a couple of Kilkenny cats when who should burst in but *ALVAREZ!* This wasn't the first time this crazy Argentine had trailed me, but this time I nearly passed out. His face was as white as a sheet and his hair usually plastered down slick was standing on end. He just let out one scream and dived for Jack. And then I saw he had a long knife in his hand. Well I never thought so fast in my life. I just had time to grab his arm or he would have plunged the knife into Jack's back. He shook me off and then the two men went to it and I passed right out cold.

When I came to I was down in the living room and they were forcing whiskey down my throat. The place was full of cops, most of them holding Alvarez and Jack, both of them covered with blood and Alvarez screaming with rage. The girls were crying and the men were trying to quiet them and at the same time get the police to take Alvarez out and let everybody go home. Finally, one of the men, Wilkins his name was, a big politician I found out later—got the cops off to one corner and gave them some kind of a song and dance after which they dragged Alvarez out still yelling and the party was officially over. Or at least I thought so—but the worst was yet to come. Hardly had the cops gone when Jack who hadn't been saying anything through all this, but was just propped up against the wall getting whiter—well Jack just folds up and falls down in the corner dead to the world. The men rushed to pick him up and then I heard one of them yell "Get a doctor quick. He's bleeding to death." Well, all the panic before was nothing to this. A couple of the men herded us girls into our coats and hats telling us we had to duck because it looked like a real scandal this time and they couldn't afford to get involved in the papers with a bunch of night club girls—that they were responsible citizens, and I couldn't help telling 'em I was a responsible citizen too and I couldn't afford to get involved in the papers with any roustabout playboys either.

Well the doctor came in just as we were leaving and I don't know yet what happened. I have been afraid to look at the papers this morning—and mother isn't speaking to me at all—it was after five o'clock when I got home. Oh if I ever get out of this mess I'll never let myself into another as long as I live. Suppose Jack is seriously injured and there's an investigation—or suppose he dies and we're all dragged into it? I'm just sick and you not home to help me either. Would you rush back if I had to cable you?

Scared-to-death!
Dixie.

(From The N. Y. World—June 3rd)
WILD PARTY ENDS WITH BROKER DYING

"Jack" Milton, Millionaire Man-About-Town In Bellevue Hospital After Mysterious Stabbing

NIGHT CLUB GIRLS HELD
Big Social and Financial Names Involved In Scandal

Although every effort was made to hush up the affair, the police learned early this morning that "Jack" Milton, millionaire broker and club man, is in the Bellevue Hospital dying of knife wounds received during a wild party in his apartments early Tuesday morning. A scandal is promised that will rock New York's social and financial circles. While the police are keeping a strict censorship apparently from instructions "higher up," it was learned that Alvarez Romano, Argentine tango dancer in the Jollity Night Club, was being held as well as a number of the Night Club girls who were in the party which started at three o'clock last Tuesday morning and wound up with the stabbing at dawn. The names of the girls are being kept secret by the police, as well as the names of the other men who were in the party in Milton's luxurious apartments overlooking Gramercy Park. It is known however that all of the men are of social and financial importance and that every effort is being made by them to keep their names out of the investigation which is already under way.

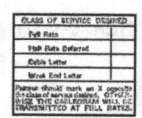

WESTERN UNION CABLEGRAM

```
                                    JUNE 3RD
LCO NITA DUGAN AMERICAN EXPRESS PARIS
                       NEW YORK 164 19 X
IN TERRIBLE SCANDAL FOR GODS SAKE COME
HOME AT ONCE AND HELP ME
                                    DIXIE
```

III

POSTAL TELEGRAPH – COMMERCIAL CABLES – TELEGRAM

JUNE 5TH

CHIGAGO ILL 416 X
DIXIE DUGAN
                439 FLATBUSH AV BKLYN NY
JUST RECEIVED CLIPPING FROM MORTON
SAYING JOLLITY NIGHT CLUB GIRLS HELD
AFTER STABBING OF NEW YORK CLUB MAN
DURING PARTY ARE YOU MIXED UP IN THIS
RUSH WIRE WORRIED
                                    DENNY

POSTAL TELEGRAPH – COMMERCIAL CABLES – TELEGRAM

JUNE 6TH

BKLYN NY 27168 Z
DENNIS KERRIGAN
            TOWER BLDG CHICAGO ILL
AND HOW
                                    DIXIE

(From The N. Y. Tab—June 6th)
BROKER FIGHTING FOR LIFE

"Jack" Milton, Stabbed By Love-Crazed Argentine in Wild Party with Night Club Girls

DENIES "DIXIE" IS INVOLVED

POSTAL TELEGRAPH — COMMERCIAL CABLES TELEGRAM

JUNE 7TH

CHICAGO ILL L59 X
DIXIE DUGAN
    439 FLATBUSH AV BKLYN NY
I HOPE YOU ARE CRAZY ABOUT HIM WHOEVER
HE WAS AND THAT HE DIES AND GOES TO HELL
        DENNY

POSTAL TELEGRAPH — COMMERCIAL CABLES TELEGRAM

JUNE 8TH

BKLYN NY 613 Z
DENNIS KERRIGAN
    TOWER BLDG CHICAGO ILL
TEMPER TEMPER
        DIXIE

(From The N. Y. Tab—June 8th)

DIXIE DUGAN WEEPS

"Can I Help It If They Were Both Crazy About Me?"
Sobs Beautiful Dancer

JEALOUS LOVER BARES ALL

Romano in Cell Tells of Passion for Beautiful
Night Club Dancer

JUNE 9TH

CHICAGO ILL L59 Z
DIXIE DUGAN
　　　　　　439 FLATBUSH AV BKLYN NY
I TOLD YOU NOT TO DANCE IN THAT NIGHT
CLUB WHEN I TELL YOU SOMETHING AFTER
THIS MAYBE YOU WILL PAY ATTENTION TO
SOMEBODY WHO KNOWS WHAT HE IS TALKING
ABOUT

　　　　　　　　　　　　　　DENNY

```
         POSTAL TELEGRAPH – COMMERCIAL CABLES
                    TELEGRAM
```

                                          JUNE 9TH
BKLYN NY 166 Z
DENNY KERRIGAN
               TOWER BLDG CHICAGO ILL
MAYBE SAYS BABY GO AND PEDDLE YOUR
CHRISTMAS CARDS I HAVE ENOUGH TROUBLES
WITHOUT YOU NAGGING ME LIKE AN OLD
WOMAN
                                             DIXIE

~~~~~~~~~~~~~~~~~~~~

<div style="text-align:right">

The Tombs,
New York City.
June 9th.

</div>

Adorada mia:

I write to tell you you are beautiful, querida mia, and my heart sings songs of you, but your little head is full of deceit and some day I will go mad and kill you, but always I will love you, diosa mia. Always and for a day! And I tell you too what I will do. So soon I get out of the clutches of these pigs in blue coats with their clubs always ready, I will find this Milton dog and I will cut his heart up into little bits and every bit into little bits because I love you, mi queridissima, and he is no good.

So what do the police tell me this morning—this Milton man maybe he will not die after all and I say "It is a great pity. I will have to do it all over again and how glad that makes me!" "You'll have to let him alone" they say, "because it is a big scandal now and if you kill him it will be a bigger scandal and you will go to the chair." And I sneer in their faces. "Who? Me? I Alvarez Romano, the son of a presidente of Costaragua?" "Which presidente?" they say and I cannot tell them because I cannot go back anymore to find out. And they say presidente or no presidente, they put you in a chair and pull the switch and socko! the electricity it fries you alive. It seems to make them very happy about talking of frying people alive but to me it is nothing for I am all afire when I think of you. It is like millions of what you call them—volts—always going through me when I think of you—to my fingers and toes and my heart bumps bumps. And then I think of this Milton dog making love to you and I sizzle all over and everything I see is red. Yes, I have made up my mind and will kill him, and you too. Both of you. Because he has money, you like him. I had money too, but the Revolution takes it all away. What do you care? Your heart is like a mirror. It shows only who is looking at it. I will smash it into a thousand pieces. I will grind my heel on it and then I will be sad and will cry and will pick up all the little tender pieces and kiss them and put them together and keep them forever in a little silver box on the piano. And when I play the sweet songs of my country, they will hear and know that I am singing them all for you, flor del Paraiso!

The food is terrible in this jail. Fit only for pigs and policemen and Jack Miltons, but no, he is in a nice hospital with only a little knife stab in his back. It is lucky for him I did not have my big knife. Ah, that is a knife! I should have pin him to the floor like a butterfly but he gets away with only a little scratch maybe two or three inches deep. It is nothing. In my country, we would not notice it. With a little knife like this in my back, I could hold you in my arms and not know it. But what does he know about love—this big, fat money chaser with his millions and his soft paws caressing you. Tomorrow I kill him. I dig my way out of here, through the wall, under the sidewalk. I tear his iron bed to pieces and beat him to death with it, but no, they will not let me near him.

My heart is breaking, for you are walking on it with your little feet. Your little high heels they dig into my heart and it hurts so—but it is good. I will die here in this awful place and maybe I will never see the sun again or the moon. And those stars of which I would fill both your hands and sprinkle in your hair. And on the moon I would let you stand and carry you from place to place. All this I would do for you but I must die here, all alone, forsaken, far from my country and my people. And even you, for which I have done all this, you do not come near me. Ah, beautiful women have no hearts! But in my heart is a song for you. It is an old song which a lover sings to his love.

*"Oh would that I could hide within my songs
And, every time you sang them, kiss your lips."*

Tuyo que no te olvida—from one who can never forget you,

ALVAREZ.

(From The Eve. Tab—June 11th)
HE DID IT FOR LOVE
(An Interview by Beatrice Heartsease)

Say not that the little God of Love no longer flourishes his deadly bow and arrow in our big, wicked city for I have just met a heart wounded by one of his dear, delightful darts. They will tell you in the cold grey Tombs where those who have loved not wisely but too well are caged like wild beasts, that Alvarez Romano is a hot-blooded killer from the Pampas. Hot-blooded, yes, but only as we girls would love to have our men. A killer, yes, but one who kills for love. Ah, how magnificent to find in this sordid city of sin a knight of old who goes forth to do battle for his lady fair! Such is Alvarez Romano—erstwhile tango dancer in the Jollity Night Club but in reality the highbred, high-spirited scion of an old and honored house in Costaragua—the son of a Presidente no less, a fugitive to this Land of Liberty, only to find himself—ironic fate—once more a prisoner. Ah, life is a cruel jest! But we must smile at it, even though our hearts be breaking.

The girl in the case, or as the French have it "Cherchez la femme" meaning "Women are gay deceivers ever" is a true daughter of the new Age, shallow as a boy, deep as a woman, with dark eyes that can light up with devilment or grow languid with love. One can see how the ardent, passionate Alvarez would be intrigued and eventually captivated by the saucy impudence of a piquant mind continually offering and as often denying the promise of a slim young body, unfolding to the first warm breath of life.

But there is a triangle here. Ah, sly reader—how did you guess it? And as every triangle must have three angles, let us seek the third angle. You will not find it in Sunny Costaragua and you will not find it in the humble Brooklyn home of an American dancing girl. No, you must go down to that grim, mysterious romantic spot which has been called the nerve center of the world: that powerful, insidious home of the mighty octopus—that narrow cavern of cruelty where hope and despair keep high court—Wall Street, with its graveyard at one end and its river at the other and all Heaven and Hell between. Here then, in one of those tiny cubicles where the crafty spider spins his web sits "Jack" Milton, millionaire broker, club man, raconteur, hail-fellow-well-met, sugar daddy, one of those modern Minotaurs who feeds on the young flesh of "girls who do not know." Today he is lying wracked on a bed of pain—stricken down by the avenging hand of Alvarez Romano, tempestuous son of a passionate south land where womanhood is a lovely and sacred thing.

Strange too that the girl who is the burning focus of love and hate in this triangle—strange too that her name should symbolize our own south land, for Dixie is her name. Dixie! Why the word is a roll of drums, a blare of trumpets with proud flags flying and tears of pride and love and devotion! And all of this too is here—in this triangle where Death keeps his grisly watch in a high hospital room, and Passion looks out of the dark burning eyes of a lover, in the grey depths of the Tombs and Youth with its tender dreams of love and all that life holds dear cowers in a simple Brooklyn home beneath the black wings of Tragedy.

(Tomorrow Miss Beatrice Heartsease will give our readers another of her poignant and searching articles entitled "She Was Young And Didn't Know.")

POSTAL TELEGRAPH – COMMERCIAL CABLES
TELEGRAM

JUNE 13TH

LR 630
NEW YORK CITY
DIXIE DUGAN
         439 FLATBUSH AV BKLYN NY
WOULD YOU CONSIDER OFFER OF FIVE
HUNDRED DOLLARS A WEEK FOR TWENTY WEEKS
OVER KEITH CIRCUIT OPENING PALACE
THEATRE NEW YORK CITY TWO WEEKS FROM
DATE
        B. F. KEITH VAUDEVILLE EXCHANGE

POSTAL TELEGRAPH – COMMERCIAL CABLES
TELEGRAM

JUNE 14TH

RLO L6
NEW YORK CITY
DIXIE DUGAN
         439 FLATBUSH AV BKLYN NY
WOULD YOU CONSIDER ENDORSING BABY FACE
POWDERS COLD CREAMS ROUGES WITH USE OF
YOUR PICTURE FOR ONE THOUSAND DOLLARS
        BABY FACE COSMETIC COMPANY

THE FASH-FORM MILLS INC.
"Makers of Maid-to-Wear Underthings."

June 14th.

Miss Dixie Dugan,
439 Flatbush Av.,
Brooklyn, N. Y.

My dear Miss Dugan:

We are sending you under separate cover one half dozen of our new Dixie Dugan Bloomers. At least we hope you will allow us to call them The Dixie Dugan Bloomers and we would even consider reimbursing you to some extent for the use of your name although we feel that the publicity that will accrue to you from the distribution of thousands of these bloomers from coast to coast is sufficient compensation.

We are very proud of the quality of silk that goes into the making of these, and the subtle pastel shades which was a real idea, our artist going direct to the natural color harmony of the flowers for his inspiration.

Anxiously awaiting your reply, we are
Sincerely yours,
Fash-Form Mills, Inc.
Per, Aaron Lipsowitch, President.

~~~~~~~~~~~~~~~~~~~~~~~~~

(The New York Evening Tab)
BEGINNING NEXT MONDAY
DIXIE DUGAN'S OWN STORY

True to its tradition of being the first with the latest, the Evening Tab announces it has secured at great expense the story of Dixie Dugan's life from her own lips.

Every father and mother will want to read this story—how a young girl who leaves her home to find fame and fortune in the wicked maze of Broadway becomes involved in a scandal which is rocking New York's social and financial structure.

This story comes from Dixie

Dugan's own lips and carries a message to the bewildered parent who today is asking that baffling question: "What will become of this young generation?"

Don't miss the first installment of this epic of night club life which Dixie Dugan has called with amazing simplicity "Ten Thousand Sweet Legs."

Order from your local news dealer!

~~~~~~~~~~~~~~~~

BELLEVUE HOSPITAL
FT. OF EAST 26 ST.
NEW YORK CITY

PRIVATE WARD 18.
June 15th

MISS DIXIE DUGAN,
439 FLATBUSH AVE.,
BROOKLYN, N. Y.

DEAR MISS DUGAN:

The first thing I saw when I came to were the roses you sent me. Only seeing you could have made me happier.

JACK MILTON.

~~~~~~~~~~~~~~~~

439 FLATBUSH AVE.
BROOKLYN, N. Y.
June 16th

MR. JACK MILTON,
PRIVATE WARD 18,
BELLEVUE HOSPITAL
FT. EAST 26 ST.,
NEW YORK CITY.

DEAR MR. MILTON:

I thought you were dying or I wouldn't have sent them. Throw them out if they annoy you.

DIXIE DUGAN.

~~~~~~~~~~~~~~~~

CHICAGO, ILL.
June 18th

DEAR DIXIE:

I hesitated a long while before writing this letter because I don't know hardly what to say. I can hardly believe that you are the girl I'm reading about in the papers. Dixie Dugan—my Dixie—going out to wild parties with millionaire brokers, being pursued by crazy Argentine tango dancers, mixed up in a brawl that may end up in a murder, and now with your pictures in all the papers, and news items saying you are going into vaudeville and into the movies, and today I see in one of the New York papers an announcement of your Life Story written by yourself. Well, you certainly surprise me.

Here I've been going along from town to town, selling Greeting Cards For All Occasions, trying to make an honest living, working hard toward the day when I can offer you my hand and my heart and an honest home where I could come home to a nice little wife who would love me devotedly and would appreciate a good home, and maybe a little house with a garden by the side of the road, and by the way, that's one of our best sellers—9M60 The House By the Side of the Road. You probably remember how it goes.

Let me live in a house by the side of the road,
etcetera.

I tell you I'm stunned and heart-sick but I guess maybe a fellow can never tell about women. They look like butter wouldn't melt in their mouths and the first thing you know they're out stabbing and shooting and raising hell in general. So maybe you had better get it all out of your system now and no matter what happens, I will always think of you.

All to myself I think of you

Think of the things we used to do
Think of the things we used to say
Think of each happy yesterday.
Sometimes I sigh, sometimes I smile
But I keep each olden, golden while
All to myself.

Your heartbroken
DENNY.

P.S. "All to Myself" is by Wilbur Nesbit and is one of our best sellers. I'm going to send you one of the samples from "Ye Sturdie Hearte of Golde" line, boxed with or without easels. It's made on glass and a little bit cracked but you'd hardly notice it. Whenever you read it, think of me thinking of you—all to myself.

D.

~~~~~~~~~~~~~~~~~~~~~~~~

<div style="text-align: right">439 FLATBUSH AVE.,
BROOKLYN, N.Y.
June 14th</div>

DEAR SUNSHINE:

Well by this time the G. F. is pretty dizzy. I haven't felt like this since I fell out of my crib and lit on my head. You should see the newspapers—great big black and red scare lines, composite photographs in the tabs showing me before and after taking—they have me all taken too. They won't believe that this little girl's motto is the same as Commodore Perry's—"Don't give up!"

Denny writes me sad notes from Chicago all full of the firm's best sellers. Why don't you ring him up at the Tower Building. He'd probably get a big kick out of taking out a chorine from the Scandals and you can tell him I still think he's a sweet boy, but he's too full of sediments. Alvarez is in jail offering me the moon and stars and a lot of hot Costaraguan pash, and then postscripts inviting me with real southern hospitality to have a knife and cut myself a piece of throat. And Milton in the hospital making sound financial passes. But the story of my life which I am writing for The Evening Tab and which I have to read every day to find out what I have written, that's the prize gag. Oh boy, what a lot of hooey! "Ten Thousand Sweet Legs" is the name of it. And I get one thousand sweet smackers for letting them write anything and sign my name to it and running as many moral photographs of me as the censors allow. And offers from vaudeville and advertisers wanting my name on their packages, and my face—no less—on their bottles. And I love it all to death but just when I am beginning to get real happy about it, I remember that Alvarez is going to be tried for murder and I'll be mixed up in it—sitting up there on the stand with my legs crossed, working the revealed knee on the jury. Well, I have a lot of faith in human nature. You've got to admit there's something in this sex appeal that they're all talking about. Look how it's hung on all through the years and then look at what's happened to those other crazes like Mah Jong and Cross Word Puzzles.

What do you think darling—I was offered a part in the biggest revue in New York and *I turned it down*, partly because I'll probably be making felt slippers in some woman's prison but principally because Walter Catlett told me I'd be swamped in it. "You'd be plumb nerts" says he, "to think of it." "Well, it's a big show," says I. "Yes," says he, "like the south half of an elephant, big but not interesting."

Hoping you are the same,

Dixie.

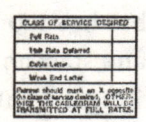

WESTERN UNION CABLEGRAM

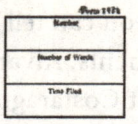

JUNE 16TH

RDO PARIS
DIXIE DUGAN
   439 FLATBUSH AV BKLYN NY
ARRIVING MAJESTIC MEET ME PIER
SATURDAY MORNING THE BIG SISTER WILL
SEE YOU THROUGH

NITA

IV

439 Flatbush Ave.,
Brooklyn, N. Y.
June 18th

Dear Sunshine:

There hasn't been so much excitement in one little girl's life since Fanny Ward was a child—and they do say that when they opened up Eighth Avenue they found one of her rattles in the same layer of mud with Peter Stuyvesant's wooden leg.

Firstly, the big sister Nita dashed back from Paris to help me through my troubles which up to then consisted principally in pasting clippings. If I were Sodom and Gomorrer, whoever they were, I couldn't have rated more white space next to pure reading matter. The dear old subscribers sure like a good hot sexy brawl with their morning Java.

Nita took hold of things the minute she got back, which I knew she would do. First thing she got busy with some of the men she knows who are way up in politics, or something and they had Romano's trial stalled off for a while to see how Milton recovers. Then she had a talk with Milton who is picking up nicely but seems to be sillier than ever about me. She says he would like to have Romano sent up but he doesn't want to get involved in any scandal himself, so he is pulling all the wires he knows to have the thing shushed.

Meanwhile my life story written by myself breezes along in the Evening Tab. Every new installment is a fresh surprise to me—the author who must pay out two cents every evening to find out what it is. It seems by the chapter today I was the bestest girl they ever had in

Sunday School and copped off all the little Golden Text Cards, which will certainly be news to mother who could never find me any time Sunday unless she sent out a posse. I mean after I learned to walk.

The next thing Nita did was to cinch that vaudeville offer Keith's made me. I get five hundred smackers for myself, and they pay the rest of the cast and expenses. The route is for twenty weeks but it seems there is a little goopher dust in the contract to the effect that eighteen of these weeks is optional on how the first two go. Well baby, if the first two don't go, all I got to say is there is no hope for vaudeville and the movies will have the field to themselves. My stunt is going to be a sketch called "Night Club" starring me. I'll sing and dance and act too. It isn't written yet but we are going to start rehearsals next Monday at Bryant Hall. Nita got hold of the man who writes a lot of these revue sketches for Ziegfeld and the Shuberts and he's working on it now. Can you see me as an actress? Get away from that entrance Jeanne Eagels—I can't have you stealing my stuff.... Who's on the phone? ... Mr. Belasco? ... Tell him to call me back, I'm in my bawth!

Whoopie! Get hot!
Dixie.

(N. Y. Herald-Tribune—June 18)
THEATRICAL NOTES

Confidential spies from this Department report that Dixie Dugan is going into vaudeville.

Pretty young things who get entangled with the law usually use the front page as a springboard into the Two-a-Day, but it seems that Dixie has something besides what her mother gave her.

It will be recalled by those of you who waste time on other departments of this paper that she was a specialty dancer in the Jollity Night Club where the Argentine, Alvarez Romano also danced before he eased a knife into "Jack" Milton, who was throwing a party up in his apartments for Dixie, and his boy friends, from which it would seem that Dixie though a brunette, suddenly went blonde.

Dixie Dugan's vehicle, in what is euphemistically called Variety, is a new sketch "Night Club." The brightest of our readers can probably deduce from this what the sketch is about. It will have a try-out out of town and then come into the Palace.

~~~~~~~~~~~~~~~~~~~~

June 20th

DEAR MISS DUGAN:

I read about you in the Minneapolis Tribune and the trouble you got into and it seems to me a girl like you all alone in the big city needs a man to take care of her. I am lonesome and affectionate and need a pal and helper, as I have a modest but successful little suburban poultry farm where I know I could make you happy. Will you marry me and help me take care of my chicken farm and my five darling little children? Their ages are from Hilda 7 yrs. to little Pete, age 9 mos.

Maybe you will be interested in knowing how I look. I am an American, age 46, but look 40; am 5 ft. 10 in. high, weight 160 lbs. and am very active. I am a Methodist and belong to the Sunday School and the Glee Club and have been a widower since Jan. Have been a country school teacher, a r.r. telegraph operator in Anoka, Minn. and all my life have been a hard worker, ambitious and a hustler. Now I am an experienced poultry man with an established egg business inventing labor-saving, sanitary brooders. I have a piano and violin and associate only with refined people who I know will be glad to entertain you as my wife, not holding your past against you.

Trusting you will snap up this opportunity, I remain

Yrs. truly,
(signed) PETER NORTON
Address: R. F. D. 4
Anoka, Minn.

~~~~~~~~~~~~~~~~~~~~

(From The Newark Star—June 21)

SPECIAL ENGAGEMENT
This Week Only
DIXIE DUGAN
In
"NIGHT CLUB"

With an All Star Cast Including
Jollity Club Jazz Maniacs.

(From Variety, Week of June 22)
STATE
(Vaude—Picts.)

Stand 'em up biz. May be due to the weather. May be due to the turns. The weather turned out better than the turns. Stand 'em up biz anyway.

Biff Magee and Pals (New Acts) opened. This is the old comedy mule stunt modernized for a lot of laughs. The Honeysuckle Four, individually heavy troupers, zipped across for an easy hit in the deuce spot. Barney and Gert, following, were a class twosome, working in 1927 tempo for a sizable score in the giggle department.

Ben Sorka and Maude are an unsubtle comedy team in "one" with Yid humor and soprano straight.

Eppus Duo—man and woman novelty perch turn in four, didn't get much of a deal. The woman's work on a high horizontal, balanced by the man, got out of range of the spot and was lost. A dull eye and low lights throughout not so good for the mob eye.

Dixie Dugan in "Night Club" was in the choice groove next to shut. A flash act that has everything—comedy, speed, girls, talent, etc. Dixie is an eyeful, an earful and means a houseful! What a girl! Where is Ziggy? The kid is clever—she's hot—she's vaudeville plus—she has all it takes—she dances like a zephyr—she has a mine of comedy—she has grace—personality—verve and sex. She's a bear. Nobody can stop her. The kid is there—she's the spirit of vaudeville. She sells it. They buy it. So be it. So be it. There it is. Take it or leave it.

Eight femmes and a pair of male hooters take up the burden when she is off. Girls plenty young to please the fatigued man of commerce.

There is a song bird in the act who ungargles a pip of a soprano.

Of course, there is a band—nicely received. Conductor, not so hot. Somebody should explain the difference between the up and down beat to the boy.

The comedy was a peppy hash of gags and stories. Some of the lines could be sent out to the laundry with the rest of the wash.

But Dixie is in. This is one tabloid scandal that dug up a live one without the aid of a bathtub.

The pic—"Hold That Girl" is one of those heavy muzzling affairs with the regular shrine in the garden finish. Ran the die-hards out of the house. Even the community petters with dark-corner specialties of their own couldn't stand it. Heigh ho!

(Early)

(From the N. Y. World—June 24)
SHIPPING NEWS

ARRIVALS:—S/S Sierra Cordoba from Costaragua, bringing among other distinguished passengers, Senor Fillippo Romano, ex-presidente of the Republic of Costaragua.

(From The N. Y. Tab—June 27)
DIXIE DUGAN DISAPPEARS
Beautiful Night Club Dancer and Stage Star Kidnapped or Murdered?

Last night the orchestra played the overture for Dixie Dugan at the State Theatre, Newark, and the curtain went up on an empty stage. The audience waited expectantly for Dixie to trip out. They waited and waited. No Dixie. The orchestra played the introductory music again. A wave of chill apprehension swept over the house. What could have happened? The curtain came down once more and an agitated stage manager hurried out and with profuse apologies to the audience explained that Miss Dugan was ill and could not appear but the show would go on. The show did go on—as usual—with lights and laughter out front. But back stage was pandemonium. Dixie Dugan was not ill. She had disappeared.

Careful search of her dressing room gave no clues. All of her street clothes were there. Her maid could give no explanation. "Miss Dugan came back here for a cigarette, just after her call," said the maid. "She was in her opening costume and made up to go on. I gave her a cigarette and she went right out that door. I haven't seen her since." The maid wept. But tears will not bring her back. Neither did any of the stage hands see her. Nor the door man, nor any one out in the street in the vicinity, so far as the police could learn.

All sorts of dark and ugly rumors are afloat. As everyone knows, Dixie Dugan is the central figure in the stabbing affray in which "Jack" Milton, millionaire broker and influential man-about-town, nearly lost his life a few weeks ago in a wild, early morning party in his luxurious apartments. It is said Dixie knows too much about the night lives of some of our leading citizens.

Rumor also connects the arrival in this country a few days ago of Senor Fillippo Romano, ex-presidente of the Republic of Costaragua, the father of Alvarez Romano, night club tango dancer, who stabbed "Jack" Milton and who until a few days ago was held in the Tombs. It is now learned that he was released a couple of days ago on bail but his attorneys are keeping him incommunicado.

On the other hand, it is rumored in financial circles that "Jack" Milton was one of a powerful syndicate of oil interests who underwrote the last insurrection in Costaragua which overthrew the Romano government. So this stabbing by Alvarez Romano seems more than just a jealous fight for Dixie. It may be an act of poetic justice!

~~~~~~~~~~~~~~~~

SCENE: *Living Room at the Dugan Home—439 Flatbush Ave., Brooklyn.*

REPORTER EVE. TAB: Are you the mother of Dixie Dugan?

MRS. DUGAN (crossly): Yes I am! What of it?

> "I am her mother," sobbed Mrs. Dugan. "Her mother who nursed her from tender childhood," and tears streamed down her honest, old face, wrinkled with care.

REPORTER: Will you tell us something about her childhood?

MRS. DUGAN: I will not!

> "Dixie was my little baby," she sobbed. And then she smiled wistfully through her tears. "And such a baby. Big brown eyes and golden curls. I've kept one of them. Would you like to see it?"

REPORTER: Can we take a picture of you?

MRS. DUGAN: No!

REPORTER (*to Photographer*): All right Mike.

MIKE, THE PHOTOGRAPHER (*to Mrs. Dugan*): Hold this please. Look at them as if you were about to cry. (*Hands her grimy pair of prop baby shoes which he fishes out of his pocket.*) Head up a little more please.

MRS. DUGAN (*proud in spite of herself over having picture taken*): Wait till I fix my hair a little, can't you?

> Her gnarled hands clutched the tiny baby shoes in which Dixie used to patter around the floor in those dear dead days of long ago when she would totter to the door and wave a chubby hand to her daddy coming up the rose-covered walk. "These are her first little shoes," sobbed the dear old mother. "Her little 'oots she used to call them. And now . . . and now . . . Where are those little feet?"

REPORTER: (*indicating three or four youngsters peering curiously through window*): Those yours?

MRS. DUGAN: Thank God, no!

(*Reporter gestures significantly to Mike who disappears and returns almost immediately with children whom he groups with professional speed around Mrs. Dugan.*)

MIKE: Now come on, kids, look up at the lady. Look sad. Put your hands on their heads, Mrs. Dugan.

MRS. DUGAN: What's all this for?

> TINY TOTS COMFORT FRANTIC MOTHER. The Evening Tab Staff Photographer pictures scene in home of Dixie Dugan when neighboring children come to console mother of missing night club star. "Where is boo'ful lady—Will boo'ful lady bing us tandy?" they prattle in childish innocence.

MIKE, THE PHOTOGRAPHER: Stop chewing that gum, will ya?

TINY TOT: Aw, go button your nose!

THIS IS STATION W-W-W BROADCASTING OVER A BAND OF NINE HUNDRED EIGHTY KILOCYCLES BY AUTHORITY OF THE FEDERAL RADIO COMMISSION. REPORTED MISSING TO THE POLICE—DIXIE DUGAN OF 439 FLATBUSH AVENUE, BROOKLYN, AGE EIGHTEEN, 5 FT. 2 INCHES TALL, WEIGHT 110 POUNDS, BROWN EYES, DARK BROWN HAIR. WHEN LAST SEEN WAS WEARING SHORT PINK STAGE COSTUME, NO STOCKINGS, BLACK SHOES. HAS SMALL SCAR ON LEFT WRIST, TWO SMALL MOLES ON BACK UNDER LEFT SHOULDER BLADE. LAST SEEN AT STATE THEATRE, NEWARK.

WHILE WE ARE WAITING FOR THE FINAL RETURNS OF THE NATIONAL LEAGUE WE WILL HAVE A SOLO BY MISS AXIE GOODYKOONZ WHO WILL SING "WOULD GOD I WERE THE TENDER APPLE BLOSSOM." . . .

~~~~~~~~~~~~~~~

The New York Evening Tab offers $10,000 reward for any news which will lead to the discovery, alive or dead, of Dixie Dugan, missing Broadway beauty and Night Club star who disappeared mysteriously from the State Theatre, Newark, on June 26th. Address Dixie Dugan Reward Editor of the New York Evening Tab.

~~~~~~~~~~~~~~~

VOX POPULI

To the Editor of the Evening Tab:

I am an old subscriber of yours dating away back two years come St. Steven's Day and probably the only subscriber you have who can spell out all the hard words under the pictures. So surely you will forgive me if I ask you to explain something in your paper which puzzles me.

You need not start so. It is not the editorial page. No. It is Dixie Dugan's life story entitled, rather pastorally I take it, "Ten Thousand Sweet Legs." How—and this is the question that burns me—do you manage to get daily installments of this story from her own lips for your Magazine Page when on the First Page of the same paper you not only admit you do not know where Dixie Dugan is but you will give $10,000 reward to any one who can tell you. Of course, if this is a professional secret like levitation or ectoplasm, or if it is something you do with mirrors, I will not blame you for treating this letter with the amused contempt it deserves.

                FAITHFUL READER.

POSTAL TELEGRAPH — COMMERCIAL CABLES
TELEGRAM

              JUNE 28TH

RE 30L 67
HARRISBURG PA
EDITOR NY EVENING TAB
         NEW YORK CITY
GIRL ANSWERING DESCRIPTION DIXIE DUGAN
TAKEN OFF TRAIN HERE WILL HOLD FOR YOUR
IDENTIFICATION AND REWARD
       POLICE DEPARTMENT

SHOW GIRL

```
                                    JUNE 28TH
SO 2L9 56
SPEEDWAY AIR FIELD
CHICAGO ILLI
EDITOR NY EVENING TAB
                        NEW YORK CITY
PLANE PASSED OVER HERE EARLY THIS
MORNING CARRYING PILOT AND GIRL WHOM
AIR MAIL PILOT EARL LANDRY CLAIMS
ANSWERED DESCRIPTION DIXIE DUGAN TRIED
TO APPROACH PLANE CLOSER BUT IT ESCAPED
IN FOG HEADED NORTH PLEASE ADVISE
            MANAGER SPEEDWAY AIR FIELD
```

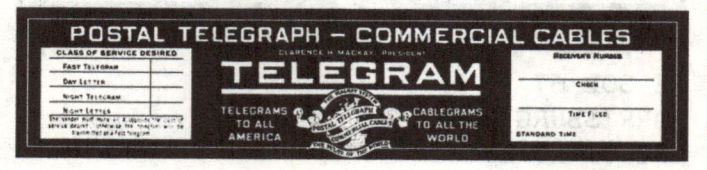

```
                                    JUNE 28TH
EG 547 33
FORT LAUDERDALE FLA
EDITOR NY EVENING TAB
                        NEW YORK CITY
WILL YOU PLEASE TAKE STEPS TO CONVINCE
LOCAL AUTHORITIES I AM NOT DIXIE DUGAN
AM BEING HELD HERE FOR SOME IDIOTIC
REWARD YOU ARE OFFERING MEANWHILE WILL
LOSE JOB UNLESS I GET TO JACKSONVILLE
WHERE ROBINSON BROTHERS CIRCUS IN WHICH
```

SHOW GIRL   87

I DO TRAPEZE ACT OPENS NEXT MONDAY WIRE
ANSWER CARE LOCAL CHIEF POLICE
                              PEARL LE MAY

                              JUNE 29TH
RL L72 50
BUTTE MONTANA
EDITOR NY EVENING TAB
                              NEW YORK CITY
DIXIE DUGAN FOUND HERE WIRE
INSTRUCTIONS
                              THE LIONS CLUB

                              JUNE 29TH
TA 444 95
DENISON TEXAS
EDITOR N Y EVENING TAB
                              NEW YORK CITY
I KNOW WHERE DIXIE DUGAN IS HIDING BUT
WILL REQUIRE SOME MONEY FOR EXPENSES
PLEASE WIRE ME TWO HUNDRED DOLLARS
                              G. F. GOLDBLATT

V

MINNEAPOLIS, MINN.
July 1, 1927

MR. DENNY KERRIGAN,
TOWER BLDG.,
CHICAGO, ILL.
HELLO DENNY:

What's the matter with your sales, ole fella? Where's the old pep? Where's the old wim and wigor?

A careful analysis of your sales reports for the last few weeks shows a slump which is not reflected in the reports of any of the other men. Business in the East and Middle West is uniformly good with steady reorders and heavy advance buying for the new lines. Watkins in Illinois and Kimball in Ohio are doing record business in Everyday cards and mottoes and especially in Ye Lyttle Boxed Gifts. In our leader—BX-11, Ye Merrie Lyttle Egg-Beater, both Watkins and Kimball have three hundred percent gain over you in the latest analysis of sales which I have made.

I can't understand this, ole fella, and I want to tell you confidentially the Old Man is getting darned peevish. He was going over the figures with me today and he said to me "What's the matter with Kerrigan?" And I said "He's all right." And the Old Man says "He is, is he? Then look at these figures." And I had to admit that the figures looked bad. "You can't tell me," says the Old Man, "that the demand for our Boxed Egg-Beater should go up in Illinois and Ohio and down in Indiana. They're still beating eggs in Indiana." And then I thought I'd have a little fun with him and I says "You know you couldn't beat eggs with those egg-beaters." And he says "Well, they don't know that in Indiana—at least, not yet. And besides, those are gift egg-beaters and you can't tell me they don't give egg-beaters in Indiana, especially when they come in a gift box with nine color off-set box top and a die-stamped hand-colored gift card attached." So I says, "Well Kerrigan is falling down on the egg-beater, but look at his sales on Wearyin' For You. Why he sold more of those mottoes, framed and cards with eps than all the other boys in the Middle West." And that sorta pacified the Old Man for a little while but he went away muttering about the egg-beaters, so I'm just tipping you off.

If there's anything on your mind, why don't you let a fella know. You know I'm one of the boys, even if I did give up juggling sample cases to park here on my haunches and kick the old sales in the tail once in a while. You can spill it to me, ole fella, 'cause I got a hunch there's something psychological about this. A good go-getter like you wouldn't fall down on a swell number like BX-11 if he didn't have somethin' eatin' his heart out.

Slip it to your gruff old sales manager.

AL.

P.S. BX-14, 3C-9, and the 5 cent Dad cards in black and white are out and won't be reprinted. Kill the dollar Mothers. There's no profit in it. We are putting in a new 75 cent retail Mother with engraved insert, as the trend seems to be toward cheaper Mothers and more expensive Sweethearts.

Tower Building,
Chicago, Ill.
July 3rd.

Mr. Al Evans,
Gleason Company,
Minneapolis, Minn.
Dear Al:

Herewith Sales Reports for week ending July 2nd.

You will note I took an increase on the Kiddy Mother-Goose Birthdays but I don't seem to be able to put my heart in the Boxed Gift Line. I think it's priced wrong and doesn't compare value for value with Buzza. I was talking to one of the Buzza men in the lobby last night and he said the whole Boxed Gift Line demand is falling off in Indiana so I can't understand what you say about Kimball and Watkins. Now you take BX-11 for instance, there's a gift item for fifty cents retail which is just a single-action egg-beater, and it doesn't compare with a similar article in the Buzza line, where they not only give them a double-action egg-beater, but the box top is done in that new Perroquet process, using water colors. I tell you I'm getting damned sick telling those dumb dealers those water colors won't last, because they always come back and say, "What of it? Nobody is going to beat eggs with the box tops. Suits us if they last long enough to get over the counter and out the door." So your Sales Strategy Board better think up a new knock for us fellows.

No, there ain't nothin' on my chest—that is, not much. I do wish I could take a week off though, for I'm not feeling so good.

Denny.

P.S. Mokowitz Brothers say they sent in a big mail order, so when I called, they weren't having any. And yet I didn't see any record of my getting any credit for this order. Mokowitz report a big Confirmation card business.

POSTAL TELEGRAPH — COMMERCIAL CABLES
TELEGRAM

JULY 5TH

DENNY KERRIGAN
X 261 LD

        TOWER BLDG CHICAGO ILL
LETTER RECEIVED OLD MAN SAYS TO COME IN
AT ONCE AND REPORT TO HIM.

        AL

~~~~~~~~~~~~~~~~~~

July 6TH.

SCENE: *Sales Manager's Office Gleason & Company*
TIME: 10 A. M.

    SALES MANAGER: He isn't down yet. Just as well.

    DENNY: What's on his chest? I mean what's eatin' him? I mean what's the big idea, huh?

    SALES MANAGER: He thinks you're layin' down.

    DENNY: Who, me?

    SALES MANAGER: He thinks you ain't got your heart in the ole Gleason line any more.

    DENNY: Who, me?

    SALES MANAGER: What's the matter? Why don't you tell a fella? You look like the last drink in the bottle.

    DENNY: I'm sick.

    SALES MANAGER: Where? 'Smatter?

    DENNY (*laying hand over heart*): Here.

    SALES MANAGER: Aw, go on! You talk like a True Story.

    DENNY: I should care what I talk like. I'm sick, I tell you. My heart aches so I can't stand it. I'm going crazy.

Sales Manager: You ought to sell Greeting Cards all the better for that. That's what we need in this Sentiment business—more sentiment. (*Suddenly.*) Now I see why you're ahead of your quota on 9M-63.

Denny: Just a Wearyin For You? That's a motto! Wish we had more like that.

Sales Manager (*triumphantly*): You're in love. That's what's the matter with you.

Denny: How did you guess it?

Sales Manager (*proudly*): Oh, you've got to be a psychologist in this business. How do you suppose a Sales Manager could hold his job if he didn't study people? Why the first principle of successful modern salesmanship is the ability to analyze the fundamental principles which underly the successful creation and stimulation of the initial desire for your product and then . . .

Denny (*wearily*): You said all that at the last convention. But I'm heartbroken just the same.

Sales Manager: She threw you down?

Denny: Not quite that.

Sales Manager: She's cheating?

Denny: Maybe, I don't know. God, how can you tell about women?

Sales Manager: That's true, too. (*Suddenly.*) Where is she?

Denny (*pacing the floor*): That's it. Where is she? If I only knew. She's gone. Disappeared. Vanished off the face of the earth.

Sales Manager: Yes? Who is she? Do I know her?

Denny: No. She's a little dancer in New York. The sweetest, the dearest, the loveliest, the cutest . . .

Sales Manager: I know. I know.

Denny (*ecstatically*): And eyes—big, brown, beautiful! And hands—like our motto Pale Hands That Took Hold of My Heart.

(*Continues rhapsodically.*)

> *I used to laugh at your tender awkwardness*
> *But that was before you took hold of my heart.*
> *And now I do not laugh any more*
> *For your hands are small and weak,*
> *But they are hurting me.*

SALES MANAGER (*suddenly, all business*): My God, I'm going to get the Old Man to turn over just the motto line to you and let you hit the big accounts. You'd clean up!

DENNY (*paying no attention*): You know she got into some sort of trouble down there in New York. She was dancing in a Night Club and she went to a party and a crazy Argentine dancer followed her there and stabbed the host of the party—a rich broker, named Jack Milton. And then she got so much publicity, she went on the stage. And the last I heard of her was an account in Variety, of her act, how wonderful she was and the next day there were headlines in all the papers of how she had disappeared, vanished right off the stage and no one knows where she is, and what's become of her even with rewards offered and everything.

SALES MANAGER: Gee, what do you know about that!

DENNY: It was bad enough before she disappeared. We sorta had a quarrel and I told her where to get off. I wasn't going to have her dancing in any night club and stabbing people in the back—I mean running around to wild parties and getting mixed up in murders and things. But since she disappeared, I've just gone crazy wondering all day what's become of her and dreaming all night she's been murdered or something and I've got so I just can't eat or sleep or nothing. I think I'll just go crazy if they don't find her pretty soon.

SALES MANAGER: But I thought you said you had a quarrel with her before that and had broken off?

DENNY: I know. But you know how those things are. Why Al, she's got to be so much a part of me, I could break off my arm just as easy as break off with her. Yeh, or a leg. That's how I am about her. Goofy.

SALES MANAGER: Well I know how you feel, but still in all the Old Man is paying you a salary and a commission to sell Mottoes and Greeting Cards and Boxed Gifts and it looks to me as though . . . here's the Old Man now. Good morning D. G.

GLEASON (*President of Gleason & Company, Greeting Cards For All Occasions*): 'lo A. E. 'lo Kerrigan. (*Shaking hands.*) I called you in to have a chat with you.

DENNY: I know.

SALES MANAGER: We were just talkin' it over.

GLEASON (*to Sales Manager*): So. (*To Denny*) Suppose I see you later, Kerrigan. (*Denny goes out.*) Now what's eatin' that young fellow?

SALES MANAGER: He's batty about some night club girl in New York. She disappeared.

GLEASON: Probably off with some other bird.

SALES MANAGER: No, I guess they were kinda fond of each other. She's been a victim of foul play or something. There's a big reward in the papers to find her.

GLEASON: That's tough, but what the hell's that got to do with Kerrigan's sales in Indiana? Did you tell him about that Boxed Egg-Beater?

SALES MANAGER: I wrote to him and he said we weren't putting enough value in the article compared with a similar item in the Buzza line.

GLEASON: My God! Is he selling Buzza goods or Gleason's. I never saw a salesman yet who didn't think he was an authority on manufacturing and costs and they can't even add up their expense accounts correct.

SALES MANAGER: I think he'll be all right when he gets over this love affair. He's young, you know, and sentimental.

GLEASON: I don't see any reason why we should let sentiment interfere with our business. Sentiment is all right on cards, to be sold in large quantities at a profit, that's all. Otherwise, it's just a damn nuisance. I know. I used to be sentimental. Then I went into this business and it took all the sentiment out of me.

SALES MANAGER: I know.

GLEASON (*wistfully*): You know Christmas is really something pretty fine, the spirit of Christmas, I mean. Christmas isn't just a day to give a lot of things away . . . I mean . . . damn these sentiments! They keep running in my mind. I remember when I was a kid and used to come down the stairs and see that tree all lit up, why it was like all the stars in the heaven on a summer night, and we used to sing songs and there would be a big turkey with plum pudding—you know I haven't seen a plum pudding since I was this high. (*Sadly.*) It would probably give me indigestion now. (*Suddenly.*) And what does Christmas mean now?

SALES MANAGER: Yeh, what?

GLEASON (*wistfully*): It means that eighteen months before it comes off, I'm going to worry whether some other outfit is going to get out a line with tissue-lined envelopes for five cents retail, and how many of the old dies can we hold over and stamp on new stock, and are we going to get any more of that Italian hand made paper. And one year before, I'm worrying all about the sample line getting out on time, and six months before, how orders are coming in and three months before, how re-orders are coming in. And about Christmas when all should be peace on earth and good-will to men, I've forgotten all about angels and camels and Wise Men and am wondering what the hell's the matter with collections. God, what a business! (*Savagely.*) That cub Kerrigan makes me sick—still sentimental!

SALES MANAGER (*soothingly*): I don't blame you.

GLEASON: A lot you know about it! Wait until you're as old as I am and you'll know what it means to be sick like I am. Envy, that's it. I wish I could get so crazy about a girl that I could forget sample lines, and sales and discounts and re-orders. And yet, what would become of this business if I did?

SALES MANAGER (*earnestly*): It would go straight to hell!

GLEASON: And a good thing too! (*Jams on his hat.*)

SALES MANAGER: Where are you going?

GLEASON: I think I'll go out and get drunk.

SALES MANAGER: What about Kerrigan?

GLEASON: Fire him. Or no, raise his salary. I don't care what you do. Don't let me hear about him any more.

SALES MANAGER (*helplessly*): I don't know what to do about him!

GLEASON (*sadly*): Neither do I. I guess you'd better send him in here. (*Sits down again. Sinks back in seat and pulls hat down over his eyes. Broods.*)

SALES MANAGER: Before he comes in, I know you'll be glad to learn that sales for the month have exceeded June of last year by twenty-five percent. That's five percent over the quota we set. We took most of the increase in with the new Song of the Heart series.

GLEASON (*far away*): Song of the Heart. Dear! dear!

SALES MANAGER (*on phone*): Tell Mr. Kerrigan who's waiting out there, to come in now. Mr. Gleason will see him.

~~~~~~~~~~~~~~~~

THE OPEN-EYE DETECTIVE AGENCY
We Never Sleep
12 EXCHANGE PLACE
NEW YORK CITY

July 5th.

To: MR. JOHN J. MILTON
67 WALL STREET,
NEW YORK CITY.
SUBJECT: *Confidential Report*

Operators 291 and 306 discovered yesterday small boy who had seen subject step into closed car at stage door of State Theatre, Newark. At time of disappearance had not been talked to by police. Boy thought nothing of the matter but when discovered by our operators remembered incident distinctly. Didn't take notice of license number. Did not see, or could not remember having seen any one else in car. Think we have clue of car. Will report.

CARMODY.

~~~~~~~~~~~~~~~~~~~~~

THE OPEN-EYE DETECTIVE AGENCY
We Never Sleep
12 EXCHANGE PLACE
NEW YORK CITY

July 6th.

To: MR. JOHN J. MILTON
67 WALL STREET,
NEW YORK CITY.
SUBJECT: *Confidential Report*

Special Operator 411 has traced whereabouts of subject through attorney who arranged bail. On arrival at address, however, found subject had just left taking all belongings in large brown leather suitcase. Found nothing in apartment but copy of Variety Magazine dated June 22nd with pages eighteen and nineteen torn out, as if hurriedly. Operator traced Variety file and discovered page eighteen contained story of motion picture combine and page nineteen, reports of three vaudeville shows in Newark, Brooklyn and Loew's Circle. Have called in operator 411 and assigned special theatrical operator to the case. Will report later.

Carmody.

~~~~~~~~~~

<div style="text-align: right;">67 Wall Street,
New York City.
July 7th.</div>

To: Open-Eye Detective Agency,
12 Exchange Place,
New York City.

Gentlemen:

    Thank you for your reports just received.

    Suspect Argentine dancer is involved in Dixie Dugan's disappearance and fear for the worst, as I know from experience he is a desperate man and would not stop even at murder.

    If anything of importance transpires, you can reach me through my private phone—Gramercy 0001. Spare no efforts or expense to locate her.

<div style="text-align: center;">Sincerely,
John J. Milton.</div>

~~~~~~~~~~

>   HOTEL HERMITAGE,
>   WEST 42ND ST. TIMES SQ.
>   NEW YORK CITY.
>   July 9th.

MR. DONALD GLEASON,
GLEASON GREETING CARD CO.
MINNEAPOLIS, MINN.
DEAR MR. GLEASON:

 I am afraid I was too overcome at your kindness to thank you as much as I wanted to for letting me have leave of absence for a few weeks until I can find Dixie.

 I guess I am like all the other fellows on the road who think you're just a hard-boiled business man with a cash register where your heart is. When I get back on the job, I'm going to work myself to death for you. Not that I haven't given my best efforts to the line up until now. But you were so darned nice—remember our 30X11—

> *They may make 'em as staunch and as foursquare as you,*
> *They may make 'em as honest and make 'em as true,*
> *With just such a mighty grand record behind 'em.*
> *But damn it old fellow! I never could find 'em.*

>   DENNY KERRIGAN.

VI

> Hotel Hermitage,
> Times Square,
> New York City.
> July 14th.

Mr. Al Evans,
Gleason & Company,
Minneapolis, Minn.

Dear Al:

Well, Al, I sure am putting in a busy session down here in New York what with this and what with that and I sure seem to be getting the low-down on this here Dixie Dugan disappearance. That is—a sort of low-down, so to speak.

Yesterday, I went down to Wall Street and met this fellow Milton I told you about. Well, it seems this broker is a sort of a broker—just what sort I don't know but he is about fifty years old and looks like a fat spider and is crawling with jack. Gee, when I sat there and looked at him and thought of him pawing Dixie, I wanted to jump over the desk and tear his heart out with my bare hands. But, he wasn't a bad sort after I got talking to him and he told me how he has a lot of detectives out trying to find Dixie and that he suspects this Argentine dancer Alvarez Romano is mixed up in it because he disappeared the same time Dixie did. But he says he'll find her if he has to spend his last dime to do it. I hope he does—I mean spends his last dime—and finds her too, for that matter.

I says to him why are you so hot and bothered about all this? And he says because I'm in love with her, he says and I says aren't we all?

But what good is it going to do you because I'm going to marry her. And then he has the gall to tell me I wouldn't be doing her any favor to marry her. You couldn't keep her in cigarettes, let alone stockings, he says and I says all the cigarettes she gets from me won't give her a cough. When I get hold of her, I'm going to make her cut out this rough and tumble night life and settle down in a nice little quiet home. And he says and raise a lot of nice little quiet kids, I suppose, with sticky faces and feet that go pitter patter. And I says that's the idea.

> *I love to hear the friendly sound*
> *Of little children pattering 'round*
> *Pattering 'round about the floor*
> *Oh how could you or I be sore . . .*
> *To hear them pattering 'round the floor,*
> *Pattering, pattering, 'round the floor.*

And then I goes on and recites the rest of it and he seems surprised that I can recite poetry, but you know I know every sediment in our line and could recite 'em all backwards which is the way most of 'em should be recited, if you ask me, because if we haven't got a cheesy bunch of poets writing our stuff, then I don't know poetry when I see it.

And by the way, that reminds me. He's got a sign over his desk on the wall that would make a swell motto. I made a copy of it while I was talking to him about Dixie. Look it up, and if it isn't too protected, let's use it. It goes like this: "Cheer Up! Remember Today Is The Tomorrow You Worried About Yesterday. Whoopie!" I can see that done in bold face lettering in gold against a black background, about 4 by 5½ say. We ought to sell a slough of them to offices and places because there's a deep thought underneath it—a kind of philosophy you might say. Am I right?

I've been picking up some very nifty ideas for the line while I've been hunting for Dixie but I've got to ring off now as I'm going to a good dancing show tonight to take my mind off my troubles. I bet I'd go crazy if I didn't get some sort of relief like this.

Best regards and tell the Old Man I hope to be back on the job soon. And I'll fill every little Indiana home so full of mottoes they'll be sweeping them under the beds to get them out of the way.

DENNY.

<div style="text-align:center">~~~~~~~~~~~~~~~~~~~~</div>

NEW YORK CITY.
July 15th.

MR. KIRK KING,
SCENARIO DEPARTMENT,
COLOSSAL FILM CORPORATION,
HOLLYWOOD, CALIFORNIA.

DEAR KIRK:

Well baby, this week has been a cuckoo. You know when I wrote you about a couple of weeks ago, I told you I was one of them there ghost writers doing my bit for belles lettres, as we call our Evening Tabloid magazine page, by knocking out a few sticksfull of bogus autobiography. Well, I'm still Dixie Dugan and my contribution to the Fine Arts is monastically entitled "Ten Thousand Sweet Legs." Boy, it's hot. With one hand I offer them sex and with the other I rap them smartly over the knuckles with a brass ruler and say "Mustn't touch. Burn-y, burn-y." Then I sling them a paragraph of old time religion and single standard and what will become of this young generation. (I hope nothing ever becomes of it. I like it just the way it is.) And then another paragraph like the proverbial flannel undershirt that is supposed to make you hot and drive you crazy, and presto! the uplifted forefinger, "But this is not what you should be interested in, children." And then a little Weltschmerz and then the old Sturm und Drang—a Sturm to the nose followed up with a Drang to the chin—the old one-two. So, as you may gather, this opus is the kind of love child that might result from an Atlantic City week-end party with the American Mercury and True Stories occupying adjoining rooms. So much for literature!

Now for facts. This Dixie Dugan person is a hot little night club dancer who got into a jam where one of those not so tired business men was stabbed in the giblets by a sun-kissed tango dancer from the coffee belt. Then she went into vaudeville and was kidnapped and that's just where the handsome speaker fell in soft, thanks to his native intelligence and that special Providence which watches over drunkards, children and newspaper men. And you have to keep it under your hat because it is one of those big office secrets. But we have so many of them, I can afford to be a little lavish with this one.

This Dixie baby was doing a vaudeville turn over at Newark and she walks out to the alley to puff a cigarette. She couldn't smoke on the stage because the fireman was either too old or too young, and she is standing out there in the alley just ready to go on, when up comes one of those long black cars we newspaper men are so fond of, and who should step out of it but Alvarez Romano, the old knife tosser from Firpo's fatherland. And who should be just behind him in a taxi but little Jimmy, the boss having sent him over to get some dope for Installment Number 12 for "Ten Thousand Sweet Legs."

Well the Spick and the little dame had a pow pow which I couldn't hear and she steps in the car presumably to finish up her smoke or her talky-talky and bingo! the car goes right away from there like one long black bat out of hell and Jimmy, that's me, says ah ha! this ain't regular, but maybe there's a story in it or maybe it's just a nice ride but anyway I'm on the expense account, so what of it? And I tells Jessie James up on the front seat to whip up which he does. Well, that Spanish caballero sure switched a mean tail light through the

Newark traffic and it seems we were always one corner and a half behind 'em, but we dashed right after 'em and then he starts to turn a corner which ain't there and it seems a truck had the same illusion and they both went socko! We pulled up just in time behind 'em to hear the swellest assortment of curses and breaking glass you ever listened to and what with the truck driver yelling curses in very bad Italian and this Spick responding with swell Spanish comebacks and little Dixie jumping up and down on the side walk, it was hotsy totsy, and up and up! Well Dixie sees me and I see Dixie and while the wop is looking for a club and Romano is looking for a knife, I takes Dixie in the cab with me and we go right away from there just two jumps away from the cops who begin to hover around the scene like country mechanics over a dead Ford and after we are some distance away Dixie tells me this Spanish influenza guy invited her into the car to finish her smoke and then kicked the gas right in the nose and told her he would do the same to her if she started to make any screams with her pretty face, that he had his plans made to take her with him out of the country and they could be married or else.

I told her I didn't blame him a bit. In fact, I was indebted to him for an idea and she says what do you mean? And I says this kidnapping. It's a great hunch, only instead of Alvarez kidnapping you, I'm going to do it and she says over my dead body and I says that isn't necessary. So then I tell her my scheme. I'll take her into New York and hide her in a swell apartment and the paper will pay all her expenses while she stays kidnapped and meanwhile the paper advertises extensively and offers fabulous rewards to anyone who can find her and my job would be to see they don't. Meanwhile, this would keep up the interest in her daily story, even more than my swell writing, if possible. And then we can cook up any kind of a yarn about how she was kidnapped by bootleggers, or high jackers or the Fascisti or the Ku Klux or the Shuberts. It won't make any difference which, because the dear public will promptly forget all about it as soon as we start something else. The public is the loveliest gift God ever gave a newspaper—it can always be depended upon to get excited one day and forget what it's all about the next. This breeds circulation and democracy, one and inseparable.

Well anyway, Dixie falls hard for the idea. She's a good scout and besides she could see all the publicity in it and the chance to have a lot of fun and be paid for it, and getting mixed up like this with the insides of a newspaper story struck her as plumb romantic. I bet new medical students feel that way about their first gall stones. Ah well, what is life without romance? Woe is me I that I can no longer capture that first fine, careless rapture! Maybe that's from Swinburne.

So as I write these few, vague, general and inadequate words to you, I and my paper have succeeded in kidnapping our star writer and from all over the country telegrams are coming in saying where they think she is. And yet if she were to lean out the window and let down her hair Rapunzel, it wouldn't reach to the sill. There's a big thought in this which you out there in Hollywood surrounded by master minds, can't miss.

More anon!

JIMMY.

~~~~~~~~~~~~~~~~~~

<div style="text-align:right">July 17th.</div>

DEAR SIS:

Well Nita, this letter is being smuggled out to you only to keep you and the folks from worrying. I am all right and living the life of Riley, right here in New York while a nation-wide search is being pushed by the paper which is paying my kidnapping expenses. I know this sounds ginny but there is nothing stronger than aspirin on the baby's breath. 1 cannot tell you any more except that I am well and happy and you are not to get excited or spill anything about this to anyone but the folks, and you are to tell them as little as possible to keep them from worrying which they may or may not do.

Well Sis, you should see Jimmy. Well what about Jimmy says you. Ah, that's what I'm trying to find out. But he sure is sweet and has lots of It. Besides that he is my ghost. That means he writes the stuff for the Evening Tab that I write only I get paid for it. And more besides, he is my jailor. Stone walls do not a prison make, nor iron bars a cage. . . . And that's not from one of Denny's mottoes either. One of Jimmy's first jobs as my abductor was to buy me some clothes as I was kidnapped with my stage costume. You should see what he bought me! What fun! Maybe if Jimmy and the paper will stand it, we can have a party up here in my solitary cell consisting of two rooms and a bath overlooking the Park. You know I've ridden many a taxi through this park and this is the first time I ever saw how it looked. Why the darn thing has trees in it with leaves on 'em just like that tree in the Student Prince. I always thought Shuberts faked it.

Have you heard anything from Denny? I wish I could write to him, but I have my literary career to consider. I bet I'll be famous if I can just stay hid long enough. One of the kicks I get out of life is getting the papers every day and reading how lost I am. You certainly have to read the papers to find out what's going on in the world.

Your loving sister,
DIXIE.

THE OPEN-EYE DETECTIVE AGENCY
We Never Sleep
12 Exchange Place
New York City

July 17th.

To: Mr. John J. Milton
67 Wall Street,
New York City.
Subject: *Confidential Report*

Nothing new to report. Operators 411 and Special Theatrical Operator working busily on clues.

We are enclosing bill for $1800, for services and expenses to date and would appreciate check.

Carmody.

Hotel Hermitage,
Times Square,
New York City.
July 18th.

Mr. Al Evans,
Gleason & Company,
Minneapolis, Minn.
Dear Al:

This is getting more and more delirious and now I don't know where I am but I'll tell you what happened up to now so you can see what I mean.

After I had that talk with Milton, I thought it over and it dawned on me that he was playing me for a sucker that he probably had Dixie hidden somewhere and all this talk of detectives being hired and his suspecting this Romano being mixed up in it, was a lot of bologny to cover himself. The more I thought of it, the madder I got. And yesterday I went down to his office and told him pretty. I says where do you get that stuff I says. And he says what stuff? And I says you know what stuff. If you think you can play me for a sucker, you're crazy and he says who's playing you for a sucker? And I says you are. And he says is that so? And I says yes that's so. And I know you've got a lot of money and you think you can get away with murder but I'm going to find out just where you've got Dixie hidden and I says all that talk about this Argentine being mixed up in it is a lot of hooey too, and he says you're crazy and I says not that crazy, and then he shows me a report on his desk from the Open Eye Detective Agency saying they were still looking for clues and he says you see they're trying to find her and the Spaniard and they haven't located either one. But they'll get them. These private detectives are smart and I says any good stenographer can write a letter like that. You don't expect me to swallow that, do you? And I started to tell him again where he got off and then who do you suppose comes bursting into the office? A tall, dark skinny bird sputtering broken English. Milton sees him and starts to duck under the desk and this guy who is nobody else than Romano which the detectives can't find, starts over the desk after him. And boy! I never felt so neutral in all my life.

Well, finally the rumpus settled down so they could hear each other talk and what do you suppose comes out? This Spaniard guy says he had Dixie in a car and he had an accident and when he looks around Dixie's gone, kidnapped from him. He says he didn't expect anything like that but he's sure he knows who did it and that guy is nobody else but Milton. Milton keeps saying he doesn't know anything about it, and he keeps saying it so hard and so fast that Romano begins to believe him.

And just then a boy comes in with a note for Milton and Milton says wait a minute, maybe this is news. And he opens the note and it is from the Open Eye Detective Agency and he reads "Shadow still following Spanish subject. Have no clues and sending bill herewith. Carmody." And then Milton gets mad and begins to do some of the swellest swearing I ever heard and then he pulls out the drawer of the desk and produces a bottle and three glasses and we all have a drink and talk it over and it seems all three of us are trying to find Dixie and now it looks as if there must be a fourth guy that's stolen her.

Boy! I never saw anybody disappear like that girl. She's just like one of those Irish fairies we used to read about when we were kids—lepracauns I think they called them. They're hard to get and you got to watch 'em all the time because the minute you take your eye off them they disappear.

And all the time we were talking, 1 kept looking at that fool motto over Milton's desk— "Cheer up. Remember Today Is The Tomorrow You Worried About Yesterday. Whoopie!"

DENNY.

THE OPEN-EYE DETECTIVE AGENCY
We Never Sleep
12 EXCHANGE PLACE
NEW YORK CITY

July 19th.

TO: MR. JOHN J. MILTON
67 WALL STREET,
NEW YORK CITY.
SUBJECT: *Confidential Report*

Operators 411 and Special Theatrical Operator are diligently pursuing clues. Think we have discovered new lead. No trace yet of Spanish subject but shadows are busy. Could we have check?

CARMODY.

SCENE: *In the office of George Carmody of The Open Eye Detective Agency.*
TIME: *Several days later.*

SECRETARY (*on phone*): Well, what does he want to see him about? ... Mr. Carmody never sees anyone without an appointment ... who? ... (*Covers transmitter with hand.*) Mr. Carmody, it's a reporter from the Evening Tab. He says he must see you right away. It's very important.

CARMODY: Don't you know I *always* see reporters? What's the idea? Send him in.

SECRETARY: All right. Tell Mr. Doyle, Mr. Carmody will see him. (*Jimmy enters. There is the usual exchange of greetings and then:*)

CARMODY: Well, what can I do for a representative of the press?

JIMMY: It's like this. We got it you're working on this Dixie Dugan disappearance.

CARMODY: I couldn't say yes or no to that. We have so many cases that we are working on here.

JIMMY: Well, as you know we're pretty interested in this case, the paper I mean, and I wanted to have a little heart-to-heart talk with you. You'd like to find her, wouldn't you?

CARMODY: Sure, but we'll find her. We never sleep.

JIMMY: Well if we found her before you did, there wouldn't be much glory in it for you, would there?

CARMODY: My boy, we'll find her. Quick as anybody. Quicker maybe. I don't mind telling you, in strict confidence, understand, I have three of our best men working on this night and day. (*Impressively.*) Night and day, mind you! (*With a pontifical gesture.*) We never sleep!

JIMMY: I heard you the first time. Listen, I've been handling this Dixie Dugan stuff for the Evening Tab since it broke. I'm writing her life's story too and I'm in a position to give you all the breaks, pictures, publicity, anything you want, provided you play ball. Is that clear?

CARMODY (*eagerly*): Now you're talking. What do I do, pitch or catch?

JIMMY: Well, give me some facts first. Who's putting up the dough for these three sleepless wanderers of yours?

CARMODY: Jack Milton, the broker. He's gone plumb nuts about this little wren.

JIMMY: And you'd just as soon have him keep on putting up, wouldn't you, just so long as he finds her?

CARMODY: Well, that's rather a crude way of putting it but I can't find any flaws in it.

JIMMY: All right. Then here's the racket. In the first place, I know where Dixie is.

CARMODY (*genuinely surprised*): Thahellyasay! How do you know that?

JIMMY: Because I put her there.

CARMODY: You mean you kidnapped her?

JIMMY: Sure. And I want her to stay kidnapped until I get ready to spring her and I want to spring her my own way. And I don't want any of your flat-footed sleep walkers wandering in on this accidentally. In other words, you come in on the party and I'll tell you where she is and if I move her, I'll keep you posted. Meanwhile, you can send all the reports you like to Milton—good ones—I'll help you write 'em. I'll put some literary invention in 'em. Instead of the usual dumb "Shadow Follows Subject," we'll just have that a part of the time and the rest of the time we'll have "Subject Follows Shadow." That'll be an innovation.

CARMODY: But where do I come in?

JIMMY: Well, when we get ready to spring her, you're going to find her, with my help and then you get yours from Milton and the paper plays you up all over the first page with close-ups of your eagle eyes and your rubber heels and everything. Why, you'll be famous over night. What say?

CARMODY: That's K.O. with me.

JIMMY: All right. Now the first thing we'll do is call in those three shadows—they're probably in that speak-easy around the corner—and I'll take 'em up to Dixie's apartment and we'll introduce the shadows to the subject and maybe throw a party—we could write some reports for Milton between drinks.

CARMODY: Say, that's all right about the girl, but what about this Argentine? We're following him too, for Milton.

JIMMY: Don't you know where he is?

CARMODY (*defensively*): Well, we've got clues.

JIMMY: That's bad. Now if you just had something important. Why the devil didn't I kidnap him too while I was at it? It would be just like him to stumble in on this and bust it all up.

TELEPHONE: Br . . . r.r.r.r.ng!

CARMODY: Yes . . . hello . . . this is Carmody . . . what? . . . well hold him there! . . . what . . . what . . . no . . . yes . . . no . . . don't tell me that . . . Oh my God! . . . (*Hangs up.*)

JIMMY: What is it?

CARMODY: Milton's office . . . the Argentine just left there . . . Milton told him about my having him shadowed and he went out with blood in his eye . . . said he'd kill 'em . . . my best detectives too. . . . (*Sadly.*) My God, I bet he finds them.

JIMMY: Aw, you can get some more detectives.

CARMODY: Yeh, but these boys are away overdrawn on salary and expenses. It'd just be my luck to have 'em bumped off owing me a lot of money.

JIMMY: I got it! Why don't you keep 'em right on the case? In that way they'll never find him—or he them, either.

CARMODY: Not a bad idea!

One Hour Later.

Tekephone: Br ... r.r.r.r.ng!

Carmody: Hello, who is it?

Voice: This is Jimmy Doyle. What the hell do you mean by double-crossing me?

Carmody: What are you talking about?

Voice: Dixie. Where did those flat-footed sleepwalkers of yours take her?

Carmody: Why nowhere! They're right here in the office now. They ain't been out all day.

Voice: Oh my God! Then where is she?

Carmody: Where is who?

Voice: Dixie Dugan, of course.

Carmody: Well, how should I know? (*Struggling for something to say.*) Isn't she there?

Voice: Hell no! She's gone. Vanished! Not a trace!

Carmody (*wailing*): Now we got to go and hunt for her all over again!

VII

Hermitage Hotel,
West 42nd St.
July 26th.

Mr. Al Evans,
Gleason & Company,
Minneapolis, Minn.
Dear Al:

Well, I'm coming back to work Al—back to the old grind. Everything is going to be hotsy totsy now, as they say down here in New York. All this sweating and fretting about women is over. They can all go to. They're all alike Al. Don't believe any of 'em.

It's just like the other night I was to one of those night clubs trying to forget my troubles with a blonde who was trying to wish hers on me instead. And after I spent enough to take the mortgage off the old farm, we started for the door and the orchestra plays "Just Another Day Wasted Away."

Well, it's like that with women Al. Every day you're with them, it's just another day wasted away. You can tell the Old Man I'm coming back and spread greeting cards and mottoes all over the state of Indiana. I'm going to strew 'em Al. No one will escape. All this energy I've wasted on Dixie is going to be turned into channels that are worthier and full of purpose.

I guess you gather from this that I'm off Dixie. Well, I am. But first, where do you suppose I found her, with detectives and newspapers and what not hunting for her all over America. I goes over to her house one evening and there she is sitting in the front room reading about herself being lost. Well, I says, I thought you was lost. Didn't you know I was down here looking for you and she says you and who else? The whole world has been looking for me. At least if not the World, the Evening Tab—newspaper joke. Heh! heh!—and then she tells me the whole story how she was kidnapped by this dancing spick, Alvarez Romano and later by Jimmy Doyle who writes her stuff for the Evening Tab and the Evening Tab kept her hid while they pretended to be hunting for her so as to make a big story. Finally she got tired of staying hid so she went home—the last place that a detective would think of looking.

So I says now that you had your fling, I suppose you're ready to settle down now and marry a good man and she says what's this, a nominating speech? Name him and don't keep me in suspense like this. But I says I don't have to name him. You're looking at him. What do you say we get married and get a little apartment in Chicago and I'll come home to you every Saturday night after my week on the road selling mottoes and greeting cards in Indiana. And she says I can depend upon you coming home Saturday night, can I? You wouldn't fool a dumb girl and sneak in on Friday? And I says no kidding now Dixie, I'm crazy about you and you know it and if you don't marry me, I'll—I don't know what I'll do and she says you can sublimate it. That's being done now and besides I don't want to marry you or anybody else, says she. I'm young and full of the devil and want to stay that way for a while. And then she says she doesn't want to get married and doesn't want to have children crawling around the floor because when she comes home late some night she might step on them and hurt them and then she'd never forgive herself. Or they might start staying out late nights or come home snozzled and she'd worry herself sick about them. And I says to her stop fooling now Dixie. What is your real reason for not marrying me? And she says do you want me to get personal? And I says go as far as you like and she says well you're a dear, sweet boy but you're no career, and that's what I want. I'm going back on the stage in a new show and I've got one of the principal parts and years from now when I am fat and famous and retired and a little slow on my feet and you want to renew this proposition, I'll consider it among my other proposals in rotation as received. Meanwhile, Indiana is calling for you and you'll be of much more value to the nation and yourself on the banks of the Wabash far away. Go back to Indiana says she and sell millions of greeting cards, and scatter sunshine through the land, says she, and forget little Hard-Hearted Hannah who loves you too much to smear your life by leading you into an ambush from which you're bound to wake up dizzy some morning with your ears full of rice.

Well Al, this sort of talk went on I guess until one or two o'clock in the morning with me sounding her out like this and finally I got it Al. This show she's going into is being financed by this broker and he's promised to make her a star. I couldn't compete with that kind of money and I told her I was going to go back home and forget I had ever met her. Do you know what she says? She says I bet you can't. Well, I'll fool her Al. The world is full of women. What is it Kipling says?

> *A woman is only a woman*
> *But a good cigar is a smoke.*

I bet that would make a good motto Al. Think of the thousands of men who would like to hang that up on the wall and look at it every day and agree.

And by the way Al, after I got home last night I wrote a little motto which I think would be a big seller.

> *I think of you through all my nights*
> *I think of you through all my days,*
> *Wherever I go*

*I see the glow
Of your sweet and lovely ways.
But every day I think of you
I to myself do say
Another day thinking of you, of you,
Is another day wasted away.*

That would look nice illustrated Al, with a border of forget-me-nots and maybe a fellow standing on a hill looking out across moonlit water as if he were looking and looking. Try it out on the Creative Department anyway Al. Not that I expect much results because they think they know everything and yet they sit up there out of touch with the world, pulling ideas out of their hats and us salesmen who are out in the world, in touch with life all the time keep sending them ideas which they throw in the waste basket.

I want to tell you Al, one of these days I'm going to throw a bombshell into this organization. I'm going to tell the Old Man just what I think of it and show him our line is losing all its vitality because of the antics of the Creative Department.

Well Al, have the old grips packed and be sure I get a complete line this time. I don't want to go out on the road and find numbers missing and then be bawled out for not sending in orders for numbers I haven't got.

I'll be in the Chicago office Monday ready to hit the ball as in the good old days before I ever met this woman who has blighted my life. There's a swell new song down here that states the case. It's from "Allez Oop" and it says "Pull Yourself Together and Smile." It goes something like this—

*Pull yourself together and smile
Troubles will pass you by
Life is like a beautiful isle*

Under a changing sky.

And then something or other and finishes up

*Pull yourself together and smile
And watch the clouds go by.*

That's me Al. S'long.

Denny.

~~~~~~~~~~~~~~~

<div align="right">439 Flatbush Ave,
Brooklyn, N. Y.
July 28th.</div>

Sunshine dear:

    I haven't written to you for ages and I've a lot of alibis, some of which are true. I suppose I could start off and tell you some little ones and gradually lead up to some whoppers and you'd be so astonished, you'd forgive me. But truth is stranger than fiction, as Denny would say, only he'd try to make a motto out of it.

    Speaking of Denny, he's gone back to Indiana after laying down the law to me saying either I marry him or go to hell. I pointed out to him I might do both but I preferred to take them separately. He is convinced that it's all off with me anyway and that I'm too full of spirits, drugstore and otherwise, and he went away saying his heart was broken. The fact is I'm real fond of Denny and I guess I'd even marry him if I had nothing else to do.

    Some day I'll get married and raise a lot of marvellous children, but right now I'm helping the City Fathers keep down the traffic. Why should I help crowd the subways? You can't get into them now. I was reading only the other day that they can't build schools fast enough to take care of the children. I'd feel terrible if I went to all that trouble only to find my children had to stand out in the rain to do their lessons.

Meanwhile, my little brain—which is one name for it—is all a-twitter and a-twirl. His name is Jimmy Doyle and he has me going around like a top. Did I tell you about him before? Maybe not. There are so many men in my life. Applause! Well anyway, he is a special writer on The Evening Tab and he's been doing my life story and meanwhile trying to add a few chapters of his own. He's as cute as a little red wagon and writes beautiful and I think he's hot dog. And he's written a musical comedy with a swell part for me and he says I'm going to be a star, so all I need now is to have all the critics and the public agree and that will make it unanimous.

I can just hear you say that's a lot of bology, but don't be so sure because we've not only got a star and the author but we've got an angel. Yes sir, little Dixie has grabbed herself an angel. Or rather, he has attached himself to Dixie and he's getting a producer and going to put up the jack for this show. I suppose you've guessed who it is. Jack Milton, the beautiful broker who threw that party for me and got stabbed in the back by Romano for his pains. All he says he wants me to do is to think sweetly of him and make good. I think he knows that I know what I think he means but if he thinks I'm selling out for a speaking part, he's due for a long buggy ride. As for the show he's going to put on, we haven't named it yet but it's all about me starting poor and winding up rich. There are all kinds of places in it where I can act all over the lot besides hoofing hot and hooting musically.

Alvarez Romano, my red hot Tamale has been playing dead for some time now. So I suspect he is up to some new devilment and will probably break into the picture and try to smear things just when I am sitting pretty. Well, he's an exciting devil. I wish Denny had some of his S. A. Denny is just too sweet and orderly to be thrilling. Now with Jimmy, you never know where you are and with Alvarez, you never know where he is. What I wish I could do is merge the three of them with Jack's money and marry the syndicate. I'd go shopping with Jack, stay home with Jimmy, tell my troubles to Denny and spend the week ends with Alvarez.

Love and kisses.

DIXIE.

67 WALL ST., N.Y.
August 1st.

MR. JAMES J. DOYLE,
% EVENING TAB,
NEW YORK CITY.

DEAR MR. DOYLE:

I have finished reading the manuscript of your musical comedy "The Girl from Woolworth's" and I have sent it to my friends, the producers Kibbitzer & Eppus with suggestions for changes which I think will improve it. I don't propose to know anything about the show business but I know what I like and if they approve of the script with my changes, you will probably hear from them within a few days.

Yours very truly,
JOHN MILTON.

KIBBITZER & EPPUS
1000 BROADWAY
N.Y.C.

August 4.

Mr. J. J. Doyle.
℅ Evening Tab,
New York.

Dear Mr. Doyle:

Will it be convenient for you to come in and see the writer 11 o'clock tomorrow morning?

Moe Eppus.

~~~~~~~~~~~~~~~

August 5—11 o'clock.

Mr. Eppus is out of town but leaves word for Mr. Doyle to come in and see him tomorrow at 11 o'clock.

~~~~~~~~~~~~~~~

August 6—11 o'clock.

Mr. Eppus was called out suddenly but will Mr. Doyle come back to see him at 3 o'clock this afternoon?

~~~~~~~~~~~~~~~

Same day. 3 o'clock.

Mr. Eppus is tied up in conference but will Mr. Doyle come back next Monday?

~~~~~~~~~~~~~~~

Next Monday.

Mr. Doyle catches Mr. Eppus going out. Mr. Eppus makes an appointment for Thursday afternoon.

~~~~~~~~~~~~~~~~~

Thursday afternoon.

Mr. Eppus suggests Mr. Doyle see Mr. Kibbitzer next Monday.

~~~~~~~~~~~~~~~~~

Next Monday.

Mr. Kibbitzer sends out word he never heard of Mr. Doyle. Will Mr. Doyle write him a letter telling him what it's all about?

~~~~~~~~~~~~~~~~~

Mr. Doyle writes a letter to Kibbitzer and Eppus telling them what it's all about.

~~~~~~~~~~~~~~~~~

The Following Day.
No answer.

~~~~~~~~~~~~~~~~~

One Week Later.
No answer.
Mr. Doyle telephones Kibbitzer & Eppus. Both out of town.

~~~~~~~~~~~~~~~~~

                                                August 27.

Mr. John Milton,
67 Wall St,
New York City.
Dear Mr. Milton:

I have received a letter from Kibbitzer & Eppus asking me to come in to see them.

I have tried to see them for weeks now with no result. What shall I do?

                                                Yours truly,
                                                Jimmy Doyle.

                                                August 29.

Mr. James J. Doyle,
℅ Evening Tab,
New York City.
Dear Mr. Doyle:

I have been talking with Mr. Eppus on the telephone and he says they wrote to you but you never came in to see them.

Feels if you are not more interested than that, they are not interested in producing your play.

Kindly go in to see them at once, unless as they say, you have lost interest.

                                                Yours truly,
                                                John Milton.

The Following Day.
　Mr. Doyle goes in to see Mr. Eppus. Mr. Eppus is out of town.

~~~~~~~~~~~~~~~~

The Following Day.
　Ditto.

~~~~~~~~~~~~~~~~

The Following Day.
　The same.

~~~~~~~~~~~~~~~~

The Following Day.
　Also.

~~~~~~~~~~~~~~~~

The Following Day.
　Likewise.

~~~~~~~~~~~~~~~~

Bulletin.
　Mr. Eppus sees Mr. Doyle and makes an appointment for tomorrow.

~~~~~~~~~~~~~~~~

Tomorrow.

Office of Mr. Eppus—of Kibbitzer & Eppus.

MR. EPPUS: I'm glad to see you, Mr. Doyle. Mr. Milton tells me you have written a play.

DOYLE: Why, haven't you read it?

MR. EPPUS: Read what? I haven't any play here of yours. (*To secretary.*) Have we a play here of Mr. Muggins?

DOYLE: Doyle is the name.

MR. EPPUS: I beg your pardon—Mr. Doyle.

SECRETARY: I don't think so. (*Pries gingerly into huge mountain of letters, telegrams and manuscripts on Mr. Eppus' desk.*)

MR. EPPUS: (*rises courteously to assist her. Looks on top layer*): Why no, Mr. er . . . er . . . er . . . er . . .

DOYLE: Doyle is the name.

SECRETARY: What's this? (*Picks up script from chair on which Mr. Eppus has been sitting.*)

MR. EPPUS: (*reading title with great surprise*): "The Girl from Woolworth's," by James J. Doyle. (*Laughs heartily.*) Well, to think I've been sitting on it all this time. It must have been there a week. (*Heartily to Doyle.*) Yes sir, at least a week because before that I remember I had one of Sammy Shipman's plays there that he had been looking for for months and it was there all the time. Oh well, that's the way it goes. (*Sitting down, suddenly all business.*) Now what is it Mr. Doyle? What did you come to see me about?

DOYLE (*helplessly*): Why, you sent for me, Mr. Eppus.

MR. EPPUS: I don't remember that. (*To Secretary.*) Did I send for Mr. Doyle?

SECRETARY: I don't believe so.

MR. EPPUS: But now that you're here, we might just as well talk. Mr. Milton tells me you've got a play. Is this it?

DOYLE: Yes.

MR. EPPUS: (*riffling through first few pages*): Cost too much money. There isn't any money anymore in shows like this. If I played $40,000 gross a week for a year, I wouldn't get my bait back. And the road—well I don't have to tell you what the road is like, Mr. Doyle.

DOYLE (*flattered*): I guess it's pretty bad.

MR. EPPUS: It's the movies what did it.

(*15 minutes elapse during which Mr. Eppus tells how the movies did it.*)

DOYLE: Mr. Milton suggested I come in and see you about this show. He said you were interested.

MR. EPPUS: We're always interested in works of new authors. I make it a point to read scripts the moment they come to my desk. I'm going to give this my very earliest attention. (*Stack of manuscripts which has been teetering precariously on desk, falls into waste basket.*) Yes sir, one never knows when a great hit is going to come into your office. Take "Abie's Irish Rose," it went the rounds of the managers for years. And "Broadway" and "The Spider" and "Burlesque." (*Picks up a couple of manuscripts and puts them on chair and sits on them.*) Yes sir, in this business we must keep one eye open all the time. (*Suddenly, briskly.*) I'm glad I met you, Mr. Doyle. Some time when you have something, bring it in and I'll be glad to read it. (*To Secretary.*) Take a letter. Lee Shubert, Shubert Theatre, New York City. It has come to my attention that your office has been making a practice . . . no cross that out . . . it's too damn polite . . . I'd like to know what the hell you mean . . . no, I'd better not say that either . . . take it again . . . where do you get that stuff . . . that sounds all right . . . Goodbye Mr. Doyle . . . where do you get that stuff trying to . . . now what was I going to write to him about anyway? (*Glances idly at script on desk. Reads.*) "The Girl from Woolworth's." That's a good title. Did you read it?

SECRETARY: Yes, it has some fly stuff in it.

MR. EPPUS: That's the one Milton wants to bankroll, isn't it?

Who's the dame?

SECRETARY: He's cracked on a little night club dancer—Dixie Dugan. You know she was mixed up in that stabbing and then went into vaudeville and made a hit before she was kidnapped.

MR. EPPUS: What did Variety say about her?

SECRETARY: Said she was swell. Wondered why Ziggy didn't cop her.

MR. EPPUS: Ziggy waits until somebody else makes 'em, then he cops 'em. I bet if I put her in this show and two critics mentioned her name, the next day Ziggy'll be calling her out of bed before she's read the papers herself. Silly like a serpent, that guy. Have Milton come in and see me tomorrow and send that script to Otto Harbach right away and tell him to call me early tomorrow morning and tell me if he can make English out of it. We've got to get something to follow "Oui Oui Wilhemina." You could have shot a machine gun through that orchestra last night and hit nothing but cut rates.

One Week Later.

KIBBITZER & EPPUS
1000 BROADWAY
N.Y.C.

September 5th.

MISS DIXIE DUGAN,
439 FLATBYSH AVE.,
BROOKLYN, N. Y.

DEAR MISS DUGAN:

Will it be convenient for you to come in and see Mr. Eppus tomorrow morning, at 11 o'clock in regard to part in "The Girl From Woolworth's"?

This show is now being cast and rehearsals start in ten days.

Yours very truly,
MINNIE NIVOTCH,
Secretary to Mr. Eppus.

VIII

THEATRE NOTES COLUMN
(Evening Tab—Sept. 17th)

A plaintive whinny has come in from the Kibbitzer and Eppus office anent the alleged scarcity of girls who can sing, dance and switch a mean gluteus maximus for the edification and solace of the wearied gentlemen of commerce.

Girls with the above qualifications are asked to report on the stage of the Alhambra Theatre at eleven o'clock tomorrow as rehearsals are now under way for "The Girl From Woolworth's." This is a new opus by a new face in the theatre, if one may be allowed to use this locution. His name is Jimmy Doyle of the EVENING TAB staff. He has written the book and the lyrics.

Among the featured players appears the name of Dixie Dugan who will be recalled as the little night club dancer from the Jollity who became involved in a stabbing fray which grew out of a party in the bachelor apartments of Jack Milton, the wealthy broker. Although several investigations were conducted it seems the only answer the police could get from those present was that they were waiting for a street car.

It is rumored "The Girl From Woolworth's" opens in Atlantic City for a week and then comes into the Globe.

~~~~~~~~~~~~~~~~~

<div style="text-align:right">

MUNCIE, INDIANA.
September 18.

</div>

DIXIE DARLING:

I see in the papers you are going into a new show so I suppose your career is going along all right and you have forgotten all about me. It is just as well, I suppose, because I am learning to forget you, as you told me to. I'm all wrapped up in my work now and getting along wonderful. We are making a big drive on box assortments of Christmas cards, 12 assorted in a box with envelopes retailing at 50¢. This is our Ye Glade Tidings seller and a big department store in Terre Haute ordered a thousand which gives you an idea. They're going to have a fellow dressed up as Santa Claus at a counter selling these. And I wrote one of the sentiments myself which I think isn't bad at all. It goes...

> *Christmas ain't a season*
> *Christmas ain't a day*
> *Christmas ain't a reason*
> *For giving things away.*
> *Christmas ain't a buying*
> *Or selling in the mart*
> *Christmas is a happiness*
> *And you're the biggest part.*

The buyer for O'Connor's Au Petit Coin here in Muncie told me she thinks that's the best sentiment she ever saw. I think she's just a little bit goofy about me, but then you've never been in Muncie so you can't imagine the scarcity of males. Anything that walks upright and combs its hair and is seen in town not more than twice a year can throw the females into a panic.

We have a motto in our line which I was going to send you because it expresses just what I have been thinking since I saw you in New York and you told me you thought more of having a career than you did of me. But then I decided not to send it although I think I'll quote you a few lines just to show you what it is like. It retails $1.50 with plain mouldings, 40, 40 and 5, 40 and 10 discount. It goes After A While I May Not Care. No. 4M11.

After a while I may not care
That the sunlight glimmers in your hair
And the dear delight of summer's skies
Is deep in the depths of your lovely eyes
And after a while it may be true
That my heart won't ache for the sight of you
And I can forget your slow sweet smile
After a while.

Of course, you've got brown eyes but the idea is just the same. I wish you would write to me if you ever get the time and tell me what you're doing. I don't see why we can't be friends. Though, of course, you don't have to unless you want to. But I never did anything to you that I can remember. You can suit yourself. Still I would like to hear from you. I am sending you my route list for the next two weeks, but if you should lose it you can send your letter to the main office in Minneapolis and they will forward it to me.

Sincerely yours,
DENNY.

~~~~~~~~~~~~~~~~~~~~

SCENE: *Office of Kibbitzer and Eppus.*

(Seated at twin desks are Mr. Kibbitzer and Mr. Eppus. Jimmy Doyle, the trusting young author of "The Girl from Woolworth's," has been called in to discuss a few changes in the show now in rehearsal.)

KIBBITZER: Mr. Eppus and I have been talking over your script, Mr. Doyle, and we think it's all right.

DOYLE (*beaming*): Gee, I'm glad to hear that.

KIBBITZER: Don't we Mr. Eppus?

EPPUS: Absolutely.

KIBBITZER: But we think it ought to be changed a little bit. I don't suppose you'd mind just a few changes?

DOYLE: Well, it's been thought out pretty carefully, Mr. Kibbitzer, and of course I'd be glad to do anything that's necessary, but don't you think . . .

EPPUS (*showing his fangs for just a flash*): Of course we think. What do you think we do in this show business? Guess? Let me tell you . . .

KIBBITZER (*soothingly*): It's like this, Mr. Doyle. Mr. Eppus and I have been talking over your script and we think the title's wrong. "The Girl from Woolworth's" is well, kinda cheap. This is going to be a swell production with the orchestra scaled at five fifty and at least two big sets and swell costumes. And how are we going to make Woolworth's look five fifty from the front? So, we thought we'd change it to "The Girl from Tiffany's."

DOYLE (*aghast*): But that changes the whole idea. I have to rewrite the whole thing.

KIBBITZER: Oh, no. You might have to change two or three scenes in the first act and change the characters around a bit. We have to throw the boarding house out anyway. We thought that scene could be played on the deck of a steamer going to Europe. (*To Eppus.*) Remember that set from the first act of "Ah, There, Paris" that closed in Newark last fall? We can get that for a song and re-paint it and there you are for one of your big sets.

DOYLE: But, my God, man the boarding house is where all the heart interest is. We got to show this girl how poor she is and where she came from and all the friends she has.

EPPUS: Can't she have friends on a liner? She can have more friends on a liner than in a boarding house. And they'd be sweller, too. And a boat gives us a chance to use a sailor chorus with a moonlight effect. And we can use those two ripple machines for the water. Have you any idea how much those ripple machines cost? And, besides, who the hell wants to pay five fifty and look at a cheap boarding house for half the night?

Kibbitzer: You see, you've got to be practical about the show business. It's all very well for you smart fellows to write a show, but we're the poor fellows who have to put it on.

Doyle (*bitterly*): I suppose if you got "Romeo and Juliet" you wouldn't produce it unless you could buy a balcony cheap.

Eppus: "Romeo and Juliet"? Pfui! I seen that once. There wasn't a hundred dollars in the house.

Kibbitzer: That kind of play don't make money. You got to stick to things people understand.

Doyle: I suppose Woolworth's and a boarding house is too deep?

Kibbitzer: That ain't the idea. You got to give them flash, so when there's nothing going on even and the jokes are bum and the singing is rotten they've still got something to look at.

Doyle: Any other little changes?

Eppus: Well, you got to get a first act finale. You got it all wrong. Thr girl is happy and having a good time. Why if we opened in New York with that kind of a first act finale the Cain's Warehouse man would be backstage measuring up the scenery. No sir, you got to have her crying, see? Her heart's broken. That's the secret of successful musical shows knowing just when to break the little girlie's heart. Yes sir, she's crying. The young buyer has gone off to France thinking she has stolen the necklace.

Doyle: What young buyer? I never heard of him before?

Eppus: Well, he's in. What the hell do you think we got Bobbie Watson for?

Doyle: I don't know. I didn't know you hired him.

Kibbitzer: Well, we didn't exactly hire him. We got him in a trade for one third interest in "The Mad Honeymoon" and the Vitaphone rights to the subway scene in "The Yes Girl." Besides, he's a swell light comedian and you haven't got a light comedian part in the book.

DOYLE: And may I ask where you got the necklace? Or is that any of my business?

EPPUS: Oh, we put it in. You've always got to have a necklace. But we've got a real novelty this time. For years they've had nothing but pearl necklaces, but Kibbitzer and I talked it over and I got the idea of the diamond necklace.

KIBBITZER: You got it?

EPPUS (*defensively*): Well, we got it together. Anyway, the girl's crying and just when their hearts are breaking out front forty or fifty young debutantes run in singing "Let's Be Happy," the hit song, and the curtain comes down on her dancing and laughing through her tears. That'll wow 'em.

DOYLE: Say, what show are you talking about? I never wrote any song "Let's Be Happy." I thought I was writing the lyrics for this show.

KIBBITZER: Well, we got two or three songs we're putting in. You're going to like them. Gee, they're swell. (*Sings to Eppus.*)

> *Oh, let's be happy*
> *Each girl and chappie*
> *Let's be happy now*

How does the rest of that go?

EPPUS (*singing a bit off key*):

> *Behind the cloud so gray*

KIBBITZER (*joining in*):

> *Little Mister Sun is chasing*
> *All the blue away.*

Doyle (*almost tearfully*): But that isn't my song and it doesn't fit in the book. It has nothing to do with the plot.

Kibbitzer (*still singing*):

> So let's be happy
> For somewhere for every chappie
> There's a little girl like you.

What did you say?

Eppus: What do you know about the show business? What shows did you ever produce?

Kibbitzer (*the old oil*): Now, now, we're all agreed. We're not going to have any trouble. Mr. Doyle here is a sensible author. He's not like those crazy authors who scream murder if you change a line. He's got a swell script here and all we've got to do is make a few little changes and everything will work out just swell. By the way, Mr. Doyle, we can buy the Tampico Marimba Band cheap and a couple of the fellows are pretty good actors. Couldn't we write the band in somewhere? I thought somewhere in the second act this boat could stop off at Mexico and the band would be on a hacienda or something. Mexican stuff is always good. Look at "Rio Rita."

Eppus (*sourly*): Well, this ain't no "Rio Rita."

Doyle: I guess you're no Ziegfeld either.

Kibbitzer: Ziegfeld is lucky, that's all. For twenty-five years just one break after another. If he went down with the Titanic he'd come up with "Abie's Irish Rose."

```
                POSTAL TELEGRAPH – COMMERCIAL CABLES
                            TELEGRAM
```
                                        SEPT. 19TH 12 NOON
RE 267 81
INDIANAPOLIS IND.
DIXIE DUGAN
            439 FLATBUSH AVE. BKLYN NY
DID YOU GET MY LETTER
                    DENNY-LINCOLN HOTEL

~~~~~~~~~~~~~~~~~~~~

```
                POSTAL TELEGRAPH – COMMERCIAL CABLES
                            TELEGRAM
```
                                        SEPT. 19TH 4 P. M.
12 NK 132
BKLYN NY. 141 P
DENNIS KERRIGAN
        LINCOLN HOTEL INDIANAPOLIS IND.
WHY
                                    DIXIE

~~~~~~~~~~~~~~~~~~~~

SHOW GIRL 137

POSTAL TELEGRAPH – COMMERCIAL CABLES — TELEGRAM

```
                              SEPT. 19TH  8 P. M.
SE 667 NITE
INDIANAPOLIS IND.
DIXIE DUGAN
              439 FLATBUSH AVE. BKLYN NY
NEVER MIND.
                                         DENNY
```

~~~~~~~~~~~~~~~~~~~~~

POSTAL TELEGRAPH – COMMERCIAL CABLES — TELEGRAM

```
                              SEPT. 20TH  12 NOON
NA 411 22
BKLYN NY
DENNIS KERRIGAN
         LINCOLN HOTEL INDIANAPOLIS IND.
SKILLABOOTCH.
                                         DIXIE
```

~~~~~~~~~~~~~~~~~~~~~

Sept. 21st.

Sunshine Darling:

You're sure lucky to be all set hoofing in the Scandals with nothing more to worry you than runs in your stockings. They've got me going around down here like a waltzing mouse these days. Jack Milton tells me he's going to have me starred. He says they have to do what he says because he's putting up most of the sugar, but Eppus says if I get featured I'll be lucky. And Kibbitzer acts as though the first thing they're going to do after they raise the curtain next week in Atlantic City is throw my trunk out in the alley. Kibbitzer isn't carrying any banners for me no way not since he made one of those ah, there little girlie passes at me and I wasn't having any. Just another big brother! Well, that's what a female gets for having Deese, Dem and Doze. Meanwhile they're running my poor Jimmy out of gas. He is getting colly wobbles and pink eye and he screams when you look at him. After rehearsal yesterday he cried all evening into my coffee. You see, he started out with a real cute book for this show, but they've changed it around so much already he can't remember what it used to be. And every day at rehearsal they change it some more. The first change was from "The Girl from Woolworth's" to "The Girl from Tiffany's." Then they changed it to "The Girl from Childs." Then Kibbitzer found a lot of Mexican costumes he could buy cheap so they changed it to "The Girl from the Rio Grande." Now it's been changed again and it's called "Get Your Girl" and it's supposed to be up in the great northwest. Jimmy has re-written all the roles half a dozen times in as many dialects. And already I have been a clerk, a French model, a Mexican senorita and now they've changed me all over again and I'm a cowgirl. Jimmy says if he ever does another musical comedy he won't write an original book to begin with at all. He'll just copy "The Merry Widow" and sell them that for by the time they get finished rehearsing it will be entirely different. The only trouble with that, Jimmy says, is that a producer like Kibbitzer wouldn't buy "The

Merry Widow." He'd be sure to say it wouldn't have a chance.

Oh, I was going to tell you Jimmy wrote me the cutest little song. It goes with a scene that thank heaven is still in where this boy and I have the last word in small apartments. It's just a piano, but it's a trick piece of furniture out of which you can open everything, a bed, a table, a bathtub and the keys are knives and forks and the pedals are golf sticks and there's a little ice box with one slice of bread and one egg. And we're supposed to be happy now that we're out of that cramped hotel room and have a home of our own where we can have a family and where we can entertain buyers from Milwaukee and everything. Here is the song. It's called "In Our Little Two By Four" and the tune is by Con Conrad and it's just darling. Here is the way the first verse goes:

> *Wide open spaces*
> *Are silly places,*
> *Dear.*
> *Full of home owners*
> *Building-and-loaners,*
> *Queer.*
> *We never knew what a home-loving heart meant*
> *'Till we had lived in a co-op apartment,*
> *Cuddled together*
> *Sweetly,*
> *Neatly.*

And this is the chorus:

> *We've a cat that folds into a kitten*
> *In our little Two by Four;*
> *Our Great Dane collapses to a poodle*
> *Which is quite a charming chore.*

> *We've a duplex first and second mortgage*
> *That we keep behind the door—*
> *We can laugh and well the banker knows it*
> *There's no room in which he could foreclose it*
> *Soon a folding stork will maybe*
> *Bring a disappearing baby*
> *To our cunning little Two by Four.*

But I think the second chorus is even cuter:

> *Oh, we keep our telescopic baby*
> *In our little Two by Four*
> *She collapses in her folding cradle*
> *When we open up the door.*
> *She is trained to crawl upon the ceiling*
> *When we have to use the floor.*
> *Of our space she fits in but a fraction—*
> *All her little joints are double-action.*
> *Raised on milk condensed in cans, so*
> *She will always fit our plans, so*
> *We are happy in our Two by Four.*

And right here I would like to rise in my large white cravat and tell you Jimmy is just what the doctor ordered to be taken after each meal. Most of the time he pays no attention to me and believe it or not I get more kick out of that than being pawed by a lot of these catch-as-catch-can taxi wrestlers. But when he does pay attention to me like last night when he took me out to dinner after rehearsal and told me all his troubles, well, you see he's got a low soft voice and he never quite finishes his sentences. Just kind of leaves them up in the air and looks at you—and ooh, sotch a geese flesh. And just when you think he's kind of falling for you he starts talking about something else as though you were a million miles away. Well, I tell you he just has me looping the loop. He doesn't even get jealous. Can you feature that? I guess I gotta learn a new technique to get Jimmy, 'cause I do so want him. I do so. Positivel.

I think I'll hurry to bed so I can dream about him some more.

Dixie.

IX

NOTICE

All members of the company of "Get Your Girl" will leave at 2:30 p. m. Sunday from the Penn Station for Atlantic City. Full Dress Rehearsal Sunday night. Curtain 8:30.

~~~~~~~~~~

Atlantic City Daily Star
(Sept. 28.)

"GET YOUR GIRL" IS HOT, SAYS EPPUS

Tomorrow evening at the Apollo Theatre, Kibbitzer and Oppus will present the premiere of their latest and greatest musical comedy, "Get Your Girl."

Dixie Dugan, the night club dancer who recently had the jury weeping in a thrilling Broadway murder trial, is being featured in this elaborate extravaganza from the pen of clever Jimmy Doyle, N. Y. Evening Tab scribe, with music, tra la, by Con Conrad, dances, hey hey, by Sammy Lee and scenic effects, and how, by Herman Rosse. Walter Donaldson and Gus Kahn have contributed interpolated numbers to this brilliant orgy of song, dance and splendor which Mr. Ippus, in an interview early this afternoon, claimed will be the most stupendous attraction to open in Atlantic City since the "Follies."

Mr. Eppus believes he has discovered a new American Prima Dona in the pretty person of Dixie Dugan and entertains high hopes for the new songbird's future.

It is the initial venture into musical comedy for the young journalist, Jimmy Doyle, but Mr. Eppus insisted it is most certainly the work of a seasoned veteran who thoroughly understands the many ins as well as the many outs of superior musical comedy production.

Dixie Dugan is to be capably supported by an enormous and high salaried cast of exceptionally talented artists which, asserted Mr. Eppus, would run high up into the hundreds if the time were taken to count them. But the management has been too busy with a million and one more important tasks in preparing "Get Your Girl" for its gala opening performance tomorrow evening at the Apollo Theatre.

~~~~~~~~~~~~~~~~~~

DRESS REHEARSAL

SCENE: *Apollo Theatre, Boardwalk, Atlantic City.*

(It is eighty-thirty p. m. and the stage is full of electricians, carpenters, property men, scenery, props and advisors. Every member of the company was individually notified that he, she or it, as the case might be, could not and must not bring any one to the rehearsal, positively and absolutely. In consequence there is no one sitting out in front except each girl's mother, her girl friend, her boy friend, her girl friend's boy friend and her girl friend's boy friend's uncle from Des Moines. Also there are performers from the night clubs who don't go on until midnight; representatives from the music publisher who is stuck for the orchestrations unless there is a hit; scouts from the ticket agencies; performers week-ending in Atlantic City full of good wishes and conflicting advice; and lost somewhere in this shuffle, the author, the composers, the scenic designer, the book director, the dance director, three backers and the producers, Kibbitzer and Eppus. We're off.)

KIBBITZER (*yelling from first row*): HEY! YOU UP THERE ON THE STAGE. HEY THERE! MIKE! JOE! JUMPING JUDAS WHERE IS THAT STAGE MANAGER? JOE!

Voices (*taking it up*): JOE! . . . OH, JOE . . . WHERE'S JOE? HEY PETE, SEEN JOE?

KIBBITZER: Well get Mike for me.

Mike (*assistant stage manager*): Yes, Mr. Kibbitzer?

Kibbitzer: What's the matter up there? Why aren't you set and ready?

Mike: We're doing the best we can, Mr. Kibbitzer. We've been trying to fix that pink baby spot.

Eppus: To hell with the pink baby spot. Get that stage clear. Set the opening and let's start. We'll be here all night.

Joe (*stage manager*): Somebody looking for me?

Kibbitzer: Now look here, Joe. Stand by there so we'll have you when we need you. Are the girls ready for the opening?

Joe: The girls are all ready, but the costumes haven't come yet.

Eppus: Well where the devil are they? Go and find out who's taking care of that.

Kibbitzer: Come back here. Get the stage clear and we'll do the opening without costumes. Call all the girls on the stage.

Joe (*shouting off stage*): EVERYBODY ON STAGE FOR THE OPENING NUMBER. COME AS YOU ARE.

Voices: OPENING NUMBER . . . EVERYBODY ON THE STAGE . . . ON THE STAGE . . . OPENING NUMBER . . . COME AS YOU ARE . . . HURRY UP.

(*Crowd of pretty young things in kimonos, bath robes, bathing suits and pink underwear struggle through mob of carpenters, electricians and property men.*)

Kibbitzer: Come on, come on. We'll be here all night. Hurry up. Line up in your positions . . . who's missing?

Eppus: That isn't all the girls. Where's the rest of them?

Joe: Well, some of them haven't shown up yet. They missed the train.

Little Blonde (*stepping forward*): Lorraine called up, Mr. Kibbitzer, and said she would be on the next train. She was awfully sorry.

Eppus: She'll be a damn sight sorrier when she gets here. Who's next to you over there ? . . . (*no answer*) . . . You with the black hair!

Fifteen Voices: Yes sir?

EPPUS: Hey, you over there. You. What's your name? Joe! Who the devil's missing over there?

JOE: That's Irene's place, Mr. Eppus. She's lying down.

EPPUS: The hell you say. Looks to me like you're all lying down tonight. I suppose we better let everybody sit down and take it easy until she's had a rest. What the devil do you think we're paying a thousand dollars an hour here for?

JOE: Yes sir.

KIBBITZER: Stop that hammering back there!

STAGE CARPENTER (*advancing slowly and menacingly*): What did you say?

JOE: Mr. Kibbitzer wants you to stop that hammering.

STAGE CARPENTER: Yeh, and who is Mr. Kibbitzer?

JOE: Why he's the owner of this show.

STAGE CARPENTER: Yeh, well he don't own much. Of all the cheap lousy building I ever saw. Every time you touch a flat it falls apart.

JOE: Well stop that hammering.

KIBBITZER: Hurry up and get your work done and get off the stage. We'll be here all night.

STAGE CARPENTER (*peering over footlights to locate direction of voice*): And who are you?

KIBBITZER: I'm Mr. Kibbitzer.

STAGE CARPENTER: Listen, big boy, if you think you can do this job any better than I can come up here and do it.

EPPUS: You're through. Get your money.

STAGE CARPENTER: Boys, did you hear that? We're through. Come on. (*All work stops like magic as entire crew starts to walk out.*)

JOE: Hey! Wait a minute. Wait a minute.

KIBBITZER: Hey, my God, you can't do that. Stop them, Joe.

(*Joe patches it up after half an hour's parley, during which entire cast stands around in full makeup waiting patiently.*)

KIBBITZER (*running up and down the aisle*): Can't we be doing something?

Eppus: Looks to me like we did. If you want to bawl someone out bawl out the cast and lay off that union labor.

Jimmy Doyle (*the author no less*): Oh, Mr. Kibbitzer. Have you got a minute?

Kibbitzer: NO! Hey you girls up there. Go and sit down some place. No, you can't come out here.

Eppus: Yes you can. Get off that stage.

Kibbitzer: Stay where you are a minute. Walk that opening number. Let's have some music.

Musical Director: I haven't got the opening number. The orchestration hasn't come yet.

Composer: You told me you were bringing it with you.

Musical Director: What are you talking about? You didn't write it until yesterday.

Composer: Well, the first one I wrote was good enough. If you hadn't belly-ached so much we'd have that.

Eppus: Now that you boys have that all settled, what are we going to use for music in the opening?

Musical Director: Search me. I've got the old opening here. Come on, boys. The first opening. Let's go.

Dance Director: Hey, wait a minute. Stop. Stop that music. What's the big idea?

Musical Director: What's the big idea yourself?

Dance Director: You can't use that music. I did a whole new routine for that new opening.

Kibbitzer: Well, we're going back to the old routine.

Jimmy Doyle: Say, you can't use that old routine. We went all over that yesterday. It finishes full stage. How am I going to get into that apartment scene from a full stage without that time in front?

Dance Director: Who the hell cares how you get into your apartment scene? It's no good anyway.

KIBBITZER: Cut out the apartment scene.

JOE: Strike the apartment!

(*And that is the cue for Dixie Dugan to come to life. The little apartment scene is one of her pet numbers. She has rehearsed it for four weeks.*)

DIXIE: Oh, Mr. Kibbitzer. The apartment scene isn't out, is it?

KIBBITZER: Yes, we can't make the change. We'll put something else in that spot for you. Hey, Jimmy! Write another scene for this spot. Something in one.

DIXIE: Aren't you going to leave it in for the dress rehearsal even?

KIBBITZER: Didn't you hear me say it was out?

JIMMY DOYLE: Well, I'm not going to write a new scene for that spot.

DIXIE: Well, if I can't have that scene I don't want to be in this show. You can have my notice right now.

KIBBITZER: Joe, take Miss Dugan's notice.

DIXIE: And what's more I'm catching the train back to New York tonight.

EPPUS: Hey, wait a minute you can't do that. You can't walk out on a dress rehearsal like that.

DIXIE: Well if you're cutting out everything I do what's the use of me staying here? Just to be near the ocean?

KIBBITZER: Let her quit if she wants to.

EPPUS (*pulling Kibbitzer down close to him*): Don't be a fool. If she walks out Jack Milton won't kick in another nickel. And we're going to take it on the chin for five thousand down here this week.

KIBBITZER: We gotta hit. If you had any sense you'd freeze Milton out now.

EPPUS: Well, I think we got a flop and it isn't honest to freeze Milton out of it.

KIBBITZER: Where is he? I thought he was coming down here?

EPPUS: He's over at the Ritz. He'll be here any minute and you know as well as I do if you get gay with Dixie he'll walk right out and take our other backers with him.

Kibbitzer: Maybe you're right.

Eppus (*sweetly*): Oh, Miss Dugan. You don't care where the apartment scene is so long as it's in, do you?

Dixie: You can throw it in the alley for all I care.

Kibbitzer: Oh, we all like it and we like you in it, but it's too early in the show.

Dixie: It isn't too early if it's out, is it?

Kibbitzer: Who said it was out? We're just moving it, that's all. It's out of the first act, that's what I meant. See, you misunderstood me.

Jimmy Doyle: Well, I'd just like to know where you're going to put it in the second act?

Eppus: Just stick around, I'll show you.

Joe: The costumes are here for the opening.

Eppus: Go on, girls, hurry up. Get ready for the opening.

Joe: Hurry up, kids, step on it.

Kibbitzer: For the time being we'll leave the apartment scene where it was.

Dance Director: Well, then, I have to change the routine again.

Kibbitzer: Is that all right with you, Miss Dugan?

Dixie: All I want to know is whether it's in or out?

Kibbitzer: It's in.

Dixie: Okay.

Eppus: Say, are we going to have a rehearsal tonight? Come on with those lights. Who's lighting this show anyway?

Designer: I'm supposed to be lighting it.

Eppus: Well get busy. Light it.

Designer: Dammit, set it first. Get all those people off the stage so you can see what the scenery looks like.

Eppus: I can tell without clearing the stage. Looks cheesy.

DESIGNER (*defensively*): You'll see it will look different with the lights on.

KIBBITZER: It's the goddamest looking scenery I ever saw.

EPPUS: Give us a pink flood and take the blues out of the foots.

JOE (*shouting to spotlight men*): A PINK FLOOD!

VOICE (*from the gallery*): WHAT?

JOE: A PINK FLOOD ... NO, NOT BLUE ... PINK ... P-I-N-K ... PINK!

DESIGNER: Terrible.

KIBBITZER: More pink. Can't we have more pink? Where's your borders?

DESIGNER: My God, you don't want pink on that set.

EPPUS: Well, let's try the blue again. Give us all the blues you got.

JOE: BRING UP YOUR BLUES ... HEY ... A BLUE FLOOD ... BLUE!

ELECTRICIAN (*in gallery*): WHAT?

JOE: A BLUE FLOOD ... B-L-U-E!

ELECTRICIAN: YOU SAID PINK.

JOE: I KNOW I DID.

ELECTRICIAN: WELL MAKE UP YOUR MIND. WHAT IS IT? BLUE OR PINK?

JOE: BLUE.

DESIGNER: Swell.

EPPUS: I like the pink better. Change it back to the pink.

KIBBITZER: The way you had it before, Joe.

JOE: KILL THE BLUES ... BRING UP YOUR PINKS ... HEY ... CHANGE THAT FLOOD TO PINK ... COME ON, COME ON ... WHAT ARE YOU WAITING FOR?

ELECTRICIAN: WAITING FOR YOU TO MAKE UP YOUR MIND.

KIBBITZER: Come on, come on. Let's get started on this rehearsal. We'll be here all night.

VOICES: HEADS UP ... LOOK OUT FOR THAT DROP ... MOVE IT YOURSELF ... IT'S NOT IN MY DEPARTMENT ... GIVE US A WORKING

LIGHT HERE . . . GET THOSE TRUNKS OUT OF THESE WINGS OR WE'LL THROW THEM IN THE ALLEY . . . JOE . . . MIKE . . . MORE PINK ON THE BORDERS . . . OH, MR. KIBBITZER . . . OH, MR. EPPUS . . . EVERYBODY STAND BY FOR THE OPENING NUMBER . . . OPENING NUMBER . . . BRING DOWN THAT HOUSE CURTAIN . . . TAKE IT UP . . . BRING IT DOWN . . . LEAVE IT THERE . . . SAY WHAT THE BLANKETY BLANK . . . BLANK . . . BLANK . . .

(*Seven a. m. the fallowing morning and Dixie Dugan has just staggered in from the dress rehearsal. Her sister, Nita, who has come down to Atlantic City to be with her for the week, is drowsing in the other bed. Dixie is pacing up and down, wild-eyed, over-wrought and hysterical from excitement and fatigue.*)

Do you really think it's going to be all right? . . . Do you really? . . . I'm so frightened. . . . Gee, I'm dead. . . . If I could only sleep. . . . Seven o'clock in the morning and rehearsing since eight last night and there's a call for eleven o'clock. . . . Four hours sleep, if I can sleep. . . . Milton wants to give me a party tonight after the opening. . . . I bet I fall asleep at the table. . . . Am I dead! . . . He left about two. . . . Said I was going to be great. . . . Do you think I am? . . . I'm so panicked. . . . Oh, if I don't go over I'll just die. . . . And they keep changing the numbers and switching things around. . . . Was that a madhouse! . . . You should have heard Jimmy and Eppus go to it this morning. . . . About three or four, I don't know. . . . Gee, you'da popped. . . . Eppus wanted to put some ducks in the show. . . . Said they'd look like swans from out front. . . . Nobody'd know the difference. . . . Wanted to tie their legs together and anchor them in a real pool of water in the garden scene. . . . Well, you'da died. . . . The ducks didn't know what it was all about. . . . The minute the orchestra started up they got panicked and started flapping their wings. . . . In three minutes that stage was so wet a fish would have drowned. . . . Then I was supposed to come out and lead that hot number. . . . On a wet stage, mind you. . . . Well, we all landed on our fannies. . . . One of the girls turned her ankle. . . . She'll be out tonight. . . . What a break! . . . Gee, I'm dead. . . . You wouldn't mind working, but the sitting around and standing and waiting while Eppus argues with Kibbitzer and the musical director fights with the composers. . . . And everybody else yelling and the girls weeping and fainting. . . . Poor Jimmy. . . . They sure did swarm all over him. . . . What's the use of my going to bed? . . . I can't sleep. . . . If I only had a drink. . . . Milton gave me a couple of drinks early in the evening out of his flask and Jimmy hit the roof. . . . He's all right now. . . . He walked back here with me. . . . Gee, he's a sweet kid. . . . I hope it goes over for his sake. . . . Do you think I'll be all right in it? . . . I'm so worried. . . . And that pink dress I'm wearing in the first act finale . . . Well, I cried when I saw what they had done with it. . . . I look that big around in it. . . . What's the use of my going to bed? . . . I got to be at the theatre at eleven. . . . At five o'clock this morning we were all staggering around in our sleep. . . . And Kibbitzer yelling come on, come on, we'll be here all night. . . . Milton's giving me a party tonight after the show. . . . I haven't told Jimmy yet. . . . Gee, I don't know what to do. . . . After all if it wasn't for Milton I wouldn't have had this chance. . . . Maybe Jimmy won't care. . . . Sometimes I can't figure him out. . . . Guess I'm falling in love or something. . . . Isn't that dumb? . . . Gee, I'm dead. . . . Oh, boy, what a bed. . . . I'll just sleep like this. . . . Take my slippers off. . . . That's a good kid. . . . Gee, it's swell to have a sister like you. . . . Where have you been all my life? . . . Guess I will slip off this dress. . . . Help me with it, will you? . . . Oooh, my feet hurt. . . . Yeh, they were going to stretch my shoes. . . . Promised faithfully. . . . They're always going to do something for you in this outfit. . . . Yes, Miss Dugan. . . . Sure, Miss Dugan. . . . Don't you worry about it. . . . Everything's going to be all right. . . . They yes you to death. . . . Gee, the sun is shining in the window. . . . What time is it anyway? . . . Can't you stop that darn ocean outside? . . . I think I'll get up and go out and swim.... Gee, I'm dead.... You know what Milton said?... Said I was so sweet he could eat me.... I'd give him the darnedest case of indigestion.... I can't stand him.... Sometimes he's all right.... But I have to be nice to him, I guess.... I wish Jimmy would say that to me.... You know what he said?... He said someday I'll break your damn neck.... Gee, it was sweet to hear him say that.... I wish he would.... He can break my neck any day.... Gee, I'm dead.... And I got to be at the theatre in a couple of hours.... Jimmy's going to take me down there.... Said I could eat breakfast with him at Childs. ... I could eat a horse with Jimmy.... Gee, he's a sweet kid.... Gee, I'm tired.... I'll break your damn neck.... Jimmy... Sweet boy... Sweet...

X

ATLANTIC CITY STAR
(Sept. 29.)

One of the most interesting conventions to be held in Atlantic City this year opens today at the Superba Hotel when the Gleason Company, manufacturers of greeting cards for all occasions, holds its annual sales convention. All the salesmen who travel the United States and Canada as well as foreign representatives will be present together with high officials of the company including President Donald Gleason, Sales Manager Al Evans and various district managers. Chief among the star salesmen of the company here to confer on business problems, as well as drink deep of the beauties of Atlantic City, is Denny Kerrigan who comes from Indiana, famous for Booth Tarkington, the Ku Klux and the Four Horsemen of Notre Dame. One of the principal speakers who will address the convention is Teddy Zest, the poet laureate of the company, responsible for most of its beautiful sentiments as well as the popular American poet whose tender verses are syndicated far and wide. Mr. Zest is also scheduled to speak tonight at the First Presbyterian Church on the subject: "I Am A Father and Why Not?" The remainder of the Gleason organization at the close of the day's business plan to attend en masse the opening tonight at the Apollo Theatre of "Get Your Girl," featuring Dixie Dugan, the Jollity Night Club Band and Fifty Hotsy Totsies.

~~~~~~~~~~~~~~~~~~~~~~~~

SCENE: *Convention Room, Superba Hotel, Atlantic City.*

The room is full of Gleason salesmen jelled into small groups of three or four each awaiting the official opening of the convention and putting in time pleasantly swapping dirty stories and giving the company hell in all departments. In each eloquent face is stuck a gift cigar, compliments of the company, proving once more that bread cast upon the water comes back all wet. Al Evans, a dynamo in breeches (a phrase variously attributed by advertising experts to Carlyle, Dr. Crane, John D. Rockefeller Jr., and Colonel Lindbergh—they can have it), breezes in and smacks the official mahogany a fast one with the official gavel. The convention is on.

AL: Gentlemen . . . boys, fellows, hey! Clucks, back to your corners. The invocation (*Groans.*) will have to be passed up (*Cheers.*) as Archie Basset, the only member of this organization who remembers his prayers is confined to his room with an ice pack and a nice brown fur-lined throat. He says he didn't have hardly anything to drink (*Yells of derision.*) so the only charitable thing to suppose is that some one spilt it on his head and it ate its way into his brain which is something you wouldn't understand. You will find a little table in front of your chairs, if that isn't asking too much of you this early in the morning, and on the table you will find some paper for making notes and pencils used ordinarily for making out expense accounts but dedicated today to a higher and nobler cause. You will also find little song books containing a few ditties which we are all going to sing together as loud as we can unless advised to the contrary by the management. Dennis Kerrigan, who has been invited by the National Broadcasting Co. to sing exclusively anywhere except over the radio, will lead you. He is a conscientious tenor. In other words, the possesor of a small still voice. Gentlemen, Dennis Kerrigan, the sweet singer of Rolling Prairie, Mishawaka and the Banks of the Wabash far away.

DENNY: Boys, pick up your song books and turn to Number Three . . . Number Three . . . in the little brown hymnbook. . . . Brother Anderson will pass among you afterwards and take up the good will offering in his hat. I hope you see he gets it—in his hat. Let's go!

SALESMEN (singing lustily):

We sell them Gleason Valentines in summer when it's hot

> We sell them Gleason Christmas cards in winter when it's not
> And whether the weather is weather or not
> In shower and in shine
> We jump right in and sell the trade
> The Gleason Wonder Line.

DENNY: Everybody. Come on!
ENSEMBLE:

> *Glory, Glory, Halleluia,*
> *The dealers all say howdy-do-ya.*
> *Glory, Glory, Halleluia,*
> *We jump right in and sell the trade*
> *The Gleason Wonder Line.*

DENNY: Second verse and not so confidential. Come on. Sell it!
SINGING SALESMEN:

> *We sell 'em flocks of Greeting Cards*
> *With whoop-dee-do and dash.*
> *For we are Gleason Wonder Boys*
> *And full of pep and pash.*
> *They sign so many dotted lines*
> *They break out in a rash.*
> *And don't let 'em tell you any different.*

DENNY: And the chorus?
SALESMEN (*lustily*):

> *Glory, Glory, Halleluia,*
> *The dealers all say howdy-do-ya.*
> *Glory, Glory, Halleluia,*

*We jump right in and sell the trade
The Gleason Wonder Line.*

DENNY (*to Al*): You can take them now. They're all in a lather.

AL: We're first going to throw the meeting open. That means every man for himself like a college glee club. If you have any deep-seated wrongs festering in your bosoms bring them out into the light of day where the bright sun and the sweet rain and the comforting zephyrs of God's Great Outdoors will heal and glorify and bring life, liberty and the pursuit of happiness—where am I? What does it matter?

VOCAL SALESMAN (*taking it up*):

*What does it ma-a-a-ter
If the skies are gray
And the sun don't shine*

AL (*rapping for order*): Throw him out, he's breaking our hearts. (*Peace as the singer subsides with a painful gurgle.*) All right, boys, you've been yapping for months now for a chance to tell the world what a bunch of bums the home office is. Well, this is field day. And now we're going to run off the preliminary and final heats in belly-aching—standing, running, and jumping with and without weights. The usual liberal handicaps for junior salesmen. Yes, Artie? I see you. First in the field as usual. Boys, Artie Crawford. Traveling out of Chicago. One of King George's spies. Can be seen almost any week-end sneaking into Canada for evidence.

ART CRAWFORD: I'd like to know why we can't go back to the old way of mounting two samples on a sheet? Now with so many sheets...

VOICES: Aw, shut up!

Sit down!

You shouldn't steal sheets!

Limit yourself to towels!

Go on back to Chicago!

Where's your gang?

AL: Hey! Hey! Give the little boy a chance.

ART CRAWFORD: When I started in this business you could carry a whole line in your pocket. Now it takes four big sample cases alone for Christmas. Now when I started in this business . . .

VOICES: Who told you you started?

Who told you this was a business?

Let's see your machine gun.

ART CRAWFORD (*paying no attention*): When I started in this business there were no hoodlums in it. Now it's full of them. And it seems by some strange coincidence we have most of them working for us.

VOICE: The boy knows his hoodlums.

ART CRAWFORD: Now I want to make it clear that I'm for smaller lines and better stuff. I've got a hump on my back from carrying the junk you fellows put out up there at the home office.

VOICES: So that's how you got that hump. We heard different.

AL: If poor Artie is getting too feeble to carry the samples we'll have to get him a bicycle. Only that might establish a precedent.

VOICE: The precedent has been established.

AL: All in favor of a bicycle for Art Crawford say "aye."

Chorus (*groans*).

AL: The motion is carried. Yes, Mr. Holmes?

MR. HOLMES: I just want to say that I don't think the office is paying enough attention to Father's Day. The Buzza Company has just got out a swell line of Father Cards—5, 10, 15, 25, and 50¢ sellers. These are all regular Fathers and besides they have novelties. Like, For the Father of My Best Friend, To My Sweetheart's Father, To One Who Is Like A Father To Me, also Father-in-Law, and Father's Father. (*By way of explanation.*) That's Grandfather, of course. Now I think it's just a matter of simple mathematics to prove there are just as many fathers in the country as mothers. Why when you get down to reason there's bound to be. And that proves the potential market is there. And fundamental constructive salesmanship tells us that once the potential market is discovered methods for tapping it can be laid out along well known principles, such as surveying the market, determining the quota and the sales unit, the dollar per capita per annum potential, the overhead, the turnover, the saturation index, and the direct as well as inverse ratio of unit promotion cost to unit sale profit. Thank you. (*Sits down completely overcome by his own eloquence. There is an awed silence.*)

LOUD DERISIVE WHISPER: They were astonished when I answered the waiter in perfect French.

AL: I think a song might cheer us up a little after what we've just been through. What say, Denny?

DENNY (*rising merrily*): All right, boys. What's the matter with Number Ten in the little polka dotted hymnal? Tune, The Song Is Ended, But The Melody Lingers On. Just the chorus.

SALESMEN (*with feeling*):

> The sale is ended
> But the helluvit lingers on
> All the commish is gone
> But the helluvit lingers on
> The deal was splendid
> And the management wrote to say
> You had a damfine day
> If their credit was just O. K.
> Then came the goods to the store
> Broken and short—was that customer sore!
> As we intended
> We returned for more sales anon

—Buyer and sales had gone—
But the helluvit lingers on.

AL: Boys, now I've got a surprise for you. Teddy Zest is going to speak to us.

VOICE: That's no surprise. I read it in the paper this morning.

AL: My mistake. I didn't think you could read. Boys, Teddy Zest, the poet all America loves, who has written most of our best sellers past, present and foture. Give him the good old Gleason Greeting Song.

SALESMEN (*singing*):

If here ain't Teddy Zest himself
Hello! Hello! Hello!
Himself no less and in the flesh
Hello! Hello! Hello!
We're glad to meet this handsome guy
And should he ask the reason why
We're proud to tell him in reply
Hello! Hello! Hello!

TEDDY ZEST: Boys, I'm proud to be with you today. I'm proud to be associated with such a fine gang of real fellows dedicated to the mission of spreading good cheer far and wide o'er all our beautiful countryside where hands are warm and souls are true and hearts are fine and staunch as yew. Each day I wander down the road and see a man beneath his load of care and worry go a while and to this man I give a smile and lo, his burden melts away, and brighter dawns another day. And once again he views the years no longer through a mist of tears, but walks erect four square and free once more the man he used to be. (*Bows, applause.*)

Why, boys, it's not given to every one to do good and get paid for it. That's the kind of a job you have, spreading cheer through all the land, spreading cheer on either hand, cheer to tots with heads of gold, cheer to dear sweet mothers old, cheer to maidens young and gay, cheer to fathers staunch and gray. So here's a cheer from me to you and three more cheers for our flag so true, the grand old red and white and blue. (*Applause.*)

The other day I was visiting a dear old couple in Battle Creek. They were celebrating their diamond wedding aniversary—their names escape me—tch, tch—and I thought really this dear old sweet couple can tell me of life for they have fought the good fight and their crowns are awaiting them. So I asked this dear old gentleman about life. But he was very old and very feeble and couldn't talk plainly. But I read in his faded blue eyes this message, this message of undying courage and fidelity which seemed to say do not falter in the battle, do not falter in the fight, learn to see your bounden duty, learn to read your trials aright, learn to face things as you find them, then resolve and plunge right in, for it's not the winning race that counts, but running the race to win. And so it goes in every field, and so it will go for aye, it's not the running to win that wins, the wreaths of laurel and bay. So give a hand to less fortunate ones, and a smile to those in doubt, for nobody knows where the other one goes—so what's all the rush about? (*Applause.*)

The other day my little boy Wilfred climbed up in my lap and rubbed peppermint candy in my moustache. (*Laughter.*) And he said, daddy, does everybody have to work and I said yes, Wilfred, everybody has to work at something or other for that is the duty imposed on us by life. And then he said, daddy, will I have to work when I grow up and I said yes, Wilfred. And then he said, but aren't you going to make enough money daddy so I won't have to work? I said no, Wilfred, no matter how much money daddy makes you'll have to work when you grow as big as daddy. What do you think of that, Wilfred? And then Wilfred thought a while and then he looked up at me with those big baby blue eyes and he said, daddy, I think that's just dandy. (*Applause.*) And that's just what work is—just dandy. It's fine to have a job to do and fine to feel you're equal to the job at hand and know the thrill of working with a right good will, and is there any better fun than seeing jobs getting done? And, boys, that is my message true, to each and every one of you, no better job in all the land, than spreading joy on either hand, and selling messages of cheer, which far and wide through all the year, will go to hovel and to dome, with thoughts of mother, heart and home. No better job for hand or heart, than this in which you have a part. And here's my old wish ever new, may God bless every one of you and make your dearest dreams come true. And that means you and you and you. Thank you. (*Thunderous applause.*)

AL: I'm sure we got a great deal out of Mr. Zest's inspiring speech and I know you fellows will all go out and sell twice as much of his stuff now that you've met him face to face and realize what a fine upstanding four square He-Christian gentleman he is. (*Applause.*) During Mr. Zest's speech I noticed our president come in and take a seat at the back of the room. (*Hearty applause.*) Will you come up and give the boys a talk, Mr. Gleason?

GLEASON (*not rising*): No, I'm going to stay right back here and listen for a while. If I talk I'll only hear what I know already. If I listen I may hear something new.

DENNY (*rising*): I have an idea I'd like to talk about. I've been thinking about it for some time and I'd like to know what Mr. Gleason and Al and all you boys think about it.

VOICE: Did Dixie Dugan give it to you?

DENNY (*hotly*): You keep your tongue off Dixie Dugan unless you want a good sock on the nose.

VOICE: Well, don't get mad.

DENNY: I don't have to get mad to sock you on the nose. It would be a pleasure.

Voices: Fight! Fight!

Al (*vigorously*): Here, here. Cut it out. If we're going to have a fight let the entertainment committee handle it and put it somewhere on the program where it will do some good. Come on, Denny. Let's have what you were going to say. Spill it.

Denny (*glowering at opponent*): Well, all I was going to say is I've been thinking about getting out a Christmas card that would have a wider appeal than just Christmas and I wrote one that I would like to submit to our creative department. (*Reads.*)

> *May the beautiful shining Christmas star*
> *Shine down on you wherever you are.*
> *Wherever you roam, wherever you be*
> *May it bring love and cheer to thee.*
> *And may the Christmas spirit never cease.*
> *Good will to men and World Wide Peace.*

(*With the natural instinct of a mother artist defending its young.*) You see, World Wide Peace is the idea. Something that will tie up with the peace and good will and the Christmas spirit.

Gleason (*taking fire and jumping up enthusiastically*): World Wide Peace . . . great . . . wonderful . . . that's a real thought for a Christmas card . . . get that one out . . . get it out right away . . . we can sell thousands of them . . . millions . . . we can get every church organization in America back of it . . . it will go in every Christian home in the country . . . World Peace . . . why you can get it out in all languages . . . French, Italian, German . . . can't you see it? . . . thousands . . . millions . . . thousands of millions of those cards going all over the world like winged messengers bringing tidings of great joy to all the peoples!

Denny (*thrilled*): Do you really think so, Mr. Gleason?

Gleason: Think it? I know it. Why you've got a magnificent idea.

An idea that comes only once in a century. Listen . . . World Peace Christmas cards . . . cards carrying a message of Peace on Earth Good Will to Men . . . going out in all languages, . . . to all nations . . . all over the world . . . why we could line up every church organization . . . every woman's club . . . you would have millions buying them . . . millions selling them. When did you get the idea?

DENNY (*modestly*): Oh, just the other day. I've been working it out at home. The details, the type of design, the numbers at different prices, discounts, distribution.

GLEASON: Fine. Not only the regular dealers, but we'll get every organized agency for good, for service, for uplift, for welfare work, for Christianity to hande them too. (*To Denny.*) Isn't that your idea?

DENNY: You bet. Why not?

GLEASON (*to salesmen*): Boys, I believe this is the biggest Christmas card idea that has ever been conceived. What I like about it especially is that it gives us an opportunity to do something noble, something inspiring in a big broad fundamental way. You know this business isn't just dollars and cents. Profits aren't everything. (*Solemnly.*) What doth it profit a man if he gain the whole world and lose his soul? Right?

SALESMEN: That's right . . . Okay.

GLEASON: You're selling Christmas cards. Are they pieces of paper with designs and verses on them? No. You're selling that which inspires thoughtfulness, you're selling kindness, you're selling friendship and love and handclasps, and heartbeats, stable commodities, not luxuries . . . necessities. That's why I say Denny's idea is far greater than just a Christmas card idea. His idea is a card that will not only be a Christmas card, but will carry a message of good will and understanding and world peace to all the peoples of all the world! The golden Christmas Star surrounded by flags of all nations. Boys, it's wonderful . . . the very thought of it thrills me. . . . I can see millions of hands reaching out for this card at Christmas . . . I can see millions of them flying like angels of peace over the whole world. We can line up every church organization, the foreign missionary societies, every woman's club, every fraternal organization. We can get the governmental agencies back of this, the societies for the propagation of world peace, the diplomatic offices, the export trade, the import trade, millions will be buying them . . . am I right?

FIRST SALESMAN: That's right.

SALESMEN (*in chorus*): Okay!

GLEASON (*taking Denny by the arm and presenting him*): And here's the man who conceived the idea . . . a magnificent idea . . . a colossal idea . . . an idea of truly epic proportions . . . the World Peace Greeting Card . . . and a greeting card shall lead them. (*Starts applause, every one joins in.*) Now, boys, I'll tell you what I've just decided to do. Denny here deserves more than just a pat on the back for this idea. I'm going to take him in off the road and make him assistant sales manager in charge of the World Peace Christmas Card movement. And I know all you boys will get together and help him put it over. Am I right?

SALESMEN: Right! Okay! (*All crowd up and shake hands with Denny.*)

AL (*rapping for order*): Boys, the old Gleason Hello Song for our new assistant sales manager, Denny Kerrigan.

SALESMEN (*in lusty chorus joined by the Old Man himself*):

> *If here ain't Denny Kerrigan*
> *Hello! Hello! Hello!*
> *Himself no less and in the flesh*
> *Hello! Hello! Hello!*
> *We're glad to greet this handsome guy*
> *And should he ask the reason why*
> *We're proud to tell him in reply*
> *Hello! Hello! Hello!*

Only a few minutes later Denny may be seen talking to the room clerk at the Hotel Superba. Would any of the "Get Your Girl" company be stopping here? Yes, quite a few of them. Would Miss Dixie Dugan be here? Yes, 1242, but she's not in. Went out early. Could one leave a note for her? Certainly one could.

THE NOTE

Dixie, You Dear Sweet Thing:

I'm in town stopping here. Tried to reach you, but you were at rehearsal. Coming to see your show tonight and if you hear a hundred men cheering for you that will be me. Can I see you after the show? Can we go somewhere and have something to eat and talk over old times? Did I say I would try to forget you? I was crazy. Leave a note saying you'll see me. I love you to death.

Denny

P.S. Got promoted today. Swell new job—assistant sales manager. Doesn't that sound good? You'll be proud of me yet.

XI

SCENE: *Room in the Superba Hotel, Atlantic City.*

It is eleven o'clock in the morning and the shades are drawn, but enough bright sunshine filters through to pick out a pair of tumbled twin beds with a dark head on one pillow and a light one on the other. The light head is sleeping soundly and if one must say it—snoring a tiny bit. The dark head is buried face down in the pillow, but not deeply enough to completely smother a sound that might be either laughing or crying. The telephone rings violently. A delicate maidenly snore stops with a little squawk and the owner bolts upright as though shot. The dark lady pays no attention.

NITA: Telephone, sis.... Hey, Dixie! Telephone.... Are you crying?

DIXIE: None of your d-d-damn business.

NITA: Dickie darling. You *are* crying. What's the matter? (*Telephone rings again.*) Are you in for anyone?

DIXIE: N-n-no.

NITA: Hello? (*Hand over mouthpiece.*) It's a man.

DIXIE: It's always a man. Damn 'em!

NITA: Sounds like Jimmy. Don't you want to talk to him?

DIXIE: N-n-no. N-n-never.

NITA: Hello ... yes ... this is her sister Nita ... oh, yes, Jimmy ... why no, she just went out.... I expect her back though soon.... Want to leave a message? ... yes ... all right, I'll tell her.... 'Bye.... ... That was Jimmy. Said for you to call him up as soon as you came back in.

DIXIE: He should live so long. He can rot first.

NITA: What's the matter with you? What happened last night?

DIXIE: Everything.

NITA: Well, do you know what time you came in here? Five o'clock. And snozzled. Were you snozzled!

DIXIE: Oh, I don't know. All my clothes are on the chair. I couldn't have been so snozzled as all that.

NITA: Well, baby, you didn't put them on the chair. They'd be hanging on the ceiling if I hadn't gathered them up.

DIXIE (*burrowing back into pillow*): I'd rather not hear any more about it. Oooh . . . my head. I've got to be at rehearsal at eleven. What time is it?

NITA: It's after that now.

DIXIE: Good.

NITA: Don't you want some breakfast? . . . wait a minute. . . . Room Service! . . . . hello . . . what do you want, sis?

DIXIE: Nothing.

NITA: Hello, Room Service? . . . two toasts, two coffees . . . is that all you want?

DIXIE : Oooh, I feel terrible.

NITA: One order of bacon . . . crisp. . . .

DIXIE: Oh, migawd.

NITA: Two medium boiled eggs. . . .

DIXIE: Eggs . . . ooh, gawd.

NITA: And some, lemme see . . . some orange juice . . . want some orange juice, Dick?

DIXIE: NO!

NITA: Two orange juices. That's all. . . . And send up the morning paper and the mail. . . . Dickie, I should think you could hardly wait to see that paper. I'll bet the review will be all about you. You were swell last night.

DIXIE: Bologny!

NITA: Well you were. I thought opening night and everything

you'd be scared to death.

DIXIE (*furiously*): I don't want to hear about the damn opening. I don't want to hear about the damn show. And everybody in it or with anything to do with it or connected with it in any way can all go to hell. And I don't mean if or perhaps.

NITA: You're just feeling rotten.

DIXIE: I'll say.

NITA: Who'd you fight with last night.

DIXIE: Let's talk of something else.

NITA: Who brought you home?

DIXIE: How should I know?

NITA: Well, I'll tell you. Denny brought you home.

DIXIE (*wide eyed*): *No!*

NITA: Yes! And he helped me put you to bed.

DIXIE: Well, that was a break for him. I hope you all had a good time.

NITA: I can tell you he felt pretty bad about it.

DIXIE: Putting me to bed shouldn't make him feel so bad. He may never have another chance to see what the well dressed young girl is wearing.

NITA: I don't see anything funny about it. How did you happen to come home with Denny?

DIXIE: Search me. I started out with somebody else.

NITA: Well, where did you meet him?

DIXIE: I don't know, I tell you. I don't know where I met him. All I know is I was on a party and I drew a blank and when I wake up I find you sitting up in bed with your hair all over your eyes asking a lot of dumb questions like where are you, and how are you, and who do you love. Anyway, your nose is red.

NITA: Never mind my nose. You should see yours.

DIXIE: Can't, thank God.

NITA: COME IN! . . . oh, it's the paper. Bring it here . . . a couple of letters for you too, Dickie . . . letters of apology, I suppose . . . hoping you'll forgive them for the way you treated them . . . how do you get away with it?

DIXIE: I treat them all too good. Anything is too good for them. . . . Well, bellboy, are you off for the day? . . . didn't you ever see two girls in bed before? . . . go home and tell your mother you're a big boy now and she can put some pockets in your pants. (*The bellboy goes right out of there with hot pink ears.*)

NITA: Dickie . . . darling, listen to this: "*A new musical comedy star swam into the firmament last night when Dixie Dugan sang and danced her way into the hearts of a representative first night audience at the Apollo Theatre where 'Get Your Girl' had its premiere. Vivacious, petite, with a gay abandon and an in—an in-sous an i-n-s-o-u-c-i-a-n-c-e—*" whatever that is—

DIXIE: Whatever it is I've got it. And a headache.

NITA: "*She carried the show on her slender shoulders to a complete personal triumph and all of this in spite of the handicap imposed upon her by tinny tunes, limping lyrics and an anemic book.*"

DIXIE (*flashing*): That's a lie! It's not anemic.

NITA: I thought you were off Jimmy?

DIXIE: I am. But he has a good book, or rather he did have one until Kibbitzer and Eppus began to re-write it.

NITA: "*. . . An adequate supporting company and one of the hottest little choruses that ever hoofed along the Boardwalk.*" What did you and Jimmy fight about?

DIXIE: What else does it say?

NITA: Did you scrap with Milton, too? I think you're a fool.

DIXIE: I care what you think. A lot you know about it. Who kissed you in?

NITA: Denny said last night he came back to see you. He was out front all evening clapping hands, yelling "whoopie!" every time you came on or went off.

DIXIE: I heard him. Had a flock of his sentiment slingers with him, too. Stuccoed to the ears. They couldn't be as enthusiastic as they were unless I was Jolson or they were blotto.

NITA: Did Denny go back to see you?

DIXIE: What did Denny tell you?

NITA: He said he did. Said he begged you to come out after the show and talk to him, but you told him you were tired and had a rehearsal and were going to bed early.

DIXIE: Then what's all this checking up for? If you know what happened why do you ask me? Why don't you draw up a chair and hear my confession? There's your bacon and eggs at the door.

NITA: COME IN! . . . right here between the beds. . . . Denny was pretty well broken up last night about you turning him down and lying to him.

DIXIE: Oh, *he* was broken up! And how about me? I suppose I laughed myself to death all night. Gay and light-hearted and full of fun. God what a party I had.

NITA: I'll sign it. . . . What happened? Can't you tell me?

DIXIE: 'Course I can tell. But what good will that do?

NITA: Want some of my bacon?

DIXIE: Bacon! That would finish me. Oooh, do I feel!

NITA: And do you look! Who did you go out with?

DIXIE: Jack. Let's talk of something else. What else does it say in the paper? How do you like eggs? What's the next train back to New York?

NITA: What difference does that make to you? You're here for the week.

DIXIE: Am I?

NITA: Don't be a nut. Of course you are. What happened to you and Jimmy last night? How did you see him if you were with Jack?

DIXIE: At the Paradise.

NITA: What did he say?

DIXIE: "Hello."

NITA: And you had a fight with him over that?

DIXIE: Didn't have any fight with him.

NITA: Well, one of us is crazy. I don't get a damn bit of sense out of it.

DIXIE: You should have had fish for breakfast. It's brainfood. Full of phosporous.

NITA: Did you have a fight with Jack, too?

DIXIE: I wouldn't call it a fight exactly. One of those elimination contests. He makes a pass at her. She ducks. Counters with how could you think that of me. He backs up. She follows up advantage with tears. Bell rings. Her round. Waiter appears. His round. Now they are back in the center of the ring. They shake hands. He leads with peck to cheek. Tries to go into clinch. She lights cigarette. They spar. Waiter appears. His round. Bell rings. Draw.

NITA: Talk sense.

DIXIE: Fourteenth round. Both groggy. O-o-o damn everything.

NITA: Dickie! You're crying.

DIXIE: I'm n-n-not.

NITA: You are too. What's the matter?

DIXIE: God, I'm miserable. I wish I was dead.

NITA (*holding her close*): Dickie, darling! Don't cry. Tell me about it. You can tell your big sister anything. What's the matter? What happened?

DIXIE: It's Jimmy. I'm so crazy about him. And I sat there in the dressing room and waited and waited for him to come back to talk to me. I thought maybe he'd want to take me out and if he did I was going to ditch Jack. But he never came back at all. Didn't even send a message back or anything. Just left me sitting there waiting all dressed up. And of course Denny came in and wanted to take me out but I stalled him. I thought maybe any minute Jimmy would come so I told him I was tired and had to get to bed early because we had an early rehearsal and to run along and be a good boy and I'd see him later in the week. And of course he was terrible cut up and wanted to know what he did that I treated him that way. And all the time I was listening for Jimmy's footsteps. And I don't know what I said to him but I kept on answering him no and yes and yes and no and tomorrow and the day after and finally he went away and then Jack came in with an armful of flowers and all pepped up for the party. And he tells me how wonderful I am and how everybody was crazy about me and how the show went over with a big bang and he loves me and everything is set for a grand celebration and let's go. And still no Jimmy. Not a sign of him. Not a peep out of him. Not even how do you do, good-bye, go to the devil, or anything. So finally I got next to myself. I should sit around and get crow's feet waiting for him to show up!

NITA: That was sense.

DIXIE: So Jack piles me into a taxi and we go to the Paradise where he has a table reserved with flowers on it and champagne in buckets and waiters three deep all around us bowing from the waist and saying yes sir, yes sir. And he starts throwing money around at head waiters and waiters and busboys and the orchestra leader and the entertainers and all the time he's saying this is the life. Am I crazy about you! Have another. I feel like a kid. Fill 'em up. Have another. Have some more. So I thought I might just as well. If I can get lickered I won't feel so bad. So pretty soon I lost count. We danced and drank and drank and danced and the place filled up and the orchestra got louder and the floor got more crowded and I could see more black coats and white arms and more waiters and more champagne and I was having a heluva time.

NITA: I bet you were.

DIXIE: Like fun. I was crying inside all the time. I kept thinking of Jimmy. Where is he? Why didn't he come back to see me? Is he mad at me? Why should he be? I didn't do anything to him. I couldn't. He could walk on me.

NITA: Silly baby.

DIXIE: Just plain nerts. Well, anyway Jack was having the time of his life. All the pretty things he said to me. How cute I was. How sweet, how young. Did I think he was too old for me. Kept telling me that he was only forty-five. That wasn't old. And did I think it was. And how crazy he was about me. And he never met anyone like me. And could I learn to like him just a little. And me saying sure, sure, sure with one eye on the door feeling somehow even then I might see Jimmy come in. And then the drums rolled and an announcer steps out on the floor in the spot light and says something about we are honored tonight by having as one of our guests the star of "Get Your Girl" and out of the fog I hear a loud voice in my ear "Dixie Dugan!" and a big yell and hand clapping and Jack beaming all over saying "Get up. They're calling for you. Stand up." So I stood up and they give me a pink spot and everybody yelled "Speech!" and the announcer takes me by the hand and leads me out on the floor and I sing "Little Two By Four" from the show. The one Jimmy wrote for me.

NITA: It's a cute song.

DIXIE: It's a piece of tripe. But it sure sounded swell in that cabaret with the saxes moaning underneath and that banjo rhythm in the chorus. And me thinking of Jimmy and smiling at everybody and all the time my heart getting bigger and bigger and my throat smaller and smaller. Gee, it was terrible. Swell, too. Know what I mean?

NITA: Sure I know. There's nothing feels nicer in some ways than a heartache.

DIXIE: Don't I know it. I had a pip. Well, I get back to the table and Jack thinks all the emoting is for him. And is he thrilled! He wanted to eat me up. And then the announcer says we have another treat in store for you tonight ladies and gentlemen because we have as one of our guests the author of "Get Your Girl." Folks, this is Jimmy

Doyle who wrote one of the snappiest shows that has opened here in years. Give this little boy a great big hand.

Nita: He was there all the time?

Dixie: All the time. Right across the floor and I hadn't seen him. Well, he stood up and took a bow and made a little speech and sat down and this dame that's with him reaches across the table and pats his hand.

Nita: Who was she?

Dixie: Ask me another. Didn't I try to find out! There was another couple at the table and I kept watching out of the corner of my eye so when the girls got up to go out I excused myself and went out, too, to get an earful. You couldn't blame me for that.

Nita: Of course not. Who were they? What did they say?

Dixie: Well, the dame that patted Jimmy's hand kept pulling Jimmy this and Jimmy that and how smart he was and how cute he was and the other one agreeing with her. And then she went on saying she always knew he had it in him and she told him so and no one else could ever be as proud of him as she was. That was the pay-off. Cora her name was. Cora. Tie that.

Nita: Who was she?

Dixie: I couldn't find out. They tipped the girl and breezed back to the table. She could hardly wait to pat his hand some more I suppose. But you never saw such jewels. Diamonds big as your eye and a square cut emerald that looked like Vanderbilt's lawn. Well, I suppose that's what hooked Jimmy. Dough. She must be filthy with it. Probably one of those Park Avenue buds.

Nita: Was she pretty? How did she look?

Dixie: That's the hell of it. I'd like to tell you she had a map like Wallace Beery, but she hadn't. She's pretty, God forbid.

Nita: I don't care how pretty she is. You've got it on her forty ways.

Dixie: You think so. But you're not Jimmy. Sat there all evening and never gave me a tumble. Danced by the table and just said hello once and sort of nodded and went on. Just hello, that's all. Well, I never thought it could feel like that. I guess that was the time I settled down to serious drinking. Also I let out a few kinks and decided to show Jack a good time. I wasn't going to let Jimmy think he was so hot I couldn't pay attention to somebody else. Well, Jack sure does respond to good treatment. I'll say that for him. He opened up like a morning glory. I guess we were getting pretty cordial and affectionate and I wasn't caring much either when I sneaked a peep across the room and caught Jimmy giving me a dirty look. Well, that was just what I craved. Duck soup. I let out a few more kinks and Jack's blood pressure jumped to 270. Everything was going crazy about this time anyway. More noise, more drinks, more dances, faster and dizzier, and more champagne and then I see Jimmy get up with his party and leave the place. With not even a look at me or good-bye or how do you do or anything. Just walked out behind this dame carrying her wrap on his arm. Never looked back. Nothing.

NITA: He might have said something to you.

DIXIE: Jack passed right out of the picture then as far as I was concerned. He kept on pawing me, but I wasn't there at all. I was following Jimmy and seeing him here and there and doing this and that and I couldn't drink enough to get him off of my mind. Then Jack got mad because I wasn't paying attention to him and we had an argument although I can't remember what he said or I said. All I know is I suddenly went cold all over and I knew I had to get away from there or I'd kill somebody. So I went out to the ladies' room and I told the maid if anyone asked for me to tell them I got sick and went home and she said okay and I slipped her a dollar. And then she said you do look sick, dearie, you better lie down a little and I did. And I went out like a light. And that's all I remember. Now go on with the story. How did I get here?

NITA: I told you Denny brought you here.

DIXIE: I give it up. Where did I find him or where did he find me? And how?

NITA: In a rolling chair on the Boardwalk. Five o'clock in the morning. There was a girl with you. One of the dancers from the Paradise. She told Denny you passed out on the couch in the ladies' room and the man you were with sat at the table and waited for half an hour for you to return and then he came back and asked for you and the maid told him you had taken sick and gone home. So he went home, too. Mad as the devil. And it got later and later and the maid tried to rouse you and couldn't, and finally everybody had gone and they were putting the chairs on the tables and she finally wormed out of you where you lived and this dancer said she'd see you got home. So she loaded you into a rolling chair hoping the fresh air would bring you to.... And you were rolling down the Boardwalk when Denny came along.

DIXIE: Was he tight, too?

NITA: No, when you ran him out he went back to his salesmen and they organized a poker party and the game didn't break up until around five and he was out trying to get a little fresh air before he went to bed when he ran into you.

DIXIE: My luck! I suppose now I can count him among my souvenirs.

NITA: Well, the girl was glad to get you off her hands so she turned you over to Denny and he brought you up here. You could walk all right, but I never saw you so out. So we both put you to bed and then he sat around and talked a while before he left. He's a darn sweet kid if you ask me.

DIXIE: Sure he's a sweet kid. Do you want him?

NITA: Well, I'd certainly make him a better wife than you would.

DIXIE: Who wouldn't?

NITA: Gee, he's crazy about you. Sat there talking about how heart-broken he was that you were in the show business and throwing your best years away helling around.

Dixie: Helling around? He's like all the other goofs who think girls don't do any work in this racket. Just wear clothes and make faces at the audience and h'ist high balls the rest of the time. Say, for the last six weeks I've been busier than a one legged man in a forest fire. Helling around! Feature that.

Nita: Well, anyway he sat here for an hour holding your hand and raving about you—when he wasn't just sitting and looking at you and crying like a big goof. Boy, I wish I could get them panting for me like that.

Dixie: That's always the way. I don't want the ones I can get and then I go and fall like a ton of brick for somebody that doesn't even want to look at me. Well, here's to men!

When you meet 'em you like 'em—

Nita: Don't be a sap.
Dixie: Don't interrupt. I'm making a toast—

When you meet 'em you like 'em—
When you like 'em you kiss 'em—
When you kiss 'em you love 'em—
When you love 'em you lose 'em—
Damn 'em!

Nita: Goofus! There's Jack. Crazy about you. Wading around in money up to his adenoids and if you play your cards right he'll marry you and eat out of your hand. And what do you do? Stand him up because you're lovesick for some one that doesn't even know you're alive and cares less. What's this Jimmy stuff going to get you? Suppose you got him. Then what? Why Jack spends more for golf balls in July than Jimmy makes all year. Marry Jimmy and the longest trip you'll ever take will be on the Staten Island ferry. Grab Jack and see the world.

DIXIE: Suppose I couldn't get along with him?

NITA: Well, you're bound to make a few months of it one glad sweet song for him and then you can take him to Paris and check him.

DIXIE: I couldn't marry a man with the idea of checking him in a few months.

NITA: I wouldn't say that out loud if I were you. People will think you're some quaint old museum piece.

DIXIE: Well, anyway, Jimmy's out. I'm through! You can hug that to your heart if it'll do you any good.

NITA: Isn't that some one at the door? COME IN! . . . Well, flowers . . . no less . . . for you of course.

DIXIE (*opening box*): Roses! Imagine having to smell roses this early in the morning. Men have no sense . . . ah, here it is. (*Reads.*) "Please forgive me and have dinner with me tonight. Will telephone. —Love, Jack." Well, now that is sweet. I wonder what he said to me that he wants me to forgive him? I can't remember what happened. Probably he can't either so I can start anywhere.

NITA: Well, don't be a fool. Don't let him get away. You're not going to get a lot of opportunities like Jack. (*Telephone rings.*) There, that's him now. Hello? . . . who? . . . oh, just a minute. . . . (*Covering mouthpiece.*) It isn't Jack. It's Jimmy . . . hello? . . . yes . . . no this is her sister . . . can I take the message? . . . she's in the tub . . . important you must see her right away . . . you're going back to New York, is that it? . . . all right, I'll tell her. . . .

DIXIE (*grabbing phone*): Hello Jimmy . . . no, I wasn't in the tub at all . . . I mean I was, but I just got out . . . are you really going back to New York? . . . oh . . . well when? . . . where? . . . I'll be there in two ticks. . . . 'Bye. (*Jumps out of bed.*) Whoopie!

NITA: Well, for God's sake. I thought you weren't going to see him any more? Where you going?

DIXIE (*throwing on clothes*): Childs for breakfast . . . with Jimmy.

NITA: But you had breakfast.

DIXIE: I'm going to have another.

NITA: But listen, wait a minute. What'll I tell Jack if he calls?

DIXIE: Tell him anything. I don't know. Don't bother me.

NITA: And what about Denny? Suppose he calls?

DIXIE: Migod woman. I don't know. Elope with him. Seduce him. Marry him. I don't care. Whoopie! Jimmy called me up. He couldn't go back to New York without seeing me. That shows something.

NITA: You haven't got a brain in your head.

DIXIE: I love it. I wouldn't be any other way.

NITA: Well, I'm going to tell Jack you're having dinner with him. If Jimmy goes back to New York you have plenty of time to see Jack.

DIXIE (*jamming on hat*): Don't talk to me about dinner when I'm just about to have breakfast. (*Grabs coat and starts out door singing.*)

Is he my boy friend?
HOW de-ow-DOW!

NITA: Wait a minute . . . well, she's gone, let 'er go, God bless her . . . didn't even look at her letters . . . wonder who they can be from. . . . Senorita Dixie Dugan (*Tries to peer through it—turns it over—reads.*) "From Alvarez Romano, care of American Consul, Sanaguay, Costaragua." Well, tie that!

~~~~~~~~~~~~~~~~

XII

Tuesday

NITA DEAR:

Just got back from rehearsal and found your note saying you had to dash back to New York. Just when the baby sister needs you, too, to bounce all her troubles off of. That doesn't sound right, but fifteen minutes a day of good reading will do wonders for me.

Must jump right in the tub and out again as Jack is taking me to dinner. Had breakfast with Jimmy. He's gone to New York. Tell you all about it later. Seems worried. So does Kibbitzer. So does Eppus. So is your loving sister,

DIXIE

POSTAL TELEGRAPH — COMMERCIAL CABLES
TELEGRAM

SEPTEMBER 30

```
NA 342 13
NEW YORK CITY NY
ABE LIPOWITZ
            RITZ HOTEL ATLANTIC CITY
ANY LIFE IN GET YOUR GIRL WIRE
            TRIANGLE TICKET AGENCY
```

```
POSTAL TELEGRAPH — COMMERCIAL CABLES
TELEGRAM
```

SEPTEMBER 30

89 NK 173
ATLANTIC CITY
TRIANGLE TICKET AGENCY
          1444 BROADWAY NEW YORK CITY
BLUE BABY.
                                          ABE

~~~~~~~~~~~~~~~~~~~

Tuesday Night

NITA DEAR:

Home from theatre. Am I dead! Saw Jack for dinner and a few minutes after show tonight. Hinted house was poor and show looks in bad way, but he'll back me to limit if I'm a good girl. And I says if I'm not is what you really mean, naughty mans, good night, and I beat it upstairs. And now for something more important. The girl Jimmy was with that night at the Paradise is Cora Brewster, daughter of the big gazook who owns the Evening Tab on which Jimmy works. I asked him if that was any reason why he had to sit and look at her all night like a dying duck in a thunder storm. And he said he was only a wage slave in a gilded cage and had to do what he was told. I thought you were your own boss, I said. No, he says, I'm just one of the poor girls in Madame Brewster's house all dressed up in the yellow kimono of tabloid journalism tapping on the window to attract customers and living only in hopes of making enough money so I can get out some day and have a house of my own.

And where does Cora fit into this scheme I says. She's just a friend says Jimmy. That is, she's been nice to me because I've been helping her a little bit. Yeh, says I. It's like this, says Jimmy, she's got a bug to write so her father's been letting her play pussy wants a corner down in the office with the telephones and typewriters and I've been showing her how to dial numbers and make her adjectives come out even. So when she happened to be here for the opening of my show and wanted to go I couldn't very well refuse to take her could I? Besides her father isn't going to get mad at me for being nice to her and as long as I have to work for her father I'd rather be friends with him. And besides all that it's nice to be nice to a nice girl. I'm nice to you don't you think? You don't have to be if it's an effort, says I. It's no effort he says to me. Of all the nice girls I know you're easily the nicest. Well, that built me right up. And though it was only bacon I was eating it tasted like bee's knees in butter.

    He dashed for the train right after that and I floated into rehearsal full of what those perfume ads call pshaw de veev. You know—like Douglas Fairbanks—all over the place. More later.

DIXIE

APOLLO THEATRE
"Get Your Girl" Company

RECEIPTS
Monday Night $1,425.00

COMMENTS
HOUSE MANAGER: Too warm all afternoon for window sale.
COMPANY MANAGER: What could you expect with such bum advance publicity? But tomorrow will tell the story.

RECEIPTS
Tuesday Night $914.00

COMMENTS

HOUSE MANAGER: If you'd been ready to give a show last night you wouldn't be off tonight.

COMPANY MANAGER: Too cool anyway. But tomorrow mat will tell the story.

RECEIPTS

Wednesday Matinee $317.00

COMMENTS

HOUSE MANAGER: Matinees are always bad here. They're all on the beach.

COMPANY MANAGER: We really don't care about the matinee anyway. It's just like dress rehearsal. But tonight will tell the story. How's the advance?

HOUSE MANAGER: There ought to be a good window sale before the curtain if it isn't too cool.

RECEIPTS

Wednesday Night $652.00

COMMENTS

HOUSE MANAGER: It's a good sign when it starts off slow.

COMPANY MANAGER: The house was dark last week so they're out of the habit. But tomorrow will tell.

POSTAL TELEGRAPH – COMMERCIAL CABLES
TELEGRAM

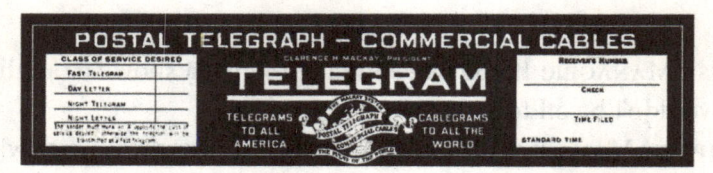

OCTOBER 1ST

RH 244 98 C
ATLANTIC CITY
JAMES DOYLE
     NEW YORK EVENING TAB NY CITY
ITS A BUST STOP CLOSING SHOW SATURDAY
STOP ITS ALL YOUR FAULT TOO.

                KIBBITZER AND EPPUS

~~~~~~~~~~~~~~~~~~~~~~~~~~

POSTAL TELEGRAPH – COMMERCIAL CABLES
TELEGRAM

OCTOBER 1ST

NA 12 763
NEW YORK CITY NY
JOHN BREWSTER
     HOTEL RITZMORE LOS ANGLES CAL
NEED FIVE THOUSAND DOLLARS QUICK STOP
LOVE

                        CORA

~~~~~~~~~~~~~~~~~~~~~~~~~~

```
                                    OCTOBER 1ST
A 14C CK 12
LOS ANGELES CAL
CORA BREWSTER
          NEW YORK EVENING TAB NY CITY
WHY STOP KISSES
                                            DAD
```

```
                                    OCTOBER 1ST
345 KD 3C
NEW YORK CITY NY
JOHN BREWSTER
          HOTEL RITZMORE LOS ANGELES CAL
SHOW WRITTEN BY JIMMY DOYLE NEEDS ONLY
LITTLE MONEY TO PUT IT OVER STOP
WONDERFUL SHOW STOP GOOD NOTICES STOP
CAN BE SAVED STOP PLEASE HELP STOP LOTS
OF LOVE
                                           CORA
```

OCTOBER 1ST

NB 113 38
LOS ANGELES CAL
CORA BREWSTER
          NEW YORK EVENING TAB NY CITY
YOU ARE OVERWORKING YOURSELF STOP COME
OUT HERE AND REST STOP LOVE AND KISSES
                                    DAD

OCTOBER 1ST

A 1OCCK 35 5
NEW YORK CITY NY
JOHN BREWSTER
          HOTEL RITZMORE LOS ANGLES CAL
CALLING YOU LONG DISTANCE MIDNIGHT
TONIGHT STOP YOURE THE DEAREST DADDY IN
THE WORLD
                                    CORA

POSTAL TELEGRAPH — COMMERCIAL CABLES
TELEGRAM

OCTOBER 2ND

```
A 65K NL 72
LOS ANGELES CAL
CORA BREWSTER
        NEW YORK EVENING TAB NY CITY
CONFIRMING CONVERSATION LONG DISTANCE
LAST NIGHT AM WIRING MY ATTORNEY
INSTRUCTIONS FOR BUYING INTEREST IN
GET YOUR GIRL AND SAFEGUARDING YOU IN
TRANSACTION STOP HE WILL PROCEED TO
ATLANTIC CITY WITH MONEY AND MAKE
NECESSARY ARRANGEMENTS IN HIS OWN NAME
STOP STILL CONVINCED YOU MUST HAVE
FALLEN ON YOUR HEAD OR ARE YOU IN LOVE
STOP GO AHEAD STOP
                                    DAD
```

POSTAL TELEGRAPH — COMMERCIAL CABLES
TELEGRAM

OCTOBER 2ND

```
354 TK 12 5
NEW YORK CITY NY
KIBBITZER AND EPPUS
        APOLLO THEATRE ATLANTIC CITY
KEEP YOUR SHIRT ON STOP HAVE A SCHEME
STOP ARRIVING MIDNIGHT
                                   DOYLE
```

```
           POSTAL TELEGRAPH — COMMERCIAL CABLES
                      TELEGRAM
```

                                          OCTOBER 2ND
NB 35 134
NEW YORK CITY
DIXIE DUGAN
          APOLLO THEATRE ATLANTIC CITY
DONT WORRY STOP SHOW NOT CLOSING STOP
ARRIVING MIDNIGHT STOP RESERVE TWO
CHAIRS BREAKFAST CHILDS
                                               JIMMY

                                                    Friday
Nita darling:

    News, news, news. Instead of the show closing here tomorrow night we're laying off next week and rehearsing and then we come into New York. Pray for us. Kibbitzer and Eppus are out—right on the fanny, and I don't mean Brice. Jimmy is running the show. He is putting it back just the way it was when he wrote it and already it's going better. We're rehearsing day and night and I'm dead on my feet, but Jimmy's heart is so set on putting this first show of his over I couldn't do less even if I wanted to.

    How? When? Where? Who? The answer is Jimmy found an angel. He won't tell me who. He says he can't. But the angel skidded Kibbitzer and Eppus out into the alley and gave Jimmy full charge. Told me all about it at breakfast after he came back from New York. Haven't seen much of him since except running up and down the aisles during rehearsal and barking at everybody. Me too. Maybe his bark is worse than his bite—what? Naughty girl, Nita, thinking such things. Tch, tch.

Have you heard anything from Denny? Me neither. I guess he has cancelled all my time. I think I'll send him a little motto something like this:

People often drink a lot
But only when they think a lot
And that's my trouble, too,
For every drink's a little think
And every think's of you.

I ought to get something for that don't you think? The chair maybe—better known as the hot squat.

News, news and more news. Dinner with Jack last night. I'm afraid he's disappointed. Been seeing too many movies where when everything else fails you get the girl down to Atlantic City and the salt air eats away her iron will and she's just A Piece of Clay in the Hand of the Potter, and Goes Down, Down into the Valley of Shame and Eats the Bitter Bread of Remorse. I guess he realizes now that's a lot of railroad propaganda to keep the week-end excursions running. I as much as told him so over our second stein of beer and good beer, too—I'll take you there if you'll come back. I says, Jack I think you're swell and I like you a lot and I don't know whether you're a bear down in Wall Street or a bull and I wouldn't know if you told me, but Dixie Preferred is one stock you can't manipulate on a margin and the mere fact that I may bite you on the ear once in a while when I'm ginny and think you're some one else must not confuse a sound business man like you. I'm just an old fashioned fool of a girl, big boy, and when I sell out it will be for value received payable in advance in the gold bonds of matrimony. Blue Skies is not an investment—it's only a song by Irving Berlin. Well, I could tell by the way he paid the bill that he felt it was just another day wasted away.

And more news by me yet. You must have seen that letter I got from Alvarez just before you left—at least the outside of it. Well, he's down in Costaragua with his father and they're both running off a revolution trying to get back into power. You remember his father was a presidente or something. Well, the whole picture was all out of shape like a banquet photo for all I could make of it until Jack chirped during dinner, do you know where your old back stabbing friend Alvarez is? No says I rolling over and playing dead, ain't never heered. What do they be saying down by the old saw-mill? Well, says Jack, his father came into see me several months ago and promised if I got up a syndicate to finance his revolution we could have the oil concession. So I got a few of my pals together and we talked it over and decided that would be the patriotic American thing to do. Our country may she always be right, but right or wrong we've got to have oil. So we sent ex-presidente Romano off with our blessing and backing and he took that tango dancing hot tamale with him, tight pants and all.

Feature that. No wonder I haven't heard from Alvarez all this time. Ever since he tried to kidnap me in fact. But his letter proved he hasn't changed a bit. Here's a piece of it. Judge for yourself.

"All day and all night we fight up the hills and down the hills and soon we will kill all these dogs who now run like rabbits when they see me and my brave soldados coming at them with blood in our eyes and knives in our teeth. Not little pocket knives like that which I stick into your fat friend Jack who thinks we fight for his oil. Ha, ha, ha. I laugh in his nose. No, we have big beautiful knives, and every time I stab I think of you, diosa mia, and cry Die Pig! You are one less dog I must kill and then it will all be over and I will be rich and happy and my country she will be free and I will come and get you, my little Dixie, and you will come back here with me or I knock your pretty little, how you say, block off, and

drag you down here to my arms which ache to hold you, querida mia...."

Whoopie! If Jack with all his dough could only talk like that and look like Jimmy. And speaking of Jimmy and dough I sure would give a pretty to know who the mysterious angel is. Some attorney is down here handling the business for him, but who's behind the man behind? Jimmy isn't telling, but I'm going to find out or bust a garter belt.

Put down that bottle!
Dixie

~~~~~~~~~~~~~~~~

<div style="text-align: right;">Atlantic City
October 3rd.</div>

John Brewster
Ritzmore Hotel
Los Angeles, Cal.
Dear Mr. Brewster:

Pursuant to your instructions I completed negotiations with Kibbitzer and Eppus, producers of "Get Your Girl," by which I secured for your daughter, Miss Cora Brewster, controlling interest in production. This was comparatively easy as "Get Your Girl" is in bad way financially and producers were glad to get out from under. In fact, they had intended to close the show Saturday night.

However, I agreed to take it over and guarantee the loss for current week and in the event the show proves successful pay them $500. a week out of the gross until they had received the sum of $15,000. They retain their interest in the stock and motion picture rights, but I do not believe these rights have any value.

The remaining interest of 40 per cent is held by John Milton, a broker with offices at 67 Wall Street. He gives me to understand he is willing to string along for the time being and take his chances with the production and this should be satisfactory for he has no desire to meddle in the management of the production itself, which according to your wishes I have turned over to the author, James Doyle.

The show will lay off next week and our office is now negotiating with Jules Murry in the Shubert office for New York theatre for the following week if possible or if a house is not available on such short notice a fill-in booking for the week with a New York house the week following. Awaiting further instructions, I remain

Very truly yours
Levinson, Aaronson, Schmaltz,
Rosenbaum and Reilly
By I. Rosenbaum

~~~~~~~~~~~~~~~~

<div style="text-align:right">
Atlantic City
Friday
</div>

Miss Nita Dugan
439 Flatbush Avenue
Brooklyn, N. Y.
Dear Nita:

I tried to get you on the phone but the clerk said you had gone home so I am writing to tell you our sales convention is over and I'm leaving for Minneapolis tomorrow. I've been in to see Dixie's show every night and they are changing it a lot and it seems to be getting better, but the attendance is brutal. I haven't tried to see Dixie although you know how much I would like to talk to her. But she doesn't seem to have time for me anymore. I guess I haven't enough hop on the ball for her. Well, she's a sweet kid, but she's young and she hasn't any sense about men. If she'd only listen to me, but I guess you're the only one she pays any attention to and I hope you'll watch over her because she doesn't know what it's all about and she thinks she's smart, but there's always some one else who's smarter and some day she may be sorry she's treated me the way she has. But I guess I'll just go on liking her just the same because that's the kind of a goof I am. "Thinking of you, why that's all that I do, all the day long, all the night through, the sound of your voice, the touch of your hand, etcetera, etcetera." That's from one of our best selling mottos.

Did I tell you I've been made assistant sales manager? I thought Dixie would get a big kick out of that—but I guess not. Wotthahel, Bill, wotthahel.

Stopping over for a day in Chicago and will look Sunshine up. Maybe Dixie has written something to her about me. Maybe not, too. Well, "Laugh and the world laughs with you, weep and you weep alone"—that's from our line, too, in two sizes, 10 cent seller and 25.

Your friend
DENNY

```
                                            OCTOBER 4TH
K7 397 B44 SANAGUAY COSTARAGUA
MILTCO NEW YORK
     DONT THINK YOUR AUNT NELLY WILL LIKE
IT HERE STOP FARM OVERRUN AND PAPA LEFT
SUDDENLY FOR HIS HEALTH STOP SONNY NOT
EXPECTED TO LIVE AFTER TOMORROW LOVE
                                             JAY
```

```
┌─────────────────────────────────────────────┐
│  RADIOGRAM  WORLD WIDE WIRELESS             │
│  CONTINENT TO CONTINENT  SHORE TO SHIP      │
│  SHIP TO SHIP           No.                 │
│  "Via RCA"  RADIO CORPORATION OF AMERICA    │
│                              "Via RCA"      │
└─────────────────────────────────────────────┘
```

OCTOBER 4TH

K7 397 B44 SANAGUAY COSTARAGUA
(DECODED)

JOHN MILTON
67 WALL STREET
NEW YORK CITY

REVOLUTION DEFEATED STOP GENERAL ROMANO AND ARMY IN FLIGHT STOP GOVERNMENT TROOPS CAPTURE SON ALVAREZ WHO HAS BEEN SENTENCED TO BE EXECUTED

JAY

XIII

ATLANTIC CITY
Oct. 4.

NITA DEAR:

Jack has just told me the dreadful news. Remember I wrote you about Alvarez fighting in a revolution down in Costaragua? Well, Jack got a cable from the company's representative down there saying the revolution has been defeated and Alvarez has been captured and is going to be executed. The poor kid. I'm just sick about it.

And I just got such a sweet letter from him. All about how he was chasing the enemy up one hill and down another and sticking knives in them and soon he was going to be presidente or something and would come back and steal me away from here and take me down to Costaragua with him. Of course he was as crazy as a brass drummer half the time, but the rest of the time he was too sweet for words. It makes me cry when I think of all the nice things he used to say to me when he was dancing with me in the Jollity Club. Maybe they won't execute him. What do you think? Jack says he can't get any more news because the government is censoring everything or something like that.

I've asked Jimmy to try and find out something through the paper he's working for. He says they have a correspondent down there and they ought to be able to get some information out of him provided he isn't hiding in some volcano planning a revolution of his own.

The show is closing in Atlantic City tonight and we all leave for New York tomorrow morning and start a week of rehearsal day and night. The first call is tomorrow night, 8 p. m., Bryant Hall.

Am writing this with one hand and making up for matinee with the other. They called overture a few minutes ago. There goes the curtain. Signing off,

Your loving sis
DIXIE.

~~~~~~~~~~~~~~~~~~

<div style="text-align:right">NEW YORK, N. Y.
October 4.</div>

MR. PHIL MASON
MILTON AND COMPANY, WASHINGTON BUREAU
WASHINGTON, D. C.

DEAR MASON:

Get in touch right away with Congressman X. Convince him of peril to American interests in Costaragua by suppression of Romano revolution. Confidentially our oil concession is a bust if we can't get some marines down there pretty quick to reinstate Romano. X should worry about that but don't fail to call his attention to persecution of American citizens and indignities to American flag. Heavy on the flag. Intervention necessary to protect life and property and sustain dignity of our great nation. Step on it.

<div style="text-align:right">Hurriedly,
JOHN MILTON.</div>

~~~~~~~~~~~~~~~~~~

Speech
OF
HON. PHINEAS FIBBLEDIBBER
OF ALABAMA
IN THE HOUSE OF REPRESENTATIVES

(*From the Congressional Record*)

(The House in Committee of the Whole House on the state of the Union had under consideration the bill (H.R. 9481) making appropriations for the Executive Office and sundry independent executive bureaus, boards, commissions, and offices for the fiscal year ending June 30, 1929 and for other purposes.)

MR. FIBBLEDIBBER. Mr. Chairman, I have been sitting here listening to the remarks of the gentleman from Iowa (MR. CORNHILL) with ill concealed loathing and disgust. I will go further and say his impudence is exceeded only by his ignorance. He has insinuated that the real purpose of my appeal for the pacification of Costaragua is to restore order so that American investors and bond holders will be secured their dividends and interest payments. This gentleman has manipulated the facts and distorted the figures and woven over and about his handiwork the mucilaginous web of falsehood and the meretricious tissue of deceit. (APPLAUSE.)

Gentlemen in the words of the poet: "Lives there a man with soul so dead who never to himself has said, this is my own my native land," and er ... and so forth. (APPLAUSE.)

MR. WHOOPS. Will the gentleman yield?

MR. FIBBLEDIBBER. I yield five minutes to the gentleman from Minnesota.

MR. WHOOPS. Mr. Chairman, I have asked for time for the purpose of reading a poem entitled "The Lone Eagle" by our former colleague, Mr. Knute Knuteson, so that it may be incorporated in the Record. The poem reads as follows:

THE LONE EAGLE

High, high up in the skies
The Lone Eagle gallantly flies,
Colonel Charles A. Lindbergh is his name
And deathless and immortal forever will be his undying name,
Across the blue to Paris he flew
Not only for me but also for you
From the Land of Liberty across the sea
To the land of Liberté Fraternité and Egalité.

Thank God again this marvelous man
Was as you might expect an American
No Frenchman, German or Englishman
But a staunch, four square son of Uncle Sam
So Lafayette we can now say adieu
For our debt has been paid in full to you.
Three cheers then for Colonel Charles A. Lindbergh so true
And three times three for the Red, the White and the Blue. (APPLAUSE.)

Mr. FIBBLEDIBBER. Gentlemen, the dark ground of Costaragua is stained with blood. The sombre sky of Costaragua flares crimson with the unholy fires of arson and rapine. God's own sun cannot shine through the pillars of smoke by day and those twinkling stars in heaven's blue canopy pale their ineffectual glow as the raging hell of war's infernal fury seethes and belches death and destruction through the dark watches of the night. Shall we sit idly by and fiddle while Rome burns? Oppressed people are calling to us, outstretched hands are reaching for the light, piteous eyes strain through the fog of ignorance and the miasma of oppression. Will our country ever fail to fight the good fight for the weak, the needy and the oppressed? I say no by the Eternal. Never! (APPLAUSE.)

MR. SINGLETREE. Mr. Chairman, will the gentleman yield?

MR. FIBBLEDIBBER. I yield to the gentleman from Nebraska.

MR. SINGLETREE. Mr. Chairman, I desire to call the attention of the House to the success we are having in Nebraska with our dairy industry. Nebraska is a land blessed with sunshine, populated with an industrious law-abiding citizenship and supreme in the development of co-operative dairy associations and co-operative cheese factories. The people of my home county were the first Nebraskans to begin the co-operative manufacture of cheese and I take a pardonable pride this morning, gentlemen, in stating ...

~~~~~~~~~~~~~~~~

POSTAL TELEGRAPH — COMMERCIAL CABLES
TELEGRAM

OCTOBER 8TH

```
12X 376
WASHINGTON D.C.
JOHN MILTON
          67 WALL STREET NEW YORK CITY NY
THE MARINES ARE COMING COMING COMING
                                        MASON
```

~~~~~~~~~~~~~~~~

Brooklyn, N. Y.
Oct. 8.

Dear Nita:

I'm getting pretty damn tired of this Cora person. Around Jimmy all the time. All day today and yesterday she was at rehearsal with him. All but sitting in his lap with her arms around his neck. Came back to Atlantic City from New York and rode back to New York with him Sunday. Compartment together all the way no less. Then he takes me out to dinner and says it doesn't mean anything—she's just interested in the show business. You can tell that to my Aunt Fanny I says to him. Then he says he has to be nice to her—it's business. Yeh, business. Hooey. Well, I'm getting all fed up. He can have the business and her, too. My God you'd think a girl who had everything—money and clothes and a rich father and the top floor of a Park Avenue hotel—would give another girl a break. Why should she try to cop the only two legged male I'm interested in? Well, she can have him and the show, too. For two cents I'd walk out on the whole racket. Can you feature me rehearsing all day and night with a dame like that sitting out front criticizing. Say I nearly jumped over the footlights tonight and gave her a facial. And then Jimmy had the nerve to come back after rehearsal and ask me to go out and have a bite to eat with him. Well, I had a break. Jack was waiting for me and we went right by Jimmy like a taxi on a wet night. What are you doing in Philadelphia? For God's sake come home. What with all this changing and rehearsing and the show opening next Monday night and Jimmy yelling at me and Cora crawling into his vest pocket every chance and the family on my neck for coming home late and looking like hell and not marrying a millionaire I'm rapidly going nuts. All I got to say is this is the damdest world I was ever in and I hate every inch of it.

Dixie.

NEW YORK CITY
October 8.

MR. KIRK KING
SCENARIO DEPARTMENT,
COLOSSAL FILM CORPORATION,
HOLLYWOOD, CALIFORNIA.

DEAR KIRK:

You'll never know anything about women till you get mixed up with a musical show. Next to saxophone players it's the craziest sex there is. I've had years of it in the last three weeks and if I had my choice between Cleopatra and Clara Bow I'd take arsenic. I wrote to you about Dixie Dugan. She's got the lead in this show of mine and she's cuter than a brindle pup. But, boy, what a temper. I mean temper. Temper is what I mean. You should have heard her yesterday in the middle of rehearsal. Three stage hands broke down and cried like babies from pure envy. It would take a book to tell you all the reasons, but briefly it's like this—The daughter of old man Brewster who owns the Evening Tab, my meal ticket, came to bat when my show was ready to close in Atlantic City with enough money to buy out the producers and give me a chance to put it back in the shape I wrote it. So naturally she's watching rehearsals and since it's part of the deal that I can't give away the secret of who is backing me Dixie can't figure what this dame is doing out front making suggestions how she thinks the show could be improved. So when Cora, that's her name, thought Dixie's specialty dance in the second act was too long and suggested cutting two choruses out of it, boy, oh boy, oh boy!

That's only part of it. The hell of it is I'm afraid I'm falling for the kid. Besides being cute and all that she's got a quick mind, a keen sense of humor and says just what she thinks. And she really thinks. No, I'm not overworked. I'm just getting to like her a lot. Maybe too much. I don't know. But it's pleasant. Darn swell, in fact. But she'll probably marry one of these rich guys that's prowling around her all the time. Prowling is the word, too. There's one Jack Milton who has an interest in the show. Just nuts about her. Filthy with lucre, too. Always pelting her with orchids or pushing her in and out of long limousines—the kind you need television to see the chauffeur.

The show has me worried nuts, too. Not the show itself because I'm sure I can get it whipped into shape, but we don't seem to be able to get any bookings. In the mornings they say see us this afternoon, in the afternoons they say maybe we'll have a house tomorrow. Meanwhile salaries go on just the same and everybody worried sick thinking maybe we won't open at all. I thought the show business was all laughter and applause and big royalty checks and silk hats and swilling tea and giving talks to schools of journalism on how I became a playwright. In your hat. It's a headache. It's a pain anywhere you sit. And then imagine falling in love on top of it. That's the pay-off.

JIMMY

THE BELVEDERE
PHILADELPHIA
October 9th.

DICKIE DEAR:

Heads up. You should fret about Jimmy with Jack at your feet. I'm here for only a day or so more and then home, but I have to sail right away on a buying spree for the firm. Just staying here long enough to check up with the local branch and then back to Paris. Wish you were going with me. That's terrible about Alvarez, but maybe he'll wiggle out of it some way. Tango dancers have slippery hips.

Love,
NITA

RADIOGRAM — WORLD WIDE WIRELESS — RADIO CORPORATION OF AMERICA

OCTOBER 10TH

K12 5B 766
SANAGUAY COSTARAGUA
MANAGING EDITOR
NY EVENING TAB NY
   YOUR QUERY RECEIVED STOP GENERAL SORILLO REORGANIZING ROMANO FORCES AND LEADING COUNTER REVOLUTION STOP RELIABLY INFORMED ALVAREZ ROMANO SON OF EXPRESIDENTE TO BE EXECUTED WITH FIFTY FOLLOWERS INSIDE TWENTY FOUR HOURS STOP HOW MANY WORDS

                                     PERKINS

RADIOGRAM — WORLD WIDE WIRELESS — RADIO CORPORATION OF AMERICA

OCTOBER 10TH

K12 5B 766
NEW YORK CITY NY
ARTHUR PERKINS
CARE AMERICAN CONSUL
SANAGUAY COSTARAGUA
    FILE FLASH ONLY ALVAREZ EXECUTION

                                     NY EVE TAB

(The Flash)

```
RADIOGRAM
WORLD WIDE WIRELESS
RADIO CORPORATION OF AMERICA
```

                      OCTOBER 10TH

L6 GS 29L
SANAGUAY COSTARAGUA
MANAGING EDITOR
NY EVENING TAB
    ALVAREZ ESCAPED
                PERKINS

Out of Which Blossomed the Story

REBELS SLAUGHTERED
IN CORRAL OF DEATH
By Arthur Perkins

(Special Correspondent of the New York Evening Tab)

Sanaguay, Costaragua. Oct. 11.— (Special): Fifty-four rebels were executed today. They were not led out at dawn and granted the last dignity of bandaged eyes and a firing squad. They were shot down one by one in a frenzy of fear and hope trying to scale the low wall of the corral in which they were herded for they were promised liberty if they could escape. This morning they were alive, bold and swaggering, tonight they are a heap of dead men, a fantastic pile in the moonlight looking for all the world like a lot of old clothes.

How was it done? Come with me. Look! There are two corrals. One holds the prisoners. From this a gate leads into the second corral in the center of which stands Herrera with a revolver in each hand. Beside him, kneeling on a blanket, his orderly with the supply of cartridges arranged in neat rows. Herrera has killed many men. He loves to kill and, because he is a valuable officer and it is good policy to keep him happy, unnecessary rebels who have been caught are given to him to do with as he likes. He is an artist. It is a point of pride with him never to repeat his formula. So each time he kills a batch of prisoners he does it differently. Today he is in a devilish mood. He will tease them with the hope of escaping. He will hold out life to them and then as they reach for it trustingly—he will blast them with death.

Soldiers with drawn guns herd the prisoners away from the gate, separate the first ten from the shrieking, cursing mob and drive them through the little gate into the corral where Herrera awaits them. As they rush for the walls Herrera fires. As fast as he can pull the trigger he pours bullets into them. As soon as one revolver is empty he drops it and his orderly fills its hot chambers with the cool bullets arranged in neat rows on the blanket. Some of the prisoners skip and duck, others crawl on the ground, others try to rush Herrera. Coolly, sardonically he shoots them all. Ten more prisoners dash through the little gate hoping to win freedom. They, too, Herrera shoots in quick succession and their bodies lay in quivering heaps from which arms reach fantastically and stiff fingers claw the walls even in death. Ten more prisoners push through the gate, stumbling, cursing, each trying to hide behind his neighbor. Herrera shouts sarcastic encouragement to them. One dashes for the wall and Herrera allows him to throw one leg over before he drops him with a bullet in the back. Some kneel and pray only to crash face downward with their open mouths in the dust. Ten more prisoners. Twelve more bullets. The revolvers are smoking hot. The orderly's fingers tremble as he fills them. The dusk is sifting down. There are fifteen men left to run the gauntlet. The troops force them through the little gate. Herrera's practiced eye counts them. Fifteen men, two revolvers, twelve bullets, three men too many. Calmly he sets to work picking off the leaders. A group of three rush him and he drops them in quick succession, the last a huge fellow so close the powder burns his face. The orderly passes Herrera a full revolver. He loses precious time fumbling with the empty one now too hot to hold. The dusk deepens. Herrera empties the second revolver. There are five men left. Two are trying to hide. Three are climbing the wall. The full revolver is not ready— there is a slight delay. The three men are half over. Herrera grabs the revolver from his orderly and fires blindly. Two men fall from the wall, one silently, one screaming horribly. The third is over. Herrera dispatches the two who prayed they were hid. Pumps one bullet into each with smiling precision. And then standing on the heap of dead bodies, looks over the wall and watches the escaped one running low against the ground like a terrified rabbit. He covers him with his last bullet and then with a loud laugh fires, but in the air.

The escaped one seems to ooze into the ground he is going so fast. Herrera's soldiers start in pursuit but Herrera stops them. He adjusts his serape, lights a cigarette and surveys his work. He is satisfied. What if one little one escapes? Herrera did not know who the "little one" was, but he knows now and already his soldiers are hot on the trail for the "little one" who cheated the corral of death was one of the leaders of the revolution, the son of ex-presidente Filippo Romano—the "little one," the lucky one, was Alvarez Romano.

"GET YOUR GIRL" FOLDING UP?
From Variety

The Main Stem hears under cover that "Get Your Girl" may fold up soon for lack of suitable house. This was a Kibbitzer and Eppus baby at first but after a poor showing in Atlantic City they picked up their doll rags and went home, leaving the author Jimmy Doyle to hold the bag with the new angel who they do be saying is the daughter of a local tabloid publisher. The show has been rehearsing in town waiting for a house and rumors of discord have been unusually brisk. The chief trouble seems to be the lady angel who wants to direct the show as well as bank roll it, with the result that her appearance in the theatre does not cause the cast to break out in a rash of cheers and confetti. The principal head on collisions have been between the little lady and the star of the piece—Dixie Dugan who made one of those sudden and miraculous hits first as one of those night club How-dowdy-dee-ows and then in a vod tab and now in "Get Your Girl"'s brief Atlantic City's stand. Dixie has all but walked out several times. Weep for the poor author-manager who may be a good newspaper man but in this Times Square racket has damp ears and a soft fontanelle. He must not only entirely revamp his piece and conduct rehearsals himself but please his lady angel and pacify his star. Well, as the young father of triplets said when he fell down the elevator shaft and was fired for carelessness, "God is love, there ain't no pain."

~~~~~~~~~~~~~~~~

October 13th.

Mr. Dennis Kerrigan
Gleason & Co.
Minneapolis, Minn.

Dear Mr. Kerrigan:

I thought it was just too sweet of you to stop over in Chicago and see me though I know Dixie must have suggested it—she's a darling and I do hope she makes a big hit in her new show altho carrying a whole show by herself must be pretty hard for her since she's had hardly any experience compared to me but then some girls get all the breaks.

I know I can say things like this to you because you are so sympathetic and understanding not like most men who don't understand girls at all and think that all they want is to be held and told how cute they are or sweet or something which is all right I suppose but that isn't everything. A girl like I just craves to be understood and you are in such a beautiful inspiring business selling lovely poetry which carries wishes and good cheer far and wide to one and all. This is very lovely and inspiring and I don't see how anyone who can be in such a noble business could be interested in just a little hoofer like I but you said you was so I must believe you because you couldn't associate all day with such beautiful sentiments and not be sincere and truthful too and besides anyway I want to believe you but then maybe I shouldn't ought to have said such a thing you'll think I'm just terrible but I'm not.

I was invited out on a party tonight after the show but I came right up to my room so I could write to you because I thought of a cute little poem which I thought maybe you could use. If you can't just throw it away because maybe it isn't any good anyway, however here it is.

> *Every day I think of you*
> *Every night I dream of you*
> *And that is all that I can do*
> *Just think and think the whole day through*
> *Of poor little me and great big you.*
>
> SUNSHINE.

KLAW THEA., 45th St., West of B'way.
Evgs. 8:30. Mats. Thurs. & Sat.

OPENING MONDAY NIGHT
James J. Doyle Presents
GET YOUR GIRL

HIS NEW MUSICAL COMEDY
WITH
DIXIE DUGAN
AND HER
GANG OF COMEDIANS, SINGERS, DANCERS, AND
The Original
JOLLITY JAZZ MANIACS

~~~~~~~~~~~~~~~~~

October 15th.

Miss Nita Dugan
The Belvedere
Philadelphia.
Nita Darling:

You can't sail Saturday. The show opens Monday night. At the last minute Jimmy got a house, the Klaw—it isn't very big but it's just right for an intimate musical which is what this has finally been worried down to. You've got to be there for the opening. I can't go through with it if you're not out front. Don't sail Saturday and leave me. I'm frantic. Everybody is crazy. The new costumes aren't ready. We're still rehearsing a lot of new business and can't possibly get it in shape for opening Monday night. I know I'm going to be a terrible flop. Jimmy is driving me mad. Barking at me all the time, snapping at this and that. I know he is half nuts with worry over the show and working all day and all night, but so am I. Put off sailing until after the opening and come and help me. I can't eat or sleep and when I do try to get a little rest at home, the family is on my neck. "Why don't you marry Jack, why don't you marry Jack—look at all the money he's got. You owe it to us—you owe it to yourself!" I wish they'd let me alone. Maybe they're right. I don't know. Did I tell you Jack wants to marry me, wants me to ditch the show and get married and go to Europe on a honeymoon? If the family ever heard that and thought I even hesitated, I'd have to sleep out in the garage. What am I going to do about Jimmy? One time I see him he acts as though he likes me and then if I make one false step on the stage he yells at me like a traffic cop. He's driving me crazy. If he'd only put his arms round me once and say "I love you," but he doesn't. Sometimes I think I'll take Jack up, marry him and go to Europe and stay there until I can forget the whole damn mess—the show and Jimmy and Cora and all the rest of it. I found out Cora is hanging around Jimmy because she's the one that put up the money for the show. She's nuts about him. I can tell by the way she looks at him and paws him every chance she gets. And he's with her most of the time—talking about the show he says. Damn the show and Jimmy and her and everybody and everything except you darling. Don't sail Saturday, sis. Please come home and stay with me till after the opening. I've got to open. I've got to make good, if for nothing else but to make a tramp out of that Cora dame who's been trying her best to get Jimmy to throw me out and get a big name star in my place. I've got to make good. You can't leave me. I've got nobody but you. Sis darling, wire and say you're not sailing Saturday. You can't leave me—I'll go mad.

DIXIE.

TELEGRAM — POSTAL TELEGRAPH – COMMERCIAL CABLES

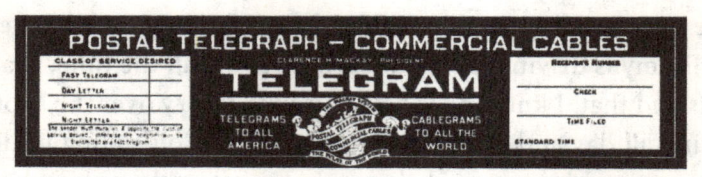

OCTOBER 16TH

DIXIE DUGAN
KLAW THEATRE
NEW YORK
DARLING CANT POSTPONE SAILING STOP MUST
BE IN PARIS FOR FIRST SHOWING OF SPRING
STYLE COLLECTIONS OR WAFFLEHEIMERS WILL
GIVE ME GATE STOP WILL SEE YOU SATURDAY
MORNING FOR NICE LONG TALK BEFORE
SAILING NOON STOP DONT WORRY YOURE
GOING TO BE A BIG HIT AND THE PRINCE OF
YOUR HEART WILL CARRY YOU AWAY IN HIS
WHITE ROLLS ROYCE AND YOULL BE HAPPY
EVER AFTER

NITA

October 16th.

MISS SUNSHINE PURCELL
℅ GEO. WHITE'S SCANDALS
ILLINOIS THEATRE, CHICAGO
DEAR SUNSHINE:

I got your pretty poem
And simply wish to state
The way you wrote the little thing
Was absolutely great.

You took me by complete surprise
It was so witty and so wise.
And yet so tender and so sweet
It would be mighty hard to beat.

How's that? Poetry while you wait. Of course you inspired it, but then I'm naturally gifted that way anyway. I often tell the creative department here—that's where all the ideas come from—ideas, heh! heh!—My God, I sneeze better ideas. I tell them let me get up some of your ideas and you'll have something that will go over the counter instead of under, but they know everything. Some of these days I'm going to fight it out with them in bare feet on a cake of ice. You've only seen me in my milder moods. But you wouldn't know me, Sunshine, when I get all wrought up. Of course, you're young yet and don't understand men much, especially men that think a lot and are complicated like me. But you certainly are an unusual girl just the same when you can write such a beautiful poem so easy-like. Why, even I would have to work on a thing like that.

Now as to coming down to Detroit, why it was funny, I was thinking of doing that very thing. Isn't that a coincidence? You see, we have some big accounts there. So don't be surprised if I show up. Of course I won't be able to see much of you as these are very big accounts and I will have to work hard on them, especially Ye Quainte Olde Tyme Nooke Gift Shoppe. They got a lady buyer there, a Miss Krunch and she has lots of sales resistance so every once in a while one of us good-looking salesmen must stop over and take her out and get her all warm and confused. The technical name for that is "contacting." You must have heard of "contact men" in advertising and merchandising? Well that's me!

Soon I will be in Detroit
And I have got a hunch

I'll see my little Sunshine, too,
As well as Lady Krunch.

DENNY.

~~~~~~~~~~~~~~~~

OPENINGS TONIGHT
THE CALL OF THE TAME—comedy at the **BELMONT**
SENTIMENTAL SUSIE—musical comedy at the **MAJESTIC**
DAMN YOUR EYES—drama at the **BIJOU**
HEIGH-HO—intimate revue at the **CENTURY ROOF**
GET YOUR GIRL—musical comedy at the **KLAW**

~~~~~~~~~~~~~~~~

POSTAL TELEGRAPH – COMMERCIAL CABLES
TELEGRAM

OCTOBER 20TH

DIXIE DUGAN
             KLAW THEATRE N.Y.
HOPE MARILYN MILLER WILL CHOKE OVER HER
COFFEE TOMORROW MORNING WHEN SHE READS
HOW YOU KNOCKED THEM FOR A ROW OF
FILLING STATIONS LOVE AND KISSES
                  SUNSHINE

~~~~~~~~~~~~~~~~

```
                    POSTAL TELEGRAPH — COMMERCIAL CABLES
                                TELEGRAM
```

                                            OCTOBER 20TH
DIXIE DUGAN
                    KLAW THEATRE N.Y.
WISHING YOU THE OVERFLOW FROM ABIES
IRISH ROSE
                                    EVENING TAB

~~~~~~~~~~~~~~~~~~~~

```
                    POSTAL TELEGRAPH — COMMERCIAL CABLES
                                TELEGRAM
```

                                            OCTOBER 20TH
DIXIE DUGAN
                    KLAW THEATRE N.Y.
I WILL BE OUT IN FRONT BUT MY HEART
WILL BE BACK STAGE WITH YOU
                                            JACK

~~~~~~~~~~~~~~~~~~~~

```
                                              OCTOBER 20TH
DIXIE DUGAN
                              KLAW THEATRE N.Y.
I WOULD LIKE TO CROWN YOU DASH WITH
SUCCESS PERIOD
                                              DENNY
```

```
                                              OCTOBER 20TH
DIXIE DUGAN
                              KLAW THEATRE N.Y.
THE BEST OF GOOD LUCK TO THE NICEST KID
EVER HANDICAPPED BY THE BUMMEST FIRST
PLAY OF THE GOOFIEST YOUNG PLAYWRIGHT
                                              JIMMY
```

RADIOGRAM — WORLD WIDE WIRELESS — RADIO CORPORATION OF AMERICA

OCTOBER 20TH

S/S LEVIATHAN
RADIOGRAM
DIXIE DUGAN

KLAW THEATRE N.Y.

SLAY EM BABY

NITA

POSTAL TELEGRAPH — COMMERCIAL CABLES — TELEGRAM

OCTOBER 20TH

JIMMY DOYLE

KLAW THEATRE N.Y.

CAME THE DAWN AND SWEETLY UPON THE
FEVERED BROW OF THE YOUNG PLAYWRIGHT
FAME PRESSED A LINGERING KISS

KIRK

```
                                    OCTOBER 20TH
JIMMY DOYLE
                    KLAW THEATRE N.Y.
CAN WE HAVE OPTION ON YOUR NEXT FIVE
PLAYS
              SHUBERTS
              ZIEGFELD
              DILLINGHAM
              THEATRE GUILD AND
              THE BOYS WHO USED TO
                  WORK WITH YOU ON THE
                  EVENING TAB
```

~~~~~~~~~~~~~~~~~~~~~~~~

```
                                    OCTOBER 20TH
JIMMY DOYLE
                    KLAW THEATRE N.Y.
HORSESHOES
                                            CORA
```

~~~~~~~~~~~~~~~~~~~~~~~~

> **POSTAL TELEGRAPH – COMMERCIAL CABLES TELEGRAM**
>
> OCTOBER 20TH
>
> JIMMY DOYLE
>
> KLAW THEATRE N.Y.
>
> IF YOU GET ALL THE GOOD LUCK I AM
> WISHING YOU TONIGHT YOULL BE WALKING UP
> AND DOWN BROADWAY TOMORROW WITH A TIN
> CUP BEGGING FOR A LITTLE MISFORTUNE
>
> DIXIE

~~~~~~~~~~~~~~~~~~~~~~~~~~

> **POSTAL TELEGRAPH – COMMERCIAL CABLES TELEGRAM**
>
> OCTOBER 20TH
>
> JIMMY DOYLE
>
> KLAW THEATRE N.Y.
>
> SUCCESS OSER
>
> KIBBITZER & EPPUS

~~~~~~~~~~~~~~~~~~~~~~~~~~

WHAT THE CRITICS SAID

"Get Your Girl" is a polychromatic pot-pourri which titivates the neuronio filaments, tickles the tympani and threads a rowdy rigadoon through the calloused convolutions of this weary old cerebrum. . . . Hammond—Herald Tribune.

This old meany played hookey last night from his perpetual pilgrimage to the grotto of Mrs. Fiske and found himself, much to his aged surprise, in the Klaw Theatre where a Night Club Madcap named Dixie Dugan danced into the whitelight of stardom. . . . Woollcott—New York World.

When I was in dear old London last year, I was asked what is the matter with the American Theatre. Twenty-five years ago, come Saint Swithins, I would have said—plague take it—what would I have said? Certainly nothing that has anything to do with "Get Your Girl" which I saw last night from my customary aisle seat. I look in my program and see the name of Dixie Dugan. Surely I will not have to consult this program again for I would know this captivating little miss if I were to meet her in Hyde Park on a foggy November day. Such esprit, such verve, such elan—speaking of London on a foggy day, etc. etc. . . . Dale—N. Y. American.

"Get Your Girl" is a mean whoop-dee-do that will keep the Klaw seats warm long after your Christmas jewelry has turned green. And Dixie Dugan is the hottest little wench that ever shook a scanty at a tired business man. Tickets on sale eight weeks in advance, and if you fall for that whoopie about getting them at the box office, you are going to be seeing Roxy ushers all winter—God forbid! . . . Winchell—Evening Graphic.

"Get Your Girl"—A Wow! . . . a sock in the nose! . . . a kick in the pants! . . . Variety.

```
                                    OCTOBER 21ST
RADIOGRAM
NITA DUGAN
                           S/S LEVIATHAN
WE WENT OVER   OPEN A BOTTLE FOR ME
                                    DIXIE
```

```
                                    OCTOBER 21ST
RADIOGRAM
DIXIE DUGAN
                       KLAW THEATRE N. Y.
I KNEW YOUD DO IT DARLING WILL YOU HAVE
HEIDSICK OR THE WIDOW CLICQUOT
                                    NITA
```

Hotel Manana,
Havana, Cuba.

Querida mia:

I write you this few words because soon I will be too busy in my own country where I return to head the new big revolution which I plan now night and day. They capture and try to kill me but I am too brave and know too much and I get away but not before I kill ten twenty thirty—how many I do not know, but it is frightful and then I come here where my father is already and together we plan a new revolution which will be bigger and better and which when I have finish killing all those dogs, cutting their throats from ears to ears and back again I will come and get you and we will be happy in my beautiful country, because then I will be the presidente and you will belong to me, flor del cielo, all of you from the top of your sweet head to the bottom of your little feet which walk all night on my heart, cruel and beautiful one.

Cari nostamente tuyo amante apasionado,
Alvarez.

```
                                    OCTOBER 22ND
RADIOGRAM
NITA DUGAN
                          S/S LEVIATHAN
HE LOVES ME   WHOOPIE
                                    DIXIE
```

```
                    RADIOGRAM
                   WORLD WIDE WIRELESS
              RADIO CORPORATION OF AMERICA
```

                                        OCTOBER 22ND
RADIOGRAM—S/S LEVIATHAN
DIXIE DUGAN
                              KLAW THEATRE N. Y.
WHO THIS TIME
                                                NITA

~~~~~~~~~~~~~~~~~~~~~

```
                    RADIOGRAM
                   WORLD WIDE WIRELESS
              RADIO CORPORATION OF AMERICA
```

                                        OCTOBER 22ND
RADIOGRAM
NITA DUGAN
                                       S/S LEVIATHAN
JIMMY JIMMY JIMMY JIMMY JIMMY THIS TIME
NOW AND FOREVER
                                                DIXIE

~~~~~~~~~~~~~~~~~~~~~

The Super-Colossal Wonder Picture Epic
of this or any other century

HOLLYWOOD GIRL

By J. P. McEVOY

Author of Show Girl, The Potters, Americana, etc.

ALL-TALKING—ALL-DANCING—ALL-SINGING

With three-dimensional technicolor television, featuring

ALL STAR CAST

DIXIE DUGAN:	Who shakes a sun-kist Scanty—with sound.
FRITZ VON BUELOW:	Colossal Director in the Leaping Lispies with more Yeth-men than Paul Whiteman has chins.
JIMMY DOYLE:	Who worked up from Ghosting on a tabloid to writing dialogue for Rin-Tin-Tin.
SOL NEBBICK:	The big producer with the rat-trap mind, the Frigidaire heart, and nerves like E-strings.
MICKEY O'KEEFE:	Who wrote the original Prisoner's Song: "I Can't Lock You Anything But Up, Baby".

I

> Brooklyn, N. Y.
> May 15th.

Miss Nita Dugan,
Hotel Scribe,
Rue Scribe,
Paris.

Dear Nita:

Still wading around in Frenchmen and Three Star? Et comment, sez you, and who wants to know? The baby, sez I, Dixie Dugan, late Star of *Get Your Girl*. I've heard of you, sez you, but not recently. Where've you been? On Broadway, sez I. Where on Broadway, sez you. Up and down, sez I—up and down, between Forty-eighth and Forty-second, looking for a job. Well, pull up your chair and take down your hair, and tell us all about it. You can weep here, and here, but not here—it's velvet. Jake, sez I, and it's like this:

The show was one of those nine-day wonders, but after that they stopped wondering and we took it up where they left off, but Jimmy hung on saying, they'll come, and they did, but not to us. After we had been running—"running"—I'm leffing—four or five weeks, staying away from our show was the rage, and all the time they were telling Jimmy, hang on, it's always like this just before Thanksgiving, and after Thanksgiving, hang on, it's always like this just before Christmas, and after Christmas, hang on, it's always like this just before Easter, but long before that Jimmy was hung. So they backed up the van and moved us up to the Whoosis Theatre, where all good shows go to die and only people go to see them who wouldn't pay more than fifty cents to see the twelve apostles in a six day bike race. And after that, old girl, we went on the road, and the road ain't what it used to be and never was. And if they tell you it's the movies that did it, how about those million Chevrolet Coupes that you never see parked on the pavements? Ah well, boys will be boys and girls will be girls, and if you want it different you can go into a Shubert chorus. Where am I?

Oh yes, we went on the road and the first place they booked Jimmy was a theatre in Toronto where the balcony was condemned. That was only the kickoff. They do say a virgin producer has a chance to stay that way in New York, but once they get him out on the road he always comes back with a brazen laugh and a set of triplets. It wasn't long before they had Jimmy frozen out and then the new gang celebrated by cutting salaries to the bone, on the theory, I suppose, that the nearer the bone the sweeter the meat. The farther we went out into the open the closer they got, until I figured if they ever got us out to the Coast they'd be throwing fish to us on Seal Rock. So one week I didn't send out the laundry and me and my shadow, and you couldn't have told us apart, crawled into an upper berth in Kansas City, and made choo-choo back to New York.

And here I am, as Jonah said to the whale. Have been trying for months now to get my feet in some trough but all I get is the run around—that nothing today my dear, but keep in touch with us, you never know what is liable to turn up. I know what's going to turn up—my toes.

Poor Jimmy is really socked—he's lost everything he made and everything he could beg, borrow or steal. He'd like to go back to the *Evening Tab* but he's afraid the boys will razz him to death. Besides, the show bug has bit him and once that happens the swelling never goes down. So Jimmy is writing another show for me and if it gets on and over we're going to take the first ten dollars that comes into the box office and get married on it. I'm for taking the first two, but

Jimmy says we ought to have a reserve. All we have now is our health and two young people of assorted sexes with a lot of health and not enough money to get married are liable to get into a lot of trouble. Wouldn't that be fun? Wishing you the same,

DIXIE.

```
                                         MAY 17
NA387 39 DL HOLLYWOOD CALIF 17 1109A
JIMMY DOYLE
CARE EVENING TAB
                          NEW YORK CITY
THE SQUAWKING PICTURES NEED FRESH YOUNG
STORIES THAT WILL SCREAM WELL STOP YOU
ARE WASTING YOUR SWEETNESS ON THE
DESERT AIR STOP WOULDNT YOU LIKE TO
COME TO HOLLYWOOD THE MECCA OF THE
LITERARY WORLD AND MECCA WHOOPEE
                                    KIRK
```

```
                                           MAY 17
SB423 19 NEW YORK N Y 17 403P
KIRK KING
COLOSSAL FILM CORPORATION
                    HOLLYWOOD CALIF
MUCH TO HIS SURPRISE THE LITTLE GIRL
SAID YES SIR AND THEN HE DIDNT KNOW
WHAT TO DO
                                           JIMMY
```

```
                                           MAY 18
NC476 DL-HOLLYWOOD CALIF 956A
JIMMY DOYLE
CARE EVENING TAB
                    NEW YORK CITY N Y
IN HOLLYWOOD INTERROGATION POINT DONT
BE SILLY STOP GO TO AMBASSADOR HOTEL
AND SEE FRITZ BUELOW COLOSSAL DIRECTOR
TELL HIM YOU WROTE THE BOOK OF
GENESIS AND BLACK BEAUTY AND ALL THE
SOUND EFFECTS FOR HER SACRIFICE STOP
ASK A THOUSAND BUCKS A WEEK TAKE FIVE
HUNDRED
                                           KIRK
```

> **MAY 19**
>
> SA486 L5 NEW YORK N Y L9 1130A
> KIRK KING
> COLOSSAL FILM CORPORATION
> HOLLYWOOD CALIF
> KIDDING ASIDE CANT YOU GIVE ME A REAL TIP BEFORE I GO SEE BUELOW
>
> JIMMY

> **MAY 20**
>
> NA502 37 DL-HOLLYWOOD CALIF 20 1033A
> JIMMY DOYLE
> CARE EVENING TAB
> NEW YORK CITY N Y
> THE SCOTCH OUT HERE HAS BEEN CUT UNTIL THERES VERY LITTLE SUSPENSE AND NO LOVE INTEREST IN IT SO THE ONLY LITERARY ADVICE I CAN GIVE YOU IS THAT WHEN YOU COME OUT BRING YOUR OWN
>
> KIRK

PUBLICITY DEPARTMENT
COLOSSAL FILM CORPORATION

May 17th.

To Miss Betty Byrne,
Motion Picture Editor,
N. Y. Evening Tab.

FOR IMMEDIATE RELEASE

Fritz Buelow, the great director who made that sensational epic *Sinners in Love* and that equally thrilling masterpiece *Lovers in Sin* is paying his first visit to New York in three years. He is not coming here to play, however, but to shoot the Coney Island sequences for his newest epic *Sinning Lovers*, which is the present title for the picture previously announced as *Loving Sinners*. It is the film adaptation of that famous poem *The Charge of the Light Brigade*. Mr Buelow and his technical staff have reserved a floor at the Ambassador Hotel.

~~~~~~~~~~~~~~~~

Better get up Fritz. That dame'll be here any minute now.
Who cares?
It's the interviewer for the *Evening Tab*—Betty Byrne.
Who sent for her?
I did—you gotta get some publicity while you're here. Whatcha got a manager for?
I don't know. What day is it?
Monday.
What became of Sunday? Anybody working today?
Kelly is shooting that skirt-blowing sequence in the Fun House over in Coney Island.
What, again?

Well, he figured out a new Ufa angle shot for it. Sez it'll be a wow with sound.

Mix me another. Any skirt is a wow with Kelly—sound or no sound. I hope I never see another.

The little one wasn't so bad. Hot, what?

They're all hot. A cold one would be a novelty. When did she leave?

How do I know? I was in conference. The ginger ale's all gone.

I'll take it straight. What's this Byrne baby like? Never heard of her!

Young.

Good!

About so high; built like this; blonde.

You needn't stay. Where's my robe and slippers?

She wants to talk about sound pictures.

And send some ginger ale up on your way out.

I'm so sorry I'm late, Mr. Buelow, but I couldn't get away from the office until after six.

You're Miss Wilkins?

Betty Byrne—from the *Evening Tab*. I had a story about you the other day.

I never read the papers. In fact, when I'm working on a picture I never read anything. All my energy is concentrated on my work. Burns you up this business.

It must.

Creating characters, pumping energy, vitality, inspiration into a lot of mannequins and marionettes. Building cities, moving armies, making wars and plagues and famines and earthquakes.

It must be wonderful!

You know, sometimes when I think of the power at my command it makes me stop and think. Last summer I took a thousand people out into Death Valley and kept them there four months. It was 120 in the shade and no shade. Fourteen died, twenty-seven went mad—all extras—and 120 mules. It was magnificent.

What picture was that?

Her First Night. Hasn't been released yet. We're putting sound in it . . . will you join me?

Well, just a tiny little bit. There, wait a minute; that's too much . . . lots of ginger ale. Heaps of it . . . tell me about your new picture, Mr. Buelow.

It's an Epic of Sacrifice. Based on that famous poem, *The Charge of the Light Brigade*. It opens with a long shot of the Cavalry Charge, then a closeup of the thundering hoofs going right over the camera—you can imagine what that will be with sound! And then lap dissolve into all kinds of animals going into the Ark. That's where the story really begins. The water rises higher and higher; it submerges the whole world and then turns red. Blood! The tide of war. The Four Horsemen appear in the sky—pestilence, famine, death. The bloody tide rolls back—devastated France. Close-up of the machine-gun spitting death. An endless belt of cartridges going 'round and 'round. Fade-in a ferris wheel. Coney Island. The War is over. Pleasure-mad crowds forget the great sacrifice. That's where we are now. Oh yes, there is a Babylon sequence. You know, Ancient Babylon! And then New York, the Modern Babylon! There's a big message there for the young generation . . . Here, let me give you some more.

Not so much . . . aren't you terrible! I guess you directors are used to having your own way.

That's what the world thinks. The world's all wrong. It's lonely on the heights. The sparrows play in the streets, but the eagle soars alone. Soars and broods—lonely—lonely—alone.

I know. (*Softly*) I think I can understand.

Yes, women understand, for they too are alone and lonely.

How do you know?

A great director must know people. He holds them in the hollow of his hand and looks through them—into them. He turns them inside out. He devours them. Out of a thousand lives comes Life; that knowledge of Life which makes everything he does live. He must break a thousand lives in his bare hands to know how that one life will quiver before the camera, so that a million eyes will dim with tears and a million throats will choke and a million hearts will stand still . . . you don't look very comfortable over there. Why don't you come over here and sit by me . . .

Nine o'clock.
. . . You're so . . . so gentle and yet so strong . . . Honestly, I never felt before I could confide like this in anyone.
Ten o'clock.
. . . Here, you didn't finish yours . . . and you've been on your own ever since? You poor little sweet . . . There . . . just relax . . . poor darling . . . Don't! . . . Mr. Buelow . . . Fritz . . . No . . . Fritzie darling . . . Oh-h-h . . .
Eleven o'clock.
. . . You don't have to say that. You don't have to say you love me . . . I don't care. I feel happier tonight than I've felt since I was a little girl. You *do* understand, don't you?
Midnight . . .
. . . and you'll call me tomorrow, Fritzie, sure?

Sure. . . There now, run along, I'm going to turn in early. Got a big day tomorrow. We do the gag faction in the *House of a Thousand Mirrors*. It's allegorical, showing things are not what they seem. The girl sees her lover multiplied a thousand times in the mirrors. She tries to reach him and crashes into his images, bruised and despairing she tries to escape. She cannot. Subtitle, "Ah Love, Love What is the Substance? What is the Shadow." A great gag, what? . . .

(From the Evening Tab—May 20th)

GREAT ARTISTS ARE LONELY, SAYS FAMOUS DIRECTOR.

By
Betty Byrne

Oh girls, guess who I saw last night—no, not Jack Gilbert, though he's ducky, too. Come, come, you're not ver' bright this morning. Don't you know who's in town girls—stopping at the Ambassador in a suite as big as Madison Square Garden? Oh, you'll be green with jealousy when I tell you that I talked to him ver' ver' long and we had the most thrilling things to say to each other. Now that you're all akimbo and agog, I'll tell you. It was Fritz Buelow. You know that Miracle Man who made "Lovers in Sin," the picture which made us all laugh and cry and "Sinners in Love" which wrenched our hearts and yet made us smile happily through our tears. Well, he's back in town after more than three years' absence. He's working now on the most gorgeous epic in his career. He was telling me all about it last night and I'm sure he won't care if I let you in on an eentsieweentsie bit of it. It has a big theme—Sacrifice—and there's a big message under it. He's shooting part of it now in the Fun House and the Mirror House in Coney Island, showing the part where life is an illusion and the only things that matter are big, deep things like sacrifice and love. Doesn't it sound gorgeous, girls?

And here's a juicy little tip for some lucky girl. Mr. Buelow is planning a great jazz-mad sequence with singing and dancing—in sound—and he's looking for a real jazz-mad type. Here's what he said to me last night in his very words, "I'm looking for a real jazz-mad type." So you see girls, that's just what he wants. Well, he ought to find what he's looking for in New York, don't you think so girls?

Oh yes, Mr. Buelow is big and burly, with those strong shoulders which thrill us girls. He has blue eyes and light curly hair, and yet his long sensitive hands betray the artist and the dreamer. "It's lonely on the heights" sighed Mr. Buelow. "The sparrows twitter in the streets but the solitary eagle soars in the empyrean alone—lonely—and broods in majestic silence." Isn't that just too thrilling, girls?

Toodle-oo, I'll be seeing you.

FAN FARE

BROWN EYES: I don't know whether Rin-tin-tin has had any pups or not, but I certainly will find out for you if I can.

JUST A FAN: Aren't you sweet to say so, but after all one should do one's best, one should shouldn't one?

BILLY: Certainly, Clara Bow always wears bloomers on the set. Go to your room.

```
POSTAL TELEGRAPH — COMMERCIAL CABLES
                 TELEGRAM
```
                                              MAY 26

SE 235 30 DL-NEW YORK N Y 26 950A
KIRK KING
COLOSSAL FILM CORPORATION
                        HOLLYWOOD CALIF
YOUR BUELOW BIRD HAS MORE SECRETARIES
THAN PAUL WHITEMAN HAS CHINS STOP HAVE
TRIED EVERY WAY OF REACHING HIM FOR A
WEEK SHORT OF TUNNELLING STOP WHAT HAVE
YOU
                                        JIMMY

```
POSTAL TELEGRAPH — COMMERCIAL CABLES
                 TELEGRAM
```
                                              MAY 26

NA 532 6 HOLLYWOOD CALIF 26 202P
JIMMY DOYLE
CARE EVENING TAB
                        NEW YORK CITY N Y
TRY PUTTING ON A SKIRT
                                         KIRK

Brooklyn, N. Y.
June 5.

Miss Nita Dugan,
Hotel Scribe,
Rue Scribe,
Paris.

Dear Sis:

Guess what I've been doing the last two weeks—riding herd on a movie director—a big megaphone and puttee man from the West. His name is Fritz Buelow and he made *Sinners in Love* and *Lovers in Sin* and who givesadam? I do and I'll tell you why. There was a blurb in the *Tab* the other night about him, that he was hot for a jazz-mad baby that could make yip yip and faw down in a new squeakie and I says to myself Fritzie I'm just what your osteopath ordered to stop that pain in your head and I owe it not only to you but Will Hays and the industry to come through and quick and pretty. So I high-heeled right over to the Ambassador and asked old Poker Face at the desk to tell Fritz the good news. Buelow, says he, there's nobody here by that name, and I says well I saw it in the paper he was stopping here and Icycle says what paper and I says the *Evening Tab* and crossed myself quick and he says we take the *Times* here and I says come, come, it's a short life at the best so why not be pals along the way and if you don't like that you can take your high hat and I only wish it were a pineapple and Buelow is here and I bet your father was an acrobat and Dixie Dugan is the name and send it up pronto. All of which didn't get me here to there with old Broad A so I picked it up and dusted it off and took it around the block. Around and around. Thinking to myself how am I gonna get to this bozo. Why isn't there a Human Fly in my family that could shin up the brick work? Then I get a big hunch. Jimmy, I says, he used to be on a paper and these birds are pelicans for publicity so I rang Jimmy, and give him the works and he laughs so loud he sounds like two Texas Guinans gone hay wire.

How will YOU get into see him says Jimmy. Tell me first how I get in. I've been tailing him for weeks with night letters of introduction and they won't even let me off at his floor. And why do you want to see him anyway, and I told him I was off the legit for a while and had a big letch for the movies now that the apple knockers could hear me as well as see me and he says well even if Buelow and I were as close as call and settle I wouldn't help you meet him and I wants to know and he says because he's a bad bimbo and I says tell mother and he says well he's one of those guys that's on the make for every dame on the lot and I says do tell, ain't mother nature the old devil and he says and what's more if I hear any more about you trying to see this guy I'll sock you right on your pretty nose. That from Jimmy, mind you, so I says there you go making love to me again over the phone but that won't stop me from trying to see Mr. Buelow whom I consider a genius and if you can't wangle it I'll certainly find somebody who can because I know that me and the screen are going to be just like that and then I hung up maddizell and went into another big huddle with myself.

And then whatcha think. The old subconscious went put-put and the old brain backfired or something for a perfectly elegant idear snuck out. Whoops says I why didn't I think of that before and I dashed to the nearest telegraph office and sent Buelow a wire saying

SENDING SPECIAL STAFF WRITER MISS DUGAN TO INTERVIEW YOU FOR FULL PAGE SUNDAY FEATURE STORY WILL TELEPHONE FOR APPOINTMENT PAN-AMERICAN NEWSPAPER SYNDICATE.

Well, Goofus, it worked like nobody's neverminds. When I called up the next day a secretary said Mr. Buelow was extremely busy but he would grant me an interview the following evening at nine o'clock in his apartment and would I be prompt as Mr. Buelow was a very important and busy man and if I wasn't exactly on time and so on and so on and I said I was going to be busy too as I had to squeeze Mr. Buelow in between Lindbergh at 8.30 and the Marx Brothers at 9.20 but I'd do my best.

And, baby, that tomorrow is today and tonight's the night. Nine o'clock is the zero hour. Block that kick, block that kick, block that kick. Hooooooooooooooooold 'em, Vassar.

DIXIE.

II

The Fuzzy-Wuzzy . . . a creep joint in Harlem. An assortment of couples in ochre, beige, Arabian sand and postum shades doing the bumpity-bump under revolving lights—red and green—while a small hot band makes dirty wah-wah. It is edging on to midnight which is only the middle of the afternoon north of 135th. At a small dishevelled table sit Dixie Dugan and Jacques Goldfarb.

GOLDFARB: He ought to be along here any minute now.

DIXIE: So you've been telling me for the last three hours.

GOLDFARB: He must have got caught in a story conference over at the studio. He's a demon for work, Mr. Buelow, and this is the most important picture he's ever directed. It's an epic.

DIXIE: What's an epic?

GOLDFARB: Well, it's something—something—(*makes eloquent gesture with hands*) like that, see? Big! It's called *Sinning Lovers*.

DIXIE: Do they sin in a big way—with sound and effects? Listen to that wench sing. Hot Dow!

> *Oh yu may leave an' go to Halli-ma-fack*
> *But mah slow draag'll bring yu back*
> *Yu may go but this* (slap) *will bring yu back.*

GOLDFARB: Mr. Buelow said for us to be sure and wait here for him, that he didn't want you to be disappointed in getting your interview.

DIXIE: What's your racket?

GOLDFARB (*indignantly*): Racket? I'm Mr. Buelow's personal representative; his general manager, and also in charge of his press relations.

Dixie (*humming*): You may go but this will bring you back. (*Absently*) Don't those boogie femmes have funny shaped fannies? (*Coming to suddenly*) Oh, I beg your pardon!

Goldfarb (*suddenly*): Say listen, Miss Dugan, d'you like this writing business?

Dixie: Writing business? No, I can't say that I do, but it's a living and a girl must live. Ask me why.

Goldfarb: You're too pretty to be writing for a living.

Dixie: That's what I often tell myself. Only this morning I said to myself, Dixie, you're too pretty to be writing for a living, and then I listened but I didn't hear anything—so that's why I'm here, waiting to interview your famous Mr. Buelow, and if he doesn't show up pretty soon he'll get a good journalistic kick in the pants from me. Are you there?

Goldfarb (*shaking flask ruefully*): We seem to have killed it. I wish I knew somebody here.

Dixie: I'll fix that. Call Charlie there at the door.

Goldfarb: Why, have you been here before?

Dixie: I laid the cornerstone, and broke a bottle of gin on it as it slid down the ways. No, that was a ferry boat. Say, Charlie, we want a quart of Scotch. He'll get it for you—he's a good egg. How do I do it? That's the power of the press you read about.

Goldfarb: How would you like to go into the movies? (*Reaching for her hand*) I can fix it up.

Dixie: You don't have to hold that—I wouldn't hit you.

Goldfarb: I think you would be cute in the movies.

Dixie: I shouldn't wonder. That's what my older brother was saying the other day, Sam. He isn't very bright. Spends all of his time writing to the papers saying I'm a little girl sixteen years old and my boy friend doesn't speak to me any more. Do you think it is because

I'm getting warts? I'm sure he is too much of a gentleman to say so. What shall I do? Shall I get another boy friend who doesn't mind warts or shall I get some more warts and not bother about the boys?

GOLDFARB: Suppose I could get you a screen test?

DIXIE: All right, I'm supposing.

GOLDFARB (*capturing the other hand*): I think you'd be a knock-out in the movies.

DIXIE: You're repeating yourself, Mister—get on—get on.

GOLDFARB: You don't seem to like me.

DIXIE: I don't see how you can say that. I'm very fond of you. I had an uncle once who looked like you. I remember I was just a little bit of a girl, and then one day a lot of men came to the house and took him away. Raise your elbow a bit—that's better. They have good Scotch here. Charlie says he wouldn't take any chances. If it's for a friend he cuts it himself. Oh, how d'you do.

GOLDFARB (*jumping up*): Oh, hello. Mr. Buelow, I want you to meet Miss Dugan.

BUELOW: How do you do. Sorry to keep you waiting. May I present Chiquita Tortilla? This is Miss Dugan. You have seen Miss Tortilla, of course?

CHIQUITA (*extending small dark hand*): I am ver' please to like you, yes? (*To Buelow with flashing black eyes*) Miss Doogan who she?

BUELOW: A newspaper writer. Writes for the—the—what do you write for?

DIXIE (*uncertainly*): The—the *All American Newspaper Syndicate.*

GOLDFARB: I thought you said the *Pan American*?

DIXIE (*laughing it off*): It's really the *All American*, but we call it the *Pan American* because we're always putting somebody in the grease.

CHIQUITA: In th' grease? What's that?

BUELOW: Miss Tortilla hasn't been in this country long. She

doesn't understand the American slang. In fact, she hasn't been here long enough to understand much about the country, have you?

CHIQUITA (*taking cue*): Ah, but I love thee grand America. Eet ees so beeg, so reech an' effrybody so nice eet make my heart go boomp boomp.

DIXIE: Is Miss Chiquita boomping in the picture you're making now?

BUELOW: She plays Lilith in the ancient story and the Red Hot Mamma in the Modern Babylon part—that's New York—you know skyscrapers, modern towers of Babylon—Babel—well, same thing.

GOLDFARB (*worried*): Mannheim was looking for you this evening . . . he was in the projection room looking at the Coney Island rushes.

BUELOW: What did he want?

GOLDFARB: He was sorter glum. Said there wasn't enough sex in the merry-go-round sequence.

BUELOW: There you go, Miss Dugan. That gives you an idea. Every time you try to do something Big in this business a supervisor pops up out of a manhole and gums the works.

DIXIE: What's a supervisor?

GOLDFARB: The gag is that he's a guy that's hired by the front office to keep Gentiles from getting too artistic.

BUELOW: And after I go and shoot the merry-go-round with allegorical dissolves that show Life is a mad carrousel going around and 'round in tinsel grandeur to the cheap blare of that gaudy Calliope called fame—this big button-hole presser yells for more sex.

DIXIE: What does he want? More It in the horsies?

BUELOW (*pouring himself drink*): I guess so.

DIXIE: You might have 'em all come alive and go on the make for each other. (*Singing with orchestra.*)

I'm not much to look at, nothin' to see

> *Just glad I'm livin' and lucky to be—*
> *I got a woman crazy for me,*
> *She's funny that way.*

BUELOW: That's good. What's that?

DIXIE: Dick Whiting's newest. Ain't it diggety? I feel like laying down a few flat arches. Who's for that?

GOLDFARB (*rising*): Come on!

BUELOW (*quickly*): Here! It's my dance. (*Holding her closely as Chiquita stares after them in angry surprise*): Say, you're different from most of these writers.

DIXIE (*singing*):

> *I can't save a dollar, ain't worth a cent*
> *She doesn't holler, she'd live in a tent,*
> *I got a woman crazy for me,*
> *She's funny that way . . .*

Who's different?

BUELOW: You are. I like you.

DIXIE: Come, come, Mister. Heads up.

BUELOW: Do you like writing for a living?

DIXIE: Just nerts. Take a typewriter to bed with me every night.

BUELOW: Is that all?

DIXIE: And some paper. Let's talk about you. Are you really a genius? Do you think talking pictures are here to stay? How long are you gonna be in New York? Does your little Mexican friend carry a knife? She's madder'n hell.

BUELOW: Say, you're a swell dancer, kid.

DIXIE: It all dates from the day I clipped that coupon. Now I make all my own clothes and speak to the waiter in perfect French. But you should see me with a typewriter.

BUELOW: In bed?
DIXIE: With a typewriter. (*Sings.*)

> *When I hurt her feelings once in a while*
> *Her only answer is one little smile*
> *I got a woman crazy for me,*
> *She's funny that way.*

There's a damfool for you.
BUELOW: Say, listen, you're too pretty to be writing for a living...
DIXIE: ... how would you like to have a screen test? Is that it?
BUELOW: Well, how would you?
DIXIE: No.
BUELOW (*stunned*): What?
DIXIE: What do I want with a screen test? Suppose it turned out good? I'd have to leave New York and go to Hollywood and make pictures. And what for? There are too many pictures now. Let's make 'em play an encore. Come on, clap hands .... No, I guess that's all. Back we go, and you better pipe down on that screen test stuff when we arrive, or your little Hot Tamale won't like it.
BUELOW: Where does she get off telling me? Why, I made her!
DIXIE: Just a little old star-maker, what?

Brooklyn, N. Y.
June 6th.

Miss Nita Dugan,
Hotel Scribe,
Rue Scribe,
Paris.

Dear Sis:

Guess what? I have a movie director on my trail and a song writer on my hands. Life is getting full of that old meaning for me and to think that just a few weeks ago I was feeling so low I would have gone away with a flag-pole sitter. And it all happened last night at the Fuzzy-Wuzzy in Harlem where I had gone to meet Fritz Buelow—you know, that director I told you about. Well, I was sitting up there with his manager waiting for him and along about midnight he staggered in with this Mex femme Chiquita Tortilla. Before that his manager, an Eskimo named Goldfarb, started holding hands and talking screen tests, but his technique was very bad and his Scotch wasn't so good either, so he didn't get anywhere. Then Buelow trotted me around the floor a bit and told me I am too pretty to be writing for a living—I was pretending to be a writer for the papers you see and why not? Who isn't? Channel swimmers, Parachute-jumpers, Flea trainers—they all wind up doing signed articles, telling how they did it, giving advice to young parachute jumpers and flea trainers.

Buelow still thinks I'm a writer and we hadn't been around the floor twice before he was feeling my ribs and talking screen tests. I guess men are pretty much alike except some of them have a lower boiling point. Being a movie director, Buelow seems to figure all he has to do is look masterful, holler allez-oop, and the little girl does a nip-up. Well, I will say, I encouraged him. After all, this bozo goes places and does things, and if he wanted to give me a lift I could be sitting on top of one of those Beverly Hills throwing rocks at Mary Pickford's cat. Anyway, he was awfully nice to me, and of course, he tried me out right away, but I went completely Winnie-the-Pooh on him and now he probably thinks I'm all seven of the foolish virgins with a touch of Ed Wynn. Anyway, he kept up his lateral passes combined with an occasional end run but the baby sister held for downs on the old one-yard line. I think we play a better open game here than in the west.

I can't say that all this endeared me to little Chiquita, but I should get flats under the eyes worrying about her. Buelow finally talked me into having a screen and talking test and I'm to go over to the studio in Astoria in a couple of days. He promised me the best camera and mike crew and he would supervise my makeup himself. And would I have dinner with him tomorrow night? Sure, says I, and coffee with liqueur in the salon. So that's that.

But that wasn't all. During the evening several people came over to the table to talk to Buelow and one of them, a song publisher, brought a cute fellow with him and introduced him to us. He was one of those dreamy kids who look a little bit shell-shocked, so you knew right away he must be either a genius or a nut. Well, he sat down with us and had a drink and asked me for a dance and then he told me he was a lyric writer and that he wrote the words for a lot of popular songs that I can't remember now, and that he had just signed a big contract to go West and write theme songs for the movies. You know, like *Ramona*, and *Diane* and *Sonny Boy*. His name is Mike but pretty soon I was calling him Mickey for short. He's kinda cute at that; reminds me a little bit of Denny, my old greeting card weakness. I wonder what's become of him?

Well, to get back to the party: it was still going strong at 4 a. m. with the dance floor jammed and all singing "She's Got Good Bread," but Buelow said he had to be on the set at nine so we all blew up to Childs on the Circle and had bacon and eggs and coffee and Mickey took me home all the way over to Brooklyn which is no way to treat even a song writer but he was very sweet—sang songs to me all the way over... his own, of course, and I kissed him on the nose and told him to call me up sometime if he knew how to dial.

And now I'm wondering what Buelow will say when he finds out I was faking and that I'm not a writer at all, but just a little hoofer who is all burning up with ambition. Gee, Sis, no foolin', I've got to get something pretty soon. Jimmy can't get his show produced which he's been writing for me. He couldn't even get me an introduction to Buelow. He wouldn't anyway—too jealous. Won't he burn up when he finds out I've not only met him anyway but am getting tests and everything? And wouldn't it be just too bad if I did get a break in the movies and went over? Oh boy! Come on Fritz. Do that thing!

Love,
Dixie.

June 7th.

Miss Dixie Dugan,
439 Flatbush Ave.,
Brooklyn, N. Y.
Dear Dixie:

This is one of those hello and goodbye letters. I'm leaving today for Hollywood. It's funny, you know, but I was all pepped up about going out there until I met you the other night and now I hate to leave little old Broadway and you. That would make a good song don't you think? I love to say hello, I hate to say goodbye, but somewhere the sun is shining and soon I'll be with you, and my blackbirds will be blue birds because I love you. That needs a little polishing up. You see, I was just sort of dummy-ing it out.

I think you're awfully sweet. I wish you were coming out to Hollywood or I were staying here where I could see you often. You know, I think you are a real inspiration. You know when I got back home the other night after seeing you I was so pepped up I couldn't go to sleep. All kinds of songs were going through my head and then I thought of a theme song that I'm going to sell as soon as I get out to Hollywood. You know that movie, *The Man Who Laughs?* Well, I was reading in *Variety* they are going to re-issue it with sound and they are looking for a theme song. What do you think of this one? It's just the chorus and it needs a little polishing up, but here's the way it goes:

> *Oh man who laughs you make me cry*
> *My Man! You're my man*
> *And I can't live without my man,*
> *The man I love.*
> *Just like a poem by Victor Hugo*
> *I will go wherever you go*
> *Laugh, Man, Laugh, but bye and bye*
> *You will learn what it means to sigh,*
> *Man Who Laughs (Ha! Ha! Ha!)*
> *You make me cry.*

I think it ought to be a big hit. You can see it's got a lot of good commercial things in it. Part of *My Man* which was a big sock and *The Man I Love* which was one of Gershwin's best, and part of *Laugh Clown Laugh*, and then at the end where I have the laughing indicated I'll have the composer pull in a strain of Pagliacci and besides all that I think those are two swell wow lines:—

> *Just like a poem by Victor Hugo*
> *I will go wherever you go.*

That's a new rhyme too. That'll hold Gus Kahn! And I bet Berlin won't be so chesty about his "valisefull of books to read where it's peaceful." Do you get it—valise-full, peaceful? That was in *Lazy*.

When I go out to the coast I'm going to team with Dick Whiting ... you know, the fellow who wrote the tune for *Horses* and *Japanese Sand Man*, and *Ain't We Got Fun* and a whole lot more? But just the same, I wish you were going to be out there. I'm going to miss you something terribly. I never fell so hard before. Say, that's not a bad start for a lyric. I never fell so hard before, until I fell for you, and there could be a swell wow line in the chorus something like this:—

> *Falling in love is old and slow*
> *I jump right in, I'd have you know.*

Will you please write to me—I don't think I could stand it not to hear from you any more. Honest, I mean it! You can reach me at the Roosevelt Hotel, Hollywood, until further notice.

Sincerely,

MIKE (*Call me Mickey*) O'KEEFE.

DIXIE DUGAN RATES TEST.
(From Variety, week of June 14th)

Fritz Buelow, the Colossal director, has been in town handing out screen and voice tests to likely-looking gals. Object: important roles in the thpeakie thequentheth of his newest epic "Sinning Lovers." The latest to rate a few hundred feet of sound track is Dixie Dugan, who will be remembered as the cute little baggage in "Get Your Girl" and before that, in vode tab out in the alfalfa zone long enough to take a few bows and get herself kidnapped for a hat full of headlines. Dixie should do well in this new racket, and when we say racket we mean sound.

```
POSTAL TELEGRAPH - COMMERCIAL CABLES
TELEGRAM
```

                                            JUNE 16TH
SB59 7 WOODSTOCK N Y 13 91 5A
DIXIE DUGAN
            439 FLATBUSH AVE BROOKLYN N Y
DO I HAVE TO READ VARIETY TO FIND OUT
WHAT YOURE DOING
                                              JIMMY

```
POSTAL TELEGRAPH - COMMERCIAL CABLES
TELEGRAM
```

                                            JUNE 16TH
NC322 BROOKLYN N Y 7 235P
JIMMY DOYLE
                              WOODSTOCK N Y
LOUDER
                                              DIXIE

HOLLYWOOD GIRL 251

POSTAL TELEGRAPH – COMMERCIAL CABLES — TELEGRAM

JUNE 17TH

SA635 WOODSTOCK N Y 19DL 1031A
DIXIE DUGAN
        439 FLATBUSH AVE BROOKLYN N Y
HOW DID YOU GET TO BUELOW WHATS ALL THE SECRECY FOR

                              JIMMY

∼∼∼∼∼∼∼∼∼∼∼∼∼

POSTAL TELEGRAPH – COMMERCIAL CABLES — TELEGRAM

JUNE 17TH

NA437 BROOKLYN N Y 11 436P
JIMMY DOYLE
                               WOODSTOCK N Y
ONE MY IMAGINATION TWO YOUR IMAGINATION

                               DIXIE

∼∼∼∼∼∼∼∼∼∼∼∼∼

COLOSSAL FILM CORPORATION

Eastern Offices
1500 Broadway
New York

June 21st.

Miss Dixie Dugan,
439 Flatbush Ave.,
Brooklyn, N. Y.
Dear Miss Dugan:

Your recent screen and sound test has been completed. Could you come in the early part of next week and have a talk with our production manager Mr. Zouftig?

Very truly yours,
COLOSSAL FILM CORPORATION.
per I. Nebbick,
Asst. to Production Mgr.

III

ON BOARD
THE TWENTIETH CENTURY
LIMITED

June 28.

DEAR DIARY:

    Now that I am beginning a new life so to speak, I am going to tell you every day just what I do and think because some day this all may be valuable and when interviewers say how did you start your wonderful career in the motion pictures I can refer them to you Diary and they can see for themselves I'm not handing them a lot of horsefeathers. I suppose too Diary we should keep posterity in mind because when they came across a word like horsefeathers and didn't know what it meant we should have it defined somewhere, so for the sake of posterity horsefeathers means a lot of cha-cha and cha-cha means what diaries are usually full of. I was reading one only the other day in one of the screen magazines and it went something like this:

> JAN. 11. Out with X last night. We took a ride. He's awfully sweet.
> JAN. 12. Saw X again. Had my hair washed.
> JAN. 13. Had the white wrap dry-cleaned. X didn't call me up. Going to have a voice test. Here's hoping.

This was advertised as a sensational secret diary and was supposed to be all perfume and hot pants. Well, it rolls off my knife. They needn't blow some my way. I think if a girl keeps a diary she should put in it only things that matter—things which reveal her real self so when in after years she reads it back it will recall all the sweet times she has had and the merry hell she used to raise which will take the curse off of sitting around crocheting diapers for the youngest generation.

Which reminds me of a poem Julius Tannen used to recite:

> Oh I wish there were some wonderful place
> Called the Land of Beginning again,
> Where all our mistakes and all our heartaches
> And all of our poor selfish grief
> Could be dropped like a shabby old coat at the door
> And never put on again.

I think that's a honey. It always socks me, especially if I'm a little ginny.

And now Diary, let us bounce right off into the facts and figures. I was born at the usual age in the usual way, of poor parents who, as I grew to a babbling child, spent most of their time wondering why they saved me and drowned the others out of the litter. I am now five feet two inches tall and weigh 110 pounds bed-side where I sleep alone, worse luck.

I've an older sister Nita who is a dear, a younger brother, Sam, who is a nut. My father is a hard worker and has been that way for forty-five years. He is also bow-legged, not from riding horseback in the park but from being run ragged by installment collectors. As a matter of fact, the only thing we ever get on the radio now is an attachment. Mother still wears petticoats and silk stockings with cotton tops and her favorite reading is glue advertising pages showing how to make artistic lamp shades at home out of those cardboard pieces the laundry sends back in the shirt fronts.

So much for my family. As for me I am nineteen years old and what is technically known as a virgin although I have been most thoroughly and thrillingly mauled on many occasions which I will tell you about in detail some other time. Just now I must tell you Diary what I should have told you at the very beginning, where I am and why and how come. Well, I'm on the Twentieth Century Limited, on my way to Chicago where I will get on The Chief Limited and ride, God knows how long, until I get to Hollywood where I am going to be a motion picture star and ride at least two Rolls Royces at a time, Roman style.

I hope you'll excuse me just a little while Diary—it is getting dark and they have just announced the fourth or fifth call for dinner. I've often wondered why they start calling dinner so early in these diners. I guess the waiters all want to get it over with as soon as possible, and they figure if they start early enough and nag enough you'll get sick of it and eat and get rid of them. Of course, I could have it served here in my compartment, and maybe I will, because if I go to the diner I may meet some people and they'll take my mind off what I've got to do on the way out West. I want to study and learn all I can about this voice control, enunciation and deep breathing etc., so that I will make good in the talkies, or as they are more affectionately known, the belchers and a week or whatever it is I will be on the train won't be any too long for me to wade through this book on Tuning in the Tonsils or Tricks on the Trachae or Marooned with the Adenoids in Movieland . . .

Well, I'm back again Diary, with a special plate dinner inside of me and two bucks less in the grouch-bag, which I call putting a light finger on me considering the re-fueling job I did. I was given one of those tables for two and was prepared not to be angry if some good-looking male was seated opposite me and his better nature tricked him into talking to me and eventually out-fumbling me for the check. But wouldn't it be little Dixie's luck to draw the only elderly minister on the train. Two bucks that cost. I can't help wondering how Sadie Thompson would have handled the situation.

It's dark outside and I can see myself in the window, except when we're going through the towns which are all alike. A few lights away off, and then a lot of lights and then a helluva lot of lights and a long platform with a lot of faces like pies looking up and over their heads a sign that says NEW SMEAR or MUTZBURG or if the train is going real fast just SKRR. I bet they wish they were on this train, and I bet if any one of those little Main Street gazelles was offered a chance to be where I am tonight she would jump right out of her bloomers. I'm still a little dizzy myself figuring how I'm here. It just seems like yesterday since I got the hunch to wire Fritz Buelow, the Colossal Director, for an interview. Of course it was just a rib to see him, as the only thing I know about newspapers is that they smell good when they're fresh and you can't believe a word in them. Why they seal them up in corner-stones I don't know. I think that fellow down in Texas years ago had the right idea. When they opened up one of his corner-stones years later a horned toad jumped out. Corner-stones ought to always have good gags in them for posterity so they'll think more kindly of us. I seem to be worrying a lot about posterity tonight. Train-riding always seems to stir up dat ole davil sex in me. It isn't just chance that New York and Hollywood are at the two ends of such a long train trip and Iowa is somewhere in the middle. There's an idea for a book or something: A Lay Of The Prairie or Made In The Midlands. I'm going to bed Diary. I'm tired and I've got such a nice new pair of pyjamas and no one to admire them.

~~~~~~~~~~~~~~~~~~~~~~~~

June 29.

Arrived in LaSalle Street Station this morning and got on The Chief this evening. So that was Chicago. Not so hot. A great big Newark I would say. New York is a jazz-band playing diga-diga-doo but

Chicago is just a big megaphone with an overgrown boy hollering through it: Look at me, ain't I big for my age. One of Nita's old boy friends took me around and showed me the park system and the lions in front of the Art Institute which are different from the ones in front of the New York Public Library because they look like lions and those on Fifth Avenue look like Adolphe Menjou. Saw a good picture at the Chicago—one of those big movie houses like a glorified carbuncle. It was all alabaster and rhinestones and mauve and orange lights with gold organ pipes and ankle-deep carpets. Something like the Paramount in New York which somebody says was Cecil DeMille's idea of God's bathroom. Well, I'm like the little girl in the New Yorker cartoon—they can call it broccoli but I say it's spinach and I say to hell with it.

Third call for dinner. I guess I'll look over the new cargo in the diner. If we didn't take on a hotter looking load in Chicago than we did in New York I'll go up and sit with the engineer.

POSTAL TELEGRAPH – COMMERCIAL CABLES
TELEGRAM

JUNE 29

```
SA354 30 DL NEW YORK N Y 29 1201P
DIXIE DUGAN
CARE THE CHIEF TWENTIETH CENTURY
LIMITED WESTBOUND
YOU EVEN HAD TO TAKE THE SAME TRAIN
WITH BUELOW I HOPE HE MAKES A BIGGER
FOOL OF YOU THAN YOU ARE IF THAT IS
POSSIBLE
                          JIMMY DOYLE
```

Can you imagine it Diary, while I was having dinner I got the snootiest wire from Jimmy accusing me of taking the same train with Buelow. That's the director who got me my screen and voice test you know after I pretended to be a newspaper woman and I was interviewing him. I didn't tell you before Diary, but Jimmy was sore as a boil about me meeting him in the first place and then letting him make a test of me in the second place. But when the company called me into the office and told me the test was good enough to give me a contract and send me out to the coast then Jimmy just burned up, said Buelow was on the make for me or he wouldn't have wasted that much time on me. I said, of course he's on the make and what of it, all men are, only some are sneaky and don't admit it and then he said well maybe you didn't sell out for a test but you certainly will have to for a role, and then Diary did I bear down on him. What do you mean maybe I didn't sell out for a test I said, what a filthy nerve you've got to talk to me like that. If that's what you really think of me you can get to hell out and if I never see you again it'll be too soon, and then he said I was a double-crosser and a sneak and I told him he was a liar and a bum and after that we began to get personal. It was the first real fight we had ever had, Jimmy and I, and the queerest part of it Diary was that I really enjoyed it. There's nothing like fighting with somebody you're crazy about to pick you right up and give you that warm glow. It's better than a cold shower and a rub-down. I felt just great but only for about an hour or two then the reaction set in. The effect began to wear off like those lushing parties where the liquor runs out about ten o'clock in the evening and about eleven you run down like a victrola record. At two in the morning I was still calling the pillow dirty names and punching it. You see, it was Jimmy. It was all soaked with tears at three o'clock. I know because I heard the clock strike three and then four and the next thing I knew I was holding Jimmy in my arms and we were whispering to each other and feeling that extra tender toward each other. You know the way people do after they've had a big fight and are making up and then Jimmy kissed me until I struggled for breath and I woke up and it was that damn pillow.

Now he sends me a wire saying that I'm on the train with Buelow and he hopes Buelow makes a bigger fool of me than I am if that is possible. What's the matter with him—is he crazy, and even if Buelow was on the same train with me, which he isn't, what of it? Jimmy ought to know by this time I can take care of myself and he knows I love him, or I did anyway. I guess maybe I still do, Diary or maybe I don't, I don't know. To hell with love anyway, I'm going in for a career. After I'm a big success I'll have plenty of time for love and probably better opportunities. Jimmy can stay in New York and burn up for all I care. Maybe I'll answer his wire and tell him so. I wonder what he's doing tonight. Out with some dame I guess. Gee, he's a sweet boy. Ah, to hell with him. I'm going to bed.

~~~~~~~~~~~~~~~~~~~~

<div style="text-align:right">June 30.</div>

Woke up this morning and it was just a little after eight o'clock and we were in Kansas City. Two good reasons for going back to sleep. Had my breakfast in my berth, dressed and left the door open hoping something would happen. Nothing did. Lunch in the diner with nothing to see outside the window except a big landing field. Asked the conductor what it was and he said it was Kansas. Lindy would love it. Took my first good look at the map today. It seems we have to go all the way through not only Kansas but Nebraska, part of Colorado, part of New Mexico, all of Arizona and all of California before we get to this Hollywood place. Ho hum!

Just finished my eighth or tenth trip through the train, trying each time to look as though I had a different reason. Saw nothing in the Pullmans except rows of closed compartment doors—some with yip-yip coming through. In the open Pullmans they were either playing bridge or sleeping with magazines over their faces. I wish my voice culture book would put me into a nice coma that would last until I get to the coast. Stuff like this ought to do it, but it doesn't.

Breathing out:—In order to secure an even and continuous air pressure three forces have to be considered:—
1. The elastic recoil of the inflated lungs and expanded chest.
2. The contraction of abdominal muscles that assist the relaxed diaphragm to return to its place and
3. The contraction of muscles that pull down the ribs.

Loads of this! Now I ask you!

It's getting dark outside but not dark enough. I hope I never see another grain elevator as long as I live. Have to kill at least an hour before I can eat. What else is there to do on a trip like this—anyway, if you're alone. Wish Buelow *was* on the train but I'm sure he's still in New York finishing up the street shots for *Sinning Lovers*. Last time I saw him was at the studio making my test. And he called me up and congratulated me on getting my contract. The last thing he said was don't forget it's full of options. You see Diary, it's a five-year contract with options every three months the first two years and every six months after that. And one of those morality clauses. I had heard a lot about them but I never saw one before. Here's the way it goes, I think it's cute:—

The Artist agrees to conduct herself during the period of her employment with due regard to public convention and morals, and agrees that she will not become intoxicated or become involved in any scandal or become the subject of comment by any publication reflecting on her character or tending to lessen her drawing ability or popularity as an actress, and agrees that she will neither do nor commit any act or become involved in any situation or occurrence tending to degrade her in society or bring her into public hatred, contempt, scorn or ridicule, or tending to shock, insult, offend, or outrage the community or public morals or decency, or tending to the prejudice of, or to the financial injury, or injury to the business of the Producer, or the motion picture industry generally and in the event the Artist violates any term or provision of this paragraph, or of the happening of any of said incidents, the Producer is given the right, at his option, at any time thereafter, to cancel and annul this agreement on giving five (5) days' notice in writing to the Artist of his intention so to do.

There doesn't seem much chance of getting into a mixup with that clause on this train. All these closed compartments may be full of possibilities but the only man I've met to talk to at all turned out to be a climate salesman coming back from his first visit to the East. And his last if he can help it, sez he. Sez I, too.

~~~~~~~~~~~~~~~~~~~~~

July 1st.

Hollywood tomorrow morning. Whoopee! All day today we have been going through the desert. Was sitting out on the observation platform and my climate salesman sat down with me and talked California sunshine and irrigation. See all that desert, sez he, all it needs is water and I sez that ain't news pa-pah. And now after thousands of years sez he it's going to get it, isn't that funny? And I sez it's plum hilarious but who wants water? If they did don't you think the place would be running over with bootleggers on camels smuggling genuine pre-war water from the Great Lakes. I hope to tell you. Yes sir. You don't get the idea, sez he. Water is what makes the desert blossom like a rose and now with the Boulder Dam going through all this you see here will be orange groves and avocados and figs and pecans, and towns springing up everywhere with lovely homes and schools. Think of that, sez he, and I told him I'd rather not. There are too many schools and homes and filling stations now I sez. I've just gone through Kansas and I ought to know. The desert is beautiful I sez and restful, and here you want to go and fill it full of vegetables and mortgages and deferred payments. People like you are a menace I sez and ought to be suppressed. Never happy unless you're starting a subdivision somewhere and he sez all joking aside you can buy big chunks of the desert cheap now before the Boulder Dam goes in. Fifty cents an acre or you can homestead a section for only sixty dollars, but you have to live on it seven months a year. In other words, the Government bets you sixty dollars against 640 acres that you can't live there seven months without starving to death or being fried alive. It isn't on record that the government has ever lost. And then he asked me where I am going and I told him to Hollywood, then he told me he lived there, and then I did get interested Diary, and asked him if he knew any of the stars and he said no. I asked him if he had ever seen any of them and he said well he thought he saw Strongheart once, but he wasn't sure—it might have been another dog. So then I stopped talking to him and watched the sun set on the desert and it was so beautiful it made me wish there were somebody with me I was crazy about so we could sit and watch it together.

 After dinner I read all the magazines in the club car and in one of them I ran across a cute poem signed by—who do you think, Diary? One guess? Wrong! It was Mickey O'Keefe, my theme song writer, the one I met up in Harlem when I was out with Fritz Buelow and his manager Goldfarb and Fritzie's sweetie Chiquita Tortilla. I swiped it out of the car and I'm going to copy it down here so I won't forget it:—

A PRAYER FOR YOUR HOUSE

(With a bow to Eddie Guest)

Oh, it takes a heap o' licker in a house t' make it home
A heap o' Scotch an' Bourbon an' ye sometimes have ter roam
Aroun' th' hull durn city 'for ye'll find a guy who'll know
Anuther guy who knows a guy who knows a place ter go.
It don't make nary diff'rence how rich ye git ter be
By matrimony, alimony, fee or legacy,
It jest ain't home though it might be th' palace of a king
If ye ain't got a lot o' gin an' rye 'n' everything.

Oh then ye c'n sit aroun' an' sing an' ye c'n romp an' play
An' learn ter love 'most anyone in any sort o' way.
An' th' roses on yer noses they'll jest blossom all th' year,
An' git ter be a part o' ye, suggestin' someone dear,
Who usta love 'em long ago when ye wuz just a souse
An' th' kind old bar-keep usta say Boys, this'n's on th' house.
An' so I say God bless yer house from cellar up to dome
But it takes a heap o' licker in a house t' make it home.

~~~~~~~~~~~~~~~~

July 2nd.

  I'm in Hollywood, Diary. What a kick. The first thing I saw when I looked out the window this morning was orange groves. I recognized them right away because I saw one once in the Music Box Revue, only that one had electric lights instead of oranges. I asked someone on the train where I ought to stop and they told me the Ambassador if I wanted to be where all the movie people go. Well, that's where

I want to be because now I'm a movie person. Maybe I'll be a star too—who knows? It makes my heart stand still when I think of it. I'm sitting here at the window looking out at all the lights sprinkled all over the hills. Those must be the Beverly Hills they talk about. I wonder which light is Mary Pickford. Maybe it's that one over there, away up high. I'll hold you up Diary so you can see it.

Wasn't that a big joke on us Diary, thinking there was nobody on the train. No movie people—no celebrities. Why when the train stopped at Pasadena the platform was full of photographers and out of all those closed compartments swarmed stars with their arms full of roses, posing for the photographers on the steps of the train. There was Norma Talmadge and Gloria Swanson and her Marquis and Eric Von Stroheim and Adolphe Menjou and several more and the platform simply seethed with chauffeurs and footmen and maids and reporters and movie photographers. And here I rode clear across the country right in the middle of all these celebrities and didn't even know they were around. Believe me, when I become a star and come west on the train I'll walk around a little bit and give the beginners something to look at. And I'll talk to them too and give them a bit of advice and tell them how it was with me when I started. Yes, you're a bit frightened at first, I'll tell them, but then if you work hard and keep your mind on your business and of course if you have some talent too you're bound to succeed just like me. And then I'll autograph my picture for them—the one I'm going to have taken holding a big black cat right next to my face. Something like one I saw once with Dolores del Rio. I've got good eyes too. They say that's one of the most important things in pictures. Well, I'll know more about it in just a few weeks. Tomorrow I'm going out to the studio. I called them up today and told them I was here. There was some dumbell on the other end of the wire—he didn't seem to understand me. I had to spell the name two or three times. He'll be the first one to go when I get set out there. I told him I was out here under contract and imagine the dirty nerve of him. What of it, he says, who isn't? So I explained to him I had just arrived from New York where I had signed a contract to act in the Colossal pictures and he says what do you want me to do about it? And I says all you have to do about it is to get somebody on the phone who understands English so I can talk to him in my native tongue. He hung up on me but I rang back and he finally let me talk to somebody's secretary who told me to come out tomorrow morning and report to the executive office where somebody would take care of me.

Tomorrow morning, Diary! I'd better go to bed early and get a good night's sleep so I'll look my best. I think I'll say a little prayer, too, before I roll in. I'll sure mean it tonight.

IV

(From The Hollywood Daily Screen World—July 4th)

BROADWAY STAR ARRIVES FOR SINGING-DANCING ROLE. DIXIE DUGAN OF "GET YOUR GIRL" HIT SIGNED BY COLOSSAL

That the movies are continuing their raid on the legitimate stage is evidenced by the daily arrival in Hollywood of more Broadway singing and dancing favourites. The latest to come to the golden west in search of fame and fortune is Dixie Dugan, petite brunette star of "Get Your Girl," a Broadway hit of last year. She has signed a five year contract with Colossal, the first two years subject to options of three months to be exercised by the studio with generous salary increases. We hope Dixie will be given the right kind of opportunities so that when her first three months have expired, Colossal will find it to their best interests to retain her. It is said Miss Dugan is a protegé of Fritz Buelow, the directing genius who discovered her in New York. He has found and made a number of our biggest stars, and Dixie can consider herself fortunate that she attracted his attention.

~~~~~~~~~~~~~~~~~~~~~~

JULY 5TH

SC448 18 DL NEW YORK N Y 22 107P
DIXIE DUGAN
CARE COLOSSAL FILM CORP
                        HOLLYWOOD CALIF
MET BUELOW TODAY A THOUSAND PARDONS FOR

ACCUSING YOU OF TAKING SAME TRAIN TO
COAST WITH HIM

            JIMMY

POSTAL TELEGRAPH — COMMERCIAL CABLES TELEGRAM

            JULY 5TH

NA224 5 HOLLYWOOD CALIF 14 702P
JAMES DOYLE
ALGONQUIN HOTEL
          NEW YORK N Y
SEE YOUR THOUSAND RAISE YOU TEN
            DIXIE

POSTAL TELEGRAPH — COMMERCIAL CABLES TELEGRAM

            JULY 6TH

SC439 6 NEW YORK N Y 12 903A
DIXIE DUGAN
CARE COLOSSAL FILM CORP
         HOLLYWOOD CALIF
AM I FORGIVEN
            JIMMY

> **JULY 6TH**
>
> NB734 15 HOLLYWOOD CALIF 22 247P
> JAMES DOYLE
> ALGONQUIN HOTEL
>
> NEW YORK N Y
>
> DO YOU THINK MY HEART IS A REVOLVING DOOR STOP GO LAY AN EGG
>
> DIXIE

> **JULY 7TH**
>
> SC558 7 NEW YORK N Y 20 DL 1045A
> DIXIE DUGAN
> CARE COLOSSAL FILM CORP
>
> HOLLYWOOD CALIF
>
> SO THATS THE WAY YOU FEEL ABOUT IT MIGHT HAVE KNOWN A LITTLE SUCCESS WOULD GO TO YOUR HEAD
>
> JIMMY

HOLLYWOOD, CALIFORNIA.
July 7th.

Dearest Jimmy Darling:

I don't mean a word of it. I don't want you to be mad at me. I'm so lonesome out here without you. I even read and re-read your wires just to

~~~~~~~~~~~~~~~~~~

Jimmy Darling:

I got your nasty wire and think it was pretty mean of you in view of the way you talked to me before I left when I

~~~~~~~~~~~~~~~~~~

Jimmy:

What's the big idea anyway of us scrapping when

~~~~~~~~~~~~~~~~~~

Dear Jimmy:

Your wire received. Will say you certainly have a nerve to

~~~~~~~~~~~~~~~~~~

Darling Lover:

I miss you so I wish you were out here. I look at your picture and God, darling, I love you so. Why are you so mean to

~~~~~~~~~~~~~~~~~~

Dear Mr. Doyle:

I think perhaps under the circumstances it would be better if we did not write to each other any more because I feel there can never be complete trust and confidence between us after what you said to me in New York before I came out here with the first real oppor

~~~~~~~~~~~~~~~~~~

POSTAL TELEGRAPH – COMMERCIAL CABLES
TELEGRAM

JULY 8TH

NA355 8 HOLLYWOOD CALIF 19 430P
JAMES DOYLE
ALGONQUIN HOTEL
               NEW YORK CITY N Y
YOU KNOW WHAT YOU CAN DO STOP WITH
SOUND AND EFFECTS
                          DIXIE

POSTAL TELEGRAPH – COMMERCIAL CABLES
TELEGRAM

JULY 9TH

SD785 9 NEW YORK N Y 10 1106A
DIXIE DUGAN
CARE COLOSSAL FILM CORP
               HOLLYWOOD CALIF
OKAY
                          JIMMY

```
               POSTAL TELEGRAPH — COMMERCIAL CABLES
                            TELEGRAM
```

                                                  JULY 9TH
NC448 9 HOLLYWOOD CALIF 9 533P
JAMES DOYLE
ALGONQUIN HOTEL
                                    NEW YORK CITY N Y
     NET
                                              DIXIE

>   Hollywood, California.
>   July 7th.
>
> Darling Nita:
>
>   I'm in Hollywood. I have a movie contract. Tomorrow I start making faces at the camera. I will be what they call out here a lens louse. I know I should have written sooner and kept you posted but I was going places, seeing people, doing things and building character. I told you about Fritz Buelow. He's the director who got me my screen and talking test. He honestly thought I was one of those chatter sisters who write movie malaky for the mags until I went into my routine and then his eyes got this big and he says but you told me and I says that was just a rib to get to you, aren't you glad I made it? I'll tell you after I hear the playback he says. You may be God's gift to the industry and then again you may be a pain in the neck. And then I learned the playback is when they have recorded your voice in a scene, you can go into the next room and almost immediately they reproduce it through the loud-speaker just the way it will sound in the theatre so the director can tell whether you're piano or forte.

First I did some silent versions. I laughed heartily at imaginary jokes, cried just bitterly enough not to mess the mascara because my lover had gone to war or had come back or something, and then I opened letters and looked surprised and walked in and out and around and sat down and looked out windows and crossed my legs and a lot of other dramatic things. Then for the sound stuff I sang and danced and recited *Mary Had a Little Lamb* and screamed for help and pleaded for love and then Buelow told me I could go home. I asked him what he thought of it and he said lousy, but just the same they called me into the office a few days later and told me I had promise and they would give me a contract and would start me modestly at a hundred dollars a week for three months with an option to renew at the end of that time for three months more for twice that if good and with further options every three months for the first two years and every six months for the next three so that at the end of five years I would be making two thousand dollars a week. I tried to see Buelow before I left to get in a couple of gloats but he was out on location somewhere with the company shooting *Sinning Lovers*, but he called me up just before I left and told me he'd see me out in Hollywood soon. I hope so. He's an exciting devil and if he wanted to he could push me along faster in this racket than I could ever go on foot or horseback.

Meanwhile, Jimmy is off me for seeing Buelow and getting a test. And did he burn when I showed him the contract! Said I would go to hell sure in Hollywood and I told him not to be putting ideas into my young head. After all, I says to him, there's nothing to stop you from coming out and going to hell with me. How would that be for a title, Hell Bent for Hollywood? Don't tell it, sell it. I left him frothing and he has been pelting me ever since I got out here with wires trying to make up. After what you said to me I says to him you can scram. So we left it that way. But just the same Sis whenever I think of him I get a toothache in my heart. Whatever it is he needs he's got. However, I've met some cute kids out here. One of the first to look me up and trot me around was my theme song writer Mickey O'Keefe. He's working for my outfit in a bungalow full of theme song writers. It used to be the hospital. Mickey took me all around the lot one day—acres and acres of western towns and colonial mansions and streets in Venice and a dozen huge buildings they call stages. In some of them as many as two or three companies were working at once, each with a little orchestra to play music for them while they emote. An orchestra usually consists of a dog house—one of those big fiddles—a little fiddle and a groan box or organ. They play all day long and keep the actors' minds off their work because if they had to think all day about the silly things they do they'd go nuts.

Over on my lot, the Colossal outfit, they have two big new sound stages where they shoot all the talkie stuff. Nobody can get near the place when they're working. They even have watchmen out with lanterns and red flags to stop trucks from going by. Sometimes funny things happen. The other day Eric Von Stroheim was working on one of the sound stages making one of the dialogue sequences with Gloria Swanson for her new picture, *Queen Kelly*. The scene was in a jungle hut away off in Africa and Kelly's aunt was dying. Between gasps and coughs she was calling out for the priest. Gloria Swanson, who plays the part of Queen Kelly, was crying and explaining the nearest civilized post was a hundred miles away. They rehearsed the scene very carefully with dialogue a number of times and then began to shoot. Just as they got going good an airplane came over the lot and a tremendously amplified voice from the clouds began to advertise Old Gold cigarettes. Of course the microphones on the set picked it all up and the playback sounded something like this:

>   Darling, it's terrible to die . . . away out here in the jungle . . .
>   HELLO EVERYBODY

  Get me the priest... quick...
  THIS IS OLD GOLD SPEAKING
  Auntie, dear, there isn't a soul within a hundred miles.
  NOT A COUGH IN A CARLOAD.

 I have to be all made up and on the set by nine o'clock tomorrow morning. I'm getting a test for the part of Tessie who runs away from a reform school and winds up as hostess in a hook shop but she has a heart of gold. It's practically the second lead part. Chiquita Tortilla, Buelow's Mex weakness, is going to play the lead for her next picture after she gets finished with *Sinning Lovers*. Gee, I hope I smack 'em. Mickey says I've got a great chance if Chiquita doesn't have me knifed in the cutting room. He says if you're too good you stand a fair chance of finding all your best footage on the cutting room floor. This is a familiar beau geste in Hollywood. I haven't been here very long but I've learned a few things. One is there isn't any more professional jealousy here than there is in the Lambs' Club in New York and if you come out here from the East and put your toe in the door the chances are you'll have to have your foot amputated.

 When do you finish your buying spree over there for Waffieheimers? I wish you were here. Have no one to tell my troubles to. Well, maybe better luck tomorrow. Kiss kiss

DIXIE.

 P.S. One of the gags out here "a producer is a guy who was born with a silver snipe in his mouth."

NEW YORK, N. Y.
July 21st.

MR. KIRK KING,
SCENARIO DEPARTMENT,
COLOSSAL FILM CORPORATION
HOLLYWOOD, CALIFORNIA.

DEAR KIRK:

I finally got to your Buelow by the simple process of reversing the field and running the other way. As long as I tried to get to him I couldn't see him for yes men so then I dug in and became exclusive. Wrote a signed story for one of the local papers saying the talkies were a menace and a bore, that none of the directors up till now knew what they were doing and there was only one hope left and that was Fritz Buelow. If he couldn't put competent talking sequences in his new film *Sinning Lovers* they would have to go back to making their pictures beautiful and dumb. And a lot more out of the same bottle. Well, it worked. Buelow's manager got in touch with me, Buelow took me to dinner and bared his artistic soul. When I told him I had never written for the movies and never would, he was interested. When I told him I had a number of offers from other companies he was aroused. When I told him he was the only director I would ever consider allowing to touch my stuff, he was astounded at my intelligence. But when I sat for two hours entranced while he told me how tired he was of making commercial pictures and wanted to do something big and inspiring—yessing him at discreet intervals—he admitted I was the most interesting writer he had ever met. The rest of it was easy. I answered no letters, was out when he telephoned, had small items planted in the various gossip columns stating I was considering this offer and rejecting that. Finally, of course, I allowed him to talk me into signing a Colossal contract.

So now, Kirk, I'm coming into your brothel. At that it is better than being on the street in this town. The Broadway racket is all shot and I will be glad to leave the gyps fighting over the corpse. Here's a clip from *Variety* which will give you an idea:

HEAT WAVE CURLS LONG RUN PIPS

Heat and Humidity, the old summer run team, is in and pretty along the Rialto these days. A lot of palookas curled up quick with the first hot blast and now the tried and true ones are turning their faces to the wall and picking feverishly at the coverlets. The North Atlantic is congested with Tyson's best customers, doing a Lindy to Ciros and even the Legion of the Condemned who storm Leblang's bargain basement at curtain time to pick cut rates off the quivering carcasses of old hits and new flops have fled to the Far Rockaways or the Kosher heights of Sullivan County, leaving Broadway—it's toasted—to the refrigerated mercies of Roxy and Nedick's.

    I don't know just when I start West but will let you know. I am banking on you to give me the real low-down when I get out there. I wonder if you would do something for me. Remember Dixie Dugan I used to write to you about—the girl I was all het up over and who starred in my show? Well, she's out there in Hollywood with a contract from your outfit and though we had a battle before she left I'm still That Way. I wish you could kinda keep an eye on her for me until I get out there and can take the job over myself.

    And remembah! You can look but you mustn't touch.

JIMMY.

(From The Los Angeles Examiner—July 27th)

SNAPSHOTS OF HOLLYWOOD, COLLECTED AT RANDOM

    Mary Pickford, her most entertaining self, writing fake headlines for this columnist . . . Renée Adorée in a blue ensemble and hat to match walking across the Metro-Goldwyn-Mayer lot . . . Carl Laemmle Sr. giving a few valuable hints on the philosophy of living . . . Carl Laemmle Jr.

listening to his dad . . . Dixie Dugan, new Colossal acquisition and Kirk King, producer on the Colossal lot, having lunch at the Montmartre.

~~~~~~~~~~~~~~~~~~~~

DEAR DIXIE:

I called the Ambassador today and they said you had moved so I'm hoping they will forward this. I can never find you on the lot and they don't seem to know where you live. I suppose you forgot you had a luncheon engagement with me yesterday? I was terribly disappointed. When can I see you again? I am working hard on the songs for *Put and Take*. I was thinking about you last night and I did a peach of a lyric. The idea of the chorus is: Put me in your heart, take me in your arms—not bad, what? I'll sing the whole thing for you when I see you.

<div style="text-align: right">MICKEY.</div>

~~~~~~~~~~~~~~~~~~~~

(From The Los Angeles Examiner—July 28th)
. . . Lupe Velez turning handsprings on Hollywood Boulevard . . . Lila Lee practicing vowel sounds for the talkies . . . Dixie Dugan and Kirk King coming out of the Carthay Circle Theatre together . . .

~~~~~~~~~~~~~~~~~~~~

(From The Los Angeles Examiner—July 29th)
. . . Dixie Dugan and Kirk King sharing a Hamburger de Luxe at the Brown Derby . . .

~~~~~~~~~~~~~~~~~~~~

DEAR DIXIE:

I don't want you to think I'm a knocker but it's only because I'm crazy about you I want to warn you not to believe everything this Kirk King tells you. He's been out here a long time and he's a smooth article, as a lot of girls out here who believed his promises could tell you, but of course you'll think I'm just jealous and won't listen to me. You stood me up again last night. Is that fair? You treat me like I was a rag doll. I'll make a song out of that some day. It's a good title—*Rag Doll*. Please have dinner with me tomorrow night, I want to talk to you. I'll call you at five—the studio finally gave me your telephone number. Why didn't you tell me you had taken an apartment on La Brea?

MICKEY.

(From The Los Angeles Examiner—July 31st)
. . . Dixie Dugan and Kirk King eating bacon and eggs at Henry's at three o'clock in the morning . . .

(From Variety, Week of August 1st)
FROM N. Y. to L. A.
Fritz Buelow
Chiquita Tortilla
Jacques Goldfarb
James Doyle

V

(From the Hollywood Daily Screen World)

JAMES DOYLE, BROADWAY PLAYWRIGHT, HERE TO WRITE ORIGINALS

James Doyle, famous Broadway playwright who wrote "Girls Gone Crazy," is here to write dialogue and original screen plays for the The Colossal Film Corporation. It is with pleasure we welcome to the local ranks this famous young Eastern author who, nevertheless, will find he has a great deal to learn in this newest but greatest of all the arts, the talking screen. Good luck, Jimmy—an' take keer of yourself.

~~~~~~~~~~~~~~~~~~~~~

(Lola Krunch, a Hollywood moving picture critic and editor, decides to call on Mr. Doyle, the newest addition to the Broadway colony in Hollywood. Object: interview.)

Q. What do you think of Hollywood, Mr. Doyle?

A. I haven't had time to think about it much. Offhand, it looks a little bit like Keokuk on a Sunday afternoon, except that the houses and vegetation seem to have been retouched by one of those disappointed virgins who go in for painting china. The buildings have an air of impermanence and the streets with their little yellow, green and blue bungalows look for all the world as though any moment a voice would yell "Strike it" and a flock of scene shifters would tear it all down and put up a New England village or an Italian hill town. As a matter of fact, the only buildings I have seen in Hollywood that look as though they were put up to stay are sets on the movie lots.

~~~~~~~~~~~~~~~~

The newest convert to Hollywood is James Doyle, the famous Broadway playwright lately arrived in our midst. "The little yellow, blue and green bungalows look for all the world like an Italian hill town," mused Mr. Doyle yesterday.

~~~~~~~~~~~~~~~~

Q. What do you think of motion pictures?

A. I think they have too much and at the same time too little. There are too many theatres demanding too many pictures from too many producers who have too many players under contract to appear in too many features by too many writers who can't write for too many players who can't act, for too many producers who can't produce. In other words, there aren't enough real producers, real actors or real writers to supply the pictures necessary to keep up with all the real estate operators who continue building chains of motion picture theatres on all the available empty corner lots in the country. The only thing I've seen enough of out here to supply the demand is film. They have lots of it. It comes in by the carload but where are the writers to supply seventy-five feature dramas and comedies for one year for just one company, and that but one of a dozen producing organizations as large or larger?

Q. What is your solution, Mr. Doyle?

A. A pogrom.

~~~~~~~~~~~~~~~~

"The thing that impressed me most about the motion picture industry," said Mr. Doyle, "is its tremendous size. Think of the hundreds of stories which must be supplied every year to keep thousands of artists working so as to supply the millions of drama-lovers throughout the world who look to Hollywood for their inspiration and relaxation. I am amazed with the immensity of it all," said Mr, Doyle, "and thrilled too." When asked to sum it up in one word, Mr. Doyle said, "It is a great program."

~~~~~~~~~~~~~~~~~~

Office of Sol Nebbick, the producing genius of the Colossal outfit, a young glacier with a dead face, the long slim fingers of a violinist, the narrow natty shoulders of a gigolo, the frame of a bantam and the guile of a Machiavelli. After cooling his heels for an hour in the outer office, Jimmy Doyle, the eager young apostle of better movies, is allowed to enter the sanctum. While waiting, he has been privileged to see famous directors and stars storm into Nebbick's office and after a few muted moments slink out. Properly impressed, he takes a chair and peers across the vast expanse of desk. The wide forehead and narrow chin of Mr. Nebbick are barely visible over the sea of mahogany.

NEBBICK (*after a few moments of chilling silence*): Who are you?
JIMMY (*nettled*): I'm James Doyle; you sent for me.
NEBBICK (*apparently groping*): Doyle? What do you do?
JIMMY (*indignant*): I'm a writer; I'm a playwright. I just arrived here from New York under contract to write originals and dialogue.
NEBBICK: I see. (*Presses invisible button. Beautiful Young Thing appears magically with notebook.*) How many of that last batch of writers from the East have we got left?
BEAUTIFUL YOUNG THING: Let me see, the last shipment was two dozen assorted, novelists, playwrights and newspaper men. There's only three newspaper men left.

NEBBICK: See that they are put on the Chief tonight and sent home. We need those offices for that new bunch of sound technicians coming in from Schenectady.

BEAUTIFUL YOUNG THING: But we took them all out of those offices a week ago and put them down in the basement of the old stables.

NEBBICK (*yawning*): I see. What are they doing down there?

BEAUTIFUL YOUNG THING: I don't know. You know you gave strict orders for nobody to go near them.

NEBBICK: That's right. I forgot. (*To Doyle by way of explanation.*) One of those Eastern novelists we had out here went hay wire a couple of weeks ago and bit a supervisor who was making a picture from his novel. Gangrene set in. Almost lost him. The novelist is back East now writing lies about the movies. Dreiser, I think the name was, or Milt Gross, I get them confused. (*To Beautiful Young Thing.*) I'll call you later. If Tierney is outside tell him he's off that picture. We're going to take Garbo out of it and make a Clara Bow special. (*To Jimmy.*) That's the new sound epic: *My Life and Work by Henry Ford*. The real hero is the Ford factory. All those machines thundering. Colossal.

JIMMY: That ought to be swell.

NEBBICK: That was the original idea. We found it made too much noise—blasted the mike—so we changed the locale to Nürnberg and it's a doll factory. Clara Bow is on one of those 'round the world university tours—collegiate angle, see?; drops into Nürnberg and falls in love with Heindrik Fjord who has the biggest doll factory in Prussia.

JIMMY: But Nürnberg is in Bavaria.

NEBBICK: Same thing. Our technical director will fix that up. (*Suddenly to Jimmy.*) Have you any ideas for motion pictures?

JIMMY (*eagerly*): I've got a swell idea—something I've been thinking about for a long time.

NEBBICK: Would it fit Rin-Tin-Tin? He's preparing now. We want to start shooting Monday. It ought to be laid in the North. There's a trapper, see. Foxes—no, that's been used. Seals, huh? He traps seals? Rinty is a wolf but they raised him from a pup so he doesn't know it. Comes the day of the big seal drive. Rinty's master surrounded by wolf pack, Rinty goes native with the wolves, turns on his master, suddenly he sees the girl. There's a girl, you see. That's the love interest, and there's the rival trapper, that's the menace. The rival seal trapper has chopped a hole in the ice and is pushing the girl into it—down, down. (*Eyes alight with creative fire.*) There's a new murder; better than the one in *Kismet*, d'you remember? Go ahead and write it up. The murder is a good place for the dialogue sequence. Will you, I won't, you will, I won't. See, it's all written. And the sound! Can't you hear the wolves howling? And the seals shuffling on the ice floes and the native songs and dances of the Eskimos?

JIMMY (*bewildered*): I don't know anything about the native songs and dances of the Eskimos.

NEBBICK: Our technical director will fix that up. All you've got to do is to put it in story shape and throw in a little dialogue. I'd do it myself if I wasn't so busy.

JIMMY: But that isn't the kind of story I had in mind at all. I can't do stories for dogs.

NEBBICK (*apparently uninterested*): What kind of a story was it?

JIMMY: It's a psychological story. It starts in the slums. Teeming with people, dripping out of the windows, overflowing the fire escapes, like a torrent in the streets. A truck thunders into view, ploughing through the crowd. People flee to the sidewalks. The little girl is left in the center of the street bewildered, the truck doesn't hesitate—the driver is drunk, comes into the camera and over. A little boy dashes out, grabs the girl, flings her out of the way and barely escapes himself as the truck crashes on. That's the beginning. As a child, the girl is stifled by the mob. I'll take you through her whole life story and show her still overwhelmed by the mob; at work, at play. She becomes rich, famous. At last she thinks she has escaped the mob. She comes back to the city to find it plastered with pictures of her, her name in a thousand lights. A mob at the train, a mob around her house, a mob in front of the theatre. She jumps out the window to escape; a mob gathers around her, follows her to the graveyard, swarms over her grave, tramples the flowers—and disperses aimlessly. At the gate the camera catches two of them talking to each other. One of them says, who was it? The other says, damned if I know. What d'you think of it?

NEBBICK (*making mental note of essentials for future reference*): Lousy.

JIMMY (*boiling*): What d'you mean lousy. What's the matter with it?

NEBBICK (*fluently*): There's no narration, no suspense, no motivation, no character analysis, it doesn't flow, d'you understand? Now I could take that story, spend a little time on it and make something out of it, but why should I? That's what you're here for. But I can't waste the company's money on stuff like that. (*Looking over a paper on desk.*) Here's something you can start on right away. We're going to re-issue *Ladies' Night in a Turkish Bath* with sound and effects. Here's the script. Take it and write the dialogue for the talking sequences. (*Beautiful Young Thing reappears magically.*) Have Mr. Doyle taken over to Rin-Tin-Tin's bungalow. (*To Doyle.*) His secretary will give you a desk there for the short time you'll be out here. (*Beautiful Young Thing disappears with Doyle but reappears in Nebbick's office almost immediately in answer to buzzer.*)

BEAUTIFUL YOUNG THING: Yes, Mr. Nebbick.

NEBBICK: Sit down. A few good ideas came to me while I was talking to that fellow. I want you to make a note of them. Let's see, er, I'll call it *The Mob*. A girl or boy is born in the slums—make it a girl, something for Janet Gaynor—stifled with people overhead and under foot and all around. She is introduced by a narrow escape from death as truck dashes down crowded street. A little boy saves her who later becomes her lover—Charles Farrel, we can borrow him—She grows up in the mob, tries to escape it, later becomes famous, returns to the city to find her name in all the lights—glass shot—a mob at the station, mobs on the street, mobs around her house—news reel shots, we'll fake the sound—more mobs at the theatre, leaps out the window to escape, mob surrounds spot, follows her to grave, swarms over grave, tramples flowers and disperses. Pan shot of faces of crowd. Closeup of two speaking. Dialogue sequence! First speaker: Who was it? Second speaker: Who can tell? Life is like that, and fame is only a bubble on the sea of life. Fade out. The end. A Colossal epic.

BEAUTIFUL YOUNG THING: That's wonderful, Mr. Nebbick.

NEBBICK (*modestly*): All in the day's work. Take a day letter to the Eastern Office, and get London on the wire. . . .

~~~~~~~~~~~~~~~~~~~~

<div style="text-align: right;">
1842 No. LA BREA AVENUE,
HOLLYWOOD, CALIFORNIA.
August 8th.
</div>

DEAR SIS:

This is the land of tomorrow. See you tomorrow, come around tomorrow, nothing doing today but drop in tomorrow. Manana. I've been here weeks now and they all give me the old run-around, camera men, assistant directors, supervisors, technicians, gate men—tomorrow, little one, but how about tonight? They'll take you out or take you in but they won't take you up. Have been going out with one of the producers, Kirk King. I just learned the other day he used to know Jimmy back East. He's really nice, been trotting me around a lot and has taken a real interest in me. He let me do one little bit in a picture he had in production and promised me something else as soon as he had a chance. Of course, I have a contract but that's a lot of bologny. I might just as well have a waffle, or better yet, a matzos. I've met a lot of kids out here with contracts and three month options. You get stalled for three months and then out you go on your sitz-platz. I thought all I had to do was walk right in and yell, Lafayette I am here. Fui.

I have a little apartment on La Brea Avenue. I was at the Ambassador until I got my bill for the first week. When I came to I was house-hunting. I had to buy a lot of new clothes and I'm still in debt. If they don't give me a break pretty soon what chance have I got to have my option taken up? I'm getting worried, Sis, honest!

I met Buelow at a party the other night. He asked me how I was coming along and I told him King had given me a small part—a couple of days' work—but that's all I had done. I can do better by you, says he, and I says why don't you? And he says, why should I? I did enough for you when I got you a contract and got you out here. Now you've got to do something. And I says how did you get me a contract. You said my test was rotten. Evidently they didn't think so. And then imagine the nerve of him. It was rotten, says he, but I told them you had possibilities and I'd take the responsibility if they'd send you out here. And I says I don't believe it. He says I knew you wouldn't that's why I didn't tell you back in New York. Besides, I wanted you to come out here and see for yourself just how far you could get without help. So I says all right I've got the idea. Now what do I do? And he says, think about it little one and call me up sometime. There's a mighty good part in *Sinning Lovers* for you. You could start work Monday.

I had a long talk with Kirk King about it later and I told him exactly what Buelow said to me. All he said was yes, I know the part Buelow means. It would be swell for you. But I can get it for you just as well as Buelow can. After all, I'm supervising the picture. But I've practically promised it to another girl. However, I suppose I could switch it. Do you want it very badly? I didn't answer right away, so he changed the subject. I guess that finishes that. God what a place. I'd hate to be broke here.

DIXIE.

P.S. Guess who just got out here? JIMMY! I saw an interview with him in one of the morning papers. He was brought out here and given a big contract by the Colossal people, the same outfit I am with. Wouldn't that be my luck—begging on my knees for a tiny little bit and he a big shot on the same lot with interviews and pictures of him in all the papers. I expect one of these days I'll be run over by his Rolls Royce. Headline: Famous Writer Runs Down Beautiful Extra. Paste a number on her back and ship her East, wisecracks noted playwright and Broadway idol.

P.S.S. Ooh, maybe I'll see him tomorrow.

P.S.S.S. The big stiff.

August 12.

Saw Jimmy today. Was having lunch at the Montmartre with Mickey. Jimmy came in with a bunch of writers and directors from Colossal, looked right at me, said oh, hello, and walked right on. Kirk was with him, stopped and shook hands with me, but Jimmy acted as though I were a wet dog trying to crawl into his lap. Tahell with him. Mickey didn't know I knew him, told me he was a new writer from the East and had a swell big contract, and was the latest big noise at the studio.

COLOSSAL
FILM CORPORATION
INTER-OFFICE COMMUNICATION

Date   August 15th

To   James Doyle

From   Efficiency Manager's Office

You are exceeding your daily quota of typewriting paper. The maximum for Writers (Classification A to F, zone 3) is 22 sheets white and 25 sheets yellow, or second sheets. Countersign duplicate copy of this for your file and return.

C. F.

~~~~~~~~~~~~~~~~

<div align="right">August 18.</div>

Was told today at the studio that I was not going to get the part I took a test for in Chiquita's next picture. Mickey said test turned out swell but that Chiquita knifed me. Asked Buelow to give me part and he countered with invitation to week-end party at Agua Caliente. I told him I couldn't spell it. He told me I'd have to learn a lot of things out here.

~~~~~~~~~~~~~~~~

Hello, is Mr. Doyle there?

This is Mr. Doyle speaking.

Hold the wire please, this is Mr. Nebbick's office. (*A long wait.*)

Hello, who's this?

This is Mr. Doyle.

This is Mr. Nebbick's secretary; hold the wire please. (*A longer wait.*)

Hello, hello, who's this?

This is Mr. Doyle speaking.

This is Mr. Nebbick's assistant speaking. Put Mr. Doyle on.

Mr. Doyle is on and has been on for an hour.

Well, don't get off. Mr. Nebbick wants to talk to you. (*A long, long wait.*)

Hello, Doyle? This is Mr. Nebbick's office. Mr. Nebbick wishes me to inform you that there have been complaints about your typewriter. Are you using a typewriter?

Certainly.

Well, stop it at once.

Why—why should I stop it?

Mr. Nebbick has been informed by Mr. Gootch, producer of the Rin-Tin-Tin epics, that ever since you have been quartered in the Rin-Tin-Tin bungalow the noise of your typewriter has disturbed Rin-Tin-Tin while he is resting there between scenes. Mr. Nebbick wishes me to inform you this cannot be tolerated. (*Click.*)

VI

  If only I had some one to talk to if I could just talk to somebody just tell them the truth you can't you can't tell the truth to anybody out here everybody lying to everybody else telling each other how important they are how everything is breaking for them sure I'm good you oughta see my test the director said to me just the other day listen he said you're a knockout this picture is going to make you he wanted me to sign up a new contract right away but I said no the hell she did she never said no to anybody out here that's how you get along say yes talk about yes-men you never hear of the yes-girls but they're the ones with the Minerva cars and three kinds of fur coats I guess I could get there too if I said yes why don't I I don't know I could yes Buelow and I wouldn't be walking up and down here now worrying about my contract if they don't let me know today it means they're not going to take up my option I'd like to be good to you says he well why don't you why don't he that's easy they'd be all talking about me she's Buelow's new girl he must have given Chiquita the air well they talk about you anyway if you're on the level they don't believe it or else they think you're a sap well maybe I am a sap I'm certainly a sap about Jimmy calling him up writing to him why I don't know why doesn't he see me if I could only talk to him if I could only talk to somebody that I didn't have to lie to he used to be so sweet I could tell him anything and he'd say don't worry Dixie all the world is cockeyed except you and me and you ain't so bright and he'd kiss me and the hair would stand up on the back of my neck I'm going to call him no I won't either why should I he's never in he never wants to talk to me I hope he'll know some day how it feels to telephone somebody and have it ring and ring and no answer out with somebody else holding somebody else and kissing her he said he'd never love anybody else aren't men the damned liars dirty damned liars well Jimmy isn't dirty but he's a liar but the other men out here cold God they're cold sure I can do something for you but what are you going to do for me there it is take it or leave it give in baby well maybe they're right girls try to use them why shouldn't they try to get something out of it they all want just one thing and if you don't like it you don't have to come out here of course you don't and you don't have to stay either there's too many of you out here now we've got to have some way to sort you out I thought Kirk was different oh you did did you yes I did more fool you now about your contract yes Kirk well it's like this the option expires tomorrow don't I know it you know I think you've got great possibilities but what you need is the right man behind you to help you along somebody who'd watch out for you and slip you into the right opportunities and build you up and battle for you on the lot and in the cutting rooms I know it Kirk of course you know I like you Dixie I think you're awfully cute and sweet I could like you a lot I could do a lot for you you know that don't you sure Kirk I know you could now he's going to put his arms around me and ask me if I could like him a lot too come over closer join the party it's coming now couldn't you like me a lot too Dixie of course I could I'll yes him a while but I can see it coming and you thought he was different oh you did they're all alike now you play ball with me baby and I'll play ball with you I take real interest in you Dixie yes you do I thought you did I thought you were sweet to me because you were Jimmy's friend I thought you were going around with me because you really liked me I like you too but my God do I have to be mauled and muzzled over by every man I go out with I'll go for a little of that all in fun but give in baby why should I just to have an option renewed you can go to hell Mr. Kirk King how do you like that be good to you huh I'll put more coal on at least you're not as cold blooded as Buelow Mr. King I'll say that for you for all your lunches dinners and talks about my future but you'd think Buelow was running a butcher's shop how much for so much no checks cashed well why not I guess my contract is cooked and yet Mickey said they liked that bit I did maybe they'll renew it how do they take up options do they wire you or telephone you do they write you letters if I could only go out and find out but that's out stay home till we call you we'll let you know don't be coming out here every day stop calling us up a hundred dollars a week just one more check and I owe my rent they charge enough if I was living at home I wouldn't have to pay any rent I can remember when you could buy eggs for twelve cents a dozen all right maw all right but I could and calico was six cents a yard well you can have it you may be glad to get calico some day young lady all right maw all right quit your nagging there goes a swell car is that a Lincoln it's a Lincoln that's what I'd like I'd sit away back in one of those seats that's hard to get up out of to the studio Simpkins I'd go right through the gate you can't park in here oh Miss Dugan I beg your pardon I didn't recognize you you have a different car today oh that's all right Joe where are they shooting over on the back lot Miss Dugan they've been waiting for you let 'em wait it's good for 'em Joe that's right Miss Dugan you'll have to go round and come through the front office Miss Swanson Miss Dugan is the only one who's allowed to drive into this lot who is that Joe That was Gloria Swanson Miss Dugan you don't tell me Joe dear dear well so long Joe good luck Miss Dugan a nice fellow but I can remember when he wasn't so nice they're nice to you when you're on top on top there's plenty of room at the top yeah there's lots at the bottom too how do you get to the top oh a little room at the top with you that would be a cute song a room with a view I'll bet there's a good view from the top a little room with you Jimmy just a little room and I'd get up in the morning and make toast on the grill still sleeping you lazy lummox I didn't sleep much last night sweet thing now is that pretty get up and eat your toast and stop talking like that you embarrass me that's swell coffee darling put your finger in it and sweeten it will you stop dunking I love to dunk with you that would be a good song too I love to dunk with you in a little room for two a little room with a view I wish you'd wear collar buttons that wouldn't make your neck green that's jealousy honey you better hurry to the office I'm gonna stay right here and watch you all day oh you are yes and I have dictaphones all over this town all along the street I'll hear everything you say why should you I don't want to miss a word don't hold me so tight God I love you crying again you damned fool that'll get you somewhere well he isn't going to see you cry your head off it might do you good there's a damn fool for you walking up and down in a lousy little apartment crying your head off over somebody who won't even talk to you when you might be driving down Hollywood Boulevard in a Rolls Royce with one of the biggest directors in the business business it's a lousy business well life is a lousy business just like the movies it's just a long talking movie that's all with a lot of sound and effects and love is just a big gag socko she's in love hit her in the heart with a custard pie klunk that's a laugh isn't that a wow now we cut to the chase she's after him he's after her he hides behind a tree she runs into it socko now we Pan through the woods it's full of couples lying under trees climbing trees falling out of trees wham socko blooey plunk kiss kiss rockabye baby in the tree top bugles over the top bang bang kiss me I must go my country calls bang bang socko what the hell am I talking about I ought to be writing movies they're a lot of hooey most of them are Dixie but wait'll I get out to Hollywood darling I'll write some movies and I'll have you acting in them Dixie will you Jimmy honest sure I will I put you on Broadway didn't I I'll say you did I'll put you in the movies too I'll go out there and open Hollywood up like an oyster I'll take mine with a little lemon Jimmy lemon is good I got the lemon all right well it's good for your hands makes 'em white you'll be whiter than that baby if you don't get a job God are they going to take up my option do I have to go round these studios and talk to a lot of fish-eyed gatemen and casting directors nothing doing kiddo better go over and see the Central Casting why should I go over and see the Central Casting I was on the Colossal lot well why didn't you stay I thought I could do better over here oh you did I did oh did you sure I did you did did you well it's kind of quiet here now we're changing over to sound you might try the Fox lot I'm not shopping around well you might try shopping baby what do you do evenings to amuse yourself my God are they all on the make sure they are well how did these other girls get there well they had a lot of pull or they had a lot of money or they had a lot you can beat this racket if you have enough money to hang on oh can you sure you can look at Sue Carol she had a lot of money back of her well how about Lillian Gish well she started away back when they were doing Civil War pictures with the original cast and there were only two girls on the lot and both of them were Gishes I should of started then you sure shoulda kid wonder how old she is she sure doesn't look it saw her coming out of Chryson's just the other day and she walked along Hollywood clear up to Western and had the car tag along behind her just a little old last year's Mercedes I'd like to have one tag around after me here Mercy Mercy Mercy now get off the sidewalk is that nice there wasn't a line in her face I looked at the corners of her eyes especially and under the chin is where they start going too it begins to sag I can see myself sagging if I don't get some work right in the middle like an old grave I've got a nice thin flat stomach now just a little bit round that's fat I have just enough there to live on for two days they say that's why women are fatter than men in the old days they were left in the cave and they had to live on their fat until the old man came home with the bear if the bear got him first they just lived on their fat until another man came along with a bear sometimes it was just a bear came along and that came under the general heading of just too bad now a girl stays in one of these little furnished apartments with a bed that goes up in the wall and the bear comes along and says hello baby how would you like to go into the movies oh I'd just love it wouldn't you just love it I sure would love it wouldn't you just I sure would what big teeth you have the better to bite you my dear wouldn't you just love to be a star oh I'd love to be a star and ride in a big car sure a big big car that's right children ist das nicht ein great big car yah das ist ein great big car what big paws you've got the better to paw you my dear wouldn't you love to have a great big house with a big garden and swimming pool ist das nicht ein gartenhaus swimming pool gartenhaus great big car great big star oh du schoenes that means beautiful oh you beautiful doll beauty is as beauty does beauty is only skin deep that's deep enough for me the skin you love to touch don't they though I love the feel of your skin darling what is this field day that sneaky feeling that people call love that's what a lot of them call love so that's love I don't believe it oh you don't no I don't you're just a sentimental fool yes and I love it you're a damn fool I guess that's right too you came out here from New York thinking you were going to knock 'em dead in the movies and where are you the lights are coming out along the street my God five thirty they're closing out there they haven't called me they're not going to call me they're not going to take up my option oh my God what am I going to do I'll call 'em up no that won't get me anywhere I'll just call up and say I was out most of the day and thought maybe you might have called while I was out they won't believe it of course they won't believe it maybe a letter's coming to me they wrote to me that's what they did they're sending me a special delivery please God make it a special delivery dear Miss Dugan we have decided to take up our option under the terms of our contract as per paragraph umpty umpty umpt please God special delivery or maybe a messenger he'll ring the bell and I'll go to the door and say yes who is it please a letter for Miss Dugan for Miss Dugan eh fancy that who is it from it's from the Colossal studios I'm Miss Dugan I'll sign for it just a minute here you are go buy yourself a new Ford dear Miss Dugan after looking again at your tests we have decided to take up our option and we are notifying you here as per umpty umpty umpt contract department there goes that spotlight Carthay Circle Theatre the Barker our screen talks sings howls hisses you saw them now hear them there goes that spot on the clouds isn't it funny THE TELEPHONE oh my God it's them please God it's them they're going to take me they're going to take me oh please God dear

    Hello (please God)
    Ish dish you Oscar dish ish Hulda Hullo Oscar
    Who do you want?
    Dish ish Hulda
    What?
    Hullo Hullo Get off de vire
    Get off yourself
    Who? Hullo Hullo I vant Oscar
    Well take him (BANG)

    Damn the telephone damn everything damn damn double damn what a name Oscar imagine having a baby named Oscar little Oscar here Oskie Oskie sounds like a yell Oskie wow wow skinny wow wow Hulda Hulda rah rah rah God almighty I'm going nuts here I'm going to call Jimmy up Jimmy darling come over here talk to me oh you won't then to hell with you no I didn't mean that Jimmy I was just fooling ha ha ha see I'm laughing ha ha ha ha ha ha ha ha ha stop that laughing you damn fool you sound like a maniac God I wish I was I wish I had a drink what time is it six o'clock six o'clock oh it's six o'clock in the morning that's wrong let me see three o'clock in the morning I used to sing that with Jimmy he used to sing when he danced what a voice like a crow hoarse and he'd sing down my neck that's a funny feeling three o'clock in the morning cheek to cheek singing into my ear it's a wonder you wouldn't shave your face it's like a file well I did shave this morning you mean yesterday morning that's right it was yesterday morning this is tomorrow isn't it I don't mind your face when it's rough Jimmy I get a kick out of it yes you do I'll say I do it must be wrong to feel like this I feel so good is everything you like wrong everything you like to eat makes you fat well I've got nice slim hips you may go but this will bring you back Fuzzy Wuzzy that's a mad place and I thought when I was sitting there talking to Buelow feeling so cocky I'd come right out here and knock 'em for a loop in the bag in your eye in your hat well that's a break there's still some left I'll take it straight it jolts you quicker I need a good sock I wanta be socked by you just you and nobody else but you boopity boop boop I wanta be socked by you alo-o-o-one ska ska boopity boop boop some girls like to be socked I wonder what kick they get out it how did you get the black eye I ran into something now don't tell me it was a door no he treats me pretty rough but it feels good afterward well maybe it does if any man ever hit me I'd cut his throat ah you wouldn't I guess I wouldn't at that but I'd certainly bend a chair over him I betcha you'd let Jimmy sock you who that big stiff I wonder how it would feel at that he's got strong hands with little black hairs on the backs of them do you like hairy men honey I don't know maybe it's a kick I don't know have another oh I really couldn't oh but you must Dixie just a little one what do you mean a little one I wanta big one whoof whoopee socko that's all right stomach I'm not mad at you look at the cars don't look out the window you might fall that wouldn't be so bad right on that banana tree what a lousy looking tree you are do you ever have any bananas how do you get bananas palm trees you're kinda silly too you're so damn dirty don't they ever dust you off everything is dusty out here and dry your skin cracks well who gives a damn about your skin look at all those cars and all the people here's the church and here's the steeple open the doors and there's the people but not in church they go to movies that's because they put pipe organs in 'em now the congregation will rise and sing hymn Number twenty four that lovely old Christmas carol *Yes Sir That's My Baby* that's sacrilegious I shouldn't have said that I oughta go to church more maybe I'd have better luck I'd love to have a baby I'd dress it like a little doll a little boy doll with a little knitted sweater and a polo shirt and we'd go out walking what a cute baby I didn't know you had a baby oh yes isn't he a honey he sure is does he look like his daddy sure he does but he hasn't any hair on the back of his hands oh he will have well he'd better have what's he going to be when he grows up oh I'm not going to let him grow up I'm going to keep him just like this well so long drop in and have tea with me some day I just got some swell Bacardi oh I never drink any more it's a bad example for junior well so long so long see you in church did you see that woman junior she's jealous of your mother I had to watch you all the time or she would have stolen you never take candy from a stranger and always look both ways before you cross the street and don't talk with your mouth full now for God's sake what did you do with those shoes you got the toes all scuffed and I put them on brand new yesterday I'll make you walk on your hands baby movie star walks on his hands down Sunset Boulevard famous son of Dixie Dugan celebrated screen artiste and James Doyle world renowned dramatic novelist and playwright world renowned that's good I wonder if he ever will be I wouldn't care if he only wrote tomato can labels just so I could sit there and watch him maybe I could get a job posing Miss Ketchup the sweetheart of the tomato hello bottle come on I'll finish you up you go here's looking at you here's to the queen of the movies and the sweetheart of the tomato skoal who do you think you are Greta Garbo down you go brrrrr gee I'm tired gee whatta lot of lights twinkle twinkle twinkle little light twinkle twinkle little star so you want to be a star oh you're a star you're a hot star dear Miss Dugan address unknown the option on your contract has expired kicked the bucket died di-dee i-die list to me while I tell you of the Spaniard who blighted my life diddy eye die secretary take a letter Colossal Film Corporation attention Kirk

King Fritz Buelow James Doyle et al and to whom it may concern go to hell very truly yours no change that to sincerely no put it this way pursuant to the terms of our understanding which is as was and will be as follows to wit go to hell kindly acknowledge receipt and I remain with renewed assurances of my greatest esteem Dixie Dugan no sign that Feoretta Flamboodle third assistant secretary to Miss Dugan put down at the bottom dictated but not read now read that back to me that's good yes that's very good that's right all right sign it and send it by airplane carrier pigeon how about a bicycle a bicycle built for two wouldn't they be funny the Colossal Film Corporation on a bicycle built for two take another letter James Doyle Colossal Film Corporation who do you think you are I was thinking about you this eve in passing no I'll tell you what you do get him on the wire and then when he answers tell him I'm in conference no when you get him on the wire I'll talk to him oh Jimmy honey it's so good to hear your voice oh Jimmy darling can't I see you tonight just for a few minutes I'm so blue I've got the yips Jimmy I gotta talk to you I gotta don't hang up on me listen Jimmy darling sweetheart listen can you hear me talk to me tell me something I'm so blue I've nobody to talk to but you I know I went out with Kirk King but I didn't care about him Mickey who why he's just a song writer I'm all alone out here Jimmy and nobody but you God it's terrible Jimmy to walk up and down in a little room and look out the window and see so many people and so many cars and so many lights and not know anybody and know that somewhere out there in all those lights is your light and you're sitting there and you won't even go to the phone and call me oh darling darling wait a minute what's that there's the bell which bell where is it it's the door bell get out of my way chair wait a minute I'm opening the door wait a minute oh for me Miss Dixie Dugan yes that's me when did it come just a minute I'll give you something here wait a minute come here come in here there you are go buy yourself a suit of clothes and have your hair cut that's a good boy shut the door after you oh I'm afraid to open it oh what'll I do I'll look quick at the bottom and see who it's from

> WE ARE NOTIFYING YOU HEREWITH UNDER THE TERMS OF OUR AGREEMENT WE HAVE DECIDED NOT TO EXERCISE OUR OPTION ON YOUR SERVICES YOUR FINAL CHECK IS BEING SENT TO YOU SPECIAL DELIVERY TONIGHT COLOSSAL FILM CORPORATION

We are notifying you decided not exercise our option final check special delivery tonight damn you dirty dogs I hope you fry in hell sizzle and fry damn you oh yes we are very interested in you Miss Dugan great opportunity give you a five year contract you have great possibilities Miss Dugan we can do more for you than anybody Miss Dugan you dirty liars you dirty stinking liars I'll send you a wire that'll burn you up I'll tell you what I think of you that'll do you a lot of good Dixie old girl that'll get you somewhere that'll get you a job well I give a damn and I'll tell Buelow too the dirty dog and Kirk King the sneaky skunk yes you will I sure will how about Jimmy he could have done something for you could he of course he could now you'll never hear from him you'll have to go back to New York and sneak in the back way oh didn't you like it out in California Dixie sure but I like little old New York better ho ho ho but I do yeah that's what they all say how's Jimmy doing out there oh he's doing all right didn't you see him well yes sort of oh I see ah hah I see well if I hear of anything I'll let you know what's Jimmy's address out there Colossal Film Corporation Colossal Film Colossal fake Colossal fools Colossal liars all liars well I'm going to start lying I'll be a liar sure I love you sure I'm crazy about you gimme gimme gimme get me into the movies mister sure I'll be good to you sure who Jimmy Doyle oh that's all over that was just a passing fancy ha ha ha don't be silly just one of the boy friends if I never see him again it will be too soon hello Fritzie I thought I'd give you a ring sure sure I'll have dinner with you why not yes that'll be just swell I'll jump in the tub and I'll be all ready by the time your car comes I'll get rid of Kirk and come right over oh he's been hanging round all afternoon yes but I like you you know that yes I know you will and I'll slay 'em in the part too that was just written for me bye sure I love you bye bye love you my eye that fat neck gives me the creeps oh well what the hell turn on the light aw leave it dark I don't want to see anything there's nothing to see nobody's coming lie down and forget it hello phone why don't you say something we put 'em right next to the bed miss so you don't have to get up and answer 'em I'll lie here and look at your funny mouth open all ready to say something talk to me say hello you're laughing that's what you're doing well I can laugh too ha ha ha ha ha ha ha ha ha crying again Dixie dry those sweet tears they're salty Buddy they run right down into the corners of your mouth taste good I bet you look like a mess well who cares cheer up little girl you're a long time dead besides when you cry your nose gets red Denny used to say that I wonder where he is now you're a long time dead oh I wish I was nobody loves me nobody cares about me nobody loves me and my hands are cold oh yes God loves you little girl and you can sit on your hands oh He does does He well why doesn't He do something about it shut up stop that noise ring your head off what do I care I know you haven't taken up the option you don't have to call me and nag me about it I won't answer you what'ye think of that ring your fool head off all right then if you must I'll tell you what I think I'll tell you where to head in hello . . . yes . . . yes this is Dixie Dugan . . . oh no it isn't it can't be you . . . oh Jimmy where are you . . . yes . . . yes I know they did I just got the telegram . . . of course you can talk to me about it where are you . . . of course I will . . . you come here . . . yes I'll be waiting for you . . . oh Jimmy I can't believe it . . . Jimmy . . . bye dear hurry up . . . oh he called me Jimmy called me he's coming here oh I must get dressed oh God I'm so happy oh Thank you God you do love me you do you do and I've been so bad oh please forgive me God I'm going to be so good I'm going to love you so oh God Jimmy is coming to see me Oh-h . . .

VII

Scene i: *Express elevator, Office Building, Lower Broadway.*

Operator: Good morning, Mr. Goldman.
Variety Reporter (*sotto voce*): Ah, that's Goldman of Goldman, Goldman & O'Brien.
Operator: Good morning, Mr. Dillon.
Variety Reporter: Ah, Dillon of Dillon & Fishback.
Operator: Floors, please. Thirty next.
Goldman: Five.
Dillon: Seven.
Goldman: I think I'll get off with you.
Dillon: Okay.
Variety Reporter: Ah, hahhhhhh!

Scene ii: *Office of "Variety," a theatrical weekly.*

Reporter (*breathlessly*): Where's Sime? Gee I got a hot tip. Swell!
Abel: Better let him alone. He's busy.
Reporter: Busy hell! I got a big story. Merger. Wall Street bankers getting together. Dillon, who's behind Fox and Goldman who controls Loew and . . .
Abel: Oh nuts. Hey boy. Take this up to the composing room.
Sime (*cheerily*):—Well, this Goldie dame is doing perch stuff with the Gertie Hoffman troupe. Cute little broad too. So last night she falls right out of the flies, smack on the fanny.
Jack: No kiddin'!

REPORTER (*breathless*): Oh Sime. I've got a hot tip.

SIME: Hold it—yeah, and the tough part is this little bimbo had just been given fifty grand and a piece of blue ice that must have been eight karats. That's what knocked her. Celebrating.

JACK: Celebrating what?

REPORTER: It's a big movie merger, Sime. I saw them talking together. Dillon and Goldman.

SIME: For God's sake, boy!—Where was I Jack?

JACK: She was celebrating.

SIME: Yeah that's it. Her husband. Hadn't seen him for five years. Met her in Chicago and next morning he walked right out of the picture and never showed up again. Couldn't find him. Tried every way. Yesterday he comes into town, looks her up. Seems he got knocked on the head, out in Chi. He picked the right town. So full of amnesia he goes out West and turns up in the movies. Probably made a director out of him.

REPORTER: This is about movies. This is movies too. It's a merger.

SIME: Shut up!—then he gets some ground, and there's oil in it, and one day he comes to and looks around and says, Where am I? Hollywood. So he gets the hell out—comes here and finds the wife, explains all and gives her fifty thousand bucks just as a start. She gets high sterical, they go out and get plastered together. When she goes on to do her stunt at the Shubert last night, she jumps for a trapeze that ain't there. Klunk! Write it up, will ya?—now what the hell's eating *you*?

REPORTER: I saw Goldman and Dillon together down on lower Broadway—looks like a merger of Fox and Loew.

SIME: Wha'd they say?

REPORTER: Well, it isn't so much what they said. It's what they didn't say.

SIME: Well, see that you quote them correct. Is the Stanley chain part of it?

REPORTER: I think so.

SIME: How 'bout the West Coast Theatres?

REPORTER: They didn't go into that.

SIME: Well I guess you can say they're involved.

REPORTER (*panting*): How much do you want?

SIME: Gimme about a column and a half and I'll break it over from the first page.

~~~~~~~~~~~~~~~~~~~~

(From Variety, Week of October 3rd.)
FOX—LOEW—FAMOUS—COLOSSAL MERGER
Four Flicker Leaders In Wall Street Omelet

The mating season for movies opened with a bang yesterday. Before very long four of the largest companies in the flicker business will either be married or living in sin together. Fox, Loew, (M-G-M) Famous and Colossal will be banded together under Wall Street auspices which means practically the entire industry wlll be taking orders from Downtown. Yesterday morning a Variety reporter had enough first hand information in Wall Street to confirm rumors which have been rampant for weeks, or ever since Kennedy and Zukor made a hurried trip West together. Among the banking firms interested in the financing of the holding company that will absorb and operate the companies mentioned are Goldman & O'Brien and Dillon & Fishback, who have been interested before this in . . .

~~~~~~~~~~~~~~~~~~~~

HOLLYWOOD, CAL.
October 6.

NITA DARLING:

I've just left Jimmy. What a sweet time we had! We're that way again—the sun is shining, the birds are singing, the stars are as big as your fist—and if this doesn't make sense, it doesn't matter.

He'd been out here almost two months, never even called me.

Said he thought I had a swelled head. Then the day they didn't take up my option, he heard about it. He called me and came up to see me and told me how sorry he was. And I cried down his neck and all over the potato salad and cold chicken wings we got from the Del. Gee, and all the time I thought he was the one who had gone Hollywood. Pictures in the paper, guest of this and that. It's a wonder you notice me, I told him. That's a lot of malaky, says he. The press department sends out a big blurb about you, one day posing you with Clara Bow, the next with Greta Garbo and pay day you find you're docked $4.50 for that dictionary missing from the reference department. By docking all the writers, they're sure to get the right one. Unless it happens to be the guy who wrote the story about you in the press department. And that's who it was too. Try to collect from one of those guys.

I told Jimmy I'd like to see where he works and he said, Why not? The boys'll be glad to get some news from the outside world. Be sure and bring them some newspapers. The last contact they had was when Balto got through with the serum, just in time to save them, too. They'd been isolated for months, working night and day on imitations of *Abie's Irish Rose*. Remember "Toplitsky of Tipperary" and "Paddy of Palestine"? For a while one whole department was devoted exclusively to the production of "Begorahs" and "Shmai Yisroales." Come out tomorrow night. We're all working double shifts now on stories for sound pictures.

So tonight I went out to the Colossal lot and battled my way thru sentries waving red lanterns outside of sound stages—you see they try to shoot most of the mike opera at night when it's quiet.

Well it took an hour to find where Jimmy and all the other writers were holed in. It was a long wooden barracks, Nita, in a far corner of the lot, built for one of the war picture sets. Remember that big delousing scene in *What Price Glory*, or *The Big Parade* or something? I forget which. Well after the picture they condemned the building and divided it up into little cubby holes and put all the scenario writers in it. One writer in each coop with his name on the door. Jimmy says they started out first by putting the names on the door in gold leaf. Then they found that was too permanent, besides it gave the writers wrong ideas about themselves, so they printed them on little cards and then as the writers got fired or had to be taken away, they stuck the new names on with thumb tacks. But that got to be too much trouble too, so now they chalk the names on the doors or just the time card numbers.

Jimmy was in one of the cells away down the hall and I had to pass about 15 doors, all closed, but the transoms were open. All the writers were dictating madly and the plots were coming out of the transoms. I wish I could give you an idea of what a madhouse it was. But this is something like—

Long shot Zulu beating Bongo Drum Boom-boom-boom sound effect. Fade in title letters dripping blood, The Red Dance, The Red Dance of Death—long shot of Girl's white body tied to stake: Camera pans slowly up from feet—slowly moves up to face. Face fills screen, then eyes. One eye. Horror! In her eye we see reflection of fire and dance of the savages. Cut to closeup of grass rope burning. She breaks away. Bongo drum beats faster—BOOM BOOM BOOMBOOM BOOM!!! Girl flees thru jungle, on trail to white trader's shack. Shot, Chaney in plaster cast, chewing orchids. Cut to chase.

Open with closeup of white legs dancing. More white legs, lots of legs. Lap into saxophones. Plant theme song. Quick flashes, breasts, hips, legs. Fade in dear old New England mother, crocheting doilies. Shot of clock: Eight o'clock. Title: 'Pears to be about bed time, Paw. Sound effect: laughter from cabaret very sarcastic coming thru organ solo played by old New England father on a little parlor organ. *Suggest*, "Lead Kindly Light." Lap dissolved into: "Lights of B'way." Electric signs UFA angles. Shots of white legs running upstairs. Black trouser legs with evening braid pursuing down long, rambling corridors of summer hotel. Cut to chase.

Closeup, Jannings's back. Huge drooping shoulders. Fade in Beer Garden in Milwaukee. Pounding steins on table and singing Schnitzelbank. Jannings crying into beer. Close up of beer with the tears splashing into. Tart pushes him playfully. Title: Putting salt in your beer so early in the evening? . . . I copped that from O. Henry, but who knows that?—L'me see—Salt—oh yeah—cut to salt mines in Siberia. Long lines of convict prisoners struggling thru snow—might show Aurora Borealis with shooting tongues of light changing to cruel whips lashing convicts—Maybe that's a symbol or something. Jannings escapes—I'll figure it out later . . . Cut to chase.

Well, sis, that gives you an idea. Farther down the hall, some guy was doing a college story—one of those Yip for Yale one minute to play hats over the goal posts sort of things. And a male collegian chorus for sound track singing Fight, fight, fight for dear old Whoozis! And next door another underworld story—Mike the Rat and Gyp the Gat and the fine clean cop who always just happens to wander in when they're unloading the Scotch or putting one of the other gang on the spot—and so on and so on and so on . . . until I got down to Jimmy. There he was walking up and down in his cell. Three steps up and three steps back, his collar off, his hair on end and a girl taking it all down. I listened a while and couldn't make any sense out of it. Then a bell rang and the girl gathered her notebook and ran down the hall. That means there'll be a story conference in ten minutes, says Jimmy. That's the warning bell. She has to have all this typed for the conference. They have conferences every fifteen minutes so we can discuss the story as it goes along. I suppose you didn't understand what I was dictating, did you? No, says I, did you? And he says sure, I'm on the Rin-Tin-Tin story now. I was faking an Eskimo song. They chant to celebrate the success of the big seal drive. It was Nebbick's idea. I thought you came out here to do your own ideas, says I. I was young, says he, and didn't know. Well only a few more weeks and I'll be out. Have you found anything? And I told him the truth, a lot of promises and a lot of tips to go to this studio and that, but all wild goose chases. And then he says, Well, cheer up. We were flops before and we can flop again and so long as we can be together while we're doing it, it could be a lot worse. Anyway, there's something stirring around here. All sorts of huddles going on and rumors about this going out, and that coming in, and shakeups all the way up the line. I don't know just what it is. Everyone has a different angle on it. We're buying somebody or they're buying us, so anything's liable to happen. I might finish up running the works, or just opening the gates, and where's that big kiss you brought me? So I delivered it, and just then a siren blew and Jimmy jumped up and said, My God! Story conference. You'll have to find your way home. I'll call you tomorrow. Then he ran down the hall without his collar, and all the other doors flew open and all the other writers tore down the hall and out over the lot looking for their conferences. I found out later the supervisors and directors try to keep the places a secret, but the older writers always know where to find them.

Love
Dixie.

Offices of Dillon & Fishback, Lower Broadway.

Hello Max, this is Dillon.

I was just going to ring you.

About that merger story?

Yeah. What is all this cockeyed nonsense. The *Times* just called me.

Me too. Something about a story in *Variety*.

Never heard of *Variety*. What is it?

It's a theatrical sheet. The *Times* said they had a story that you and I were merging three or four movie companies.

That's what they told me, too. I told them it was a lot of nonsense.

Me too. But it gave me an idea. Maybe they're ripe for a merger and this was just a feeler.

Think so?

Shouldn't wonder. Wouldn't do us any harm to talk it over. What do you think?

Well, I know our bunch don't want to merge.

We don't either. But the other guys might. Wouldn't do any harm for all of us to get together and talk about it anyway.

How's your golf?

You'd be surprised. Who is the Warner outfit?

Fineman put out their last issue.

We might have a talk with him.

He's been playing a pretty good game lately. Eighty-two last Saturday.

I think Milton would be a good feller to talk to.

That's a good hunch. They'd never suspect him. Jack is okay. He's dabbled a bit in the theatre, too.

Sure enough. He had a piece of that show last year. What was the name of that girl he was crazy about? Dixie? Dixie something?

Dugan. But Jack isn't bragging about it. She certainly took him for a ride.

Well, it could happen to any of us.

Sure. Anyway Jack could do a lot of the ground work for us. Think it over and we'll get together sometime.

How about making up a foursome Saturday? I'll try to get Fineman.

Okay. You wouldn't like to come in on Chrysler, would you?

It's all yours.

You'll be sorry.

You're too good to me. S'long. 'Bye.

~~~~~~~~~~~~~~~~~~~~

Stage Five, Colossal Lot, Hollywood.
Chiquita and her leading man, Harold Strongface, are doing the big murder scene in the allegorical sequence of Sinning Lovers. *Strongface as Good Man is drowning Chiquita, Bad Woman, in the glittering gold fish fountain in the Patio of Passion in the House of Sin.*

BUELOW (*hoarse from yelling all morning*): Gimme something, will you; Strongface, you big ham! I want indignation, virtuous horror. You're drowning the little bitch—can't you give me that?

STRONGFACE (*mechanically*): All right, Mr. Buelow. (*To Chiquita.*) The son of a so and so. (*Softly.*) Am I hurting you, Sweet Thing?

CHIQUITA (*meltingly*): I love your hands on my neck—sooo strong.

BUELOW: All ready—action—now Chiquita, as he is pushing you down into the fountain, rage at him—spit at him—he squeezes your neck tighter—you're choking—take it BIG—let me have it—Music!—Camera!

STRONGFACE (*registering hate while talking thru his clenched teeth*): You come over to my house after you've seen the rushes tonight.

CHIQUITA: Ye—es, darling!

BUELOW (*yelling*): Give me hate, will you? Damn you!

STRONGFACE: Ah, tahel with him. He'll be dragging his tail up and down Hollywood looking for a job before the week's out.

CHIQUITA: Who? Fritzie?

STRONGFACE: Sure. Haven't you heard?—there's a big merger and Colossal is going to close down and everybody is out except directors with stage experience and actors on contract.—Hurting you, Honey?

CHIQUITA: Ye—es, it's nice. Tonight I weel hurt you—Oooh!

BUELOW: Cut! Move up for the closeup—Shot of hands on throat . . . That was lousy but we're behind schedule. Hey Joan . . . where thahel's that script girl. Joan! There, run out while we're making this set up and get Mickey O'Keefe over here. We're going to do that theme song tonight. And hurry back.

VOICES: Rest your lights . . . give us another broad here . . . Hit her with 248 . . . Try a silk on it . . . Hey, Mike, put a few of your goddam tourists to work on these props, will you?

~~~~~~~~~~~~~~~~

(*The sound-proof cell of Mickey O'Keefe, number seven in a row of two dozen cubicles all occupied by theme song writers, sad exiles from Tin Pan Alley.*)

MICKEY (picking the keys with one finger):

> *When I begin*
> *To fall in*
> *To sin—umpty ump, a loving sinner, winner,*
>   *dinner, finner, skinner*
> *Oh is it a sin to love. Oh I love to sin with you*
>   *my loving sinner—*

Oh, hello Joan—how's that?

JOAN (*running a slim warm hand through his curly hair*): How's what, Mickey?

MICKEY (*singing*): Oh is it love—oh is it sin— when I love to sin with you—just you. Umpty bump bump—just you. Now I'll work backwards on the middle part.

JOAN: Gee, that's hotsy. When will you be finished? Buelow sent me over for you—they're going to shoot sound tonight—the theme song.

MICKEY: I'm still writing it. Say, baby can you keep a secret? Listen I got it straight today from a guy who just came from New York that there aren't going to be any more pictures made out here after this month—all the production with this sound stuff can be done inside and they're gonna move everything back East so as to be near the actors in New York and the electrical experts in Schenectady. Hello Broadway, here I come.

JOAN: I heard different.

MICKEY: But this is straight—he got it from a guy downtown. He says buy Western Union.

JOAN: Western Union?

MICKEY: Because they're behind the whole thing—buying all the film companies so they can control the television when they get ready to release it—I got it straight—it's all perfected and they're just holding it back till this is put over.

JOAN: You wouldn't fool a dumb girl?

MICKEY: You ain't so dumb.

JOAN: I wish I was as smart as you—could write songs and everything. It must be wonderful. And you get it all out of this curly head!

MICKEY: Get away closer—that's better ... aren't they cute? You know baby, I can remember when knees were away uptown ...

JOAN: Fresh!

(*Soda fountain in Drug Store across the street from Colossal Lot. Dixie is getting an earful from Delight Moran, doing a small bit as one of the Seven Deadly Sins in Buelow's super-epic* Sinning Lovers.)

DELIGHT: I got seven bucks and a half a day just as atmosphere. Now when I get a part all I can chisel is ten.

DIXIE: Ten bucks is better than nothing.

DELIGHT: Sure, I know, but doing a part like Pride is worth more than ten bucks.

DIXIE: There's a lot of kids in this town that would commit murder for ten bucks. Starving, the poor devils.

DELIGHT: Yeah, it's tough and this sound stuff is making it tougher.

DIXIE: How do you mean?

DELIGHT: Used to use a lot of us kids when they were having a big fight or a frolic but now the guy goes to the window and says "Voila, Sacre Bloo. It's the Revolution. Ecouté the bloodthirsty mob coming up the road to Versailles." And then four or five huskies do a huddle over in front of the mike and make mob noises like Walla, walla, walla. You can see the dough they save. But how about little me!

DIXIE: Or little me for that matter.

DELIGHT: Yeah! The whole racket is in for a fall if you ask me. Ya know I got a boy friend who works over at Grauman's Chinese—he's that big, tall, good looking egg who stands out in the middle of the patio in the gold kimono . . . well, he overheard Joe Schenck tell Sid Grauman that the U. S. Steel Company has got control of some patents where they make pictures in three dimensions, life size and in natural colors, and they're going to produce them in Pittsburgh, and all the companies out here will have to close down. I might just as well have stayed in Akron. I wouldn't have that long haul back across the country. (*Climbs down off stool, shakes out long white robes of Pride, and pats down diamond tiara.*) Well, back to the factory. I hope they get to me this afternoon. They spent the whole morning shooting closeups of a doorknob. Say, I heard Fox is looking for a girl that can lead numbers. They're doing a revue. Know Schmeck over there?

DIXIE: No. Do you?

DELIGHT: And how! I'll take you over there tonight when I wash up here. Thanks for the coke. S'long.

DIXIE: 'Bye. (*Paying check.*) Schmeck! Well, he might be my luck. Here goes the last ten spot and not another in sight. I'll be climbing palms and chewing holes in cocoanuts. (*Goes out singing softly.*)

 I can't love or anything, but give, Baby

Say, that's a good theme song for this here Hollywood.

~~~~~~~~~~~~~~~~

(*Express Elevator, Office Building, Lower Broadway*)

OPERATOR: Good morning, Mr. Goldman, good morning, Mr. Dillon.

GOLDMAN: Hello there, Dillon.

DILLON: Hello, Max.

OPERATOR: Floors please. Thirty next.

GOLDMAN: Five. Say I lined up Fineman for that foursome.

DILLON: Six. I got Jack Milton. Had lunch with him yesterday. Say, you know he's still nuts about that Dixie Dugan gal. Says she's out west in the movies now. Got steamed up right away on the chance he might go out there.

GOLDMAN: Saturday morning is on then?

DILLON: Yes, same time. We'll meet at the club.

GOLDMAN: Okay. 'Bye. Out five.

DILLON: S'long. Six out.

~~~~~~~~~~~~~~~~

VIII

Hello Diary:

No news for today. No work from Colossal. No jobs. Nothing but a letter from *Le Dernier Chic* wanting to know when I'm going to pay for those dresses. Now if I knew that, diary, wouldn't I be smart? I guess this is the beginning. They'll all be bearing down on me as soon as they hear Colossal didn't take up my option. When I first came out here all the shops were crawling into my lap. Sure honey we want you to have anything you want. We know you're going to be a big star and we want you to be with us. You don't have to pay for it now. Don't say a word about it. It's all right. Well that was just dandy, diary. And I went plumb loco. Oh well they can't hang you. And they should have known better anyway. I'll learn 'em. I only hope they don't come in here and start seizing things. I wouldn't even have a coat of tan. Mickey sent me a cute new song yesterday. A new theme song for a comedy called *Chiropractic Papa*. He's been awfully cute, diary. Taking me out to dinner and trying to get me a job. Although why you wanta work in this madhouse he says I don't know. And I says to him you get me wrong Mickey. When I came out here I wanted to work for fame. Now I just want a job for eats. He's doing swell out here. They like him. And he's sore as the devil. He's been eating his heart out to get back to Times Square. So the last few weeks before they were to take up his option he wrote the worst stuff he could think of. And believe it or not, it went over with a yip! The supervisor was just nuts about it. So they took up his option and now he's got to stay here nine more months. Here's *Chiropractic Papa*, diary: The verse starts like this—

Sufficient I've been getting—oh
Of many kinds of petting—oh
I've tried it graeco-roman style and other ways galore
I've had the gay and ginful kind
The sinuous and sinful kind
But none could neck
Enough to wreck
My cool esprit de corps;
But, oh, the thrill
That warmed my chill
Platonic pneumogastric
When my matter-of-fact-ic
Chiropractic
Papa got gymnastic.
I entertained emotions no girl should be denied,
Though many times a bridesmaid, but never yet a bride.

And here's the chorus—

> *Oh, chiropractic papa!*
> *I love your sinful digits,*
> *For when they steal along my keel*
> *I get conniption fidgets.*
> *Chiropractic papa!*
> *Take me for your own,*
> *And you may play my vertebrae*
> *Just like a xylophone.*

Dear Diary . . . Lunch today with Jimmy at the Montmartre. Sidewalks outside door lined up with tourists saying ah! and ooh! There goes Dolores Del Rio. There goes Marion Davies. But I didn't hear the excited mob yell: There goes Dixie Dugan! Well they will, damn 'em. Jimmy and I had a table over in the corner where we could watch all the stars and the near stars and the former stars waving at each other or snubbing each other. Each one trying to be the most popular. And the little baby stars bouncing in and out in Deauville sandals, tennis socks, and batik skirts with panties to match. Alice White and Sue Carol and Sally O'Neill and Nancy Carroll and Lupe Velez—there's a hot little bimbo, diary—and, of course Gary Cooper and Conrad Nagel and Alan Hale who looks like a big ice man we used to have and George Bancroft with that permanent wave curl on the back of his neck—I could like him in a big way. And over in another corner the table where all the chatterers sit—the girls who write Hollywood gossip for the newspapers and magazines. And not very far away a round table of Colossal supervisors and directors. Jimmy used to lunch with them but now they got a new writer from the East. They always fete 'em before they give 'em the works, Jimmy says. The condemned man ate a hearty breakfast. I asked Jimmy if he was still doing Eskimo songs for the Rin-Tin-Tin epic. And he said no they had put him on *Sinning Lovers* doing dialogue for the Babylonian sequence. Just then Lola Krunch, one of the big local movie chatterers, stopped at the table and spoke to Jimmy. She interviewed him when he first came out here and he introduced me and she introduced a woman who was with her. Well, diary, I nearly fell off my chair. Who do you think it was? Hedda Natchova. And I used to be so nutty about her. What a knockout she was. And only a few years ago too. I often wondered what became of her. And here she was in the flesh. We chattered a while but I was so rattled I don't know what we said. After they passed on Jimmy said you're going too, of course. I says going where? What? When? To Natchova's house for tea Saturday. Didn't you hear Krunch say she wanted me to come? You get the idea, don't you? And I says no, being still dizzy and he says that's too easy. Natchova's trying to stage a comeback and Krunch thinks I'm in pretty over at Colossal and can do something for her. I suspect Krunch is nicking the lady. That's part of her racket. So she's staging a tea and there's enough glamour in the Natchova name to make anything she does stand up in the gossip column. It's kinda sad, you know. Five years ago she would have started a panic if she walked in here and look at her over there now bowing and smiling to everybody. I bet her face aches. But Jimmy I says she's still beautiful. Sure she is says Jimmy but they want 'em young out here now. Anyway we'll have tea with her Saturday. Her house will give you a kick. It's as big as Madison Square Garden and just about as homey.

Can you wait till Saturday, diary? I can't hardly. This will be the first really big mansion in Beverly Hills that I've had a chance to get into. We really ought to know how it looks, diary. We might want to take it over some day. I can hear that guide on the rubberneck now. To your right, the palatial home of Dixie Dugan! And then a bus load of ahs! and oohs!

~~~~~~~~~~~~~~~~~~~~

Dear Diary . . . I've just come back from tea at Hedda Natchova's house, and I'm going to try and put it all down, diary, as near as I can remember it. I only wish I could write, like a real writer and use a lot of swell words. I read lots of stories with less in them than five minutes of that tea. First there's the house, diary. Enorm! That's all, just enorm. Sits away back in the middle of huge grounds, half the side of a hill. You drive through big iron gates, up a driveway lined with palm trees, a narrow strip of cropped lawn and the rest wild. There was a butler at the door and a maid to take care of your things upstairs and then you come down the marble staircase into a huge living room with a fire burning at one end. You can get sunkist plenty outdoors here in California and still freeze to death in the house. Jimmy was to take me but he got tied up in another one of those damn conferences and couldn't get away. So he called me and told me to go alone. Natchova was very sweet to me. She didn't remember who I was, but that didn't matter. She didn't seem to know hardly anybody that was there. And they didn't pay any more attention to her. They just sat or stood and speared the cocktails off the trays as they went by. I asked one of the girls who they were. And she said well that dark-haired egg over there is a gag man on the Christie lot. I don't remember his name. And the little blonde is Myra Kelley. She's in the quickies on Poverty Row. But I don't place any of the others. And I says what are they doing here? She says what are you doing? What am I doing? What are we all doing? We're drinking drinks and putting away the tid-bits. And I says who did you come with? She says I came with me, silly. I heard there was a tea and my thirst was aroused. We'll lap them up until they stop circulating and then we'll go places and do things. Want to meet anybody? And I says sure. And she says well go ahead. Nobody will mind. And if you don't meet them they won't mind either. So, I stood around, first one foot then another while a couple of dozen girls and men dashed in grabbed a flock of drinks and hurried out. Everybody talked to everybody else but hardly anybody talked to the hostess. She wandered around smiling bravely and trying to find out as delicately as possible the names of those she was entertaining. I guess I must have looked as bewildered as she was because when it grew dark and there were only a few people left around a tray which they took forcibly away from the Filipino, she came over and sat down beside me. Some bird in a uniform went around and pulled down all the shades and lit the light. Away off in the corner we could hear a struggle going on over the last of the cocktails and then some doors slammed and it got very quiet. You'll pardon me says she very softly if I don't remember your name. It's Dixie Dugan. A sweet name says she. Who are you with Dixie? So I lied bravely. I'm with the Colossal. I've got a five year contract. Yes, says she, they'd like you. You're young and pretty.

I'll never be as pretty as you were. Or are I mean, catching myself quickly, but not quick enough. So I rattled on. You're beautiful and the way you can act. You used to tear me to pieces. I'm just a little punk alongside of you. It's sweet of you to say that Dixie. And I says well it's true. But I suppose you're awfully tired of having people tell you how wonderful you were . . . are, I mean. And she took my hand and said were, Dixie, leave it were. Then I didn't know what to say so I said well you've got a swell lay-out here. I mean you've certainly got a beautiful place. Wonder if I'll ever have a place like this? And she says sure you will. You may have this one. And I says don't be silly. Even if I ever did make enough money to buy a place like this I couldn't keep it up. And she says that won't stop you. It didn't stop me. I don't know why I'm talking to you like this. I guess it's the drinks. Or maybe it's because I'm just so tired of lying to everybody. And there's something about you sitting here, young and pretty and full of confidence, that reminds me of myself at your age. God it all looked grand. And it was, too. You know I used to pretend I didn't hear them in theatres and restaurants and on the street saying ooh! there goes Hedda Natchova! Isn't she stunning! But just the same I heard every word of it and I loved it. Now they say, look, she looks sort of familiar, who is that? And somebody will say that's Natchova and then somebody else will say well, well, I often wondered what became of her. That's how fast you go up and down in this business. But you're beautiful, I says, and you can act. Why compared to all these little squirts that are starring now—why there just isn't any comparison. And she says listen Dixie they've got one thing I haven't got—youth. They've got young necks and young legs and young eyes. And nice slim, soft young bodies. And you can't fool the camera when it comes to those things. And that's what they want out here in this business. Youth. Young flesh. And they feed it into the machine and out comes thousands of feet of young eyes and young legs and young bodies. Reels and reels of it. And that's what people want to see. Men go there and watch them hungrily all evening and then go home and close their eyes when they kiss their wives. And women go there and watch them too, but they're looking for those first lines around the eyes or if their arms are getting fat. And aren't they happy when they find what they're looking for. Beginning to look her age isn't she? And did you notice how fat she was getting in that last picture. Well, she hasn't anything I didn't have. Just lucky, that's all. If I could have got somebody interested in me when I was her age—when I was young. And I says Natchova—and she says you can call me Hedda and I says but listen Hedda what's all this old stuff—you're still young. And she says I'm thirty-two and in this business if you're over thirty you're older than God. If you're a woman. Men get away with murder. Men always had all the luck. Oh, well with all this talking stuff coming in I may get a break yet. Lola Krunch was bringing a New York playwright here this afternoon who was going to do a screen play for me with dialogue. I had stage experience you know. He's over at the Colossal lot. I don't remember his name. But he didn't show up. Plenty of others did though. Say didn't I meet him with you at the Montmartre. Sure I did. And I says do you mean Jimmy Doyle. And she says Doyle that's the name. Do you think he could do something for me? And I thought to myself Jimmy has all he can do doing something for himself. And I couldn't help thinking what a cockeyed business this was. Where playwrights are doing sound effects for dog stories and former stars are trying to use these same playwrights to help them come back. Everybody lying to everybody else. And then I remembered the lie I told her. So I says listen, Jimmy can't do anything for you. He's just hanging on over there now by his eyebrows. And I told you I had a contract, too. But I'm just a liar. They didn't take up my option and I haven't got anything. And Hedda says you mustn't worry about a little lie. It's all make believe out here and make believe is lying. You get so used to working in lies you never notice when you're living in them. You see this house. Looks grand, doesn't it? It's a big lie. I could take you through it and show you forty guest rooms that haven't any guests—I locked them up long ago. Couldn't afford the help to keep them dusted. Come here I'll show you something. See that big swimming pool. You couldn't swim in it. There isn't any water. There hasn't been ever since the pump in the filter broke down. I can't afford to get it fixed. But I tell everybody I'm installing a new ultra-violet filter. Laugh that off. Why did I have tea today? Because Krunch said she'd bring somebody here who could help me. Another lie. Why do I let all these other people come here to eat and drink and run? Because I'd go mad in this big place all alone. Why don't I sell it and get out then? 'Cause everybody would say poor Natchova, had to sell her house. I guess she's all through. Well, we sure had some swell parties up there. Say, are you going over to Lily Whooziz tonight? She's throwing a big party, to celebrate her first starring picture. Oh, everybody'll be there.

I guess you better run along home, Dixie. I'll have Michael take you, in the car. Don't mind if he goes rather slow. The tires are not so good.

So that's how I came home, diary. In the big Rolls Royce with the very thin tires. And I don't know whether it was the cocktails or the swimming pool full of dead leaves or Michael driving carefully to save the tires—there was no spare—or the gloom of that big empty shell of a house on Beverly Hills, but whatever it was I had a lump in my throat all the way home.

Office of Jack Milton, broker, 67 Wall Street

MILTON: Miss Leff? Busy?

MISS LEFF: No, Mr. Milton.

MILTON: Take a few letters, and then see about getting me some transportation to the Coast.

MISS LEFF: The Coast?

MILTON: Yes, I am going to Hollywood. What would you like me to bring back to you?

MISS LEFF: Jack Gilbert.

MILTON: If I can't get him, would Navarro do?

MISS LEFF: Did you hear that Hollywood story about the young fellow who told his girl maybe I can't kiss you like Gilbert or hug you like Navarro—have you heard it?

MILTON: No, what is it?

MISS LEFF: Well, don't stop me if you've heard it—I want to tell it anyway—he said to his girl maybe I can't kiss you like Gilbert, or hug you like Navarro, but I can bite you like Rin-Tin-Tin.

MILTON: Ha! ha! take a note to Goldman, Goldman & O'Brien—

"Confirming our understanding on Saturday will leave for Coast latter part of week to make preliminary survey of physical properties of list of companies involved.

Very truly yours,
MILTON

P.S. *I took five in that bunker—not six."*

MISS LEFF: How did you come out Saturday?

MILTON: Oh, the boys got so busy talking about this movie merger, they almost spoiled the game, but we all did pretty well after we decided to chuck the discussion and hold it in the shower room. Goldman and I were two down at the turn, but we trimmed them coming back.

MISS LEFF: That's good.

MILTON: Then we had our shower and Scotch and while we were having a rub, we merged Loew, Fox, Colossal and United Artists.

MISS LEFF: I thought Radio was coming in on it.

MILTON: Fineman didn't get back from the fight out in Chicago—he's got a sweetie out there—so that's why we decided to take in Colossal instead of Radio. If you have a few dollars, you better pick up some of that Colossal Common. We'll probably split it up three for one of the new stuff. And by the way—when you wire to Hollywood for hotel reservation, ask our office out there if they know which outfit Miss Dixie Dugan is working for.

MISS LEFF (*archly*): As if you didn't know.

MILTON (*confused*): Ask them anyway, and take a memo to Dillon of Dillon & Fishback.

"For your information, the Equity and Assets as at date of last public statement showed the Consolidated Balance Sheet of Colossal Film Corporation and Subsidiary Companies, after giving effect to current financing, as prepared by independent auditors, reveals net tangible assets of approximately $71,053,000, an amount equivalent to $5,921 for each $1,000 of Notes, due April 1st, 1930, and net current assets of $18,743,000.

Very truly yours,

MILTON

P.S. Do you know where I could pick up a half-dozen cases of Bushmill?"

~~~~~~~~~~~~~~~~~~

November 5.

NITA DARLING:

Remember old man Schmalz who ran the del around the corner and how he used to say efry day I find more py Jimminy Chrismus oudt? Well, me and Schmalz, especially since I came out here to this land of the leaping lispies. You know when I first hopped here from New York I sat down in a nest of headlines, Dixie Dugan this and Dixie Dugan that, with pictures taken before and after and all the movie chatterers telling me I was the cream in their coffee and to button up my overcoat and eat an apple every day. Well, that didn't last. Pretty soon all I got was silence and very little of that.

I was telling Jimmy the other day. What to do I says, what to do, I'm that flabbergasted. And Jimmy says you've got to come out of your dugout, you're hiding your light under a bushel. Ever hear of the fellow who went away out into the woods and started making mouse traps? Sure, I says, and I always thought he was a sap. Well, sap or no sap, says Jimmy, he became the head man in the mouse trap industry with branch offices all over the world and why? I never knew why, I says, just imagine! I don't know why either, says Jimmy, but that's my story and I'm stuck with it. How about a kiss? So after a while I sort of remembered something and said, we were talking about a mouse trap, or were we? Yes, said Jimmy, and what I started to say before I was so rudely interrupted was this, the fellow who made better mouse traps in the middle of the woods and the world beat a path to his door wasn't doing his stuff in Hollywood. He could make them right on the corner of Hollywood and Highland and nobody would ever find it out unless he had a press agent. So then I said, well put your arms around me and we'll think it over. And after a while we came to a conclusion which I think was pretty cute of Jimmy.

You'll have to get some publicity, says Jimmy, people out here don't know you're alive unless they read about you in the local papers. Take Max Reinhardt. Known only in Europe, Asia, Africa and all points in America east of Mulholland Drive. But he had never had his face in the Montmartre or his name in the Hollywood Daily Citizen, so of course he couldn't amount to anything out here, and he was really on his way back to Salsburg when he got off at Pasadena. And take Morris Gest. No, I says, it's your turn. I took Max

Reinhardt. Well anyway, says Jimmy, the point is the same, you've got to get some publicity. Get acquainted all over again with the gals in the verb and adjective racket out here. Throw a little party for them and the boy friends. What will I use for money, I says. I'm flatter than that. I'll help you, says Jimmy, the darling, and I'll help you get them there too. I don't know just how I'll do it but I will. It needn't be a big party, just a little get-together and that'll break the ice again. After that, if you cultivate the right ones in the right way you'll find yourself breaking into the local journals of opinion with sufficient regularity to impress such studio executives as can read—and you'd be surprised how many of them can.

So that's on, Nita. Jimmy is taking care of the invitations and is going to help me with the party which I am going to throw up here in my one-room apartment with kitchenette. Refreshments will consist of Scotch and sandwiches, Gin and sandwiches, Scotch and Gin and, for those who like to talk, just plain Scotch. X marks the spot. Wish you were here.

DIXIE.

IX

HOLLYWOOD PARTY

*A Talking, Singing, Dancing Picture
with Sound and Effects.*

We open with a LONG SHOT of apartment building. CAMERA TRUCKS UP to building, up wall for ten stories and we DISSOLVE into the apartment of Dixie Dugan. It is a single room modestly furnished with a kitchenette and dining alcove opening off one side. CAMERA PICKS UP flowers on table and TRUCKS TO CLOSEUP of portable victrola playing *You're the Cream in My Coffee* (Sound Effect). Through open door we get a LONG SHOT of Dixie Dugan preparing sandwiches and putting ginger ale and White Rock bottles in the ice box. Motor of ice box starts (*Sound Effect*) but over it we hear Dixie singing to victrola accompaniment.

DIXIE (*singing*):
>You're the fly in my coffee,
>You're the tack in my shoe
>You will always be
>My calamity
>I can do without you
>You're the lumps in my oatmeal
>You're the thumb in my soup

(*telephone rings*)

Even worse to me
　　　　　Hello?
What a curse to me
　　　　　What? Hello!

CLOSEUP of Dixie at telephone. We hear not only Dixie's side of the conversation but the strident mechanical noise of the voice in her receiver. Victrola continues to play under conversation.

Gee, that's too bad.

(W-a-a-a W-a-a-a W-a-a-a)

But I counted on you so.

(W-a-a-a W-a-a-a W-a-a-a Waaaaa W-a-a-a Waaaaa)

All right. I'll give you a rain check and you can come some other time.

(W-a-a-a W-a-a-a-a W-a-a-a W-a-a-a W-a-a-a Waaaaaaaa)

Gee, that'll be swell; sure! Go ahead and bring your party over later tonight.

(W-a-a-a W-a-a-a)

Okay, 'Bye!

(W-a-a-a)

Hangs up, door bell rings, Dixie opens door and is greeted by half a dozen guests. Her first arrivals. Confused greetings, cries of hello, how are you, well well well, where's the drinks, as girls and men remove their wraps and follow her into the kitchenette.

CLOSEUP of ice box, DISSOLVING into kaleidoscopic shot of hands opening ginger ale bottles, pouring liquor into glasses. Clinking six highballs together, three black sleeves, three white arms against background of round kitchen clock showing 9 o'clock.

We DISSOLVE into office of Max Shamus, a producer on the Colossal lot. He is best described by his contemporaries who assert that if his nose were filled with nickels he could retire for life. He is presiding over an earth-shaking conference on *Sinning Lovers*. Lying on the couch is the great German director Karl von Krankenhaus. Sitting on the radiator is the great Swedish trick photographer Gustaf Axelson. Pacing up and down is the great French actor Pierre Lapin. Brooding at the window is the great Polish sound technician Jan Pormorski. Sitting on the edge of a straight-backed chair is the completely bewildered American playwright Jimmy Doyle. Max Shamus is speaking in his general direction:

SHAMUS: Colossal has decided to make *Sinning Lovers* into the great American super epic of all the ages. (*To the others.*) Nicht wahr?

VON KRANKENHAUS: Ja wohl.

LAPIN: Mais oui.

SHAMUS: So, to make sure, we have taken all the Americans off the picture except you. Where are you from?

DOYLE: New York.

SHAMUS: That's all right. You will work with von Krankenhaus. He does the story, puts the epic in it. And the motifications too, then you'll make it into dialogue.

JIMMY: English?

SHAMUS: No, American. I told you this is going to be the big American super epic.

VON KRANKENHAUS: Aber mit klang.

SHAMUS: Sure, klang—lots of klang.

JIMMY: Do I write the klang too?

LAPIN: Il est necessaire que j'ai un rôle dans lequel je puisse être délicat, leger et heureux.

SHAMUS (*to Jimmy*): Lapin has lots of fastidicality. You want to work it in.

AXELSON (*sonorously*): De Stora byggnaderna—Vi maste fa med de Stora husen och broarne!

PORMORSKI (*excited*): Gdy byłem we Warszawie, zrobiłem film—

JIMMY: I wonder if I could telephone.

SHAMUS: And disturb this important conference just when we're getting somewhere? Certainly not!

A door flies open and uniformed Attendant dashes in with official-looking communication. All gather around as Shamus opens envelope. They read: Closeup.

COLOSSAL
FILM CORPORATION
INTER-OFFICE COMMUNICATION

Date   November 14th

To   All Departments

From   Peter Schmilick

The mailing room has been changed from M-11 in the Administration building to Room 134, building F, street S. Dial 5.

~~~~~~~~~~~~~~~~~~~~

We DISSOLVE to clock in Dixie's kitchenette. It is eleven o'clock. CAMERA TRUCKS BACK to a LONG SHOT of kitchenette. It is crowded with men and women—some in evening dress, some in sports costume. The table and sink are overflowing with bottles, empty and otherwise. CAMERA PANS around kitchenette into living room, also completely jammed with drinkers standing, sitting, leaning and lying. Through the hubbub of talking, laughing and singing we hear the victrola and the telephone and the door bell. DIXIE is standing by the telephone talking to girl in pink nightie holding hot water bottle next to her stomach.

MAN (*answering phone*): Hello! What? Yes wait a minute! (*To Dixie.*) It's Lola Krunch, she says she's on another party and says can she bring them all over with her.

DIXIE: Sure! Why not?

MAN (*to phone*): She says, sure, why not! And if you know of any other parties bring them along.

Hangs up. Door bell rings. Door is opened and a party of ten or twelve crowd in waving hands to everybody. Cries of hello, hello, where's the drinks.

DIXIE (*to Pink Nightie*): What's the matter with your tum-tum?

PINK NIGHTIE: Gee, I don't know. I wanted to stay in bed but Bill called up and said I had to come over to his party. I told him I wasn't dressed and he said come as you are, so this is how I was, and then when I got over there he says come on, we're all going over to Dixie's, and we did. Who are you?

DIXIE: Why, I'm Dixie.

PINK NIGHTIE: Whose party is this?

DIXIE: Mine, or at least it started out to be. I don't know hardly any of these people.

PINK NIGHTIE: You're lucky. But maybe we'll all go somewhere else pretty soon. Hey there, you in the puttees, fill this hot water bottle again for me, will you? No, not gin, hot water. Yes, I know, I'm funny that way.

(*Telephone rings.*)

DIXIE (*on phone*): Hello, Hello! Is this you, Jimmy? No? Oh damn! Oh hello Mickey—yes come on over—who? Sure, bring Buelow with you—and Chiquita too. Seen Jimmy? Double damn! Wait till I see him, I'll tell him what I . . .

We DISSOLVE into conference in Max Shamus' office. Shamus at the telephone speaking heatedly. Jimmy lying on the couch and around him gesticulating violently are von Krankenhaus, Pormorski, Lapin and Axelson.

KRANKENHAUS: Als ich bei Neu-Babelsberg war machte ich den Film *Ersatz für ewig* und ich hatte eine solch herrliche Szene—
JIMMY: Ja wohl. Sehr schoen.
PORMORSKI: Ja przecież nie mogę grać rolę miłosną w lokomotywie i równocześnie eliminować hałas maszyny.
LAPIN: Sans blague!
SHAMUS (*on the phone*): Well, seventy-five a case is plenty and you can take it or leave it! How much for Bacardi? WHAT? Robber! (*Hangs up.*)
JIMMY: I've really got to telephone, Mr. Shamus.
SHAMUS (*chewing cigar silently for a moment*): I got it. Hedda Natchova. She's sympathetical. And exotical too. (*Pushes buzzer. Girl staggers in dead for sleep.*) Take a wire, Hedda Natchova, Beverly Hills. Report my office tomorrow. Have important part for you in new super American epic *Sinning Lovers*, signed Shamus. (*Picks up phone.*) Wilshire 1074. (*To Jimmy.*) Don't forget, we gotta have lots of suspension in the picture—and pathetics. (*To phone.*) Hello, Quaker Box Lunch? Let me talk to Mike. Oh Hello Mike . . . Shamus again . . . a case of Vermouth too. (*Hangs up.*)
JIMMY (*desperately*): Could I use the phone just a minute?
SHAMUS: My God man, is this a conference or ain't it?

Uniformed attendant dashes in again with official communication, this time on pink paper, hands it to Shamus, salutes and exits. Conference pauses while all gather around to read it. Closeup:

COLOSSAL FILM CORPORATION
Attention following executives and department heads.

Mr. Nebbick	Mr. Caucus
Mr. Shamus	Mr. Krankenhaus
Mr. Kirk	Property Room
Mr. Babcock	Stage Door
Mr. Pormorski	Recording Room
Mr. Axelson	Mike—projection room
Mr. Schmoos	Jack— " "
Mr. O'Riley	

TEST SCHEDULED FOR THURSDAY, 15th NOVEMBER—3 P. M.
SUSIE SLOTZ (Ingenue)
Test No. 2027
Requested by Mr. Shamus

Charge "Love In A Fog"
Cameraman—Mr. Schmoos
Sound Supervisor—Mr. O'Riley
Monitor Man—Mr. Caucus
Directed by Mr. Babcock

SOUND AND SILENT—Stage "C"
PETER SCHMILICK.

THE ABOVE TEST HAS BEEN CANCELLED
PETER SCHMILICK.

We DISSOLVE into succession of short vivid shots showing Dixie's party has overflowed her tiny apartment.

SHOT of apartment building, lights blazing in the windows, radios and phonographs going in a mad blur of jazz.

SHOT of cars parked solid along curb both sides of the street in front of house and as far down the block as we can see.

SHOT of late arriving parties pouring out of cars dancing up the walk to apartment house entrance.

SHOT of crowded elevators.

TRAVELLING SHOT up stairway. CAMERA PICKS OUT couples parked on stairs and landings in various stages of amorous amusement. (*Caution here—CENSOR*)

SHOT of hallway outside of Dixie's door showing adjoining apartments and those across hall have been thrown open and party is circulating from one to the other.

FLASHES of dancing, love-making, fighting, drinking, laughing, yelling, screaming, crying.

CLOSE UP of Eastern author weaving in front of mirror and haranguing himself as he gestures uncertainly with slopping highball.

AUTHOR: Look'it yu! Whatchu doin' here in thish monkey cagsh, thish inellekshule shrility. (*Takes deep drink spilling most of it—then speaks to himself in glass tenderly.*) Yu mush write book 'bout all thish—all thesh shilly peeble. (*Sags forward, rests elbows on dresser and looks at himself with new interest, makes faces at himself.*) Yesh, you've got fine forred. Whoor yu? Where yu come from? Where yu goin' huh?—thash big big big shought. Thesh shilly peeble don't shink—mush exposh 'em—flay 'em—'shkurriate 'em—shilly foolsh. (*Head droops in arms, falls asleep.*)

We CUT to group in Dixie's apartment including Dixie, Buelow, Chiquita and Mickey. The rest of the party has mysteriously disappeared into the other apartments.

DIXIE: But I oughtn't to leave my own party.

MICKEY: Come on! They've left you already. They don't even know you're here; by this time they don't even know whose party it is.

DIXIE: But I never saw a party grow like this!

BUELOW: That is Hollywood. Parties just go on joining up with other parties as long as they can find one. I started out with a little dinner party of six one night and wound up at five o'clock in the morning with two hundred and fifty. You'll like the one I'm going to take you to now.

DIXIE: Where is it?

BUELOW: Down at my beach house.

DIXIE: We won't be gone long, will we?

MICKEY: You should worry! This party will be going on until morning—it's only one o'clock.

BUELOW: We'll go in my car—I'll go find the chauffeur. Come on Chiquita.

DIXIE: Oh look Mickey! There's Hedda Natchova. Hello there, when did you come? I'm so glad!

HEDDA: I had a little party at my house but somebody called up from here and said we were all invited over. That was sweet of you.

DIXIE (*recovering quickly*): Oh, sure, sure!

MICKEY: Come on Dixie, we've gotta go.

DIXIE (*to Hedda*): 'Bye! I'm going out with Fritz Buelow, but I'll be back soon. Make yourself at home. The party's all over the building, but they'll be trooping back here. You won't be lonely.

HEDDA: I've got the blues tonight, Dixie. Parties always give me the blues.

DIXIE (*throws her arms around Hedda and kisses her impulsively*): Ah, don't be blue, Hedda. Cheer up! I'll see you soon. 'Bye. Hey Mickey, wait for baby! (*Goes out leaving Hedda alone in apartment. Hedda walks over to the window, and is standing there looking out over the city as we* FADE OUT.)

FADE IN bungalow on roof of Dixie's apartment building. Most of the party have joined another party up there. Huge living room.

Everyone sitting in circle around room. The host, Charley Williams, famous director, has just succeeded in quieting down all the guests and is finishing instructions to them for a new game he has invented.

WILLIAMS: Now remember, the whole success of this depends upon you being absolutely quiet, sitting perfectly still and not making a sound. In a few moments, the lights will go out and when they come on again, well, you will see something.
VOICES: What? What will we see?
WILLIAMS: Never mind. You'll be surprised. Yes indeedy.

We CUT TO bedroom, in wing of bungalow and discover Jack Milton and two other men in evening dress.

FIRST MAN (*taking off coat, tie and collar*): Come on, let's join the party, we're late as it is.
SECOND MAN (*removing coat and vest and taking off his shoes*): Come on, Milton, get ready!
MILTON (*frankly puzzled*): What are you doing? What's the idea?
FIRST MAN (*now in shirt sleeves taking off shirt*): Well you can't go down to the party like that all dressed. We told you we were going to take you to a real Hollywood party, didn't we?
MILTON (*aghast*): But my God man, you don't mean . . .
SECOND MAN (*pulling off trousers*): Certainly! You don't think you're going in there with your clothes on do you? Why, they'll think you're crazy.
FIRST MAN: Sure, this is a real party. Everyone in their B.V.D.'s.
MILTON (*incredulous*): The girls too?
SECOND MAN: Listen to him! I thought you came from New York? You sound more like Kenosha. Hurry up, take 'em off!
MILTON (*gingerly removing coat*): But listen, I never did anything like this before.

FIRST MAN (*in his B.V.D.'s carefully adjusting top hat*): There's lots of things you'll do out here you never did before. We're not asking you to do anything we wouldn't do ourselves are we?

MILTON (*taking off shirt*): That's right too. Well, I'll try anything once.

SECOND MAN (*also in B.V.D.'s and top hat*): That's the spirit. Stick with us and you'll have something to tell them back home. This is going to be some party.

MILTON (*woozily*): Well, I must have a lot of liquor aboard to be doing this.

FIRST MAN (*handing him flask*): You'd better take on some more if you're going to feel bad about it. (*Milton takes long pull from flask, knock is heard on door.*)

VOICE (*outside*): Hey, hurry up, will you!

FIRST MAN (*putting* MILTON's *topper on him and taking him by the arm*): Coming!

SECOND MAN (*taking other arm*): We'll walk in with you if you feel you need our moral support. Let's go! (*They open door and step out into dimly lighted hall.*)

We CUT BACK to Dixie's apartment. Hedda Natchova is discovered still standing forlornly at the window. Jimmy Doyle dashes in with his hat and coat on.

JIMMY (*breathlessly*): Hello. Where's Dixie? Have you seen Dixie anywhere? Where's everybody?

HEDDA: Why, I don't know. They're all over the building.

JIMMY: Where could I find Dixie? I've been trying to get her all evening.

HEDDA: Let me think! I haven't seen her for quite a while. She was going out with somebody—with er—let me see—who was it—let me think now.

JIMMY (*suspiciously*): Who? Where?

HEDDA: Oh, I know now. She told me she was going somewhere with Fritz Buelow.

JIMMY: Oh Buelow! That dirty dog! Where did they go?

HEDDA: I don't know. She said she'd be back in just a little while. Maybe she's with the rest of the party somewhere in the building.

JIMMY: But what did she go away for? Why did she leave her own party?

HEDDA (*wearily*): I don't know. Why does anybody do anything? Why does anybody care what anybody does?

JIMMY (*stormily*): Well, I care!

HEDDA: It won't do you any good. Go and look for her. Maybe you'll find her and maybe you won't, and if you're wise it won't make any difference. Wait a minute. Bring me a drink before you go, will you? You'll find it in the kitchenette. (*As Jimmy enters kitchenette he stands appalled by litter of empty bottles, soiled dishes and cigarette butts.*)

We DISSOLVE into hallway just outside door of Charley Williams' living room in roof bungalow. Milton and his two friends all in their B.V.D.'s and top hats have paused just before opening door.

FIRST MAN: Here we are, come on, let's go in!

MILTON (*with bravado*): All right, let's go! (*Second Man opens door and together with his friend they push Milton into darkened living room, snap on the light and close door quickly after him. Milton suddenly finds himself blinking in the middle of a brilliantly-lighted living room. All around him seated and standing are the other guests fully clothed. They regard this sudden apparition in underwear and silk hat in one petrified second of silence and then before Milton has a chance to take the situation in completely, there is a tremendous guffaw of raucous laughter. Shrieking hysterical guests crowd around the poor playboy from the East as he struggles desperately to get to the door. He finally makes it and flees across the roof and dives down the first stair-*

way which brings him to the landing in front of Dixie's open door. He ducks in, pursued by all the guests, dashes into bathroom, slams door shut and locks it from inside.)

The crowd is baying outside the door like a pack of foxhounds when Williams appears on scene, together with Milton's two friends in their bathrobes. They succeed in coaxing Milton out of bathroom and getting most of the crowd to come back upstairs, all but a few of Dixie's original party, who have wandered into the kitchenette and busied themselves with the remains of the liquor.

Hedda has remained gloomily aloof from the excitement—party jokes are an old story to her.

We hear voices laughing and talking in kitchenette, then Jimmy's voice.

JIMMY: Anyone seen Dixie upstairs?

GIRL: Didn't you know—Buelow's got her down in his beach house. Told her there was another party there. Ha! Ha!

SECOND GIRL: Well, if there wasn't there will be. That Buelow guy works fast. Hey Jimmy! Where you going?

JIMMY (*dashing out door*): I'll kill the son of a—

GIRL (*going back to kitchenette*): Okay, big boy. (*Sees Hedda at window.*) Come on, Hedda, have a drink!

HEDDA: No, I've had enough for one night. I'm through.

GIRL (*gaily*): Okay grandma. (*Goes into kitchenette.*)

SECOND GIRL (*voice*): Let her alone, Joan. The old girl has got the yips.

THIRD GIRL (*voice*): They ought to have a home for these old dames instead of letting them run around to parties like a lot of wet blankets.

MAN'S VOICE: Aw, Hedda's all right. Boy, what a knockout she used to be.

SECOND GIRL (*laughing shrilly*): Used to be, is good. Well, I hope when I'm through I'll have sense enough to know it. Mud in your eye!

THIRD GIRL: Here's to hell! May the stay there be as gay as the way there.

CAMERA TRUCKS UP slowly to Hedda and registers her reactions to above conversation as she overhears it. We see her lips move and hear her repeating, brokenly:

HEDDA: Used to be, what a knockout I used to be. (*Gazes out window. The distant electric sign comes closer, growing larger, spelling out HEDDA NATCHOVA. Closer, larger, and out of the darkness blooms the glowing facade of a theatre, with HEDDA NATCHOVA flashing over it in the sky. Huge colored spotlights are playing on the building and against the clouds. Red plush ropes hold back the crowd waiting for her arrival. It is a grand premiere night. She steps out of her limousine, a voice cries HEDDA NATCHOVA, and the crowd takes up her name with a roar of welcome . . .*)

Hedda is standing on the windowsill lost in the vision of her former greatness. The French windows open softly as she smiles and waves to her admirers. Radiant and happy she steps forward to greet them. The vision vanishes. She screams as the sidewalk rushes up to meet her with tremendous speed.

A flash of red—blood red.

Then black.

FIRST GIRL (*enters from kitchenette and holds out extra highball*): Come on, Hedda. It'll do you good. (*Sees open window and stops. Screams.*) Hedda, Hedda! (*The rest of the party tumble out of kitchenette. All rush to window and look down. Ten stories below they see something on the sidewalk, something dark and shapeless, something terrible and still. SLOW FADE OUT.*)

X

(From the N. Y. Evening Tab—NOON EDITION—Nov. 15, 1928)

HEDDA NATCHOVA DIES IN HOLLYWOOD ORGY
(Story on Page 2.)

(From the N. Y. Evening Tab—3 O'CLOCK EDITION—Nov. 15, 1928)

AGED SHEIK STEALS RABBIT GLANDS
(Story on Page 2.)

NATCHOVA DEAD IN HOLLYWOOD!
(Story on Page 5.)

(From the N. Y. Evening Tab—5 O'CLOCK EDITION—Nov. 15, 1928)

SIAMESE TWINS ELOPE!
(Story on Page 2.)

SHEIK STEALS GLANDS.
(Story on Page 5.)

EX-MOVIE STAR DEAD.
(Story on Page 28.)

```
                                                   NOV. 15TH
NA462 15 HOLLYWOOD CALIF 15 1102A
NITA DUGAN
439 FLATBUSH AVE
                              BROOKLYN NEW YORK
IN TERRIBLE SCRAPE STOP GOING TO BE
MARRIED STOP CAN YOU COME STOP LETTER
FOLLOWING
                                            DIXIE
```

~~~~~~~~~~~~~~~~~~~~~~~~~

```
                                                   NOV. 15TH
SD533 4 BROOKLYN N Y 15 106P
DIXIE DUGAN
1842 NO. LA BREA AVE
                              HOLLYWOOD CALIF
ARE YOU CRAZY
                                             NITA
```

~~~~~~~~~~~~~~~~~~~~~~~~~

```
                POSTAL TELEGRAPH — COMMERCIAL CABLES
                            TELEGRAM
```
                                                NOV. 15TH
NA396 5 HOLLYWOOD CALIF 15 446P
NITA DUGAN
439 FLATBUSH AVE
                                    BROOKLYN NEW YORK
CRAZY AS A JUNE BUG
                                                DIXIE

~~~~~~~~~~~~~~~~~~

November 15th.

Darling Nita:

You've heard about Natchova. Sending you local clippings. I was having a party and she came and I went away and while I was gone she either fell or jumped out the window. Ten stories. I didn't know anything about it till I got back to my place around dawn. I was having troubles of my own. Plenty of them. I don't know if I can tell it to you straight or not. But here goes!

I wrote you about Jimmy suggesting a party for the local gossip-writers. He loaned me the money and pulled strings to get them to accept. Well it was a big success. Those who didn't come direct to the party came from the parties they were out on and brought the parties along. Those who came got on the phone and invited others. I have one room and a kitchenette but everybody there knew everybody in the building and pretty soon all the other apartments were opened up and the party was all over the house. They came from all over Hollywood. Cars were parked all around the block. Everybody was there, it seemed to me, except the one I wanted. Jimmy never showed up. Not till long after, but that part of the story comes later.

Around one o'clock or so Fritz Buelow, the director, who came with Chiquita and Mickey O'Keefe, the song writer, invited me to drop in on another party down at his beach house in Santa Monica. I was feeling full of the devil and couldn't see any harm in it. Besides, my party was going so well, they'd never miss me. Most of them didn't even know it was my party and didn't care. So I went with Mickey and Buelow and Chiquita. Just as I was leaving, I saw Hedda Natchova. She was standing over by the window, the same one she fell out of or jumped out of. She was having the blues and I remember throwing my arms around her and kissing her just before I went out, telling her to cheer up I'd see her soon. Gee, she was a peach, Nita. Sweet, and so sad. She'd been such a big star in her day and somehow it had all gone by her. Well, I hope she's happy now, God love her.

Anyway, I got into Buelow's car and we drove miles and miles to his place down on Santa Monica beach. When I got there he let us in and I noticed it was all dark and I says to him where's the party, and he says oh they're around here somewhere. We'll look for them as soon as we've had something to drink and I says well I don't know how you feel about it, but I've had enough and that goes for Mickey too. Mickey was wall-eyed by this time, but he came to long enough to object. He held on to the table and declared I got too much, I always get too much but never enough, and with that he smiled a beautiful smile and fell over in a heap, so I held up his head while Chiquita got a pillow from the divan and put it under him and then Buelow says to me, come on, we'll get him something to revive him, so I goes along with Buelow, not thinking anything. The house was all dark except the living room and he was snapping on the lights as he went along. Then we came to a room and we went in and I expected him to put on the light, but instead of that he closed the door behind us and then grabbed me. I tried to hold him off but it was like fighting a gorilla, he was so strong. I bit and kicked and scratched and called him every name I could think of. Finally he clamped one paw around my throat, held me against the wall and with the other started ripping my clothes off. All the time he kept saying you thought you were going to be cute and out-fox me, didn't you. Well, I always get anything I go after and I've been after you ever since I saw you in New York.

What happened after that is all mixed up. I know his voice began to sound away off and then the light went on all of a sudden and Chiquita was there tearing at Buelow's face with her finger nails. She must have heard me scream, and she's a jealous wildcat anyway. I slipped out while they were going to it and ran out of the house without my coat or hat, and my clothes in rags. You've never been out here Nita so you can't imagine where you are when you are at Santa Monica beach at 2.30 in the morning without a car, or a taxi, or a street car for miles. I climbed up to the top of the palisades and started to hoof it in the general direction of Hollywood. Well, I nearly died! Finally I got to a car line and discovered the next car to Hollywood didn't leave till around 4.30 so there was nothing to do but wait for it and I got home around 5.30, came up to my apartment and who should be sitting there waiting for me big as life in the middle of the most Godawful mess of empty bottles and over-turned chairs and cigarette butts—none other but Jimmy!

Well Nita, all the fights we ever had before were nothing compared to this one. He said he knew where I'd been all night and who I'd been with, said he always suspected Buelow and me from the very beginning in New York, and now he was sure I was this and that and worse. Said he waited there all night just to tell me what he thought of me and that he never wanted to see me again, then out he went, slamming the door behind him. I was so sick and stunned I couldn't even say yes, no, how do you do, go to hell or anything. I just pulled down the bed, threw myself on it and passed right out of the picture.

When I came to, the room was full of police and reporters and photographers and it wasn't until then that I learned my party had wound up with Natchova's death. They kept asking me how it happened and I told them I didn't know, I wasn't there, and they said this is your apartment isn't it, and I said yes. And it was your party too, wasn't it, and I said well, it started out that way, but I went away and didn't get back until morning, and I don't know what happened while I was gone. And they said well, sometime around three o'clock that morning Hedda Natchova was found dead on the sidewalk under that window and she either fell or jumped out. Some say one thing, some say another. Did you see her at the party and I said sure. Did she seem happy or depressed, and then I thought right away well if I tell the truth and say she had the blues they'll say she committed suicide, so I said she was gay—everybody was gay—it was a helluva party, and one of the cops says I can see that. So then they talked some more and went around snapping photographs and then who should come in—Nita, you'll die!

It was Jack Milton. I looked at him for a moment and said well, if it isn't Jack Milton I'm going to stop drinking. What are you doing here, and he says wait a minute Dixie, and he gets the photographers and cops and reporters out and shuts the door and looks all around and says well, are you surprised to see me? And I don't know what it was but all of a sudden it seemed so good to see somebody from home that wasn't mad at me I just threw my arms around his neck and started to cry and he kissed me and patted me on the back and says, come on, you'll be all right, I read all about it in the paper this morning and as soon as I saw your name mixed up in it I came running. But the funniest thing is that I was here last night and didn't know it. I says where, and he says right here, or rather in that bathroom. And in my B.V.D.'s, believe it or not. I didn't know it was your apartment. So then he told me he was at a party upstairs and some friends played a trick on him, told him everybody was going to be in their underwear and got him to strip down to his B.V.D.'s, pushed him into the dark living room, snapped on the light and left him there in the middle of a crowd of guests all seated around the room in immaculate evening dress. As soon as he got his breath he dashed out of the room, across the roof and down the stairs and ducked into my apartment because that was the only open door he saw. The guests all tumbled down after him and finally coaxed him out of my bathroom. All this happened while I was fighting my way out of Buelow's house and just a little while after that Natchova jumped or fell and the party broke up with the women screaming down the streets and the men trying to catch them and herd them into their cars to get them home. When the police came there was hardly anybody left, and no one who knew anything about anything.

So then I told him about Buelow and he asked me about my work and I told him I couldn't get anywhere and he asked me if I had any money and I told him no, and then he took me by the shoulders, shook me a little and said look here, you know I've always liked you and I know you don't care very much for me, but I like you enough for both of us. Why don't you quit all this nonsense, come back to New York and marry me and we can be as happy as a couple of bugs in a rug. Then I thought to myself why not. I haven't any job, I haven't any Jimmy, I haven't any money, I haven't any prospects and I'm just plain licked, just going down for the third time in the middle of the ocean and along comes the Leviathan and the captain says you can have either a lift or if you prefer you can have the boat. What am I supposed to say? To hell with you and your boat, this is my party and I want to sink?

Well Nita, all this went through my head just like scat. Here's Jack Milton, filthy with money, overflowing with love, begging me to take him and here am I, nobody with nothing in the middle of nowhere. So I says all right Jack, you can have it your way. I'm not going to tell you I'm crazy about you but I do like you a lot and I'll be good to you and on the level and don't expect miracles. Well, he nearly broke my ribs and when I got my breath I said there's only one thing I'm going to hold out for. I'm not going to leave this town licked. 1 want just one chance at this movie racket. I've worked and ached for it and I deserve it and if you can help me get it you can have all the rest of me all the rest of the time. So Jack says if I can help you! Don't you know what I'm doing out here? And I says running around to parties in your underwear aren't you? And he says, oh that was just a lark but my business I mean, and I says how would I know; something to do with money I'll bet. And he says well it's confidential but we aren't going to have any secrets from each other from now on, so this is it. I'm out here representing a syndicate of Wall Street bankers and as soon as I report back to them we're going to merge all the big companies out here and me and my gang will run the works. I can get you anything you want out here, that's all I can do for you. Give you a studio if you want it. Close it up if you say so. Hire anybody you like, fire anybody you don't like. Aside from that, I can't do a thing for you—except love you to death.

And I says, all right Jack, that'll come later. You do your part and I'll do mine—and then we'll do ours. And—and—well that's all Nita. Wishing you the same.

Your delirious sister,
DIXIE.

(From the N. Y. World—Nov. 22nd, 1928)

MONSTER MOVIE MERGER
Wall Street Banks Create Cosmic Films Inc. To Absorb Fox, Loew, Warner Bros., United Artists, Famous and Colossal.
JOHN MILTON HEADS EXECUTIVE BOARD.

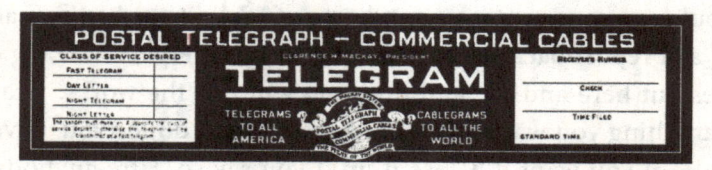

```
            POSTAL TELEGRAPH — COMMERCIAL CABLES
                         TELEGRAM
```

NOV. 23RD

```
SA298 50 NEW YORK 23 1053A
COLOSSAL FILMS SUBSIDIARY
COSMIC FILMS INC
                        HOLLYWOOD CALIF
STOP ALL WORK SINNING LOVERS JUNK
SILENT VERSION START PREPARING
IMMEDIATELY SINGING TALKING DANCING
VERSION TYPE BROADWAY MELODY STOP
LOCATE DIXIE DUGAN SENT OUT THERE ON
EASTERN CONTRACT CAST HER IN LEADING
ROLE AND SUPPLY HER WITH SUPERLATIVE
SUPPORTING CAST STOP MUST START
SHOOTING WITHIN THIRTY DAYS STOP WIRE
CONFIRMATION
           EXECUTIVE BOARD COSMIC FILMS INC
                      JOHN MILTON CHAIRMAN
```

> **POSTAL TELEGRAPH – COMMERCIAL CABLES**
> **TELEGRAM**
>
> NOV. 23RD
>
> NC592 39 HOLLYWOOD CALIF 23 315P
> JOHN MILTON
> COSMIC FILMS INC
> 1 WALL STREET
>   NEW YORK CITY
> WE HAVE THREE HUNDRED THOUSAND DOLLARS
> SUNK NOW IN SINNING LOVERS BELIEVE WE
> SHOULD SALVAGE RATHER THAN SACRIFICE
> STOP DO NOT AGREE WITH YOU THAT DIXIE
> DUGAN HAS SUFFICIENT EXPERIENCE TO
> CARRY LEADING ROLE IN REVISED
> PRODUCTION PLEASE ADVISE
>   MAX SHAMUS

> **POSTAL TELEGRAPH – COMMERCIAL CABLES**
> **TELEGRAM**
>
> NOV. 24TH
>
> SA432 19 NEW YORK 24 1105A
> MAX SHAMUS
> COLOSSAL FILMS SUBSIDIARY
> COSMIC FILMS INC
>   HOLLYWOOD CALIF
> YOU ARE RELIEVED OF FURTHER DUTIES AND
> RESPONSIBILITIES AS OF DATE STOP
> REPORT IN PERSON EASTERN OFFICE AT ONCE
>   MILTON

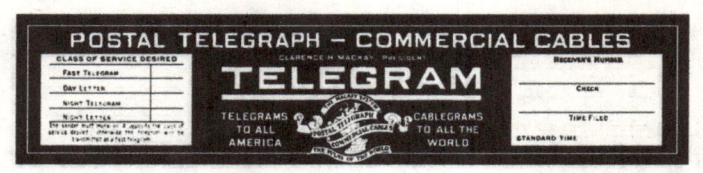

POSTAL TELEGRAPH – COMMERCIAL CABLES
TELEGRAM

NOV. 25TH

```
NC356 51 HOLLYWOOD CALIF 1205P
JOHN MILTON
COSMIC FILMS INC
1 WALL STREET
                    NEW YORK CITY
HAVE JUST SEEN TEST OF DIXIE DUGAN
CONGRATULATE YOU ON YOUR CHOICE BELIEVE
SHE IS REAL FIND AND AM ENTHUSIATIC
OVER YOUR PROPOSAL TO MAKE SINNING
LOVERS THE GREATEST SINGING DANCING
TALKING PICTURE EVER MADE WOULD LIKE TO
START IMMEDIATELY REHEARSING MISS DUGAN
AND ASSEMBLING SUPPORTING CAST HAVE I
YOUR OKAY
                         SOL NEBBICK
```

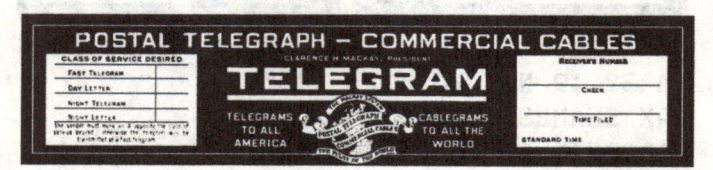

POSTAL TELEGRAPH – COMMERCIAL CABLES
TELEGRAM

NOV. 25TH

```
SB672 8 NEW YORK 25 426P
SOL NEBBICK
COLOSSAL FILMS SUBSIDIARY
COSMIC FILMS INC
                         HOLLYWOOD CALIF
```

ASSUME CHARGE IMMEDIATELY DIXIE DUGAN
PRODUCTION SINNING LOVERS
                                        MILTON

~~~~~~~~~~~~~~~~~

(From The Hollywood Daily Screen World—Nov. 25th, 1928.)
DIXIE DUGAN WINS COLOSSAL PRIZE
by Lola Krunch.

Isn't it the irony of fate that just when Colossal had decided to cast poor Hedda Natchova in the leading role of "Sinning Lovers" that the Grim Reaper should touch her with his grisly hand? But it's an ill wind that blows nobody good. Yesterday out of the Colossal offices came the startling announcement that "Sinning Lovers" would be made into the greatest Singing, Dancing and Talking picture of the century and although every girl in Hollywood has been considered for the coveted role, Sol Nebbick, the young producing genius of Colossal, after exhaustive tests, has selected little Dixie Dugan to star in this new epic. Dixie Dugan came out here three months ago and bided her time. Wise little girl. Well she knew that by refusing inferior roles she would make herself all the more desirable.

Congratulations Dixie! Congratulations Colossal! And congratulations to you, Sol Nebbick, whose infallible sense of showmanship has again led you to choose the right girl for the right role. And congratulations to the industry which again has proven to the carping critics and the sneering cynics that true ability will always find its just reward out here in Hollywood, the real land of opportunity.

Who will write and direct the new version of "Sinning Lovers"? I don't know, but Fritz Buelow who began the picture is no longer with Colossal. In fact, one little bird told me that in some mysterious way he incurred the displeasure of the Big Boogeymans in Wall Street and would not be allowed to direct another picture on the Colossal lot, but I have heard too that Buelow is not in sympathy with these mergers. He feels they are crushing the individual genius of such men as himself, and is planning to produce independently.

Max Shamus, who was in charge of the production of the picture, has been called east on an important conference relative to the 1929 production program under the new merger. His friends confidently predict he will return in a more important capacity than ever.

A number of writers have been spoken of as working on the preparation of the new version since James Doyle, the New York playwright, who wrote and produced Dixie Dugan's Broadway success,

"Get Your Girl," is no longer connected with Colossal. Differences between Dixie Dugan, the new star, and Doyle who was working on the picture are said to have resulted in a complete break with Doyle refusing to have anything further to do with the story. Doyle has a number of offers from eastern producers to return to New York and write musical comedies there and is expected to shake the dust of Hollywood any day now.

Well well, they come and go, but Hollywood, fair beautiful Hollywood, remains as bright and gay and hospitable as ever with arms ever open to those with the courage and the talent and the pluck to fight the good fight for glory and riches and everlasting fame.

~~~~~~~~~~~~~~~~

November 26th, 1928.

Dear Dixie:

I am going back to New York tomorrow night, but before I go I want to see you if only for a minute to apologize and beg your forgiveness for all the rotten things I said to you the other day. I might have known that none of them were true but I was so crazy jealous. Met O'Keefe and he told me all about what happened at Buelow's that night. I can't blame you if you refuse to see me and never speak to me again, but I won't be happy until you know how low and contemptible I feel about it, how abjectly sorry I am and how I long to see you just once more and tell you what I find it impossible to write.

I am glad you are going to get your opportunity with Colossal. They are wildly enthusiastic about you out there and are going to do everything to make your picture a tremendous success.

I suppose they told you I was writing it, but when I heard you were going to be in it I told them I would not have anything to do with anything you were in. You see, Dixie, I was still sore. Heartbroken too. I could not even work on the same lot and see you every day, so I just quit. I guess they would have fired me anyway. But you are going to be gorgeous in the picture. I know it, and you deserve all your good luck and more. You're the sweetest thing that ever lived and I am the lowest—but I'll be watching your success from New York and will be pulling for you every minute. Not that I can do anything for you except wish you luck. I've been a big flop out here and am going back a failure but I am honestly glad that, if one of us was to make good, it turned out to be you. There I go saying "us"—well, it used to be, didn't it? And nice, too!

Won't you see me just once, won't you please let me tell you how sorry I am, won't you please let me hear you say you forgive me? Please, Dixie!

Just a bum,
JIMMY.

Nov. 27th.

DEAR DIARY:

I feel like the Siamese Twins when they are assigned a room with twin beds—completely baffled. Here I am engaged to one man and in love with another but mad at him—plenty mad. Maybe I'm not in love with him either. I am until I remember how rotten he treated me, then I don't care if I never see him again. I guess I'll write and tell him so. He's going back to New York tonight he says, and he wants to see me before he goes. Oh you do, do you? Well, Jimmy, Jimmy, Jimmy, you can rot first. I'm going to marry Jack Milton and I'll tell you so, too.

But how am I going to tell you if I don't see you? I guess I ought to see you just to watch how you take it. Won't you burn? Well, it'll serve you right. Still, it must have looked kinda queer to you at that, me ditching my own party, staying out with Buelow until daylight and coming in all rags and tatters. Guess you had a right to be sore, but you didn't have to talk to me that way. I don't have to take that kind of lip from anybody. Not even from you Jimmy Doyle, and I'll tell you so, too. I guess I'll let you take me to dinner just so as I can tell you.

But maybe I'll weaken when I see him, Diary and then what'll I do—engaged to Milton and everything. You better let well enough alone Miss Dugan. Gee, but it couldn't do any harm to see him just once more, could it, Diary? I'll just eat and run and he'll get on the train and that'll be that. I won't even go to the train with him, Diary. Come to think of it, I couldn't anyway. Jack is telephoning me from New York tonight. He calls me every night now since he got back. Checking up on me I guess. Now was that pretty, Dixie? It's your own dirty mind.

Will I telephone and tell him he can take me to dinner? The phone is right here, Diary. Look, all I have to do is reach out and pick it up. I really ought to see him, Diary. He wrote such a sweet letter. He's really sorry, terribly sorry. And he hasn't any job and he's going to New York feeling he's a big flop and this is the end of everything. Maybe he'll think I'm just high-hatting him if I don't see him. I wouldn't have him think that for anything, Diary. Yes, that's just what he'll think. I guess I better see him, Diary. Don't you think so too? Sure, what harm can it do? It can't do any harm. Well, here goes—and if anything *does* happen, it's your fault, Diary. Remember that. I talked it all over with you and you said it was all right, or at least you didn't say it wasn't. Did you? No, you didn't. . . . I'll tell you all about it tomorrow.

~~~~~~~~~~~~~~~~

SCENE: *Willard Café on Pico Boulevard. A honeycomb of tiny booths, each cell just large enough for two to snuggle in. Through the windows they look down upon a rolling sea of twinkling lights. Hollywood! Above the clatter of dishes and the bumble bumble of voices a radio loud-speaker, pleasantly ignored, drools and cack-*

les with the idiotic insistence of a half-witted relative at a family dinner.

JIMMY (*in tiny booth just under loud-speaker*): I'll order later. I'm waiting for someone.

WAITER (*hovering*): The dinner is very nice tonight.

JIMMY: I can wait for it.

(*Waiter floats away leaving an aroma of hurt pride.*)

... MY DEAR FRIENDS OF RADIO LAND REMEMBER FOREST LAWN IS A PLACE WHERE LOVERS NEW AND OLD SHALL LOVE TO STROLL AND WATCH THE SUNSET'S GLOW WHERE MEMORIALIZATION OF LOVED ONES IN SCULPTED MARBLE AND PICTORIAL GLASS SHALL BE ENCOURAGED BUT CONTROLLED BY ACKNOWLEDGED ARTISTS NICHES AND URNS VARY IN PRICE ACCORDING TO SIZE AND LOCATION AND EVERY PRICE INCLUDES PERPETUAL CARE MISS ETHEL WOCKLE WILL NOW SING BUTTON UP YOUR OVERCOAT.

> *Button up your overcoat*
> *When the wind is free*
> *Take good care of yourself*
> *You belong to me*
> *Eat an apple every day . . .*

DIXIE (*brightly*): Oh hello, been waiting long?

JIMMY (*lying like a gentleman*): Oh no, I just got here.

DIXIE (*lying like a lady*): I was tied up at the studio.

JIMMY: Oh, that's all right.

> *Be careful crossing streets*
> *Oooh-ooh*
> *Don't eat meats*
> *Oooh-ooh*

JIMMY (*politely*): What are you going to have?

DIXIE (*studying menu helplessly*): I dunno. What are you going to have?

JIMMY (*ditto*): I dunno. Now let me see . . .

DIXIE: Let me see . . .

> . . . *And ruin your tum tum*
> *Keep away from bootleg hootch*
> *When you're on a spree*
> *Take good care of yourself*
> *You belong to me.*

IN MAKING THOUGHTFUL PROVISION FOR THE SELECTION OF A FINAL RESTING PLACE WHICH SOONER OR LATER MUST BE CHOSEN NO ONE NEED INCONVENIENCE HIMSELF FINANCIALLY BY MEANS OF THE FOREST LAWN PLAN OF MONTHLY PAYMENTS FAMILY LOTS SECTIONS IN THE MAUSOLEUM OR NICHES FOR THE ASHES OF THOSE WHO PREFER CREMATION MAY BE RESERVED AND PAID FOR OUT OF INCOME REPRESENTATIVES ARE ALWAYS READY TO GIVE DETAILED INFORMATION AND . . .

WAITER: Is that all?

JIMMY: That'll be all.

WAITER (*in hurt voice*): No dessert? The deep-dish apple pie is very good.

JIMMY: THAT'LL BE ALL.

(*Waiter shudders and then sadly totters away.*)

JIMMY: I wanted to see you, Dixie, before I left the coast. I'm going back to New York, you know.

DIXIE: Yes, you wrote and told me.

JIMMY: I was going tonight, but when you called and said you'd have dinner with me, I postponed it until tomorrow night. I wanted to tell you how sorry I was, but . . .

DIXIE: Oh, that's all right.

JIMMY: Are you going to forgive me?

DIXIE: I suppose so.

JIMMY (*impulsively taking her hand across the table*): Gee, that's sweet of you, Dixie. Gee, and I was so rotten to you, too.

DIXIE: Oh, that's all right. We'll just wash it up and forget it.

JIMMY (*drawing her across table*): Let's have a kiss then.

DIXIE (*disengaging hands gently but firmly*): No, that's cold.

JIMMY: Cold? how do you mean?

DIXIE: I mean finis. Capoot.

JIMMY (*incredulous*): Quit your clowning.

DIXIE: No, Jimmy. This is the fade out.

JIMMY: But you said you forgave me.

DIXIE: I do, Jimmy, but the rest of it is—well, it's just finished.

JIMMY: Ah Dixie, you can't mean that.

DIXIE (*taking a big breath and jumping off the dock*): You might just as well know it now, Jimmy, I'm going to be married.

JIMMY: Sure you are—to me.

DIXIE: No, not to you. (*Smiling sadly.*) Not this time anyway.

JIMMY (*angrily*): Who to? To who?

DIXIE: Jack Milton. He came out here on a big deal and I saw him and . . .

I AM THE SPIRIT OF FOREST LAWN I SPEAK IN THE LAUGHTER OF THE DUCK BABY HAPPY CHILDHOOD AT PLAY I SPEAK IN THE CONSUMMATE ART OF THE MAUSOLEUM COLUMBARIUM WHERE LIGHT AND LIFE REPLACE SHADOW AND DARKNESS I SPEAK IN THE LOVING EYES AND EMBRACING ARMS AT BABYLAND TELLING OF BECKONING HANDS AT THE GATEWAY OF LIFE AND NOW WE WILL HEAR FROM MISS ETHEL WOCKLE AGAIN.

> *A man showed me a lavalliere*
> *And he said it's yours if you kiss me dear*
> *Oh tell me—is there anything wrong in that?*
>   *(Boop-id-oop-id-oop-boop)*
> *I kissed him once and he asked for more—*
> *Next week he's bringing me the jewelry store*
> *Oh tell me—is there anything wrong with that?*

DIXIE (*continuing*): So you see, that's how it is.

JIMMY (*dully*): Yes, I see. (*Pleading.*) But you don't love him, do you?

DIXIE: Of course I do. (*Looks into Jimmy's eyes and wavers.*) I mean yes. Sure. Well, I like him a lot, respect him and admire him.

JIMMY: And you don't like me any more? Not even a little bit, is that it?

DIXIE (*taking his hand across the table*): Oh Jimmy, don't keep on saying things like that. Of course I like you. I'll always like you. But everything is different now, that's all.

JIMMY (*pushing dishes back*): Well I'm glad I'm going to New York. I couldn't stay around here and see you every day and realize you belong to somebody else without committing murder or something.

DIXIE (*brokenly*): Jimmy! Listen Jimmy, you're not really going back to New York, are you—honest?

JIMMY: Of course I am. What'll I do out here? Ache for you all the time and have you saying "Mustn't touch! Burny, burny." Besides, I haven't got any job. I've got to live. And don't ask me why.

DIXIE: Oh, you can get a job out here. You've got more brains than nine tenths of these saps that are getting by out here with murder.

JIMMY (*bitterly*): Yes, I've heard that song before. I've sung it myself, but brains have very little to do with this racket out here. It's like juggling a barrel on your feet or pulling rabbits out of a hat. If you know how to work the trick you're a movie writer. If you can pull rabbits out of a hat while you're juggling the barrel on your feet, then you're a director or a supervisor. And if you can do both and get gas on your stomach at the same time you're an executive.

... THIS IS K.F.S.G. THE CHURCH OF THE AIR BROADCASTING FROM ANGELUS TEMPLE AIMEE SEMPLE MCPHERSON PASTOR THE ROBED CHOIR IS SINGING AND EVERY SEAT IN THIS HUGE TEMPLE IS FILLED WHILE HUNDREDS PACK THE AISLES AND THE ENTIRE MULTITUDE JOIN IN WELCOMING SISTER MCPHERSON WHO IS EVEN NOW WALKING DOWN THE LONG STAIRS TO THIS PLATFORM OF PRAYER ROBED IN HER WHITE GOWN AND CARRYING AND ARMFUL OF BEAUTIFUL AMERICAN BEAUTY ROSES ...

DIXIE: Gee, I saw Aimee once. Remember, I told you—when I was dancing in Jimmy Durante's night club?

JIMMY: I remember.

DIXIE: She was investigating Broadway night life with a bunch of reporters and had just come from Tex Guinan's. They'd make a good team—Tex and Aimee, the Whoopee Sisters in Ten Minutes of Clean Fun.

JIMMY: Yea, whoopee is Guinan's religion and religion is Aimee's whoopee. Listen, let's get the words.

> *There's a long long trail awinding*
> *For all us sinners here below*
> *And its sweet and precious message*
> *Makes our sad hearts glow*
> *Oh it's not the broad broad highway*
> *To perdition and woe*
> *It's the straight and narrow pathway*
> *That we love to go.*

OH MY DEAR BROTHERS AND SISTERS THAT WAS BEAUTIFUL THAT WAS A GLORIOUS OUTPOURING OF THE SPIRIT AND NOW I AM GOING TO TELL YOU ABOUT A WONDERFUL THING THAT HAPPENED THOUSANDS OF YEARS AGO TO A WONDERFUL MAN NAMED DANIEL OH HE WAS A WONDERFUL MAN HALLELUJAH YOU HAVE ALL HEARD OF DANIEL I WANT YOU TO THINK ABOUT DANIEL TONIGHT I WANT YOU ALL BROTHERS AND SISTERS WHEREVER YOU ARE LISTENING IN TONIGHT ON THE RADIO I WANT YOU TO THINK OF DANIEL . . .

JIMMY: I know it's the best thing for you, Dixie. I'm not crazy. Look what Milton has done for you already. Why he's got them all jumping through hoops for you out there on the Colossal lot. I couldn't do anything like that for you in a million years.

DIXIE: Jimmy dear, stop rubbing it in.

JIMMY: I'm not rubbing it in, Dixie. I'm just telling you.

DIXIE: You're not telling me anything new.

JIMMY: And with what you've got and all of Milton's money and power behind you why you'll be on top of the heap in no time.

DIXIE (*suddenly*): I want to go home.

JIMMY: Now don't, honey, don't be like that.

DIXIE: Well, don't be like that yourself.

JIMMY: I'll be on the train this time tomorrow night.

DIXIE: Will you shut up for God's sake. Talk about something cheerful.

JIMMY (*bitterly*): Yeah, be cheerful. Leff klun leff!

DIXIE: You sound funny talking yiddish with that Kilkenny map for a face.

. . . YOU CAN IMAGINE HOW DANIEL MUST HAVE FELT A DEN OF LIONS IT SAYS HERE IN THE BOOK AND YOU CAN BELIEVE ME THOSE WERE LIONS THEY HAD LIONS IN THOSE DAYS NONE OF THOSE PUNY LITTLE LIONS YOU SEE OUT AT GAYS LION FARM NONE OF THOSE

MOVIE LIONS THEY HAVE OUT IN CULVER CITY YOU'VE SEEN THAT BIG LION ON THE METRO GOLDWYN TRADEMARK WELL HE WOULD JUST BE A CUB BESIDE THOSE LIONS THEY HAD IN JUDEA YOU COULD HEAR THEM ROAR FOR MILES AND THE HILLS TREMBLED POOR DANIEL I'M SORRY FOR DANIEL WHAT IS HE GOING TO DO IN THAT DEN FOR THERE IS NO WAY OUT LISTEN WHAT IT SAYS THEN THE KING COMMANDED HE DIDN'T ASK MIND YOU OR REQUEST OR SUGGEST NO SIR HE COMMANDED AND THEY BROUGHT DANIEL AND CAST HIM INTO THE DEN OF LIONS AND A STONE WAS BROUGHT AND LAID UPON THE MOUTH OF THE DEN AND THE KING SEALED IT WITH HIS OWN SIGNET AND WITH THE SIGNET OF HIS LORDS THAT THE PURPOSE MIGHT NOT BE CHANGED CONCERNING DANIEL THE KING WAS TAKING NO CHANCES IF HE HAD HAD A YALE LOCK HE WOULD HAVE PUT A YALE LOCK ON IT POOR DANIEL ALL ALONE ALL NIGHT WITH THOSE LIONS AH I CAN SEE YOU TREMBLE AND WITH MY MIND'S EYE I CAN SEE THOUSANDS OF MY BROTHERS AND SISTERS LISTENING IN TO MY WORDS TONIGHT AND TREMBLING FOR DANIEL I CAN HEAR THEM SAYING SISTER MCPHERSON TELL US QUICKLY WHAT HAPPENED TO POOR DANIEL WE HAVE TUNED OUT ALL THE JAZZ BANDS AND THE FRIVOLOUS THINGS OF THIS WORLD AND WE ARE THINKING ONLY OF YOU AND YOUR BURNING MESSAGE BUT FIRST WE WILL HAVE A SONG ALTOGETHER AND THEN I WILL TELL YOU WHAT HAPPENED TO DANIEL HALLELUJAH

> *Yes sir here's salvation*
> *No sir don't mean maybe*
> *Yes sir here's salvation now*
> *Goodbye sin and sorrow*
> *Welcome bright tomorrow*
> *For we've got salvation now*
> *I believe I believe*
> *I have faith and never more will grieve*

> *Yes sir here's salvation*
> *No sir don't mean maybe*
> *Yes sir here's salvation now.*

JIMMY: I'm going to be thinking about you on that train Dixie. All the way back to New York, alone! Three long days, four long nights.

DIXIE: Jimmy ... please!

JIMMY: And after I get back I'll be alone—going alone to all the places we used to go together, Jimmy Durante's, the Cotton Club, down to Barney's!

DIXIE (*feverishly*): Don't you think Jimmy Durante is the funniest man in the world? I just love him when he sings Down where the cows go woof woof and the little birdies ickle ickle and the little froggie yahckny yahckny.

JIMMY: And the Casino in the park where we used to sit afternoons and have tea and watch the rain outside. Oh God, Dixie, I'm going to miss you.

DIXIE (*crying*): I shouldn't have come. I shouldn't have seen you. I was a damn fool.

JIMMY (*crying*): Dixie! Darling!

WAITER (*suddenly from nowhere*): The deep-dish apple pie is very nice tonight, sir.

JIMMY: Get the hell out of here, will you?

WAITER (*plaintively*): Yes sir. (*Backs away in sorrowful defeat.*) Thank you, sir. ...

```
                                    POSTAL TELEGRAPH – COMMERCIAL CABLES
                                              TELEGRAM
```

                                                  29TH NOVEMBER
FB365 25 ALBUQUERQUE NM 835A
DIXIE DUGAN
1842 NO. LA BREA AVE
                              HOLLYWOOD CALIF
THE TRAIN WHEELS WERE SINGING ALL NIGHT
I WANTA BE LOVED BY YOU BY YOU BY YOU
BY YOU BY YOU I WANTA BE LOVED BY YOU
ALONE
                                            JIMMY

```
                                    POSTAL TELEGRAPH – COMMERCIAL CABLES
                                              TELEGRAM
```

                                                  30TH NOVEMBER
KC374 34 NEWTON KAN 745A
DIXIE DUGAN
1842 NO. LA BREA AVE
                              HOLLYWOOD CALIF
THE LITTLE CANARY DONT SING ANY MORE
THE FOLKS ASK ME WHY YOU DONT CALL AND
THE WHOLE HOUSE IS BLUE THEY WANT YOU
ONLY YOU BUT I MISS YOU MOST OF ALL
                                            JIMMY

1ST DECEMBER

```
FB656 24 CHICAGO ILL 1102A
DIXIE DUGAN
1842 NO. LA BREA AVE
                    HOLLYWOOD CALIF
MAYBE YOURE BETTER OFF OUT THERE WHERE
YOU FAW DOWN AND GO BOOM HERE THEY GO
BOOM AND YOU FAW DOWN KEITH CIRCUIT
JOKE LEFF KLUN LEFF
                              JIMMY
```

1ST DECEMBER

```
SC278 9 HOLLYWOOD CALIF 412P
JIMMY DOYLE
EN ROUTE 20TH CENTURY EASTBOUND
LETS NOT CLOWN ANY MORE MY HEART IS
BREAKING
                              DIXIE
```

NEW YORK CITY
December 3rd, 1928

DIXIE:

I won't clown any more. I've been sitting up here in my room for hours writing long letters to you and tearing them up. I was afraid you would think they were sappy or something. And then I thought of a poem by Carl Sandburg which I read a few years ago. I loved it then but never dreamed it could hit me as hard as it does now. I am copying it out for you. It will be the letter I cannot write.

The sea rocks have a green moss.
The pine rocks have red berries.
I have memories of you . . .

Speak to me of how you miss me.
Tell me the hours go long and slow.

Speak to me of the drag on your heart,
The iron drag of the long days.

I know hours empty as a beggar's tin cup on a rainy day,
  empty as a soldier's sleeve with an arm lost.

Speak to me— . . .

JIMMY.

XI

HOLLYWOOD DAILY SCREEN WORLD

PAGE FOUR THURSDAY, DEC. 20, 1928

STUDIO SHOOTING SCHEDULE—REVISED DAILY

STUDIO	STAR	DIRECTOR	TITLE	SCENARIST	STATUS
Chas. Chaplin 1420 N. LaBrea HE 2141	Chaplin	Chaplin	"City Lights"	Chaplin	Shooting
R K O (formerly FBO) HO 7780	Gloria Swanson	Eric von Stroheim	"Queen Kelly"	von Stroheim	Shooting
Paramount HO2400 5341 Melrose 11 A. M. to 1 P. M. (Fred Datig-casting	Clara Bow	Dorothy Arzner	"The Wild Party"	Sheldon-Herbert-Weaver.	Shooting
Colossal	Dixie Dugan	Josef von Nebbick	"Sinning Lovers"	Conrad Nebbick	Preparing

~~~~~~~~~~~~~~~~~~~~~~

COLOSSAL
FILM CORPORATION
Subsidiary
COSMIC FILMS, Inc.

INTER-OFFICE COMMUNICATION

To All Departments   *Date*   1/3/29

PRODUCTION #F-11—"SINNING LOVERS"
THE FOLLOWING CONSTITUTES THE
STAFF LINE-UP FOR THE ABOVE
PRODUCTION:

PRODUCER	MR. SOL NEBBICK
DIRECTOR	JOSEF VON NEBBICK
DIALOGUE DIRECTOR	JULIUS NEBBICK
ASST. DIRECTOR	MAX NEBBICK
2ND ASST. DIRECTOR	JULIUS NEBBICK JR.
UNIT MANAGER	SAMUEL NEBBICK
SOUND SUPERVISOR	BERNIE NEBBICK
TECHNICAL DIRECTOR	HUGO NEBBICK
CAMERAMEN	DMITRI NEBBICK
	MIKE DONOVAN
	(temporary)
	IVAN NEBBICK
ASST. CAMERAMEN	HENRY NEBBICK
	MENZ NEBBICK
	TIM O'RILEY
	(temporary)
STILL MAN	NICOLAI NEBBICK
PROP	PAUL NEBBICK
GRIP	OSCAR NEBBICK
ELECTRICIAN	BEN NEBBICK
SCRIPT CLERK	SOPHIE NEBBICK
CUTTER	SARAH NEBBICK

Office of Sol Nebbick, the boy wonder producer of the Colossal lot. Dead black eyes in a dead white face. A rat-trap mind, a Frigidaire heart and nerves like E strings. Director Von Nebbick and Scenarist Conrad Nebbick are discussing a new sequence for Sinning Lovers, *and coiled in his chair Sol Nebbick watches them with the cold cordiality of a cobra.*

Scenarist (*aglow with creative fire*): This gives us a great spectacle, with color and poetry and historical value. A marvelous musical pageant of the lovers of all the ages beginning with the Garden of Eden and coming down through the centuries to the present day.

Director: The old reincarnation gag. It's always good. I used it in *Ain't We Got Fun*, a Christie release. Remember, with Chester Conklin and Louise Fazenda? It was a sock.

Scenarist (*irritably*): This isn't a comedy sequence. We've got to have something big and beautiful in that spot.

Director: What's the matter with Louis Wolheim? Say, by the way, that's not a bad hunch. Louis Wolheim for Adam! Make a note of that.

Scenarist (*furious*): You've got to keep your same pair of lovers, that's the whole idea. They're reincarnated from one age to the next. You see, Mr. Nebbick, you have Dixie Dugan and Buddy Rogers—they're Adam and Eve. When you see them again they're Hero and Leander, then they're Paris and Helen, Romeo and Juliet and then the Sinning Lovers of today. Can't you see that with gorgeous scenery and costumes in technicolor, and a marvelous theme song going through the whole thing? What do you think, Mr. Nebbick?

Mr. Sol Nebbick (*regards him evilly for a moment and then presses thin bloodless hand to tortured stomach*): Hiccough!

THREE BELLS—SILENCE

In Which The Garden of Eden Is Shot with Sound and Effects on Sound Stage "A," Colossal Lot, Hollywood.

DIRECTOR: Now listen, Dixie, you too Buddy, get this! You better listen in on this, Julius. You too, Max. Hey there, Bernie! You can go down to Agua Caliente when we get finished. Paul, for God's sake. What are those things on that tree? Apples? They look like avocados.

PAUL: They *are* avocados, Mr. Nebbick.

DIRECTOR: Well, for Chrysler six! Who the hell ever heard of avocados in the Garden of Eden? That's an apple tree and I want apples on it, d'you get me?

PAUL: Ike, get some apples.

IKE: Izzy! Epples! Vos? No, not nipples, epples!

DIRECTOR: Now listen, Buddy, get this! We lap in on you standing under the tree, see? You've got an apple in your fin, see? This is the apple tree in the Garden of Eden, see? Then you look up and you see Eve. She's a swell broad, see? You take it big. Maybe you could drop the apple. What do you think, Max?

MAX: Sure, Mr. Nebbick.

DIRECTOR: Guess you'd better hold it—for the closeup anyway. You see the dame. You say to yourself, there's a hot item. That's where we cut to you, Dixie. You're lying on the grass, counting your toes or what have you. I don't care. Then you look up and see him. Hot Dog! The theme song goes right on, see? Whosit or whatever his name is, is into the chorus by this time. We're shooting him on another sound track and we put them together later. All this first part is pantomime, see? Got it?

DIXIE: When do I come over to Adam?

DIRECTOR: You watch me. I'll give you the signal. Max! Gimme some more light on that tree.

MAX: Ben! Hit that tree!
BEN: Another two thousand here!
DIRECTOR: Too much.
MAX: Too hot.
BEN: Put a silk on that broad.
MAX: I dug up that fellow for you, Mr. Nebbick. He's here now.
DIRECTOR: What fellow?

MAX: You know that fellow that does birds. I thought you'd like to have some birds whistling during this garden shot, and you know real birds, you can't depend on them, and the damn things don't sound like birds over the mike. I'll bring him over.

DIRECTOR (*eyeing sad individual with instinctive distrust*): What kind of bird are you? (*Bird man shakes his head.*)

MAX: He doesn't speak English.
DIRECTOR: What the hell does he speak?
MAX (*apologetically*): I don't really know—I can't understand him.

DIRECTOR (*furious*): Well what kind of a bird noise does he make?

MAX (*to bird man*): Bird, bird. (*Whistles.*) You know. (*To director.*) That always starts him.

BIRD MAN (*nods head with a slow smile of recognition. Slaps thighs with hands and crows.*) Cock-a-doodle-do. (*Bows all around to imaginary audience.*)

DIRECTOR (*to Max*): So that's the big bird effect you were digging up for over a week! Get him away from here before I kill him. (*Bird Man is led away crowing with growing enthusiasm.*)

IZZY (*sauntering up*): Here's the epples, Ike.
IKE: Hey, Paul, epples coming up!
PAUL: Where d'you want the apples, Mr. Nebbick?
DIRECTOR: Well for cripes—on the tree, sapadillo.
MAX: How'll we fasten them, Mr. Nebbick?

DIRECTOR: Let me see, how about some wire?

MAX: Oscar, some wire here!

OSCAR: Hey Ike! Get some wire.

IKE : Izzy! Vire!

MAX: D'you thing it looks better with three apples here and two above, or the other way?

DIRECTOR: Try it the other way. That's it! Now hold them there while I go back and look. (*Goes into camera booth and squints long and earnestly at composition.*) No, I think it's better the other way. That's it—now wire 'em up at that height—exactly. How long will we have to wait for that wire?

MAX: I guess he's getting a requisition.

DIRECTOR: Ben, save your lights.

BEN (*yelling*): REST 'EM! (*All except working lights click off.*)

DIXIE (*to colored maid*): Isn't that Mr. Milton coming over there? I better touch up my make-up. This heat has it running all over my face.

MAID: Yessum, Miss Dixie.

DIXIE: This sitting around and sitting around gets my goat.

MAID: Don't harrass yuahself honey. Miss Natchova used to say, Pheeney . . .

DIXIE: Did you know Hedda Natchova?

MAID: I wuz her maid for yeahs. Why honey, I'm older'n Cecil DeMille. Miss Natchova used to say Pheeney . . . .

DIXIE (*touching up mascara*): Where'd you get that name, Pheeney?

MAID: Well dere wuz fo'teen of us, Miss Dixie, an' when I came along Mammy wuz all run outta names so she said I'll jest call this 'un Pheeney 'cause they ain't gonna be no mo'. How dee do, Mister Milton.

DIXIE: Hello Jack!

MILTON: 'Lo darling. Can I watch my new star work? (*Hungrily.*)

God, you look gorgeous!

DIXIE (*airily*): Never saw me in a fig leaf before, did you?

IZZY: Here's the vire, Ike!

IKE: Hey Oscar, vire comin' up.

OSCAR: Is this where you want 'em, Max?

MAX: I think they ought to be a little higher.

(*They wire the apples on. This takes thirty minutes.*)

DIRECTOR (*meanwhile, to script girl*): What dialogue follows this scene?

SCRIPT GIRL (*in colorless voice between cigarette puffs*): Adam hello there you beautiful creature what are you Eve I am a woman and what are you Adam I am a man Eve what a beautiful garden you have here and what kind of a tree is that Adam oh that is the tree of knowledge of good and evil Eve give me a bite Adam oh no you mustn't touch because it is commanded that of every tree of the garden thou mayest freely eat but of the tree of the knowledge of good and evil thou shalt not eat of it for in the day that thou eatest thereof thou shalt surely die.

DIRECTOR: Who wrote that dialogue? It doesn't make sense. JULIUS! HEY JULIUS!

DIALOGUE DIRECTOR: Yes, Mr. Nebbick.

DIRECTOR: Did you rehearse Adam and Eve in this dialogue? (*Indicates place in script.*) All this mayest and eatest stuff?

DIALOGUE DIRECTOR: Sure!

DIRECTOR: Well, that's out. What kind of dialogue is that?

DIALOGUE DIRECTOR (*huffy*): Well, it's pretty good. It comes right out of the Book of Genesis.

DIRECTOR: Yeah? And we're paying Conrad Nebbick a thousand a week to write original dialogue and he cops all this old eatest and mayest stuff! This is a modern picture and I want up-to-date dialogue. Get Jimmy Gleason on this.

DIALOGUE DIRECTOR: Well, there's nothing very modern about

the Garden of Eden.

DIRECTOR: There will be when I get finished with it. (*Suddenly, with complete change of manner.*) Oh, how do you do, Mr. Milton. Here Max, get Mr. Milton a chair. (*To script girl.*) Get up and give Mr. Milton your chair.

MILTON: Don't put yourself out. I just got in from New York this morning and thought I'd come over and see how Miss Dugan is getting along.

DIRECTOR (*throwing up both hands*): Marvelous! You ought to see the rushes. Have you seen the rushes? Say, are they good! Max, are they good?

MAX: They're wonderful, Mr. Milton.

SCRIPT CLERK: She's got everything, Mr. Milton. (*To director.*) You know that closeup on the terrace?

DIRECTOR: Is that a closeup!

MAX: You sure got her angle that time, Mr. Nebbick.

MILTON: I won't be disturbing you if I sit here and watch a little bit? I like to see how these sound pictures are made—very interesting.

DIRECTOR (*laughing heartily*): Disturbing? It's a pleasure, Mr. Milton. Shall I go ahead.

MILTON: Why, certainly—don't mind me. I'm only going to stay a few minutes.

DIRECTOR: Miss Dugan? Buddy?

MAX: Miss Dugan on the set! Mr. Rogers on the set!

VOICES: Miss Dugan! Miss Dugan! Mr. Rogers! Mr. Rogers!

DIRECTOR: Stand by now everybody for rehearsal. Dixie, Buddy! Say Max, is that guy ready on the song?

MAX: Yes, Mr. Nebbick.

DIRECTOR: Orchestra ready? We're gonna run this together now for timing but we'll take them separate. Now what the hell do YOU want?

SINGER: I can't see the orchestra, Mr. Nebbick.

DIRECTOR: Well, they can't see you either so that makes it jake. Bernie, what's this guy belly-aching about?

SOUND SUPERVISOR: Well, Mr. Nebbick, he's supposed to be on the stage singing, and the orchestra's in the pit, but we have to have a dummy orchestra there because if they both use the same mike the orchestra drowns him out . . .

DIRECTOR (*muttering*): And a good thing, too!

SINGER: So this guy goes and puts the orchestra away over in the corner under another mike and builds screens around 'em and I can't see 'em.

SOUND SUPERVISOR: Well, if I didn't, they'd leak over on your mike.

SINGER: Well, how the devil do you expect me to follow the tempo?

SOUND SUPERVISOR: Are you going to start telling ME how to do this?

SINGER: Somebody ought to tell you.

DIRECTOR: Give me some screens here. C'mon screw, boys, screw and take some of these goddam tourists with you. Oh, I don't mean you, Mr. Milton.

MILTON: Well, I've got to be going anyway. See you later. (*Goes over to Dixie.*) You're having dinner with me tonight at the Cocoanut Grove. Don't work too hard.

DIXIE: I love it, Jack. I can't thank you enough.

MILTON: I'll give you a lot of opportunities to try, anyway. 'Bye dear!

DIRECTOR: Three bells. Lights, Ben. (*Electric bell makes hideous uproar, signalling for silence.*)

BEN: Hit 'em! (*Lights go on with blinding glare.*)

VOICES: THREE BELLS! THREE BELLS EVERYBODY! SILENCE ON THE UPPER STAGE.

MAX: SILENCE!
JULIUS: SILENCE EVERYBODY!
IKE: SILENCE!
IZZY: SILENCE!
DIRECTOR: Shut up yelling silence will you?
VOICE (*far off*): SILENCE OVER THERE!
DIRECTOR: All right, Buddy, all right, Dixie, stand by. This is the rehearsal. CAMERA!

(Orchestra goes into introduction. Singer in pink silk troubadour costume takes place on stage strumming lute and singing narrative to accompany Adam and Eve pantomime. Dummy orchestra in pit saws and blows noiselessly while singer watches relay of directors beating time all the way back to where real orchestra is hidden behind screen.)

SINGER:

>*Love was born in a garden*
>*In that olden day*
>*When Adam stood beneath the tree*
>*And first saw Eve so gay.*
>*The flowers bloomed, the birdies sang*
>>(bird effect in orchestra)
>*And all the world was new*
>*Now love is old, the moon is cold*
>*But I have you.*

Adam (Buddy Rogers) and Eve (Dixie Dugan) go through pantomime as directed while song continues under action. Director Nebbick decides to change the camera angle.

ONE BELL (pandemonium breaks loose)

THREE BELLS. They do it again.

Sound supervisor discovers orchestra is now one half beat behind singer and must be moved.

ONE BELL.

Three quarters of an hour elapse while they move orchestra.

THREE BELLS. They do it again.

Monitor man reports weird noise interference coming into the play back.

ONE BELL. The mikes are moved, new deadening put on floors and the scene is rehearsed three more times. Interfering noise continues. Sounds like an airplane far off but it doesn't seem to come any closer or go any further. An hour's search is made and they finally discover an electrician asleep and snoring above the set.

DIRECTOR: We're going to go this time everybody. This is the take. Stand by! Three Bells!
MAX: THREE BELLS. SILENCE!
VOICES: SILENCE EVERYBODY! SILENCE! SILENCE!
JULIUS: QUIET ON THE UPPER STAGE!
MAX: THIS IS THE TAKE! STAND BY EVERYBODY!
IKE: SILENCE!
IZZY: SILENCE!
SOUND SUPERVISOR: On the red!
MAX (*to Assistant cameramen*): Lock 'em up.
(*Camera men are locked up in their sound-proof tanks and assistants stand by to signal when cameras are in "sync."*)
ASSISTANT CAMERMAN: On the blue . . . up to speed!
(*Tell-tale lights, red and blue, show mikes are open, the Sound Department and the three cameras are synchronized and running. Dixie and Buddy go through their pantomime while singer and orchestra record and all around them dozens of workmen, electricians, carpenters, property men, technicians and visitors stand rooted in par-*

alyzed silence.)

SINGER:

> *Now love is old, the moon is cold*
> *But I have you.*

Adam sniffs apple.
Polishes it on lion skin pants.
Sees Eve—takes it big.
Holds apple and poses for count of five.
(*Director signals.*)
ONE BELL.

STILL MAN (*to Adam and Eve*): Hold it for the still. (*Levels camera on them and Director goes into booth to check up on scene for dissolve, comes out swearing.*)

DIRECTOR: Who the hell wired up those apples?

MAX: What's the matter, Mr. Nebbick?

DIRECTOR: What's the matter? Go and look at it. They're all wired too high. They're out of the camera. That might as well be a eucalyptus as an apple tree.

MAX: W'ell, I put them where you told me. I sure did.

DIRECTOR: Dammit! We have to do the whole scene all over again.

MAX: Once more, everybody!

JULIUS: Everybody back on the set.

VOICES: ONCE MORE EVERYBODY! BACK ON THE SET! ON THE SET EVERYBODY!

MAX: THREE BELLS.

VOICES: SILENCE! SILENCE EVERYBODY! QUIET ON THE UPPER STAGE!

(*And then—the noon whistle blows!*)

Max: Lunch, everybody! Back on the set at one sharp for the take on this scene. Well, we've done pretty good this morning don't you think, Mr. Nebbick?

Director (*straightens bow tie and spanks script girl playfully*): Damn good. I didn't think we'd get anything done.

XII

HOLLYWOOD,
8th February, 1929.

MISS NITA DUGAN,
439 FLATBUSH AVE,
BROOKLYN, N. Y.
NITA DARLING:

We finished shooting today. They've got it all up in the cutting rooms now and most of it is on the floor. The rushes keep looking worse and worse. Von Nebbick has been giving all the closeups to Chiquita who got second lead. She's the little Mex who used to be on Buelow's string, but not any more. They merged him into the alley and he's down in Poverty Row now doing quickies. Chiquita lost no time taking a run-out power on him and moved right in on von Nebbick with her It and everything. The net is closeups, lots of closeups for her—but every time they cut to me I'm going away some place.

Five weeks of it Nita. On the set and made up at nine o'clock in the morning. Then hours and hours of sitting around and rehearsing and taking the same scene a dozen times. And then the last two weeks every night till ten, eleven and twelve o'clock; sometimes two and three in the morning, and then back on the set the next morning at nine dead for sleep with big flats under your eyes and three cameras finding the lines in your face like a bank teller looking for silk threads in a dollar bill.

Jack Milton has been running around like a wet hen trying to rush the picture so we can get married and hop off on our honeymoon. He keeps on muttering in his long blue whiskers about Hawaii and Honolulu and a trip around the world or maybe it's a trip to the moon. I don't know. When the time comes I'll just shut my eyes and say I do and shove off. Still, he's damned sweet Nita, and turning the whole place upside down for me out here, so I guess I'll have to go through with it, though sometimes I feel like that bimbo in the Bible who sold out for a mess of pottage. I guess that was something like a New England boiled dinner. Imagine giving in for that!

When Jack isn't running around merging studios and firing a lot of broad-hipped executives who got that way from sitting pretty, he's on the set with me or in the projection room looking at the rushes. Sometimes he thinks they're swell and sometimes he isn't sure. Well, he doesn't know anything about pictures, but who the hell does? Answer me that one. Maybe Sol Nebbick. He's the only one that isn't always yapping around here. He just appears miraculously from nowhere, nursing his indigestion, watches the action a while and either grunts or says lousy, and then disappears again.

Don't ask me what the picture looks like. I haven't the slightest idea. I've seen pieces of this and heard bits of that and then we'd retake the scene and throw the retake away and use the worst pieces of the other negative and junk that and retake it again until everybody is so mad and so dizzy they don't know whether they're working on *Sinning Lovers* or *Uncle Tom's Cabin*.

Sarah Nebbick, the head cutter, told me today they'd have the negative cut and assembled the first of the week and we'd have the answer print—that's the first complete print from the edited negative—in time for the secret preview which will be a week from Monday night. She doesn't know the house but it will be some out of the way place where they specialize in horse opera. The studio will slip the picture in and try it on the dog before the real opening. Maybe there won't be any real opening—maybe it'll be so bad they'll throw it all in the ash can. And then again maybe it'll be a wow. Nobody knows. Neither do I. But Mickey, who wrote the songs and has seen a lot of the rushes, says the talk around the studio is that it's all set and in the bag. God, Nita, I hope so. It means so much to me. I'll wire you or call you long distance as soon as I find out. Keep your fingers crossed.

Your dizzy sister,
DIXIE.

P.S. I suppose you haven't seen Jimmy, have you?

~~~~~~~~~~~~~~~~~~

<div style="text-align: center;">
ALVARADO THEATRE
LAURA LaPLANTE
<i>in</i>
"HER BIG NIGHT"
WITH SOUND
ALSO BIG FEATURE PREVIEW TONIGHT
</div>

~~~~~~~~~~~~~~~~~~

POST MORTEM

SCENE: *On the sidewalk outside the Alvarado Theatre, Alvarado Street, opposite Westlake Park, Los Angeles.*

TIME: *10.30 P. M.*

(*The preview of* Sinning Lovers *which started at 8.30 has just finished. The mourners who occupied the last two rows reserved for the Colossal executives and cast have sought the open air and stand huddled in dejected little groups, talking, talking, talking.*)

Boys, it looks like we laid an egg.

They sure weren't having any, were they?

I told you that damned lovers of history gag was a wet smack.

Yeah? It was all right if you had shot it the way I wrote it.

Yeah? If I had shot it the way you wrote it they wouldn't have just sat there and taken it. We'd have had to fight our way out of the theatre.

What did you think about it, Julius?

Who, me? Sonk!

Still, you can't tell by one audience. It got a lot of laughs.

Yeah? But they were in the wrong place.

The trouble with this picture is what I've said all along. Supervisors!

Well, I don't think it was so bad. I mean I think we can salvage a lot of it.

Sure, we can save the sound track and make another picture to run with it.

Well, I never saw such a bum job of cutting. You could take that whole cabaret sequence out and never miss it.

I didn't do the numbers, baby. I just cut 'em.

I'll say—with an axe!

Where's Dixie? Wasn't she here?

I saw her sitting away back with Milton. They ducked out just before the lights went up.

I guess she feels pretty bad, poor kid.

Well boys, I'm going home and roll in.

Who's for home?

Going my way, Max? Give you a lift.

Goom bi, slaves—see you in the factory tomorrow.

Oh, hello Abe! How did it hit you?

Right in the pit of the stomach. Oof!

Dixie's apartment. Midnight. Telephone rings. Dixie, who has been pacing up and down makes a dive across the room and grabs it.

OPERATOR: On your call to Brooklyn New York, we are ready.

DIXIE: Hello, hello! Who is this? Oh, is this you Nita? Hello darling, this is Dixie. What time is it there? Three o'clock? It's just twelve here. Midnight. I can hear you so plain. Just like in the next room. Oh Nita, I don't know how to tell you what happened. We had the preview tonight. Everything went wrong. It was too long and it was cut bad and the sound didn't work half the time. It was just a mess. I don't know what they're going to do with it. I was so sick I couldn't sit until the finish. I walked out on it at the end and came home. Jack was with me. What? MILTON. He came home with me and we had a row. A row!—a FIGHT. Jack and I. I'm NOT always fighting, but he said it was a flop and even if I was all right on the stage this proved that I didn't get over in pictures, and I asked him what he thought ought to be done and he said he was for putting it on the shelf and forgetting it and charge it off to experience and I says to him that's all right for you to talk about the money that way but how about me and my time and all the grief and the heartaches I put in it. And he said he couldn't help that—that was the business and there was no use in throwing good money after bad. The company was in the bag for half a million dollars already on the picture. What? A HALF A MILLION! I know it's a lot of money. That's what Jack said too but I told him I didn't cost all that. They were in half of it on the other one before they even started with me and he said well the stockholders don't give a damn who was in it or what. All they are interested in is dividends and if it was his money it would be something else again but it wasn't. It belonged to the corporation and he had gone as far as he could go. And I says well what are you going to do then and he says what do you want me to do and I says what difference does it make what I want. I don't think the picture's so terrible that it couldn't be saved. He says well I don't know anything about pictures but the audience tonight told you that they didn't want it. They were walking out on it and I says well won't you try to do something about saving it. He says I'd like to but I can't. I've gone ahead and spent all this money on my own responsibility and I says well I thought it was your money all the time and he says don't be silly. I just represent the men who have got their money in this—the banks and other big corporations—you don't think I'd gamble half a million dollars of my own money in the show business, do you? I may be crazy but I'm not a complete damnfool, and then I says well what are you going to do Jack and he says well there's no use in kidding yourself Dixie. It's a flop and the cheapest and most sensible thing to do now is to wash it up and forget it. I'll go out to the studio tomorrow and settle the whole thing up and you pack up and come back East with me and we'll get married and go away on a nice trip and forget all about the movies. What do you say? And I says well what can I say Jack? You're the boss. I certainly haven't any money to put in it, but if you really loved me it looks to me like you wouldn't quit cold like this before it's really had a chance. Do you remember, you wanted me to do the same thing in Atlantic City just because the tryout was a flop you wanted me to jump the show and run away with you and get married and then you know what happened. Jimmy stuck to the job—dug up some more capital, fixed the show up and we came into New York and it was a hit, and he says well how much money did it make and I says well it didn't make much money and he says well that's it—there you are. And I says well what do I care if it makes money or not. Lots of good pictures don't make money and Jack says so far as the bankers are concerned if it doesn't make money it's not a good picture and I says what about *Caligari* and he says I never saw it and from all I've heard of it I never want to see it and that hasn't anything to do with the subject anyway. We're talking about *Sinning Lovers*. I saw that. I saw it tonight and it's a flop and then I says to him, in other words I say it's spinach and I say to hell with it. Is that what you mean? And he says well that's putting it bluntly but that's the idea. We won't talk about it any more tonight but I'll see you in the morning when you've had a good night's sleep and you feel better. A good night's sleep, Nita! Can you feature that? Then he said goodnight and went out as matter of fact as though he had just brought in the groceries. A good night's sleep! I've been pacing up and down ever since he left. I put the call in right away. Did I wake you up? What? I bet Ma was scared to death when the telephone rang at three o'clock in the morning. How is she? That's good. Don't tell her anything about it yet. Tell her everything is getting along fine. Pa too. What'll I do, Nita? What? I KNOW Jack is sensible but I hate sensible men. What? It ISN'T time I got sense. I want sense when I'm so old it doesn't interfere with my fun. Sure I've been having a lot of fun working like a dog from nine o'clock in the morning until midnight for weeks, then to have it flop like this. It'll be all over Hollywood tomorrow. I can't bear to think of facing them out at the studio. I don't know what I'm going to do. What? I KNOW I'm on long distance. WHAT? I KNOW IT'S COSTING A LOT OF MONEY BUT DAMMIT I'VE GOT TO TALK TO SOMEBODY. What? I'm not crying. I'M NOT. Well, what if I am? What do you expect me to do? Laugh and clap hands and yell whoopee? WHAT? All right Sis. I guess you're right . . . All right, I'll try . . . All right . . . I'll write to you tomorrow. You write to me. Soon as you hang up. Air mail. Please. Please, I haven't anybody left but you. I feel so alone out here. All right Sis. 'Bye. What? Nothing. I just said goodbye. Goodbye darling. (*Dixie slowly hangs up the receiver, throws herself on bed, buries her head in the pillow and cries quietly, steadily. Telephone rings.*)

    Dixie (*blubbering*): 'Lo, whu-whu-what?

    Operator (*cheerily*): The charge on that call will be twenty-two dollars and seventy-five cents for thirteen minutes.

(From The Hollywood Daily Screen World—Feb. 20th)
MAY SHELVE "SINNING LOVERS"

John Milton, Chairman of Production Board Cosmic Films said to be disappointed with preview of Dixie Dugan's first starring vehicle—Colossal Executives mum.

```
                    POSTAL TELEGRAPH — COMMERCIAL CABLES
                              TELEGRAM
```

FEBRUARY 20TH
EN ROUTE THE CHIEF EASTBOUND
DIXIE DUGAN
1842 NO LA BREA AVE
            HOLLYWOOD CALIF
WAS CALLED BACK SUDDENLY TO NEW YORK
TRIED TO REACH YOU ALL DAY YESTERDAY
AND TODAY BEFORE TAKING TRAIN BUT YOUR
PHONE DIDNT ANSWER STOP PLEASE WIRE
AND TELL ME YOURE NOT ANGRY WITH ME
STOP SURE YOU MUST REALIZE WISDOM OF
NOT GOING AHEAD WITH PICTURE STOP WIRE
ME CARE CHIEF AT ALBUQUERQUE OR GALLUP
STOP WHEN ARE YOU COMING TO NEW YORK OR
SHALL I COME BACK FOR YOU STOP ALL MY
LOVE
                                    JACK

Offices of Sol Nebbick, Colossal lot. Dixie Dugan, paralyzed with awe and cold with terror has just entered and stands waiting for Mr. Nebbick to look up from his reading and recognize her.

DIXIE (*finally*): You sent for me Mr. Nebbick.

NEBBICK (*looking up slowly and allowing a faint flicker of recognition to ripple his mask*): Oh yes. (*Sharply.*) Never mind sitting down. I won't keep you very long. I had a talk with Milton before he went back East about *Sinning Lovers*. I suppose you know how he feels about it?

DIXIE (*trembling*): I know. He told me.

NEBBICK: He told me too, and when he got finished telling me I told him.

DIXIE (*bravely*): Well, I suppose there's nothing more to be said about it.

NEBBICK: Not much. Report tomorrow morning at nine o'clock on stage "A."

DIXIE (*astonished*): For what?

NEBBICK: For the retakes of course.

DIXIE (*slowly*): Retakes! Did you say retakes?

NEBBICK: I've taken von Nebbick off the picture. Another director starts tomorrow on a schedule of retakes. I'm changing some of the production numbers, throwing out the others, rearranging the sequences and cutting the running time down to one hour and ten minutes. It's all laid out.

DIXIE: But Milton said he was going to junk it.

NEBBICK (*slowly*): I told Milton if he wanted to save the money he's got in this thing to get on the train and go home and turn it over to me and let me handle it alone. He replied that the appropriation for *Sinning Lovers* was exhausted and there wouldn't be any more money. I asked him what he wanted to do and he said put it on the shelf so I said all right. That's the way he left it.

DIXIE: But I still don't understand.

NEBBICK: I saw the picture in preview. It was lousy but there's plenty of good stuff in it. All it needs is cutting and re-making in parts and re-editing and it's got a good chance. I know pictures. Milton doesn't. (*With an evil smile*.) In fact, I think so well of its chances that I'm going ahead with it.

DIXIE (*bewildered*): Maybe I'm crazy. When? How? Where?

NEBBICK: I don't know why I'm telling you all this except that I want you to go in there tomorrow and give us the best you've got. But it's this way. When Milton said he was going to junk the picture I told him my reputation as a producer was involved and I'd rather dig up enough money to finance the re-making of it myself and release it independently than take such a black eye right at the beginning of my connection with the new merger. So he named a price and told me to wire him in New York if I could swing it. I wired him today that the deal was closed. Tomorrow morning at nine. Stage A., Miss Dugan. That's all. (*To Beautiful Young Thing at door*.) Send von Nebbick in here. And bring me some more bicarbonate.

~~~~~~~~~~~~~~~~~~~~

```
POSTAL TELEGRAPH — COMMERCIAL CABLES
              TELEGRAM
TELEGRAMS              CABLEGRAMS
TO ALL                  TO ALL THE
AMERICA                    WORLD
```

```
                           FEBRUARY 25TH
SC352 53 NL HOLLYWOOD CALIF 1103 P 25
NITA DUGAN
439 FLATBUSH AVE
                           BROOKLYN N Y
ITS ON AGAIN STOP MAKING RETAKES NIGHT
AND DAY STOP FINISHING UP END OF WEEK
AM SO TIRED IM SILLY STOP THIS TIME IT
HAS GOT TO BE GOOD STOP BEAR DOWN ON
```

YOUR PATRON SAINT FOR ME STOP MINE IS
IN CONFERENCE LOVE
                                    DIXIE

FEBRUARY 26TH
FL 735 22 DL BROOKLYN NY 1020A 26
DIXIE DUGAN
1842 NO LA BREA AVE
                        HOLLYWOOD CALIF
THE WORLD IS A BIG CAFETERIA WHERE GOD
HELPS THOSE WHO HELP THEMSELVES STOP
THAT GOES FOR PATRON SAINTS TOO LOVE
                                    NITA

FEBRUARY 27TH
SB 456 19 HOLLYWOOD CALIF 435P 27
NITA DUGAN
439 FLATBUSH AVE
                            BROOKLYN NY
I HAVE CORNS ON MY HIP FROM CARRYING
TRAYS IN YOUR OLD CAFETERIA WISHING YOU
THE SAME LOVE
                                    DIXIE

POSTAL TELEGRAPH — COMMERCIAL CABLES
TELEGRAM

FEBRUARY 27TH

NA840 16 NEW YORK NY 1230P 27
DIXIE DUGAN
1842 NO LA BREA AVE
                      HOLLYWOOD CALIF
NO WIRE FROM YOU IN CHICAGO NO MESSAGE
FROM YOU HERE WHAT DOES IT MEAN
                              JACK

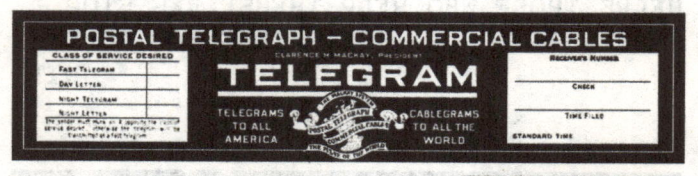

POSTAL TELEGRAPH — COMMERCIAL CABLES
TELEGRAM

FEBRUARY 28TH

SC355 2 HOLLYWOOD CALIF 856A 28
JACK MILTON
67 WALL STREET
                    NEW YORK CITY N Y
GUESS
                             DIXIE

XIII

COLOSSAL
FILM CORPORATION
Subsidiary
COSMIC FILMS, Inc.

INTER-OFFICE COMMUNICATION

To All Departments   Date   3/11/29

Pursuant to a request from the Hays office that the title *Sinning Lovers* be changed so as to forestall any possible objections from the censors, the picture will be released under the title *Loving Sinners*.

SOL NEBBICK.

~~~~~~~~~~~~~~~~~~~~~~

(From The Hollywood Daily Screen World—March 14th)
"LOVING SINNERS" BOOKED INTO GRAUMAN'S CHINESE
House Will Be Dark While Elaborate Prologue Is Prepared.

~~~~~~~~~~~~~~~~~~~~~~

(From The New York World—March 26th)

The Screen.

Enter Dixie Dugan.

Dixie Dugan, starring in "Loving Sinners," a singing, dancing, talking picture, opens at the Astor Theatre next Friday night simultaneous with its premiere in Hollywood. These double "world premieres" for Hollywood, and Broadway are the newest racket.

Our Hollywood spies report this picture as something unusual. Dixie Dugan was caught only a few months ago in one of the movie raids on Broadway after clicking in "Get Your Girl" in a short but snappy run at the Klaw Theatre last season.

POSTAL TELEGRAPH — COMMERCIAL CABLES
TELEGRAM

MARCH 29TH
SB 462 24 HOLLYWOOD CALIF 956A 29
NITA DUGAN
439 FLATBUSH AVE
                    BROOKLYN CITY N Y
THEY ARE THROWING ME TO THE LIONS
TONIGHT IN SENSATIONAL WORLD PREMIERE
GRAUMANS CHINESE THEATRE ALL HOLLYWOOD
WILL BE THERE PRAY FOR ME
                              DIXIE

POSTAL TELEGRAPH — COMMERCIAL CABLES — TELEGRAM

MARCH 29TH

FC255 31 BROOKLYN N Y 320P 29
DIXIE DUGAN
1842 NO LA BREA AVE
        HOLLYWOOD CALIF
YOUR PICTURE OPENING IN NEW YORK ALSO
TONIGHT NEWSPAPERS FULL OF PUBLICITY
YOUR NAME IN BIG LIGHTS OVER ASTOR
THEATRE ON BROADWAY WE WILL BE THERE
LEADING THE CHEERS
        NITA

POSTAL TELEGRAPH — COMMERCIAL CABLES — TELEGRAM

MARCH 29TH

NA374 22 NEW YORK N Y 243P
DIXIE DUGAN
1842 NO LA BREA AVE
        HOLLYWOOD CALIF
IN THE MOB AT THE ASTOR THEATRE TONIGHT
PULLING HARD FOR DEAR LITTLE DIXIE
DUGAN WILL BE THAT DIRTY BUM
        JIMMY DOYLE

```
        POSTAL TELEGRAPH – COMMERCIAL CABLES
                    TELEGRAM
```

                                    MARCH 29TH
NC533 42 NEW YORK NY 1156A 29
FELTS PALACE OF FLOWERS
HOLLYWOOD BLVD
                        HOLLYWOOD CALIF
DELIVER FIFTY DOLLARS WORTH AMERICAN
BEAUTY ROSES DIXIE DUGAN TONIGHT
PREMIERE GRAUMANS CHINESE THEATRE AND
ENCLOSE CARD SAYING DEAR DIXIE COMMA
WARM HANDS COLD HEART DASH BUT WISH YOU
ALL THE LUCK IN THE WORLD SIGNED JACK
MILTON
MAX SCHLING FLORIST SAVOY PLAZA NEW
YORK

(Denoting time lapse of twenty-four hours)

(From The Los Angeles Times—March 30th)

WOW OF A SOUND FILM ON SCREEN
Dixie Dugan in "Loving Sinners" Sets New Pace For Talkies.

Clever Plot, Songs and Dance Capture at Premiere

Grauman Show Dazzles at The Chinese

BY EDWIN SCHALLERT.

Say it with singing, dancing harmony. That's the new language of the screen. Rhythmically, spiritedly, pathetically and gayly, "Loving Sinners" will make you believe it, even if you don't.

This is a picture! It's an eye-opener and an ear-opener. It's right off the grill of the latest in sound development, and, oh, what a wow! . . .

(From The Hollywood Daily Citizen—March 30th)
"LOVING SINNERS" IS CINEMATIC TRIUMPH
Dixie Dugan Thrills Blasé Hollywood
BY DORIS DENBO

Through a drizzling rain and in spite of it, executive and professional Hollywood turned out last night to attend what probably will be rated as the greatest evening's entertainment Sid Grauman has offered in his new Chinese Theatre, Dixie Dugan in "Loving Sinners" Colossal talking triumph, and a prologue which surpasses anything Grauman has ever attempted . . .

~~~~~~~~~~~~~~~~~~~

(From The Los Angeles Times—March 30th)
"LOVING SINNERS" REVELATION IN THE WORLD OF SHOWMANSHIP
BY MONROE LATHROP

Hollywood had another long evening of thrills last night provided by the champion thrillmaster of the show world, Sid Grauman.

Thrills for those (a) who love to be a part of the hurly burly of massed humanity; (b) for those who react like moths to a blaze of light; (c) for those who revel in the fame, fortune and admiration that movie wealth bestows; (d) for the sightseers (with umbrellas) who get an awesome eyeful of the cinema idols; (e) for those who gorged upon one of Grauman's plethoric banquets of entertainment; (f) for the champions and devotees of the triumphant talkies.

Item (f) refers to the sensational Dixie Dugan who overnight stepped into the white light that beats on the throne of stardom with her first vocal superfilm "Loving Sinners". . .

~~~~~~~~~~~~~~~~~~~

(From The Los Angeles Examiner—March 30th)

"LOVING SINNERS" PREMIERE MARKS NEW MILESTONE IN FILM HISTORY

BEAUTY FINDS EXPRESSION IN MADAME MODE'S LATEST

Another brilliant premiere at Sid Grauman's Chinese Theatre with fashion, celebrities, kleig lights, huge sun arcs playing against towering jets of steam, a dazzling pyrotechnics of colored beams that glowed over half of Hollywood and a gloriously gowned and groomed audience comprising the creme de la creme of the beauty and chivalry, the wit, wisdom and the charm of Moviedom.

White gowns, pale blue, with rich dark furs, were the tones most exquisitely expressed in chiffons and velvets. Green, sparkling with crystals, and peach and apricot tones in satin were among the lovely gowns. Mere description is vague because line and grace can scarcely be described adequately. But pretty women, distinguished men, Madame Mode's latest creations, all go to make a picture of fashion and beauty and interest to be held no place outside of Los Angeles.

Among those present last evening were:

MRS. SOL. NEBBICK, gold and brocade wrap over gold lace gown.

MRS. HARRY RAPF, white ermine wrap over white satin evening gown.

MRS. JOSEF VON NEBBICK, green chiffon bouffant gown with matching velvet wrap trimmed with white fox.

MRS. BERNIE HYMAN, ermine wrap over gold chiffon gown.

MRS. LARRY WEINGARTEN (Sylvia Thalberg), blue satin and lace frock with white wrap trimmed with white fox.

MRS. PAT ROONEY, red chiffon with ermine coat.

MRS. CECIL DE MILLE, red velvet evening gown under brocaded velvet wrap.

MRS. WILLIAM DE MILLE (Clara Beranger), deep blue taffeta Parisian frock with sable wrap.

MRS. FRED NIBLO (Enid Bennett), white satin gown with Burgundy velvet wrap.

MRS. KING VIDOR (Eleanor Boardman), watermelon chiffon frock with ermine and sable wrap.

DIXIE DUGAN, Adrian designed frock of white tulle trimmed in a leaf pattern of sequins with white gardenias worn at hiptop, short cape of tulle.

RENEE ADOREE, white chiffon evening gown under black chiffon velvet coat with white ermine collar and cuffs.

JOAN CRAWFORD, white brocade frock with white gardenias under ermine wrap.

AILEEN PRINGLE, black velvet ensemble silver trimmed, with silver evening cape.

DOROTHY SEBASTIAN, yellow souffle, crystal trimmed with ermine wrap.

NORMA SHEARER, Delft blue taffeta ensemble with silver trimmings.

MRS. JAMES GLEASON (Lucille Webster), black lace and chiffon gown wrap of black velvet trimmed with white fox.

LILA LEE, corn colored crepe,

chiffon frock with corsage in three shades of orange, cloth of gold wrap.

CLARA BOW, emerald green chiffon frock under wrap of white ermine.

LUPE VELEZ, red brocaded wrap over matching chiffon gown.

MARY PICKFORD, coral velvet cape with white fox collar over matching chiffon dress.

ALICE WHITE, pale green chiffon embroidered with pearls and brilliants, green velvet wrap.

JANET GAYNOR, white chiffon trimmed with crystal beads, silver wrap with black and white fox fur collar.

GLORIA SWANSON, embroidered jade chiffon, with matching wrap.

MRS. HAROLD LLOYD, white georgette, corsage of white gardenias, ermine coat.

MRS. JACK WARNER, pink beaded chiffon, wrap of pink moire, corsage of pink camelias.

POSTAL TELEGRAPH — COMMERCIAL CABLES
TELEGRAM

MARCH 30TH

NC422 56 BROOKLYN NY 906A 30
DIXIE DUGAN
1842 NO LA BREA AVE
        HOLLYWOOD CALIF
YOUR NEW YORK OPENING WAS A RIOT AND WORLD TIMES AND HERALD TRIBUNE CARRY RAVES THIS MORNING STOP WRITING AIR MAIL TODAY ENCLOSING ALL CLIPPINGS STOP THEYRE MARVELOUS YOU SLAY EM BABY WE ARE ALL PROUD OF YOU SAW BOTH JACK AND JIMMY AT PREMIERE LAST NIGHT BUT DIDNT GET CHANCE TO TALK TO THEM LOVE
        NITA

(Full Page Ad From Variety, Week of April 10th)

CRASH!!!!

went all records for a single day's business in any Pittsburgh theatre when LOVING SINNERS rolled up Saturday gross at the Stanley $2,000 over best previous figure for any house!

SMASH!!!

CHICAGO—DIXIE DUGAN in LOVING SINNERS smashed all house records at Roosevelt first week. Opening day of second week surpasses opening of first week, making new history for this theatre. —Max Balaban.

BIFF!!

First week at New Grand Central, St. Louis, K.O.'d all previous records in spite of opposition from three other sound attractions.

SOCKO!

$50,000.00—ADVANCE SALE—$50,000.00 Astor Theatre, New York—lines for two blocks all day long on Hollywood Boulevard, Grauman's Chinese Theatre.

DIXIE DUGAN
IN
LOVING SINNERS

is rolling up a national record never approached in the picture business

It's a COLOSSAL Super Sound Epic
"COLOSSAL Leads in Sound"

SOME NEWS ITEMS FROM LOS ANGELES AND HOLLYWOOD NEWSPAPERS

Dixie Dugan was signed yesterday to a long term contract with sensational salary increase by Sol Nebbick, who will produce independently but release through Colossal.

It is rumoured the Beverly Hills estate of the late Hedda Natchova has been leased by Dixie Dugan, the new Colossal star.

The Pig 'n Whistle is featuring the new Dixie Dugan sandwich.

Dixie Dugan, the sensational Colossal discovery, will be mistress of ceremonies at the regular Saturday Tea Dansante at the Roosevelt Hotel tomorrow.

It was "Dixie Dugan Night" last night at the Montmartre where the new Colossal star judged the regular weekly dancing contest.

The subdivision formerly known as La Brea Pits has been renamed Dixie Dugan Vista by the enterprising firm of realtors, C. C. C. Tatum.

~~~~~~~~~~~~~~~~~

HOLLYWOOD, CALIF.
April 12th, 1929.

NITA—YOU BIG STIFF:

I love you and I'm crazy with excitement and I feel marvelous. Boy, if I felt any better I'd be a national menace. I'd be a scourge. Baby, I thought I knew Hollywood, but I was just a little stepchild with my nose flattened against the window looking at the pies and cakes inside. And that was only a few weeks ago. Now I'm inside with a pie in each fist and a face full of cake and everybody saying oh, so *you're* Dixie. Well, I'm so glad to meet you. I saw your picture and you're marvelous—won't you come to tea or dinner or breakfast or a cocktail party or a bull fight or what am I offered. Hot cat! Wait till I brush a few butlers off me. Where am I? Oh doctor! Is it a boy or a Rolls?

There are at least fifty Hollywoods out here, Nita; the lowest one away down in the sub-basement next to the boilers and then one by one going up and up to the roof garden where the stars sit in rose lights and munch caviare and flip cigarette butts down on an adoring world. I've been tossing my share over the rail this last few weeks and boy how I love it. This is la vie. Get away closer!

You should see me rolling around in a town car making important noises through speaking tubes at an imported chauffeur all dressed up like a Moose on parade. You can rent anything out here—even Mooses, or is it Meese? Mail pouring in asking for my picture or a few kind words or a check for a nursing home for waltzing mice or could they name the triplets after me or is it true that my second husband is the King of Siam. I have two secretaries—one who has nothing to do but say yes and the other one no. Me, I have nothing to say. My publicity representative speaks for me. He also writes stories about my lowly origin, how I started at the age of five in a factory in Brooklyn, working fourteen hours a day making those little straw hats for horses, and how through sheer pluck and determination and grit and will power and love for my mother and devotion to the flag, I fought my way up and up to the heights but still remain the simple sweet little home girl at heart—an ideal for all American womanhood who realizes fame is only a bauble and who secretly yearns for a little nest full of kiddies and things. I don't allow him to show me any of the god-awful stuff any more—I busted all my combies laughing.

The clips you sent me from New York were great and reviews have been pouring in from all over the country—marvelous! I read them and wonder who this Dixie is they're talking about. It can't be the same little punk who only a few weeks ago was pacing up and down in a panic wondering if her option was going to be renewed. What a difference! How quick you go up in this business. And down too, I guess. Express elevator service. No stops between the tenth and thirty-fifth. This car going to the basement only—crockery, tinware, remnants, odd lots. Especially odd lots. You certainly see them around this town. Violinists who came out here to play symphonies sitting on sets scratching Hearts and Flowers by the hour. And now with the new yappies they haven't even a set to sit on. Hard-faced mothers from all over the country dragging their little girls around to studios ready to sell them out to anyone from an assistant director to a property man just to make a little money off them. Agents with young girls tied up under long term contracts at a hundred a week leasing them to studios for ten times that and pocketing the difference. Hundreds of pretty kids from small towns, nice family girls, church girls, even society pets going broke and desperate, waiting tables, selling notions, peddling box lunches on the street corners— I could tell you stories that would curl your hair. For instance, you know a lot of people in the East retire and come out here to the coast to spend their last few years. When they die their relatives back East usually want the body shipped home and the railroad companies won't take the corpse unless there's a passenger on board accompanying it, so every year a couple of hundred tickets for railroad passage to eastern cities are turned over to an organization here that helps stranded girls and the girls ride back east with the bodies. Tie that one!

When I see you I'll tell you a lot of other things that you wouldn't believe if I wrote them. Would you believe that Tom Mix has a marble tennis court? And the great mystic Dareos who advises all the stars is an Irishman with a brogue you could cut with an axe? And he has a crystal that is about as clear as a beer bottle and his shrine looks like the office of an eye, ear, nose and throat doctor minus the couch—and it is in the Bank of California Building with hours on the door 12 to 5 p. m. and 7.30 to 9 p. m., so you can see he has his ghosts punching the clock. I wonder if he docks them if they show up late with a hangover. I didn't tell you, Nita, but when I was feeling so low I thought I would go for one of those seances and I gave him three bucks and he told me I was psychic and not to make any important changes for the coming year, and that I had been deeply in love and would be again. He certainly must have reached away out into the astral world for that one. Show me a girl that hasn't been in love and won't be again and I'll show you a bearded lady. But it's a great racket. How the dames fall for it. If I were a man I wouldn't be anything else but a mystic. But I'd get a better crystal.

And now the scene changes. We are back in the studio with Dixie Dugan, the new Colossal star who has a special hamburger steak named after her at the Brown Derby on Wilshire Boulevard and who lunches in the Colossal executive bungalow and has tea with Mary Pickford and Douglas Fairbanks and is the week end guest of Marion Davies in her beach house down at Santa Monica.

Pickfair, where Mary and Doug rough it with nine or ten house servants and three or four on the grounds, overlooks all the Beverly Hills and most of the Pacific Ocean. The house used to be a club house—two long wings in a V shape with a flagged terrace in the V. Kind of an English-looking place with shingled walls and no one to wait on the table except the head butler named Albert and an assistant butler and an assistant butler for the assistant butler. I couldn't help thinking of our town house in Brooklyn, Nita, and how Mary and Doug would have envied us our Ole, imported specially from Sweden and installed in our basement at great expense to all the tenants. The table is set every night for ten or twelve whether they come or not—I'm talking now about Mary's table, not ours. And Mary sits at the head of the table and Doug sits to her left. Well, we had tea on the terrace and Mary was charming to me. I call her Mary. And Doug was nice too. And the lawn was green and sloped away down the hill for what seemed days and the bees buzzed in the flowers and the birds warbled in the trees and I looked down on Hollywood and tried to remember what it was like to be down there, hungry and out of a job. It was quite an effort.

But Marion Davies' beach house, Nita! Just a little dove-cote right on the ocean. Only twenty-five bedrooms, Nita, but it's home and we love it. Two garages with six cars and chauffeurs to match. Chefs, butlers, footmen, maids, valets all connected to push buttons that you can reach from anywhere you sit, stand or lie. It's run like the Ritz would love to do things if they could afford it. But don't get the idea, Nita, that it's swank. Everything is so unbelievably marvelous, so beautiful, so rare, exquisite and in perfect taste that no one has to waste any time trying to impress anybody. Just to give you a slight notion, darling. The upper hall is papered with this Zuber paper, with marvelous reproductions showing the history of America. I asked one of the thirty or forty guests who was trying to get up enough energy to look at the ocean if he had any idea what that stuff cost and he said well, about four hundred and fifty dollars a set, and then I went around and counted the sets, Nita, and there were about twenty-five of them. Twenty-five times four hundred and fifty. *You* do it! And believe it or not, it's all finished with a special finish so that guests can lean against it in wet bathing suits. Guests are certainly taken care of in this country. Marion was nice to me, too. And what a darling she is—and smart! Baby! I'd like to have a brain like hers. It doesn't seem fair to be so pretty and have so much sense too. Well, maybe when I have this aged face lifted I can get them to boost the old brain up a few notches while they're at it.

Tomorrow I am flying in a private Sikorsky Amphibian on a party to Agua Caliente down in old Mexico for a bit of diversion. Heigh Ho! How is the dear old B.M.T? Give my love to all the rush hour sardines and tell them to cheerio that maybe in their next incarnation they will be real sardines and then they won't have to stand up.

DIXIE

(From The Los Angeles Examiner—April 16th)
BREAKFAST CLUB PLANS GALA ENTERTAINMENT

There will be two guests of honor tomorrow morning at the Breakfast Club. Dixie Dugan, the new meteoric star of "Loving Sinners," the Colossal Film triumph that is sweeping the country, and Teddy Page, New York millionaire sportsman and young society aviation enthusiast who is out here looking over airport sites for a new trans-continental air route. Mr. Page has just returned from a brief pleasure trip to Agua Caliente where he took a small party of friends in his Sikorsky Amphibian, the same ship, incidentally, in which he flew across the country from New York last week.

XIV

NEW YORK CITY.
April 14th, 1929.

DEAR DIXIE:

I saw your picture at the opening in New York and was thrilled with it and more than thrilled with you. Did you get my flowers? I had them sent to you at Grauman's Chinese Theatre. I haven't heard from you. I knew you were angry but I hoped you would get over it. Can't I do anything to get back in your good graces? I thought everything was fixed up between us and I was walking on air for weeks. Just to think that I would have the loveliest, cutest darlingest little girl in the world for my very own. And then this came along. Honestly, I thought I was doing what was best. I didn't want you to come out in a picture that would hurt you. I didn't care so much about the money. You know that. How could I tell that Nebbick would make such a wonderful picture out of the mess I saw? He certainly is a genius. And I know how you must feel about me and the way I almost wrecked your career, even though I helped you start it. You must admit that.

I miss you dreadfully. I never was in love before, honest. I know you believe all I think about is money but that isn't true. I think more of you than anything in the world. I'd do anything for you. I don't know why I'm writing all this except maybe because I'm so full I have to pour it out. I've had a lot of time to think back here. Everything I see reminds me of you. Every paper I pick up I see your name, Dixie Dugan. It seems every theatre I go by your picture is in the lobby, your name is in the lights, I can't get away from it. I thought at first when you didn't answer my wires I would just forget you. I've tried awfully hard. I am still trying, but I can't. Won't you write to me? Write and tell me you forgive me and everything will be once more the way it used to be. I had such a wonderful trip mapped out for us; all through the Orient and then Europe. I wanted to show you Paris. All my life I've wanted to be in Paris in the spring with someone I loved. You don't know what it means to want something all your life, to have it just within your reach when you had despaired of ever getting it, and then to have it snatched away from you. I know this must sound very silly and sentimental. I'd probably tear it up myself if I kept it until tomorrow but I'm going to send it to you because I want you to know just how I feel.

I was so happy with you just those few days in Hollywood. I'm so lonely here without you in New York. I had a beautiful apartment leased for us; five rooms with a terraced roof garden on the twenty-fourth floor of a new building overlooking the East River. It was up in the tower and the terrace was on all four sides. You could see almost all of Manhattan Island at your feet; the Hudson River to the west, the East River clear up to Hell Gate and down to the Battery. I walked all through it yesterday. I could see you in every room. I'll never be so happy again as when I found this place for us. And I don't think I could ever be sadder than I am now when I realize I will never see you in it.

Or won't I? Is there a chance? If only you would write or wire me and say, come back and get me Jack, I'd be on the next train. Train nothing, I'd charter a plane. I've watched every mail. All day long I'm snatching telegrams away from my secretary and opening them myself, hoping they are from you. If only I could see one signed Dixie! Just one little yellow telegram saying: "It's okay Jack. When do we start on that trip?"

Write to me Dixie darling. Wire me, phone me, anything, but let me hear from you. Don't torture me.

Always, with all my love,

JACK.

APRIL 17TH 1929
NA244 180 HOLLYWOOD CALIF 1253P 17
JACK MILTON
67 WALL STREET
NEW YORK CITY
YOUR LOVELY LETTER RECEIVED DREADFULLY
SORRY YOU FEEL THE WAY YOU DO I DONT
DESERVE TO HAVE YOU FEEL THAT WAY YOU
ARE EVERYTHING THAT IS NICE AND SWEET
AND WHILE YOU MAY THINK NOW I AM WHAT
YOU WANT WE WOULD BOTH LEARN VERY
QUICKLY THAT IT WOULDNT WORK OUT AND
THEN YOU WOULD BE WORSE OFF THAN YOU
ARE I AM VERY SELFISH THOUGHTLESS AND
FOR ABOUT NINETY FIVE PERCENT OF THE
TIME A DEVIL ON WHEELS YOU MIGHT THINK
IT VERY CUTE FOR A WHILE BUT YOUD GET
DARNED SICK OF IT AND I WOULD GET SICK
OF YOU BEING SICK AND WE WOULD BOTH
HAVE CHRONIC INDIGESTION AND SPEND ALL
OF OUR TIME SNAPPING AT EACH OTHERS
HEELS NOW WE ARE GOOD FRIENDS IM NOT
MAD AT YOU ANY MORE AND YOU WONT BE MAD
AT ME AFTER A WHILE AND WE CAN BOTH BE
VERY FOND OF EACH OTHER AND THAT WILL

```
BE NICE MUCH NICER THAN YOU PUNCHING ME
IN THE NOSE AND ME KICKING YOU IN THE
SHINS TILL DEATH DO US PART
                                    DIXIE
```

~~~~~~~~~~~~~~~~

(From Walter Winchell's column, N. Y. Evening Graphic, April 19)

... O. O. McIntyre is phffft ... H. I. Phillips is phffft ... F. P. A. is phffft ... Paul T. Frankl has designed a modern Scotty with square hips to fit his furniture ... Jimmy Doyle, back on the Evening Tab after a short parole in Times Square and Hollywood, and Betty Byrne, moom pitcher gel on same rag, are That Way....

~~~~~~~~~~~~~~~~

HOLLYWOOD, CALIF.
17th April, 1929.

NITA DARLING!

I am parked out here on my patio, getting a lot of useless information from a book called "Believe It Or Not." One of the tid-bits for instance is an item about a Mr. Neils Paulsen of Upsala, Sweden, who died in 1907 at the age of 160 and left two sons, one nine years old and the other 103 years old. It doesn't say what he did with the rest of his spare time at home. He should have met Madame de Maldemaure just a few pages previous who gave birth to one child the first year, twins the second year, triplets the third year, quadruplets the fourth year, quintruplets the fifth year and the sixth year, so says the book, the good woman bore six children. I'll say she was good. Twenty-one children in six years! Then she called it a day. Bored, probably. It's a swell book, Nita, but incomplete. It needs a chapter about the Breakfast Club out here in Hollywood. Believe it or not, you wouldn't believe it if you didn't see it. To begin with, here is their motto:—

        F V N E M?
        S V F M
        F V N E X?
        S V F X
        O I C V F M N X!

Try miltgrossing it and then you'll get it. The first lines are really:

        HAVE WE ANY HAM?
        YES WE HAVE HAM

Puzzle out the rest of it if you haven't anything worse to do, which I hope you have.

It's ten a. m. and I've just come back from a party out there. Try to imagine getting up at dawn to go to a party, which is all over at ten o'clock in the morning. The same morning! I was a guest of honor. Co-guest with me, and sharing with me the riotous roses flung by an applauding multitude—what the hell am I talking about. Well, anyway, co-guest of honor with me was Teddy Page, *THE* Teddy Page of the Page millions, of the Page Polo Ponies—look under P in the social register, look under the Ritz Bar in Paris. Look under the bed. What have you got? Teddy Page. A fourteen-room pent house on Park Avenue, twelve hundred acres at Cold Spring Harbor all under intensive cultivation, entirely devoted to the raising of whoopee. Three airplanes, Nita. He piloted one out here from New York by himself with ten guests aboard, two paid pilots and a steward. He told me he kidnapped the steward from Sloppy Joe's in Havana and smuggled him into Miami on a rum-runner. He's only thirty years old, Nita, his clothes fit him everywhere, and when the coat collar gets dusty he gives the suit to his Jap and buys three more. Handkerchiefs made to measure—and it would be much cheaper to use ten-dollar bills. Reeks with money, darling, but inoffensively. Blow some my way, Teddy. He dances, he talks, and he's been out here less than a week and all the Hollywood females are in a panic. Me too, Nita. Plus. My god, and why not? Looks, money, brains, position, youth, and full of hell. What else does a girl want? This girl doesn't want anything else. I decided that the first time I met him. I was invited to join a party he was taking down to Agua Caliente in his Sikorsky—flew down and flew back—and then the next time I saw him where should he be but sitting right next to me at the Breakfast Club this morning. It seems to me I started out to tell you something about it, or did I? I'm all mixed up. Every time I look for a word I find a Page. Joke! Awful! His first name is Teddy so everybody calls him Teddy. Nice, ain't it? Sounds a little bit of all right. Teddy, Teddy, Teddy, Teddy! I'm used to it already. I'll tell you who he looks a little bit like. William Haines. Only better looking. Kind of sassy, but unspoiled if you know what I mean. Maybe he bats around too much but I can snap him out of that. Oh you can, can you, says you. Sure I can says I. I'm getting very serious now that I'm a star. I'm acquiring a sense of importance, besides, a girl can do wonders for a man if she loves him. Where did you read that? Well, it's true. Mickey, that's my theme song pal—I tell him he's so hot he themes (talkie lisp)—well anyway, Mickey says Teddy's got an international reputation as a chaser and a hell-raiser in general, that he's always in scrapes but I can see why. It's only because he hasn't met the right kind of a girl. I really didn't seek this nomination but I'm going to step right up and take it just the same. I think he likes me, Nita. We had lots of fun at the Breakfast Club. That's a local organization which meets every week and entertains visiting celebrities or something. They all get together at eight o'clock in the morning. It's out near Griffith Park. They sit around a horseshoe table and sing songs and eat ham and eggs and have a lot of fun. The whole thing is broadcast, which I call the height of optimism. Imagine anybody getting up at eight o'clock in the morning to tune in to a radio program. Imagine anybody thinking anybody would do it. Well, they do stranger things than that at the Breakfast Club. One of the first things they do is all sing the Ham and Egg song. It's the tune of Tammany. Try to imagine two hundred and fifty men and women sitting around a table at the indecent hour of eight o'clock and singing as loud as they can to the accompaniment of a brass band a song like this:

> *Oh you Ham*
> *Oh you Eggs*
> *I like mine fried golden brown*
> *I like mine fried upside down*
> *Oh you Ham*
> *Oh you Eggs*
> *Flip 'em, flop 'em*
> *Flop 'em, flip 'em*
> *Ham and eggs.*

After that, Mr. DeMond, the toastmaster, yells, Hello Ham, and they all yell Hello Egg, and then he gives them a little speech of welcome to the Shrine of Friendship, this temple of idealism and sentiment. Welcome, says he, in the spirit of the Breakfast Club's golden shovel, and then he digs under the table and comes up with a little shovel and explains how this is used to bury all mistakes. It looks rather small, I says to Teddy, and he says keep quiet, maybe you'll learn something, and then Mr. DeMond comes up with a little oil can and says, I welcome you in the spirit of the oil can which smooths over all troubles and lubricates the wheels of progress or something like that, and after that has time to sink in he comes up with a hatchet and says, I also welcome you in the spirit of this buried hatchet. By this time it looks like a notion counter but he goes right on with a lot of announcements to which no one listens. The only one I remember was an announcement to the effect that the Academy of Czecho Slovak Culture will be inaugurated at Bovard Auditorium with a special program of typical songs. For instance, I says to Teddy, and he says how about I faw down and go Slovak. And I says Czech! Well after that, we got along just beautifully. So when the *Sea Song* came along we were right in the mood for it. They do it this way. The guests and members put their arms around each other's shoulders and when they are all linked together they sway in a long line from right to left and back again keeping time to the song. So Teddy had his right arm around my shoulders and I had my left arm around his neck and we swayed back and forth. It was a silly song but it felt like a national anthem before we got finished. Here are the words:

> *Sea, Sea, Sea,*
> *Oh why are you angry with me*
> *Ever since I left Dover*
> *I thought the boat would go over*
> *Dear oh dear,*
> *I've a queer sort of feeling in me*
> *If I once reach the shore,*
> *I shall say au revoir*
> *To the Sea, Sea, Sea.*

I had to untangle my arms from around Teddy's neck soon after that—much too soon—because he had been introduced by the toastmaster who went on at great length about his interest in aviation and how he had come out to the coast to look for an airport. At which point Teddy whispered to me, that's a lot of apple sauce. I came out here looking for you, and I says, contact. And he says how did you hear that, that's a flying expression, and I says I've got a colored maid named Pheeney who's always finding an excuse to say Miss Dixie, I'd like to go out tonight and contact some gin. He was still laughing when the applause stopped and he suddenly realized he had been called upon to talk and they were all waiting for him to get up. So he did and made a cute speech about the future of aviation and civic pride and airports and how glad he was to be with them and then he sat down beside me and wiped the perspiration off his forehead. The only thing that makes me happy about this whole thing, said he, is that you're next. And then was I in a panic? You don't mean I have to get up and make a speech do you, and he says either that or juggle or do flying splits. They expect something from you. And sure enough, while he was still talking about it, I heard the toastmaster say Colossal star, little beauty, talented girl, sensational triumph, *Loving Sinners*, here today, and a lot of cheers and yip yip and Teddy was pushing me up on my feet. So I thanked them kindly and wondered what the devil was next. I opened my mouth and nothing came out, so I thanked them kindly again, and then suddenly I realized this sort of thing couldn't go on indefinitely, and Teddy whispered, why don't you sing them a song which was a ducky notion, so I did—the theme song from *Loving Sinners*—and then I did a dance for them and they were all steaming, especially Teddy who had never seen me pick it up and strut it around. After I sat down he said, listen to them applaud. It's like an earthquake. And I said, you must never say that out here on the coast. It's always a fire out here. And he says do they really have quakes out here and I says if they do, and mind you, I said IF, it's very very unusual, and not polite to take notice of it, and then I told him the story Eddie Sutherland told me at one of his parties one night. It seems when he married Louise Brooks he brought her out to the coast. She had never been out here before and didn't know anything about these little quakes, so one night they were sleeping and one came along and shook up the house which is on the side of Laurel Canyon. All the dishes fell off the sideboard and the pictures off the wall and Louise turned to Eddie sleepily and said, "Eddie, behave yourself, will you." And I says to Eddie after he told the story, "Bragging again, aren't you?"

There was another song about this time, a quartette of Hollywood millionaires had to get up and sing *Hallelujah I'm a Bum* and pretty soon everybody was singing the choruses with them. I suppose you've heard it:

> *Rejoice and be glad*
> *For the springtime has come*
> *We can throw down our shovels*
> *And go on the bum*
> (Chorus)
> *Hallelujah, I'm a bum*
> *Hallelujah bum again*
> *Hallelujah, give us a hand out*
> *To revive us again.*

There are a whole lot more verses, always winding up with Hallelujah I'm a Bum, Hallelujah Bum again. I think one of the cute ones is:

> *I went to the door*
> *And I asked for some bread*
> *And the lady said bum bum*
> *The baker is dead*

I couldn't help but get a kick out of Teddy throwing back his head and singing *Hallelujah I'm a Bum*—he and his three airplanes, and a Bond Street tailor and a couple of banks and a steamship line and a railroad company. And I pictured myself as Mrs. Bum—Mrs. Hallelujah Ima Bum, At Home—Hardly Ever—To Nobody.

The Breakfast Club went on with a lot of speeches and compliments about Teddy and myself and how happy they all were to have us as guests and meanwhile we talked and talked and he told me all about roughing it along the Riviera in his steam yacht, and I told him all about Hollywood and what a dangerous place it was for girls under eighteen and men over forty—that's how I found out how old he was. Kinda cute of me wasn't it, Nita. And then I told him about meeting Chaplin at tea in Henry's and how Chaplin spent all of his time at the table totaling up the ads in the New Yorker trying to figure out how much money they made every week. And then he told me about the time Chaplin met Paderewski, and they didn't have hardly anything to say to each other because all the time Chaplin was looking at Paderewski's hands and Paderewski was looking at Chaplin's feet.

Teddy brought me home in his Mercedes. It was so long I could hardly see the chauffeur through the fog on Los Feliz. And I'm to have dinner with him tonight. Then tomorrow we're going to fly out over Death Valley just for fun. Nita dear, he doesn't know it, but I'm flying right now. I haven't had my feet on the ground since I met him. This is the real thing Nita. If this is love, I'm going to love it. What's going to become of me? I hope so.

DIXIE.

(From The New York Evening Tab—April 24th, 1929)
(By P & A: A. T. & T. transmission)
"SO HAPPY I CAN'T TALK"—

That's what Dixie Dugan, Colossal star, giggled yesterday after Park Avenue's pet playboy, Teddy Page, celebrated conclusion of marriage ceremony with impetuous bear-hug that made her gasp. They were wed by Roger Foley, justice of peace, at Las Vegas, Nev. where Teddy eloped with his Dixie in his own huge Sikorsky Amphibian. This is telephoned photo of couple a few minutes after the ceremony. Honeymoon will have to wait, Dixie said, as I am working on a production. Teddy just laughed in his gay, masculine way, so you may be sure he will have something to say about it too.

(From The N. Y. Times—April 25, 1929)

 The William K. Pages sailed suddenly for Europe last night on the Leviathan. They refused to discuss the elopement of their son Teddy with Dixie Dugan, the movie star. But it is common gossip that young Page by this escapade has finally estranged himself and that he and his young bride will not be welcomed in the ancestral home. It will be remembered Teddy Page was reported engaged to Joan Devore, beautiful young society heiress. This match was near and dear to the hearts of the Page family. When informed last night of his parents' sudden departure just as he was about to bring his new bride east to meet them, Teddy Page replied "We don't care. Dixie and I would be happy together on a bare rock in the middle of the Pacific." To which remark Dixie acquiesced gaily and with a roguish smile added "and don't think we haven't got one reserved, in case." If Broadway, Park Avenue and Wall Street rumours are to be believed, the young couple might just as well go out to their rock now and settle there.

The End

(From the N. Y. Daily News, June 7.)

MARRIED, BY JIMMY!

MAYOR JIMMY WALKER officiated last night at wedding of Dixie Dugan, talkie star, and Theodore de Peyster Page, clubman, polo hope, and aviation enthusiast. Here's the wedding party at dinner in the apartment of Quarles Smith, the new talkie magnate. L. to r.: Nita Dugan (bride's sister), maid of honor, Mayor Walker, bride, bridegroom, Mrs. Walker. And, of course, every film fan knows the peach on the right.

Messrs. Simon and Schuster
invite the attention of
The Reader
to this new novel
"Society"
by Mr. J. P. McEvoy
published
Nineteen hundred and thirty-one
Three eighty-six Fourth Avenue
New York

Mauboussin
New York Paris

To
ALORS

I

                        LAS VEGAS NEW MEXICO
THE DUGANS
439 FLATBUSH AVENUE
BROOKLYN NEW YORK
THE BABY WAS MARRIED TODAY TO A
SWEET BOY WITH LOTS OF JACK STOP
RUSH COPY WHAT EVERY YOUNG GIRL
SHOULD KNOW TO MRS TEDDY DIXIE DUGAN
PAGE UP IN THE AIR AND WHAT I MEAN
                                    DIXIE

~~~~~~~~~~~~~~~~~~~~

                        BROOKLYN NEW YORK
MRS TEDDY PAGE
LAS VEGAS NEW MEXICO
WE ARE ALL CRAZY WITH JOY AND DYING
TO SEE YOUR NEW HUSBAND STOP WHEN
YOU COME EAST INVITE US TO THE RITZ
STOP MEANWHILE REMEMBER YOUR OLDER
SISTER AND KEEP AN EYE PEELED FOR
SOMETHING IN PANTS NOT OVER EIGHTY
WITH SOFTENING OF THE BRAIN
HARDENING OF THE ARTERIES AND
YEARNING TO HAVE A LITTLE FEMALE
PATTERING AROUND THE OLD TOWN HOUSE

ON FIFTH AVENUE STOP WILL PATTER OR
PITTER TO ORDER AND AM IN NO MOOD TO
DICKER

              NITA

~~~~~~~~~~~~~~~~~~

            Agua Caliente, Mexico.

Dear Nita,

 The new husband and I are down here in Old Mexico spending our honeymoon, as I understand it is still called in the old-fashioned circles where I used to circulate. Teddy is a darling, a darling, a darling, a darling. Handsome, and rich and young and full of hell, just the type I would cast for the husband of Dixie Dugan. And just what I would get for you if there was another one, but there aren't any more Teddys. Just the same though I will keep a sharp lookout in this new society jungle and if I see an old rogue elephant with good ivory I'll do my very best to bag him for the dearest sister and the swellest gal in the world. You know it makes me feel rotten sometimes to think that I get all the breaks, and you don't get any, but maybe now that I have my foot in the door I'll be able to do something for you in a big way.

 This wouldn't be a bad place to start operations. Agua Caliente means hot water, and HOT is the word. Racing and gambling all day, lickering and loving all night—if all the rest of Old Mexico is like this, the great white father in Washington did us dirt, when he didn't let Villa take us over. The place is full of young bloods, rich and careless and handsome, most of them belonging to a polo crowd down here with George Dixon who owns the string of horses that have been cleaning up the track this season. We got very yippy together—Teddy and I, and Dixon and his gang, one of whom is an international ten goal man, whatever that means, and a house guest on his enormous ranch where Teddy and I are invited next week to continue our honeymoon. The polo boy carries his own string of ponies around with him in a special train, which gives you an idea of the way the Dixon's mob strew it about. Would you like a polo boy, Nita? I'll do what I can for you. He went right on the make for me—didn't seem to mind that I was on my honeymoon. Teddy didn't either. Seemed flattered if anything. Well, maybe I'll learn.

For the time being however, I am so dizzy that I don't know whether I'm riding or flying. Teddy's society patter is a new routine and so far I don't know where the laughs are. I hear about Newport, and Aiken, and White Sulphur, and the Old Girl, and Hell-on-the-Hilltop and closing the town house and opening the country house, or maybe it's the other way, and there seems to be a little shooting-box in Scotland, and a couple of yachts lying around collecting barnacles in the Sound—one of them is practically a canoe—just a skeleton crew of six or eight—I gather they do the marketing in that for the other boat which is an old scow according to Teddy with a crew of twenty, all brass buttons and brass rails, and brass cuspidors and brass hats and the crew speaks only to the captain, and the captain won't speak to anybody, and the family doesn't dare to cross him or he will run the damn boat on the rocks and quite frequently does. In fact it seems from Teddy's disgusted remarks that is where the boat spends most of its time, especially if there is a big party dated up for a cruise to Nassau or Havana or the Riviera. If this sounds cock-eyed as I retell it, you can imagine how it sounds to me, whose longest boat ride up to now has been on the Staten Island ferry, and who is called upon now to sit around in a two hundred dollar suit of pyjamas on a dear delightful bed with a panting new husband and decide between kisses whether we shall dash over to Antibes on the old scow, or take the suite de grande luxe on the Ile de France, and poke around Paris while I pick up a few trifling Chanels. And I used to think a Chanel was something you got greased to swim across.

Anyway I'll let you know what it's all about as soon as I find out. All I know now is that Teddy has a mother who is an old bulldog with a pearl collar, who sits on the doorstep at Newport and bites anyone who tries to get in. Her favorite pastime is chasing the new rich down Bellevue Avenue and off Bailey's Beach. This of course doesn't take all of her time because she has the energy of a dozen maniacs. So when she isn't raising Hell with her servants she is raising Hell with her family, which consists as nearly as I can guess of Teddy, two daughters and Teddy's father, who was married for his money, and has millions, and millions and millions in Oil Companies, Railroads, Automobile Factories and Banks, here and abroad.

The older daughter is called Serena Page, age 18, and at present one of Miss Chapwell's choice backward students who will be brought out and unloaded on society at great expense (Teddy's father's) in November when the big annual deb unloading season opens in New York. You see how fast I'm learning. I didn't know November was anything except football season, but I'll know it this year, because Teddy says I'll have to be at the Ritz when the debut comes off, because I'm a young society matron now, and I am in the Page family, which because of Papa's millions and Mamma's blue and very acid blood can sit in the golden horseshoe at the Opera on Mondays. It seems the rest of the week is a total loss and not to be spoken of in polite society—why, I don't know. Why, a lot of things I don't know. But when I find out I'll tell you. If I ever find out. When I ask Teddy why do you do this and why do you do that, he answers, how do I know, I do it because it's done. Done?—done by who I says. Everybody who is anybody he says, and who is this anybody I says. You'll find out he says, wait until you get back East and meet the Old Girl, and Aunt Polly and Aunt Julia, and sit through a few formal thirty-six cover dinners at Hell-on-the-Hilltop. And what is Hell-on-the-Hilltop, says I? That's home, says Teddy. Home sweet home—or one of them anyway—forty-six rooms, fourteen baths, three dining-rooms, a ballroom, a picture gallery, and not a laugh in the place. That's why I stay away from it as much as possible. That's why I'm here. But we'll both have to go back some day and meet the family and then you can see for yourself.

So that's how it stands now. After our honeymoon we are going back East to meet Teddy's father and mother and sisters and cousins and aunts, all of whom are quite insane he tells me and will make me very glad to get on the boat and go to Paris, and we'll be lucky if they don't trail along, says Teddy, and if they do says he, we'll push a few of them overboard. The aunts especially says Teddy. How about the sisters I asked him. Oh, they're in school he says and they can't get out, and a good thing, too, because Serena the older one is a wet smack and dumb as a duck, and the younger one Patricia, is only sixteen but it takes a personal maid and a private detective to keep her from running away with chauffeurs, grooms, night club doormen, elevator starters, Roxy ushers—anything that will get her away from home and school, and especially society which she hates with a great hate, and I don't blame her. She sounds all right to me I says, I'll bet I'll like her. She'll like you says Teddy, and the old man will like you too. How about your Mother I says. Don't worry about her says Teddy. She doesn't like anybody. She'd bite herself only she knows she'd get blood poisoning. Serena won't like you either. Neither will Aunt Polly, and neither will Aunt Julia, and none of their friends will like you. I can see where I have a swell life cut out for me says I. Oh, we'll have lots of fun says Teddy. Keep your chin up. If they bark at you, bark back. Anyway you married me. You didn't marry the family. I wonder, I says. I bet I did and I don't know it. Well, I don't care Nita. Teddy is swell. I don't have to sleep with Aunt Polly. They may scare me to death in Newport, and all up down the Riviera, but I'll try not to let them know it. If they get too hard, I can get hard too. I didn't kick up my heels in the chorus without learning to kick a few shins if necessary, and I've been back stage on Broadway and in Hollywood, man and girl, and I've yet to be photographed in the daisy chain.

DIXIE.

~~~~~~~~~~~~~~~

<div align="center">Miss Chapwell's School, Ltd.

New York, N. Y.</div>

Dear Dixie,

I am sneaking this chance in school to write to you. I was going to write to you from home but Mother caught me, and said I was not allowed to write you until she had learned more about you. I told her I knew a lot about you already because Theodora's aunt invited Theodora and I to go with her to the Rialto to see you in your picture "Loving Sinners" on Saturday afternoon, because that is the only day we are allowed to go to matines, and when I told Theodora you were married to my brother she was livid with jealousy, and Mother said jealous of what, and I said you wait until you see Dixie in pictures. She can sing and dance and has the sweetest haircut, and I'm going to have my hair cut that way too, and Mother said you'll do nothing of the sort it's bad enough for one member of the Page family to disgrace us getting mixed up with a show girl, and don't let me catch you going to any more pictures she's in, and what you see in all these vulgar pictures is beyond me anyway, and from now on you shan't see any more, so I kept quiet after that but made up my mind to write to you first chance I got and tell you how much I liked you in the picture and how crazy all of us girls in the school are about you and how envious I am of you out there in Hollywood with all those swell looking stars, and me cooped up in this stupid place where they won't let you wear high heels or jewelry or even decent clothes, nothing but uniforms like we were convicts or something and bottle green too of all colors. Believe me I tear it off when I get home in the afternoons and get into something gay and high heels too, the highest I can find at Delman's.

I'm dying to hear all about Hollywood and how Teddy met you and if you're going to make any more pictures and if you think I could get into the movies or on the stage like Fifi Lambier who is in "Fifty Million Frenchmen," or do something exciting because I'm sick of this school and lessons and you can't do this and that isn't done, and wait until you're out and all the lip I have to take from Serena just because she's two years older and coming out this winter. My God you'd think the world was coming to an end just because she's making her debut. Mother has even promised to let her have Pierre and the Hispano for her own and up to now Mother wouldn't have let Pierre drive the Prince of Wales. This summer I'll be lucky to get Cassidy, the third chauffeur, and the old Ford station wagon. Well, Serena needs all the help she can get and I tell her so too when she gets too overbaring, because she has about as much chance marrying first year out as I have to be Queen of the Rumanians. Honestly Dixie I had three times as many bids from Groton, Hotchkiss and Pomfret boys for the holiday dances and was allowed to go to only two of them and with a different boy the second time, because the old dingbat told Mother Cyril, the Pomfret boy, was rushing me just because he tried to leave her waiting in my car and sneak me off in his. Well she was too wise and she couldn't be bribed and she couldn't be coaxed, so I had to go home with the old dingbat and this cute boy just dying to take me to Childs for bacon and eggs at daylight. What kind of a life is that to lead? Do you blame me for wanting to get away from it all and come out to Hollywood with you. Please write and tell me all about it. I'll be passing out until I hear from you. Have you ever met Clive Brook? Some of the girls prefer George Bancroft, but Clive Brook's smooth technique when he makes love is what keeps me awake nights. I know I'd just pass out if I ever met him. Well, some day I will. I'm not going to stay cooped up here and submit to all this forever. Do you blame me? Here comes my French mademoiselle with a hatfull of irregular verbs. Mon Dieu how I hate all this. Say hello to Teddy for me, and tell him I said he's got more luck than sense to get a girl like you.

All my love. Toodle oo,

PATRICIA.

<div align="center">~~~~~~~~~~~~~~~~~</div>

NEW YORK CITY.

DEAR SON,

I suppose you read in the papers that your Mother and I were sailing to Europe upon hearing of your elopement with Dixie Dugan, the movie star, and that we were very angry about the whole thing, and especially put out because you didn't marry Joan. The truth is, I'm at the town house with the girls, and your Mother has finally stormed down to the Aiken cottage with a psychoanalyst and a trained nurse and all the hysterics she couldn't unload on us. It was she who had her heart set on you marrying Joan. As for me, I had just about decided to stop paying off chorus girls, manicurists, cloak models and night club hostesses and let you go to Hell and stay there. I hope now you have settled down. From all I can hear Dixie will probably make just the kind of a wife you need. I hope she can do something with you. I never could. Is she going on in the movies or are you both coming back East and settle here? You can go into any of my factories or branch offices, or any of my banks, here or abroad. You can have any kind of a job you want if you will work at it. Let me hear from you. I don't expect miracles, but if you stop helling around and drinking and do buckle down to something serious, I'll be more than glad to get back of you and Dixie with everything I've got.

DAD.

<div align="center">~~~~~~~~~~~~~~~~~</div>

DEL MONTE, CALIFORNIA.

DEAR NITA,

Well here I am, but where am I? I'm sitting in a private car, one of three, on a side track after an all night run and a party every inch of the way from Los Angeles. There is a lot of out-doors outside and pretty soon we are going to get a lot more because we are waiting for a fleet of motor cars to take all of us up to Dixon's Ranch, high up in the hills of Monterey. Some of us will walk out of the cars here, but most of us will have to be syphoned. What a party—what a night—what a head. Let me see if I can jot down some of it real fast before we push off, because I understand where we are going is twenty miles from the nearest post office and most of it straight up in the air. So you won't be hearing from me until after this Ranch party which if it keeps on going the way it started will probably wind up with bacon and eggs in a mad house.

Dixon took quite a shine to me in Agua Caliente and besides he is mixed up in some big way with Teddy's father, something to do with coal mines which incidentally supply most of the coal for the railroads which my polo boy owns a big hunk of. Hence his private car which is hooked on behind ours and then there is another one hooked on behind his with brass beds and valets and maids, and chefs, and polo players and movie gals, and a little bar in every car.

Seriously I am beginning to get worried about Teddy. I never saw anybody drink the way he does. And this gang of Dixon's is a hard riding, hard drinking bunch. I have been trying to slow him down a bit, but what chance have you got, every time you turn around there is someone standing there holding up a bottle like the statue of Liberty. I thought I had seen drinking in New York and Hollywood, but that was only a little Scotch each morning—a little gin each night. Here it's champagne, and champagne and champagne, cases of it in the aisles, cases of it under the beds—one stateroom full of it with Corsets sleeping in the middle of it trying to keep some sort of guard over it. Corsets is Dixon's licker secretary on these parties, she also keeps track of his horses, jockeys and trainers, and the Ranch Hands, consisting so she tells me of thirty real cowboys with feathers on their wrists, a retinue of twenty-eight servants, every one a different nationality, a guest house of twenty-two rooms, and twelve baths, a Ranch House forty-six rooms and eighteen baths, set in the middle of a hundred thousand acres of mountain ranges, and eighteen miles from the lower Ranch House where the superintendent lives.

I asked her what this party was going to be like, and she said she didn't know, as everyone of them was different. I can tell you about some of them, says she, and also I can tell you a lot about a lot of things you are meeting up with for the first time and I says I wish you would and then she says, well I've been in this social secretary racket for fifteen years and I'll tell you as much as I think will help you, because I can see right now you've got a lot to learn. Just don't try to learn it all at once says she. Come to me when you want to know something and I'll try to steer you. Well tell me something about these people, I says. Who are they? Who is Dixon? Where are we going? How long do these parties last? What do we do when we get there? Do you know anything about Teddy's family? I can't make head or tail of them. I just got a letter from his kid sister. She wants to run away from Miss Chapwell's school, whatever that is, and come out to Hollywood. I wrote and told her she was crazy to think of it. She wired and said she was coming anyway, to look out for her. Suppose she does—then what? The family will blame me. What have I married into anyway? Is Teddy's mother the old hellion he says she is—is Teddy's father so rich and important? If so, how? And why and where and who is Aunt Polly and Aunt Julia? I'll tell you all about it on the way up to the Ranch says Corsets. We ride up a narrow trail road with only two wheels on the ground, and what I can tell you of your Aunt Polly and Aunt Julia will make the drop down to the valley look inviting. There is only one thing I want to warn you about before I forget it. You know your Teddy was engaged at one time to Joan Pratt. I never heard of it, says I. You will, says Corsets, for she is Dixon's house guest at the Ranch, and she hasn't given Teddy up yet. Oh she hasn't says I? Well, we'll see about that. I'm just telling you says Corsets. She'll make it as tough for you as she can, and believe me she has developed husband stealing into a fine art. You know, don't you, that you grabbed one of the catches of Society when you got Teddy, and you're a rank outsider and a poacher from her point of view, and she'll never forgive you, never. Oh yeah?—says I. Yeah, says Corsets.

So you see Nita I have practically nothing to worry about on my honeymoon. Here come the cars. We're off! It's going to be all quiet on the Western Front.

Yeah!

DIXIE.

11

Rancho San Pedro
Monterey, California

Dear Nita,

Well, well, it's jake to have money. Don't let anybody tell you different. And it's all right to have a lot of it, too. And when it comes to wallowing around in millions like these playboys up here in the hills—well, that's just too bad. Brooklyn seems a long way off from this glorious ranch. It always seemed a long way off, even from across the Bridge, but imagine what Flatbush Avenue must look like from up here on top of the world, with a hundred thousand acres of mountain ranges like ocean waves under your feet, and every comfort, luxury and devilment that mind can conceive or money can buy from Hispanos to champagne hangovers, from polo ponies to pyjama parties night and day—and all over the place.

Teddy and I have a suite of our own in the guest house, and who should be parked next to us but Joan Pratt, the husband stealer I told you about who was engaged to Teddy until I came along and took him right out of her web without even knowing it. Seems she is a Pratt of the Newport Pratts—and why not?—and has never heard of the Dugans of Brooklyn. Well, I never heard of her either so that makes it even. But baby, she is going to hear a lot of me from now on, if she doesn't lay off of Teddy. She went right after him as soon as we got here. Seems she heard we were coming up as Dixon's house guests almost as soon as we did, and managed to get herself invited so as to be here, and crab our honeymoon. Wanted to take him out riding with her right after luncheon—the very first meal we had in the house. I said Teddy isn't going out riding, he is going for a walk with me, and Joan says walk? and sniffed, and I says yes, walk, and then she says, Oh, yes, of course, you don't ride, do you, but then, how could you be expected to know how to ride? Then I said, Oh, riding is much easier to learn than good manners, you must have found that out, so then Teddy said, that will hold you Joan, run along now like a good egg, and let Dixie and I wangle our own honeymoon. Well, Joan nearly choked, but she managed not to let Teddy see it. She merely turned to me and said very sweetly, Dixie, what a charming name—Southern, isn't it? And I said, just as sweetly, that's remarkable intuition Joan, unless someone told you. Of course a girl like me who didn't get around the world, would have thought it was Esquimo. And just to answer your next question, which you are a bit slow in getting arranged in your mind, I don't come from an old Southern family. I'm a Dugan and the Dugans were Kings in Ireland, when the Pratts were eating nuts in the trees. Really, says she? Really, says I. You must know the old saying; Ireland was a Kingdom when England was a pup, that is, if you read anything besides the bright sayings for children in Town Topics. Which disposed of Joan for that afternoon, anyway. But we are not finished with each other I can tell you that. And she isn't finished with Teddy, either. Corsets warned me against her, you know, Dixon's social secretary, and Corsets was right. If she can make trouble between Teddy and I then she has a chance to get him back—not that she's crazy about Teddy, but according to Corsets, Joan is desperate for money. It seems there are society girls who are poor as church mice and yet have to keep up a swank front and be seen everywhere in the swellest clothes and what they won't do to get by would put a Follies girl's gold digging into the "come into the drug store with me while I get some powder" class. Did you know that Nita? I didn't. And that explains a lot of those face powder and bedroom testimonials in the magazines, with pictures of Miss Uppity Hyphen Hoorah of Newport, Bar Harbor and Cannes, whose aristocratic beauty and fragile charm is enhanced by Baby Face Night Cream. The girl needs the dough and is selling what she's got. And why not? How does that differ from what other girls do who are not so Newport? Did you know there are plenty of society girls in New York and upper crust, too, who dress plenty smart from the rake-offs they get from the swell shops into which they steer the not-so-ultra but filthy rich on the lower rungs? That explains Joan and her yen to sleep with the Page millions and why she hates little Dixie Dugan hyphen Dugan of the Dugan-Dugans of Kilkenny.

Call for cocktails down below in the lounge. I am sitting in the balcony writing this, and the room below which is enormous is filled with men and women in swanky riding togs just coming in from the trails, which extend all over the mountains which Dixon owns farther than the eye can see. You wouldn't believe this place Nita, you can hardly believe it when you do see it, and I haven't seen hardly any of it yet. Only the mountains, the canyons, and lakes, and thousands of cattle grazing on the ranges which we passed on the twenty mile drive up here from the entrance gate.

There comes Teddy. Running! He has just speared the biggest whiskey and soda I ever saw. Must get down there quick and try to keep him inside the quota. Ahhh. Here comes Joan, old fashioned in hand and heading right for Teddy. Must admit she's a swell looker, Nita—slender, blonde, chic and snooty as the devil. Claims twenty-three, but I give her thirty. There she goes—pawing Teddy already. The war is on. More later. Kiss. Kiss.

DIXIE.

RITZ-CARLTON HOTEL

NEW YORK CITY

Miss Georgiana Totten,
478 Madison Avenue,
New York City.

Dear Madam:

    Complying with your kind request, we take pleasure in herewith making the following definite reservation, viz:

Mrs. William K. Page
Debutante Supper and Ball
Main Ball Room Suite
Thanksgiving Eve, November 26, 1930.

    Our estimate for dinner for 250, ball, supper and breakfast for 2000, rental of Main Ball Room suite and Persian Room, floral decorations, Meyer Davis Music, etc., is approximately $25,000.

    Appreciating your written acknowledgment of this reservation and assuring you of our best efforts at all times, believe us to remain

Respectfully yours,
For the Ritz-Carlton Hotel
W. M. Willy
Maitre d'Hotel
Banquet Dept.

Miss Chapwell's School, Ltd.

New York, N. Y.

Dearest Dixie,

    I guess the human brain can stand just about so much before it breaks down completely and that's where I am at this point so I'm writing to you to warn you that almost anything can happen and probably will as I am pretty well fed up at this point being picked on at school and stepped on at home just because I'm two years younger than Serena and the whole family is in an uproar over her coming out this fall as if she was the first one who ever came out. Well it won't make any difference to society whether she comes out or not because if I do say so she's pretty dumb only you wouldn't suspect it until she starts to talk because she looks very queenly and regal and can squash Princeton boys with her eyebrows. I don't think Princeton boys are so hot anyway. They haven't any class. One of the older girls in school here says Princeton is a country club for little boys who'll never grow up. Well anyway it isn't a jail like this place and I'll be glad when I'm out of it which will be sooner than you expect because Theodora and I are working out a most elegant plan and don't be surprised if we come trooping up to your door one of these sunny mornings and ask for a job in the movies. Oh boy think of playing opposite Clive Brook. What girl wouldn't rather do that than stick around here knowing that the only fate that could possibly befall her would be a debut at the Ritz or the Colony Club and after that gardenias and saps and saps and gardenias. I won't go through it. I won't. It is more than flesh can bear.

All my love,
Patricia.

Rancho San Pedro

Monterey, California

Darling Nita,

    I wish you were here. I wish somebody was here I could talk to. I don't know what to do. I think I'm going crazy or something. I've been talking to Corsets but she's so hard boiled. God is she hard! Don't be a fool, she says, stick it out. You've got to be hard boiled in this racket. You can't be sentimental. But this is a honeymoon, I says. All the more reason she says. Honeymoons are nothing to this gang. Just a big laugh. If you can't laugh too you're going to be damn miserable. And I says well that's all very well but what would you do if your husband did something like that to you and she says, did what? disappear with another dame for a few hours and turn up crocked? Say, he'll do that plenty. Not to me he won't I says. All right then be a sap, she says, run out now and let Joan get him, that's what she's playing for. You don't think this whole thing was just accident do you? Joan figured it all out. Oh yeah, I says, well I'll get even with her. You're going about it in a very silly way she says. You made a fool of yourself by showing how angry you were. One of the first things you must learn with this bunch you're traveling with now is to hide your feelings. Feel as you like and think as you please but never let them know. When you're having a good time act bored. When you're having a miserable time be gay. Of course there's another clique that acts bored all the time. I guess that's better yet even. And I says, that's all very well but you don't expect me to act bored when my husband goes riding off in the hills with some dame and stays out most of the night with her up in a cabin and we have to send cowboys out to get them and bring them home both cockeyed. And she says, well I don't expect you to act bored, you haven't had the training and the experience but you're getting it now so why not profit by it? I'll break her goddamned neck, I says. Temper, temper, says Corsets, be nonchalant. Light a pipe. Nothing happened to him. He's just as good as he ever was. Or just as bad.

Damn it, Nita, there's no use talking to Corsets. It's been so long since she was young she's all curdled and clabbered inside. Maybe I'll get that way too some time but meanwhile I'll handle things my own way. I haven't talked to Teddy yet or Joan either. He's still up in our room sleeping it off. He was sore as a pup because I moved out on him. I got Dixon to give me another room. That's where I am now. What am I going to do? I guess I'll leave him. I can't take a thing like that lying down. Imagine here we were sitting around most of the night waiting for them to show up. They were supposed to be back for cocktails and then dress for dinner like all the rest of us in pyjamas so there we were twenty or thirty of us sitting around in pyjamas having cocktails and more cocktails while we waited and waited and eight o'clock came and nine o'clock and ten o'clock and Mrs. Dixon frantic because the dinner was spoiling and the guests all famished but being polite saying no we'll wait and still no Teddy and no Joan and then Dixon said they might be lost on one of the back trails and everybody laughed except me. I guess I tried to laugh too but I'm sure it didn't sound convincing but finally the bunch really began to get worried, that is the few who were sober enough to worry about anything and Dixon called in the cowboys and sent them out on the various trails with revolvers to see if they could locate them by shooting and listening for answering shots from Teddy if he was actually lost. So there we all sat in our pyjamas out on the veranda and drank champagne and listened to the shooting all over the hills and finally about midnight back come the cowboys with Teddy and Joan. Teddy was weaving in his saddle soaked to the gills and yelling yippy and Joan looked like the cat who had just eaten the gold fish damn her cold, hard heart. One of the boys had found them up in a little cabin in the mountains. Well we all sat down to dinner which was ruined but it was ruined for me anyway and everybody was laughing and kidding and Teddy tried to make up to me but I told him to go butter his ears. As for Joan I didn't even speak to her and I'm not going to either. I'll cut her heart out. Or maybe I should ignore her what do you think? Maybe Corsets is right after all? Maybe I should have been very nonchalant and continental and lifted my eyebrows and said how did you like him? I'll kill her that's what I'll do. But what am I going to do about Teddy? He doesn't mean to be like that. He wouldn't have done it only Joan kept after him. Or maybe he would. Maybe he's just no good. Maybe I've married a drunkard. Well maybe he's married one, too. I can get just as wild as he can. If this is going to be a contest we'll see who comes out on top. But what kind of a life is that Nita? God I don't know what to do. Teddy is so sweet and cute and looked so sorry when I slammed out on him last night and took a room to myself. I peeked in a little while ago and he was sleeping all curled up with his hair all over his eyes. He looked just like a bad little boy. Well he is a bad little boy, and when he wakes up I'm going to break his goddamned neck. I'll show him he can't get away with that stuff with me society or no society.

Desperately,
Dixie.

The Oaks

Westbury, Long Island, N. Y.

To Whom It May Concern:

This is to notify you that I have decided to imbark upon a career as I am quite depressed by continuously being treated as though I was a mere child and I am quite convinced from my study of Freud that being repressed all the time like this is playing havock with my ego so I have decided quite seriously upon a career which will give me opportunity to express myself as an individual and have my own money so I won't have to borrow from chauffeurs and maids like I am doing just now to get enough to get away from this crushing invironment and go where I can have a career and make fame and fortune even though it should take me to foreign lands. So do not worry because I am plenty able to take care of myself. Why good grief, Joan of Arc was commanding armies in France at my age and what was she? Just a peasant. So I guess if there is anything in all this Page blue blood that I've been hearing about ever since I was an infant I ought to do pretty well. And I will too. Goodbye and don't worry. Once I have established myself I'll write you and have you send me a few things which I haven't had time to pack because I have had to sneak out like a thief in the night instead of with banners flying the way I'm coming back, believe you me. As for you Serena I bear you no grudge. I only feel sorry for you knowing that while I am having a thrilling time you will be one of those flop debs doomed to buy your own gardenias.

PATRICIA.

~~~~~~~~~~~~~~~~~~

THE MEMOIRS OF PATRICIA PAGE
by
PATRICIA PAGE
(To Be Opened Fifty Years After Her Decease)

CHAPTER ONE

I am writing this in Chicago, the second largest city in the United States of America, New York being the first and much larger. As I raise my eyes and gaze out the window I see Michigan Avenue and thousands of people going up and down and it makes me very sad to think that all of them will be dead when human eyes other than mine read this. I will be dead too but I will have made my mark in the world deo volente (latin for God willing). And if you think latin is easy, you're crazy.

Today is my first day all alone in the world. Although I am sixteen years old I've always had somebody tagging around after me, a nurse or a governess or something equally poisonous and all spies taking everything back to the family who love me in an animal way I fancy but do not understand my depths. Even Theodora my best friend whom I trust most implicitly what did she do? Got scared and ran home like a rabbit leaving me all alone here in Chicago to face the world and Hollywood where I am going to make fame and fortune in the movies like Dixie Dugan my sister-in-law who married my brother Teddy who is a bum, but quite nice.

I tried to point out to Theodora who ran away from New York with me on the money she got from selling a bracelet and what I could borrow from Cassidy the third chauffeur who runs the station wagon and it's a crying shame too, because he deserves the Minerva at least and I have promised to let him drive mine as soon as I have made my fame and fortune in Hollywood although I was very careful as you might suppose not to let him know that's where I was going with the money I borrowed from him. I told him I wanted to buy a nice big dog as I was tired of all those little sniffling pekes which Mother has around the place and which may cost a lot of money but look like neumonia germs to me. So Cassidy was very pleased that I was going to get a big dog, a great dane maybe and promised to take it riding with me on the station wagon when we went down for weekend guests most of whom do not deserve such luck as to ride with a great dane such as I told Cassidy I was going to buy and I can assure you gentle reader that I became so intreegued with the idea

I almost did go and buy one and then where would my career have been and what is more these Memoirs which I have firmly resolved will faithfully mirror the age in which I live as well as what life in society means to a young girl who is tired of all this idle folly and is firmly resolved to carve out her own destiny in the great world of do and dare.

So goodbye I said to Theodora as she got on the train to go back to New York and Miss Chapwell's school and all those things which I have escaped from, I will go on to the golden West. I have just about enough to get me there but don't worry about me. You have chosen a craven's part and it's you who are to be pitied so she waved goodbye to me through the window and I must admit my heart went down into my boots to think that here I was all alone in Chicago the second largest city in the United States with my family all in an uproar by this time over my dramatic disappearance. I am sure the police in every large city in the land are looking for me now and they can go right on looking because I'm going to stay tucked away here in this little room to throw them off the sent and then I'm going to Hollywood and after I've made a staring picture or two I will laugh at them if they should try to drag me back to the horrible life of a school girl and a sub-deb in New York. I will now go out and make a complete but guarded screwtiny of Chicago and maybe take in a movie so I can put it all down faithfully in these my Memoirs of which this is Chapter One.

                        MONTEREY CALIFORNIA
NITA DUGAN
439 FLATBUSH AVENUE
BROOKLYN NEW YORK
TERRIBLE BATTLE WITH TEDDY STOP CANT
STAND THIS MUCH LONGER STOP WHAT
WILL I DO STOP
                                    DIXIE

~~~~~~~~~~~~~~~~~~

                        BROOKLYN NEW YORK
MRS TEDDY PAGE
RANCHO SAN PEDRO
MONTEREY CALIFORNIA
GROW UP
                                    NITA

~~~~~~~~~~~~~~~~~~

                        HOLLYWOOD CALIFORNIA
439 FLATBUSH AVENUE
BROOKLYN NEW YORK
LEFT TEDDY LAST NIGHT STOP AM GOING
BACK TO THE MOVIES STOP LETTER
FOLLOWING EXPLAINING ALL STOP
HEARTBROKEN
                    DIXIE AMBASSADOR HOTEL

~~~~~~~~~~~~~~~~~~

III

HOLLYWOOD, CAL.

NITA DARLING,

I guess maybe I'm crazy. Anyway I don't care I'm happy again. Don't pay any attention to my telegram. Besides this isn't the letter following this is another letter. I tore up the first because just as I was sending it to tell you I had left Teddy forever and would never see him again he came dashing into the room and threw his arms around me and started to eat me all up. I forgot to be mad at him about Joan and humiliating me the way he did up at the Ranch. I just laughed and cried and chewed his ears and we made up so nice it was almost worth the fight and everything. He told me how sorry he was and he would never drink like that any more and was going to break away from this mob of playboys and girls and was going to take me away on a real honeymoon to Paris and he was never going to see Joan again and he was so heartbroken when I left he hopped on the next train and came tearing down after me and he'd never let me go again and then I told him I was glad and he told me he was sorry and then I told him I was sorry and he told me he was glad and then he kissed me some more and then it didn't seem like any time at all before it was all dark outside and the lights were lit and we were hungry but didn't care much. Oh he's my sweet boy, Nita, he's so bad and he's so good and when he puts his arms around me—he's just like catnip. Imagine us in Paris, Nita! Because that's where we're going to be in just no time at all. We're taking the train tomorrow to New York and Teddy has wired ahead to his lawyer to get our passports rushed through and he's reserved a big suite on the Ile de France and off we go to make love in Paris buy clothes and drink on the side-walks like they do in the newsreels, and see the racing and putter around the ruins. Teddy is looking over my shoulder as I write this and he just said he was going to putter around me and I said I'm no ruin and he said you will be and I said that's a promise.

See you soon. Hot cha cha.

DIXIE.

~~~~~~~~~~~~~~~~~~

The Study of WILLIAM KELLOGG PAGE, *The Oaks, Westbury, Long Island. The heavy door opens softly and a sleek-haired, ferret-eyed, tight-lipped secretary oozes in.*

SECRETARY: Mr. Carmody is here, Mr. Page.
PAGE (*alert*): Carmody?
SECRETARY The Open Eye Detective Agency.
PAGE (*eager*): Send him in. At once.

CARMODY *clumps in, black derby, black cigar, black shoes, black eyebrows—one of those fiction detectives who can be found only in real life.* CARMODY *seats himself solidly, pushes back his derby, crosses his thick legs and swings a heavy shoe with commendable pride.* CARMODY *waits.* CARMODY *is on the job.*

PAGE (*crisply*): I sent for you because I heard you were discreet.
CARMODY (*proudly*): We never sleep, that's our slogan.
PAGE (*impatiently*): That doesn't concern me. What I want to know is, can you do a very delicate job for me and keep the newspapers from getting hold of it?
CARMODY (*with simple pride*): You can trust the Open Eye Detective Agency, Mr. Page. Once my men get on the job they never

let go. It may take weeks, it may take months—but they hang on like bull dogs. Why, do you know, Mr. Page, we trailed a car once from New York to San Francisco up to Seattle back to St. Paul down to Omaha and then where do you suppose they went?

PAGE: Look here, Carmody, I don't care where they went. I called you in here to find somebody.

CARMODY: Who?

PAGE: My little daughter.

CARMODY: Just a minute. (*Takes soiled envelope out of pocket and fishes up stub pencil which he holds poised with blunt fingers.*) What's the name?

PAGE (*helplessly*): Now what would my daughter's name be? Page, of course.

CARMODY (*nodding sagely*): That's right. (*Writes carefully.*) Well I've got that. (*Ponders result and then looks up brightly.*) Married or single? What I mean is, was she married and living somewhere else or single and living with you?

PAGE: Suppose you let me tell you my own way.

CARMODY: Check.

PAGE: My little daughter Patricia is sixteen and she and a schoolgirl friend of hers went to a matinee yesterday afternoon, gave the slip to Mrs. Page's maid who was with them and disappeared. When Patricia didn't come home for dinner last night we naturally supposed she was with Theodora and they had just slipped away from the maid and chauffeur for a lark, but then when she did not come home after dinner and we did not hear from her we called up and learned to our astonishment she wasn't there and neither was Theodora. Now naturally we cannot allow anything of this to get into the newspapers. The girls are both probably all right and somewhere in New York City because neither of them has any money so they couldn't get very far. We are worried, of course, but it is only a childish prank, I am sure—only I want you to find her and bring her home as quickly as possible without spreading a general alarm and letting the newspapers learn about it as they would immediately if I notified the police in the regular way. Publicity like this the way the tabloids would play it up would be disastrous to a young girl like Patricia. Now how soon can you get on the job?

CARMODY: I'm on it right now, Mr. Page. When I stepped in that door I was on the job. Right now my brain is working top speed. Inside of an hour I will have a network of operators combing New York with a fine tooth comb. Why, your little girl has no more chance of getting out of New York once the Open Eye Detective Agency is on the job than I have of—of—well, I'm a man of few words, Mr. Page, and I make all of them count. I've been in this game man and boy for nigh on forty years, and you can hardly name a big case I haven't had my finger in some way or other. Take the Ruth Snyder case, for example. Did you know the real truth of the matter is that she used to carry around a little bottle . . .

PAGE: Look here, Carmody.

CARMODY: Sorry, Mr. Page. Enthusiasm! Love of one's work and vigilance, eternal vigilance. We never sleep. That's our slogan. . . .

THE MEMOIRS OF PATRICIA PAGE
by
PATRICIA PAGE
(*To Be Opened Fifty Years After Her Decease*)

CHAPTER TWO

Oh I have met Dimi and I am in love and it's the most wonderfull thing in the world!! I wonder if anyone has ever felt like this before?

Probably not. It is so sweet and so sad and you want to laugh because you're happy and you want to cry because you're sorry for yourself and you don't know why because you aren't really and when you see him coming down the street your heart beats so fast you think you are going to swoon so what do you do? You say something perfectly idiotic instead of saying all the beautiful things which he inspires in you.

One of the things we learn from Life is that the most romantic things happen in the most unromantic fashion. I must develop this thought later. For instance what could be more unromantic than the way Dimintri or Dimi as I will always call him and I were thrown together by Fate? It was in the MacVickers theatre on a calm Sunday afternoon no different from any other Sunday afternoon apparently and yet it is a day that will always be written in letters of fire in the calender of my heart. I had had my luncheon, a modest repast, in a quainte little restaurant on North Clark Street and had strolled over the bridge gazing idly down on the river as I passed not knowing I was on the most fatefull journey of my life and awaiting me at the other end of the rainbow was Life and Love and all that matters! As I walked through the Loop, as they call the business district here, wondering why they didn't clean it up a little, I saw a big movie theatre and a big sign saying Clive Brook in something or other. You see I have forgotten already and yet there was a time when I would have memoirized every gesture because I thought he was just too grand but now I can see that that was only a childish crush to be laughed off lightly. Oh dear how quickly one grows out in the world. Isn't it thrilling! And isn't it a wonderful world to live in? Yes!!! But I degress. I entered the lobby and bought my ticket and was quickly and most politely ushered through the lobby and inside where without a moment's notice and coming with quite a shock after all this bending and bowing I was shoved in with a lot of other people behind a rope which two ushers held so tight we were all herded together like a bunch of sheep and there in that unromantic situation with the motley hord stepping on my toes and poking their elbow in my eyes, I met Him! How we started talking I don't know. It is all a blur now but such a dreamy delightfull blur in which I can only see two enormous dark eyes and hear a soft mellow voice with a slight touch of Russian accent saying— Stop crowding this young lady or I'll poke you right in the nose. My hero! My knight! After an endless dream in which I seemed to be floating through miles of marble corridors and forrests of gold pillers we arrived together way up in top of the theatre sitting together and peering over the railing as though from the parapet of heaven. Way down was a tiny little picture going on with an insignificant Clive Brook making love in his usual tawdry fashion. But we hardly noticed him because from the very first Dimi and I seemed to know we were made for each other from the beginning of the world so we talked and talked all through the picture and everybody saying shush and Dimi glaring back at them in his masterfull fashion and saying Oh yeah? And believe me they didn't peep because they could tell from his ringing tone that here was a man who was master of his fate and captin of his soul and would stand no nonsense.

After a while we floated down miles of steps to the street and walked all over the Loop which seemed to have changed magically and become bright and fair and sparkling in the summer sun, and then we got on a boat and were wafted over the blue waves of Lake Michigan one of the five Great Lakes to Jackson Park and there we walked over miles of grass and listened to the birds sing and watched the little children at play and Dimi told me about when he was a little child in Russia which he could just barely remember and how he came to this country in the steerage when he was eight years old and that was ten years ago so you can see he is only two years older than I but centuries older in wisdom because he has lived. And from New York he drifted to Chicago where now he works all day long in a hatefull job but spends all his nights and holidays planning and working with his comrades for the Great Day when the workers will arise and crush the capitalistical system which has its golden shod heel on the neck of downtrodden Labor. Imagine how thrilling it was to me to hear all this for the first time and from the man I love! How long has this sort of thing been going on, I wonder.

And now how can I tell about the rest of the day? How can I describe the magic hours which Dimi and I spent in White City riding on roller coasters up to the stars, eating candy like snowballs that melted in your mouth and laughing and chaffing like all the silly heedless people around us and then sitting and talking seriously together over our hot dogs and cocoa cola with Dimi's black eyes smoldering with anger over the wrongs of the working classes and then lightening up with Fire as he pictured the world to be. What a wonderful world it is going to be and how glorious it would be to walk all the rest of my life through this world hand in hand with Dimi. Then there would be no Junior League and no Miss Chapwell's School and no horsey set in Aiken and no Newport and no Bar Harbor and those other dreary places and Dimi too will be freed from his galling chains as he so aptfully expresses it and won't have to spend his days of precious sunlight down in the dark shipping room basement of the True Faith Book Concern nailing up huge boxes of badly written religious tracks to be sent all over the world to unfortunate heathens who are much better off without them and know it too but can do nothing about it because they too, as Dimi says, are under the heel of the Church and state and all this other capitalistical nonsense which Dimi and his comrades are going to abolish!!!

Right now as I am writing these Memoirs in my little room Dimi is toiling down there in that dark basement but soon I will see him again because we have a date for dinner at the Pure Food Cafeteria on Wabash Avenue. There we will carry trays around which I think is the only way to eat. There we will sit and talk or rather I will make Dimi talk and I will listen because I haven't told him the truth yet about myself because I am sure if he once knew I was the daughter of W. K. Page he would shun me as though I were a viper because he says all big business men and bankers and whatnot are merciless monsters which is rather hard for me to believe about poor old daddy who looks so worried around the house all the time and seems to jump right out of his skin when Mother yells at him. Poor Daddy, I hope he isn't worried too much about my leaving home to make my career which I am postponing for a few days as what would Hollywood be without Dimi? Dimi! I close my eyes and see him—those big, somber dark eyes, that black, curly hair, that proud baring and that defiant glance like a wounded eagle. And musing in this fashion I will close Chapter Two of My Memoirs.

OPEN EYE DETECTIVE AGENCY

```
To W. K. Page
Wall and Broad Streets,
New York City, New York.
```

                              In re: Case No. 1,784

```
    Pursuant to telephone advice from your
secretary this morning that your daughter was
last seen in Chicago by her friend who returned
to New York last night, I have wired our Chicago
office to canvass all railroad stations, hotels,
girls' clubs, and rooming houses. In this way
we will spot her if she is still in Chicago. If
that fails we will be able to pick her up if she
tries to leave for Hollywood, as I am also
covering principal cities on all trunk lines
west and have operatives stationed at Pasadena
```

and L. A. to intercept her if she has already
left Chicago and has passed through the
aforementioned cities. This has all been handled
with the splendid secrecy for which this agency
is internationally noted. So you need not worry
about our ultimate success for I have only to
refer you to our slogan "We never sleep".
Meanwhile may I take the liberty of enclosing
our initial bill to cover disbursements?

Carmody.

```
                              HOLLYWOOD
CITY EDITOR
CHICAGO TRIBUNE
CHICAGO ILLINOIS
FEEL YOU WOULD BE INTERESTED TO KNOW
THAT DIXIE DUGAN SENSATIONAL STAR OF
LOVING SINNERS IS EN ROUTE TO EUROPE
ON SECRET HONEYMOON WITH TEDDY PAGE
INTERNATIONALLY KNOWN SOCIETY AND
SON OF W K PAGE AND BOTH OF THEM ARE
ARRIVING SANTA FE CHIEF TOMORROW AND
WILL STOP OVER AT DRAKE HOTEL FOR
DAY BEFORE LEAVING FOR NEW YORK
KINDEST REGARDS
                      COLOSSAL FILM CORP
                      DEPT PUBLIC RELATIONS
```

(*Above*) Dixie Dugan, who has deserted the movies for society and is en route to Europe on her honeymoon with her new husband, the well-known Teddy Page. Dixie was snapped yesterday in their suite at the Drake in the newest lounging pyjamas from Hollywood. When asked about her career she replied with wifely simplicity, "Teddy is my career now."

~~~~~~~~~~~~~~~~~~~

Dear Dixie,

I know you very well and I know your husband better than you think but you have never met me and yet it is very important that I see you right away and see you alone because you can do something wonderfull for me as I am in great distress so when I saw your picture in the paper this morning it was like Provadence because I have spent all my money and must do something right away and you can help me and if you only knew who I was I am sure you would rush to help me with open arms but it is very necessary that I be discreet so I cannot come to your hotel so if you will please meet me at the Pure Food Cafeteria on Wabash Avenue at noon today it will be just too wonderfull of you because this is a matter of life and death. But you must come alone and above all do not bring Teddy.

<div style="text-align: right;">Just Me.</div>

~~~~~~~~~~~~~~~~~

CHICAGO ILL

```
MRS WK PAGE
THE OAKS
WESTBURY LI
ARRIVING NEW YORK TOMORROW CENTURY
WITH DIXIE EN ROUTE TO PARIS FOR OUR
```

HONEYMOON SAILING ILE DE FRANCE
FRIDAY STOP WANT TO BRING HER OUT TO
MEET YOU AND REST OF FAMILY BUT MUST
BE SURE FIRST YOU WILL BE NICE TO
HER STOP SURE YOU WILL LOVE HER WHEN
YOU KNOW HER AS SHE ISNT ANYTHING
LIKE YOUR IDEA WILL TELEPHONE YOU
FROM MY APARTMENT ABOUT NOON LOVE TO
ALL
                                    TEDDY

~~~~~~~~~~~~~~~~~~~~~

                             CHICAGO ILL
CARMODY
OPEN EYE
NEW YORK CITY
OPERATIVE TWO SEVENTEEN COVERING
DRAKE AS PER INSTRUCTIONS PICKED UP
SUBJECT THREE OCLOCK THIS AFTERNOON
INQUIRING AT DESK FOR MRS TEDDY PAGE
STOP HOTEL MANAGEMENT TIPPED OFF
INSTALLED SUBJECT IN SUITE ON
PRETEXT AWAITING RETURN OF MRS PAGE
WHO LEFT FOR NEW YORK CENTURY TODAY
STOP HOLDING SUBJECT INCOMMUNICADO
AWAITING INSTRUCTIONS
                      MULLIGAN CHICAGO

~~~~~~~~~~~~~~~~~~~~~

                              NEW YORK N Y
MULLIGAN
OPEN EYE
CHICAGO ILL
FATHER SUBJECT NOTIFIED COMING
PERSONALLY TO TAKE HER HOME LEAVING
BY PLANE THIS AFTERNOON ARRIVING
TONIGHT STOP TIP OFF HOTEL BUT NOT
SUBJECT STOP ABOVE ALL KEEP PRESS
OFF TRAIL STOP GOOD WORK
CONGRATULATLONS
                                    CARMODY

IV

(From the New York Evening Tab)
SOCIETY STARTS WALKING OUT ON NEWPORT

Newport's loss is Europe's gain as the surprising exodus from this fashionable stronghold continues to land the Queen City's foremost social lights on foreign shores.

Princesse Miguel de Braganza, the former Anita Stewart, has turned a figurative key in the lock of The Moorings, her rambling white frame dwellings at Newport, and is sailing on the Ile de France tonight to visit her daughter, Nadejda de Braganza, who has been studying dramatic art in Germany under Max Reinhardt for several months.

No eastbound boat this season has been more crowded with elegantes than the Ile de France. When she sails at 7 o'clock tonight among those on board will be Mr. and Mrs. Lawrence Copley Thaw, Prince and Princess L. Hohenhof, Prince Pio Pochito, Mrs. John Barry Ryan Jr. the former Margaret Kahn, Mr. and Mrs. Gordon Auchincloss, Grace Bristed, Mrs. Roswell Eldridge, Mr. and Mrs. Marcel Labourdette, Mr. and Mrs. Clarence H. Geist and family, and the young Teddy Pages. Teddy, who was one of Park Avenue's gayest blades, and his attractive young wife, who was Dixie Dugan of Broadway and Hollywood fame, will spend their honeymoon in Paris and the smart places of Europe, returning in September in time for the Lipton Cup races.

~~~~~~~~~~~~~~~~

THE MEMOIRS OF PATRICIA PAGE
by
Patricia Page
(To Be Opened Fifty Years After Her Decease)

CHAPTER THREE

I see very little reason for going on with these Memoirs. Life is finished for me now and all I see ahead is one cold grey day after another until the tomb opens to welcome me and I shall be no more. And to think that only a few days ago I was so happy in Chicago that magical city by the shores of beautiful Lake Michigan and my Career was all spread out before me and my life's work had just begun. But now it is ashes. Nothing but ashes. And my Career is ended. And I am imprisoned in this big blank house looking out over Long Island which I detest and dispise. Well I suppose Edna St Vincent Millay is right

Life must go on I forget just why

But that's all very well for her. There was no Dimi in her life. Oh Dimi Dimi when I see your name written down here your vision comes up to stab me and my heart breaks into a thousand little pieces and each little piece hurts worse than the other. What must you think of me dropping out of your life like this without one word of explanation? But how could I explain Dimi dearest? I was held a prisoner by that loathsome hotel manager who smiled so sweetly and yet was a serpant in disgise— Come right upstairs, Mrs. Page will be here directly says he and then they ushered me into a luxurious suite overlooking beautiful Lake Michigan which smiled trecherously at me just like the manager who knew all along Dixie had left for New York and was merely holding me there so he could send for my father. A viper that's what he was. A snake in the grass. I will never trust another hotel manager as long as I live. How I pleaded with him, using all my feminine wiles but to no avail. He was adamant which describes it perfectly. Well someday when daddy is feeling real good I'm going to ask him to buy the Drake Hotel in Chicago and then the first thing I will do is to have that loathsome creature discharged without any references and then I will dedicate a good part of my life to hounding him and having him dismissed from one position after another the way the police do to criminals who are trying to go straight always showing up just as they are about to make good and marry the boss's daughter and they have the same trecherous smile as this hotel manager who wrecked my career, blighted my life and robbed me of all that is dear to me. Well so much for my Revenge. But now the question is what am I going to do now? I won't go back to school that is certain. I put my foot down on that last night. What a grand home coming that was. I will write it out in detail later. Mother said they wouldn't have me back in school anyway because I had made a scandal running away and I said anything that would liven up the old place was a blessing in disgise and they should be grateful to me. But gratitude is something one must never expect in this life. I guess there's no use expecting anything. I guess I'll just sit with folded hands and wait for death for what is life to me now without Dimi the one person who understood me and who I could talk to as one understanding soul to another. And just to think that now while I am sitting up here in this luxurious prison, this sented cell, he is toiling down there in that dark shipping room basement nailing up countless boxes of True Faith religious tracks to be sent away to all kinds of heathens who are better off than I am because at least they will be able to touch the same tracks that Dimi touched. But me, I am cut off from him utterly and completely without even having been able to say goodbye to him just leaving him standing there vainly waiting for me at our tryst in the Pure Food Cafeteria on Wabash Avenue. I can see him standing there now with his dark somber eyes and proud defiant baring scanning each passerby eagerly vainly looking for me who will never see him more. Well, he's going to hear from me just the same. I'll smuggle a letter out to him some way even though I am being watched with such vicious determination. They can watch me until they are blue in the face but Cassidy is my friend and as soon as I can when he drives the station wagon down I will give him a letter to post for me and if he is descreet and faithful to me in this my hour of need I will reward him handsomely as soon as I am back in the good graces of my family and can invegle some money out of them. Daddy asked me all the way back on the train from Chicago how I got the money to run away but I would be torn to pieces with red hot pinchers before I would let them know that Cassidy befriended me in my hour of need and loaned me the money out of his savings though how he can manage to save anything out of what he's paid which is something like $25 a week is beyond me because I found by experience in Chicago money just melts away when you're out in the world and faced by the problem of paying rent and eating even in a cafeteria where you carry your own tray and always load up twice as much as you can eat especially deserts because as Dimi says the eye is more greedy than the stomach and that is what is the trouble with the world today because the rich want everything they see and rob the workers like Dimi who are planning secretly to revolt against this inhuman capitalistical system which Dimi says is riding for a fall. Oh how inspiring he was! Where will I find another Dimi??? Nowhere!!! There will never be anyone else in my life. "The song is ended but the melody lingers on" I only began to realize now how beautiful that song is. I never thought before that the words meant anything but Life teaches one much. It is a better school than Miss Chapwell's. Of that there is no doubt.

I must not close this chapter without mentioning Dixie who married my brother Teddy and for why I don't know when she was a movie star and didn't need to be dragged into this family which Teddy brought her over to meet last night of all nights just as daddy got back from Chicago with me and the whole place was in an uproar. She must have a fine opinion of us and I daresay it's deserved but I liked her right away as I knew I would and she liked me too which is something as I haven't a friend in the world except Daddy who doesn't dare to be too friendly because Mother blames him for encouraging me and she also blamed Dixie last night too which was a complete surprise to Dixie because she hadn't received my note which I wrote to her in Chicago and when I told her I went to see her and was held captive by that snake at the Drake she said she was dreadfully sorry and I knew she meant it because she's the kind of person who says what she thinks and I'm sure once she gets over being in awe of Mother there is going to be fireworks and I'd like to be around when they come off. Well they're going away on their honeymoon Dixie and Teddy off to Paris to buy beautiful clothes and dine in the Bois which must be heaven when you are in love and with the one you love and while I wish them every happiness I cannot help but think how different it is with me alone and a prisoner in this grate gloomy house far away from my loved one who doesn't even know where I am or who I am and probably thinks I am false and heartless and is hating me while I sit here alone with my thoughts, alone and lonely loving him and yearning for him with streaming eyes and breaking heart and so in utter desolation I bring to a close this the third and most sorrowful chapter of my Memoirs.

```
                                    HOLLYWOOD CAL
   MR & MRS TEDDY PAGE
   S S ILE DE FRANCE
   FRENCH LINE PIER N Y C
   BON VOYAGE AND BEST WISHES FOR
   HONEYMOON HAPPINESS
                          SOL NEBBICK
                          COLOSSAL FILMS CORP
```

```
                          WESTBURY LI
MR & MRS TEDDY PAGE
S S ILE DE FRANCE
MAY THIS BE THE BEGINNING OF A
GLORIOUSLY HAPPY VOYAGE ON THE WIDE
BLUE SEA OF LIFE ALL MY LOVE
                          PATRICIA
```

~~~~~~~~~~~~~~~~~~~~

```
                          BROOKLYN  N Y
MR & MRS TEDDY PAGE
S S ILE DE FRANCE
GOOD BYE GOOD LUCK GOD BLESS YOU
              PA MA NITA & SAMMY
```

~~~~~~~~~~~~~~~~~~~~

On board
SS Ile de France

First Day

This is my first trip to Europe. I must remember to refer to it as a crossing. Wonder should I tell people it's my first. It seems from the way they talk all around me that unless you have made at least a dozen crossings you simply don't rate. And yet any one of the stewards make twice that many every season and don't brag about it. It's like that story daddy used to tell about the member of House of Commons in Ireland who was bragging about the number of his children and another member rose in his place and replied he didn't see why the gentleman should be so proud of himself in such a special department of activity in which every jackass was his equal and every jackrabbit his superior. Guess I'll tell them this is my first. I'll tell them it's my first honeymoon too although that seems to be equally gauche. That's a new word I've learned. It's French slang for wet smack. I've started learning French. Made up my mind I must know French, bridge, and the last names of people who are always being referred to as Alice and John and Mary and Grace when Teddy and his society friends get together. So far as I can gather this far anyway, society conversation consists of first names, bridge hands, places one should not be seen and French words like gauche. This boat is a good place to start learning French. Chaud means a hot water tap, froid the cold water, bain is a bath but you pronounce it like a sheep singing mammy. Wouldn't that slay you? Teddy's been over half a dozen times but he doesn't even know that much. Says you don't need to know any other language but English. You holla hey and hold out money, and they understand you miraculously. So there is a universal language. I guess I'd better learn English. That will keep me busy. I must learn to say Oh really like Joan. You roll it around in your tonsils before you let go of it. Oh rrrrilly? Oh rrully? With a kind of hitch kick at the end. And the eyebrows! They must go up. You can get by with an awful lot if you can do that. It seems to be the complete answer to almost everything. And gives the impression that you could really slay them with a wisecrack but you are really too tired of it all to make the effort. Sick-making is good, too so if you don't like something you say, my dear isn't it just sick-making. Divine is good, too. When you like something—a hat or a horse— you just say it's divine. Well this boat is divine. Teddy and I have the most divinest suite, a bedroom with real twin beds in it and a living-room in which we can dine if we want to and a bathroom with so many kinds of strange apparatus in it it looks like a power house. Two kinds of bath water salt and fresh, feature that. And a gadget

I never saw before. Teddy says you find them all over France. Very well. The French they are a funny race parlez-vous? I've got to learn the rest of that verse. Can't find anyone who can tell me what it is. That's one of the worst things about being a girl you don't hear any good stories until they're so old you know the men have heard them already and they're only listening to you with polite interest. The dining-room is called salle à manger but it's pronounced like Adolphe Menjou. I wonder what became of him? All the stewards here look a little like him. Must have been a great traveller in his youth. That isn't bad. l must spring that one on the Princess Hohenhof-Coburg-von-Schnitzlebank and shock her out of a few hyphens. That isn't her real name. It's Hohenhof. I saw it on the passenger list but I added the rest on to make it look better. Teddy knows her and says I'm going to meet her. There's a lot more society people on board. Names I've read in the society columns ever since I was a kid. I wonder what they're like? I wonder how I should talk. Better keep my mouth shut I guess. I guess they'll be full of rrillys and gauches too although they look different from this gang on Dixon's Ranch. More refined if you know what I mean. I guess I'll have to start learning refinement too. Refinement, French, bridge and how to ride a horse. I tried it out on the Ranch so I could go out with Teddy instead of Joan, but honeymoons and riding lessons don't go together. As Moran and Mack used to say, I found that out. I will now write down the menu we had for dinner and call it a day.

Crême de Céléri
Potage Ambassadeur
Consommé Croûte au Pôt
Consommé Froid Rubis en Tasse

———

Striped Bass Poché Sauce Nantua
Noix de Ris de Veau Glacé aux Tomates Farcies

Epinards Frais aux Fleurons

Haricots Verts Frais au Beurre Fin

Caneton de Long Island à la Broche
Apple Sauce

Salade de Saison

Bombe Nesselrode

Gateau Laurencia

Fromages

Corbeille de Fruits

Thé de Chine et Ceylon—Thé Orange Pekoe
Tilleul—Camomille—Menthe—Verbeine
Café Filtré à la demande
Café—Café Américaine

What price Childs' Fifth Avenue now!

On board
SS Ile de France

Second Day

I must try to set down everything I see and hear on this trip so I will always remember what it was like. The ocean is smooth and blue and all the gulls have disappeared. There are no boats in sight and everybody is walking around the deck or sitting in chairs and looking at everybody else as though they were sure they weren't going to like them. You sit away back in the chair and hold your legs out and the steward wraps you up so tight in a rug it would take a caesarian operation to get you out alive. It's really called a caesarian section but who knows that? I read it some place. Funny how you read so many things that don't matter and remember all of them. They publish a newspaper on board and everyone sits around and reads it all the way through. This is one of the hot items:

Weather Breeders Through the Ages
300 B. C. by Theophrastus (whoever he was)

"It is a sign of rain if the raven searches for lice perched on the olive trees." 1453 (MS Harl) "Yf Chrystmas day on the Fryday be, the fyrste of winter harde shalbe, the chylde that ye borne that day shall longe lyve and lecherowus be aye." And here's an American Indian one: "When the locks turn damp in the scalp house surely it will rain." You can see how useful all that is. There are also ads "felt hats for 100 francs your own hat shall be made on your head by Chez Comme Ci" and a list of unclaimed radiograms for a Miss Kountze and Ben Lissberger—"please apply to the wireless office main hall pont B." It seems pont is bridge. Well live and learn. There is also a very comical page of jokes from Punch and I will put one down so it won't be lost to posterity.

"Please, 'm, Muvver says will you please give me the broom you borrored orf of 'er lass Toosdy fortnight?"

"Yus, but don't forgit to bring it back."

Are you hysterical? I asked the steward if there were any more papers like this and he said you'll get a new one every day. I can hardly wait.

Handy phrases for shipboard—as the boat goes down the river you begin asking each other when does the bar open and you try to guess how long it will take at this rate to get outside of the twelve mile limit. All the cocktails have American names so that simplifies the French problem enormously. If you want one you say "un" and hold up your finger. "Un" is pronounced like getting hit in the stomach—ugh. When you want two you say "deux" and hold up two fingers. If you want two of the same you say "le même chose deux" and two fingers. Teddy says this will take you across the ocean on a French boat and everywhere in Europe except Czechoslovakia and London. In London you simply cannot get along without English and since Americans can't learn it they don't go there if they can help it, excepting those who go to shoot grouse and they go to Scotland where the best Scotch whiskey comes from although they've learned to do pretty well in Brooklyn since Prohibition. Teddy and I have a little table for two right in front of the captain's table and we dressed last night which was the second night out because you don't dress the first night out or the last either—it just isn't done, Rrrully! I had a very simple, long tight-fitting white dress with orchids which Teddy's father sent me and I floated down the grand staircase into the dining salon and certainly would have been a sensation only I came down too early and there was hardly anybody there. Now I know better. To be real elegant you stay in the smoking-room and drink cocktails until nine o'clock and then you walk down the grand staircase—if you can—looking very blank and haughty which gives the rabble something to talk about through dessert which they are bolting while you are still toying with your caviar d' astrakan.

In the smoking-room Teddy and I had a new blue cocktail, le Cocktail Bleu, which starts out like a kiss from your mother and winds up like a sock in the jaw. It was after two of these I first met Teddy's Newport playmates, the ones I was so scared of, the Bristeds, Auchinclosses, and a young Italian Pio something or other who was very I kiss your hand madame and looks like hot stuff. Well, all but the Prince were frigid at first but by this time I am getting to be quite an expert on eyebrows. I can time them so that I know before their owners when they're going to start up. In fact I've been practicing on my own in front of the glass and a few more weeks and a few more bleus and Dixie will be able to hold her own with anything short of a duchess.

People on the boat are beginning to look either more human or less so. They seem to be dividing up into groups, snoozers who lie in their chairs all day and read a magazine until it hits them in the face and wakes them up—hikers who go around and round the deck. They wear rough sport clothes and the women walk like men and the men lope along like camels, but very English. Then there are the hideaways who don't come out until cocktail hour in the evening and finally the serious drinkers who sit in the smoking-room and keep one eye on the bar and the other on the hat pool which is some kind of a system for betting how many miles the ship goes every day as though it wouldn't be a simple thing to ask the captain, who by the way is a swell egg and has invited me up to the bridge. Teddy says there is one more class—passengers who don't show up until the last day and come up out of the scuppers looking like stowaways.

Teddy got hooked into a bridge game with the Princess Hohenhof after dinner and I sat in the bar and talked with a Norwegian shipbuilder who has been around the world dozens of times in sailing vessels and has a weather-beaten face that looks like it was chopped out of a block of oak with a hatchet. He told me all about boats and fish and how they live in Norway and I did the big brown eyes stuff and listened so hard he thought I was talking. He told me the Bremen was built with a bulbous bow because all the fastest fish were like that and not sharp-snooted like other boats and he told me he learned how to design ships not by going to school but by sailing them and working on them and that all the Norwegian colleges were like American colleges—overcrowded with boys who couldn't be educated because they didn't have enough brains and would rather wear white collars and starve as bum lawyers than put on a pair of overalls and make a good living as competent workmen. Then he asked me what my husband did and I said he flew aeroplanes, golfed, played polo, made love, and drank like a fish, but he was going to work after he got back to America but he really didn't have to because he had more money now than he knew what to do with. And then he asked me if that's all I ever did too and I said no I was just a Brooklyn Dugan who kicked up her heels in the chorus and made faces at a movie camera and who up to a few weeks ago didn't know anything about society except what I read in the society columns and pictures in the rotogravure sections showing Miss Consuelo Whoosis crossing her legs on Palm Beach and Bailey's Beach and the Lido Beach and that's just what I was going to do too from now on. Well, says my grim old Norwegian skipper, you'll find playing all the time isn't going to make you happy and I said I've tried working all the time, too and that isn't so hot either. So we split another bottle of Pol Roger and I began to feel sorry for poor Teddy playing bridge in the salon so I went out to drag him off to bed when believe it or not to my great astonishment there was no bridge game and no Teddy in sight. I made a tour of the boat and finally wound up on the top deck where there were plenty of couples in corners pretending to be interested in the moon, but still no Teddy. Just as I was about to give up I heard a phonograph going and rounding a corner I found Teddy taking a buck dancing lesson from the two Sterling twins, a sister act which was going over to London. There were empty champagne bottles in buckets all around and all three of them were cock-eyed and kicking up crazy and here I had been sitting around feeling sorry for Teddy stuck in a bridge game and he drinking champagne all that time and dancing his head off in the moonlight with these two girls. Well I got him away and put him to bed and sat up for hours looking out the porthole at the moonlight on the sea and wondering if the rest of my life was going to be running after Teddy and dragging him away from other women and putting him to bed and forgiving him in the morning.

V

L'ATLANTIQUE

S. S. Ile de France　　　　　　　　　　　　　　　　　Mercredi

SHIP TO SHORE AIR MAIL SERVICE

THE
HYDROPLANE
WILL BE CATAPULTED
TOMORROW MORNING

Passengers wishing to mail letters for the plane are kindly requested to . . .

EAT MORE FISH!

The French know how to propagandize as well as do the Amercans. A "train du poisson" (fish train) recently ran over the State Railway making stops at . . .

IMPORTANT NOTICE

Every night the clocks will be set ahead one hour at midnight.

FROM PUNCH

Enraged Caller. "That car you sold me has split into two." Motor Merchant. "Really? I'll make a note of it. Meanwhile you need only continue the instalments on one."

IRIS Private Post-Office, 22, rue St-Augustin, Paris. Established in 1890, will receive your mail and forward it to you. Without travelling at all, you can send postcards or telegrams from anywhere you like. Ask for circular.

RAILROAD TO LONDON AND PARIS

Please get your railroad Ticket at the Information Desk.

— pour —
soigner votre estomac
combattre votre diabète
éliminer votre acide urique

BUVEZ

l'eau naturelle de

POUGES

la plus agréable
des eaux de table

HOW DO YOU RATE?

1. Who wrote "The City Mouse and the Country Mouse"?
2. Where is the Roger Williams University for colored students?
3. What game of cards took its name from the fact that the players keep silence?
4. What is the title of an earl's wife?
5. Into how many parts is the ear divided?

EVENTS OF THE DAY
PING-PONG

Semi-Finals
At 2:45 P. M. in the MAIN HALL
Miss Bristed vs Mr Orlandi
Mr Conill vs Mr Zagah

At 3:15 P. M.
Finals

At 3 P. M. in the CHILDREN'S ROOM
GUIGNOL—Punch and Judy

At 3:30 P. M. on the SUN DECK
CLAY-PIGEON SHOOTING
Final

At 4 P.M. on the SUN DECK (Weather Permitting)
WRESTLING
BOXING
FENCING
EXHIBITION

DAGO AND SIBRAN
Featherweight

FENCING EXHIBITION
Georges VELTER and Jean LE BOZEC
Amateurs

LELAGADEC AND BLONDEL
Welterweight

WRESTLING

DAMAS, Ex-Champion of Paris Amateur
and
BOURHIS, Champion of Brittany Amateur
ROSAPE, (Middleweight) Champion of the French Navy in 1921
and
PAUMELLE, (Middleweight) Ex-Challenger for the French Middleweight Title.

At 5 P. M. in the GRAND SALON

CINEMA-MOVING PICTURES
Adolphe MENJOU
In
DARK or FAIR
BRUNE ou BLONDE

At 6 P.M. in the SHOOTING GALLERY

RIFLE AND PISTOL SHOOTING CONTEST
FINALS

At 9 P. M. in the SALON DE THE

CONCERT

At 10:15 P. M. in the GRAND SALON

CONCERT DE GALA

DON CUMMING
(Boy Champion Roper)

Joan ELTON and Alexis RULOFF

The Sarah Belle and Evelyn
STERLING TWINS

DIXIE DUGAN
(Mrs. "Teddy" Page)

LE MEGOT AND MARCEL
DANCING

Please reserve your table from the
Chief Steward

Miss Dixie Dugan,
Suite Chantilly, Pont A

Dear Miss Dugan,
 Rehearsal for the Gala will be held in the Salon Mixte at 5 o'clock. Could you please arrange to be there at your convenience with your music for the orchestra?

Respectfully,
Villar.
Chief Purser

Dear Dixie Dugan,

I have taken the liberty of arranging a special dinner in your honor tonight before you appear in the Gala to which we are all looking forward with great anticipation and would be most happy if you and your charming husband would give me the pleasure of your presence.

Pio Pochito.

DINER

Offert par
Prince Pio Pochito
à
Mlle. Dixie Dugan

MENU

Caviar d'astrakan
Blinis de la Petite Russie

⚜

Tortue Claire au Xérès en Tasse

⚜

Délices de Sole Veronique

⚜

Suprême de Volaille Bergère

⚜

Asperges Sauce Chantilly

⚜

Coupe de Foie Gras Thais
Coeurs de Laitues Parisienne

⚜

Omelette Surprise Néron

⚜

Mignardises

⚜

Corbeille de Fruits

⚜

VINS

Clos Gaensbroennel Grand Cru 1924
Chateau Rabaud-Sigales 1921
Moulin à Vent 1919
Pomméry Nature 1921

SS. ILE DE FRANCE

~~~~~~~~~~~~~~~~

NITA DARLING,

I've seen England! It's all green and just outside the window. Soon we'll be at Plymouth and the people who are getting off there are racing around the boat hunting baggage and saying goodbye to everybody, or at least everybody who isn't still in bed sleeping off the Gala and the parties which followed it last night some of which kept right on going until nine o'clock this morning when the mail plane was catapulted. I tried to stay up for that too but I fell dead in my tracks about five a. m. and just managed to get to bed. Teddy hasn't been to bed yet so I suppose he stayed up to see the plane go and is roaming around the boat some place. I'll go out and run him down as soon as I finish this letter which I'm trying to get off with the mail at Plymouth so you'll get some idea of what this trip has been like— that is if I can sort it all out which I certainly doubt.

First the special dinner which the Prince gave me last night—a young Italian, handsome as the devil and twice as hot—with a special menu printed with my name on it and a lot of dishes I can't pronounce and never saw before and a different wine with every course. Well it sure was a mean meal. We started off with a toast which they all drank to me standing, emptying the glasses with one swallow and then breaking them on the floor. I never saw that done before either, but the waiters seemed to be used to it. After that we played a cute joke on Teddy. It seems for years he had been telling this bunch at Newport and Palm Beach and other places he met up with them that some time in his life he would like to have one dinner in which he ate nothing but caviar and drank nothing but Chateau Yquem so we fixed it up with the waiters—stewards I mean—to bring him just that, so when we had soup he got a little pot of caviar and when we were served fish he got a bigger pot and when we got the entree he got a still bigger one. But he was game and never peeped—just went on eating it but finally when we got to dessert and they brought him an earthen jar as big as a soup plate level full of caviar and opened the third bottle of Chateau Yquem he gave up and hollered for help. Well it was a gay dinner and what with all the food and the wine and all of us kidding Teddy and the Prince whispering into my ear how lovely I was and how happy he was to have me so close to him all evening I almost missed the Gala. But finally we got to the Salon and the Prince had the best table reserved for our party and I rushed off to get into my costume.

Back stage there was a big scrap going on as usual and as usual it was the orchestra's fault, they were playing too fast or too slow or they didn't keep an even tempo. The twins were all around underfoot going ska ska and doing time steps as though they had never been on before and Le Megot was cursing them and everybody else but especially her partner in French English Italian and possibly Greek. What her poor partner puts up with from her is nobody's business. I got a good sample of it during rehearsal in the afternoon. She treats him like the dirt under her feet and yet he's so crazy about her he takes it without a whimper. Villar, the purser, told me quite a bit about them while they were rehearsing. It seems she was one of those cocottes who sit around the tables at the Bal Tabarin in Paris, the girls there called her Le Megot, which is about the same thing as a cigarette butt or a snipe. Marcel who was a professional dancer met her there and fell in love with her and took her out of it and taught her everything she knew and made her his dancing partner and soon they were one of the sensational teams in Europe dancing in the night clubs in Paris and London and Berlin and the smart places like Deauville and Cannes. Well you'd think that would satisfy her and she'd be grateful and nice to him instead of that she was always picking up with other men and flaunting them at Marcel and spending all his money on them and still he was so crazy in love with her he couldn't break away or do anything about it. In a way you can see why, Nita, she certainly is one of the sexiest little devils I ever saw with a wild shock of hair, a slim lazy body, big black eyes and a red mouth that must drive men crazy. She certainly knocked them for a loop on the boat with her specialty, which was danced in a costume to resemble a wildcat—ears, tail and all. I got by pretty good if I do say so but when I got back to our table all the men at our party were looking across at her—all except the Prince who never took his eyes off me all evening, or his hands either for that matter. Well I didn't mind much toward the last, because for all the attention Teddy paid me I might as well have been on another boat, so I was glad to have someone to dance with and the Prince and I danced nearly every dance together after the Gala and then the party sort of scattered every which way and I don't remember things very clearly after that. Every once in a while Teddy would come back to me and then go off again and I'd see him with the twins or with the Megot dame and then I wouldn't see him at all and all the time the Prince was hanging right on, handing me champagne and trying to get me to go places with him. I know about three o'clock in the morning we were all sitting around in the smoking-room and it was as crowded as though it was 5 o'clock in the evening, everybody shouting and singing and phonographs going all over the place and the Princess said she was dying for bacon and eggs but the steward said the kitchen was closed so I said I thought that was silly there must be somebody down there and I was going down to see and I did and of course the Prince tagged right along and tried to kiss me going down the steep iron stairway and nearly broke his princely neck. But finally we got down into the kitchen which was the whole width of the boat and looked like it was half as long and we wandered all around in our evening clothes until we found one good-natured little chef with a white hat on his head making rows and rows of little doodads on toast for luncheon the next day. Well, I got to talking to him and found he used to know a girl in Brooklyn who he visited when he got off the boat so that made us great friends and he switched on one of the electric ranges and let me scramble a big dish of bacon and eggs which the Prince and I carried up into the smoking-room very proudly and to loud cheers from everybody especially our party who ate until they had eggs in their ears. Meanwhile Teddy had disappeared entirely and the Prince had gotten me off in a corner and said he didn't see how a spirited girl like me could be happy with an American because Americans really didn't know how to make love and I said who told you that and he said oh everybody knows that. European men are the only ones who know how to make love. And I said tell me all about it, begin at the beginning and he said oh you mustn't make fun of me like that. This is a grand passion. And I said you don't have to give it any fancy names I know what it is. It's dat ole davil sex. And he says I don't know what you mean but I love you madly and I says tell me more. Tell me how good you are. What do you know that the poor little American boys can't find out? And he says it's no good to tell you I'll show you and I says no tell me about it first. Give yourself a good press and show me your medals. Tell me about all the little girls you mowed down in America and then he said he wasn't going to talk to me any more that I had no heart—no soul that I was just a beautiful body but all ice inside but he was at my feet and I could walk on him. Feature that, Nita, walking around on princes at four o'clock in the morning out on the top deck in the moonlight. Or maybe it was five. I guess it was because the sun was beginning to come up and there I was just a little girl from Brooklyn with a real live Prince kissing the palms of my hands and nibbling around my neck in a wistful way. So finally I said, Listen Prince or Pio or Pochito or whatever the girls call you, you may be God's gift to the famished females of Italy but to me you're just a good-looking lad on the make. And he says I don't know what you mean on the make and I says oh you know what it means all right but you just don't know how to say it. I'm going to bed now. If you see my husband you can send him along after me. And he says, your husband I hate your husband. If it wasn't for your husband maybe you could care for me, is it not? And I said, it is not. Now run along be a good boy and get some sleep—you aren't nearly as peppy as you talk. Maybe you've been cheering up too many unhappy wives in New York, is it not? And he says you make fun always but always I will adore you. And I says you say that to every good-looking girl don't you. And he says certainly and smiled so cute I almost kissed him. Almost.

Oh here comes the boy for the letters. And here comes Teddy with that Megot dancer and her partner. I remember now the purser said yesterday something about them going to dance at the Kit Kat Club in London so they must be getting off here at Plymouth. Good riddance—I don't like that woman—she gives me the creeps. The boat has stopped—must close. Love and kisses. Will write from Paris.

DIXIE.

```
                              LE HAVRE FRANCE
    NITA DUGAN
    439 FLATBUSH AVENUE
    BROOKLYN NEW YORK
    LAFAYETTE I AM HERE
                                          DIXIE
```

ILE-DE-FRANCE BRINGS 1,300 SUMMER VISITORS TO FRANCE

THOUSANDS GATHER TO WELCOME BIG LIST OF FRENCH FLAGSHIP

More than a thousand persons awaited the arrival of the special trains from the Ile-de-France at the Gare Saint-Lazare yesterday and were in turn greeted by a flood of 1,300 friends who poured out of the trains from 10:44 to 11 a.m.

Prettiest and most dashing of all was Dixie Dugan, famous movie star, who tripped out on the arm of her new husband, Teddy Page, the internationally known society playboy. Dixie expressed herself with being more than pleased with what she had already seen of France from the train windows and bubbled with excitement over the prospect of shopping in Paris for those countless fripperies which so delight the feminine heart.

PRAISES HOOVER

Michael Noonan, member of the City Council of Chicago, who came over to study the traffic problems in European cities, spoke with enthusiasm of the new tariff bill. "I have every confidence in the constructive engineering mind of President Hoover," he said, "and would also like to take this opportunity to state that the crime situation in Chicago is greatly exaggerated by her enemies . . ."

OTHER ARRIVALS WERE:

Tytus Filipowicz, Polish ambassador to the United States, Senator Bronson M. Cutting of New Mexico, Prince Pio Pochito. . . .

Hotel Ritz, Paris

15, Place Vendome

Darling Nita,

 This is it. Dizzy that's me. Yesterday England, a week ago Brooklyn, this morning a suite in the Ritz with push buttons everywhere and flunkies bouncing in and out making strange noises. Outside a million taxi horns going quonk quonk like geese and baggage all over the halls and interviewers calling up and champagne cocktails for breakfast and lists of places for hats and dresses and pyjamas and perfume and the floor still weaving under me and a blur of strange signs and white roads and tall green trees and little villages with thatched roofs and dogs pulling carts along the road and women cutting wheat in the fields and Paris and miles of grey houses, iron balconies, red roofs, and green trees along the streets and side-walk cafes and crazy taxis jumping around like water bugs. So this is Paris! Stop it, I love it.

 Already the boat trip is a blur, a gay blur too, of jazz and caviar and champagne and moonlight and dinner parties, cocktail parties, supper parties, bacon and eggs at dawn, Teddy chasing girls, me chasing Teddy, a hot young prince chasing me and hours and hours of Park Avenue scandal, Southampton scandal, Newport scandal, Deauville scandal and the English at Le Touquet and the Americans in Paris and the Argentines in Biarritz and the grouse in Scotland and the Wagner festival in Bayreuth and the Passion Play in Oberammergau and the bull fights in San Sebastian and Olivier at the Ritz and Julien at Ciro's and Brick Top in the rue Pigalle and Joseph at the Duck Bar in Juan les Pins and Zographos the Greek syndicate gambler and Solly Joel and baccarat and coupe and cocottes and Chateau Yquem and yachts and villas and diamonds and pearls and Grande Semaines and seasons and plages and cures and seductions—does that give you an idea? I don't wonder any more that Teddy is so dizzy. A year of this and I'll be in the madhouse myself.

    Tonight Teddy is taking me to the Ambassadeurs for dinner and after that we are going to some night clubs up in Montmartre and tomorrow he is taking me over to Mary Novitsky's for beach pyjamas and shoes and things so I will be as smart as any of them when I go to Deauville and Le Touquet and all the other places he has promised to take me. He can be so sweet when he wants to be and already he seems to have forgotten everybody on the boat and is all wrapped up in showing me a wonderful time in Paris and everywhere. Sometimes I don't think he loves me at all and then in a minute he seems to change completely. I don't understand him. In a way he seems just like a kid that you can see right through and then again he's so blasé and bored and fed up he gives you the idea that you are just another toy that he has picked up to play with and when he gets tired he is going to let you drop and walk away without even turning back to look if you fell on your feet or your face. Well I guess you can't have everything when you're married. I shouldn't complain. Just think of how envious I would be if I were sitting in Brooklyn wishing I were here. Just the same I wish you were here anyway. It's all so new here and so strange. And I'm so far away from everything and everybody. Maybe I'm getting homesick. Isn't that silly? Plumb ridic, I calls it.

                                Oo la! la! (French for whoops!)

                                                          Dixie.

                              PARIS FRANCE
LE MEGOT
KIT KAT CLUB
LONDON
CHARTERING PLANE AND FLYING OVER
THIS AFTERNOON A BIENTOT
                                    TEDDY

VI

                                              LONDON

MRS TEDDY PAGE
HOTEL RITZ
PARIS
DREADFULLY SORRY DARLING BUT I AM
DELAYED HERE FOR A COUPLE OF DAYS
ON STUPID BUSINESS ONE OF THE OLD
MANS IMPORTANT ENGLISH RACKETS CANT
EXPLAIN IN DETAIL BY WIRE BUT WILL
TELEPHONE YOU SIX OCLOCK TONIGHT AND
WILL HURRY BACK TO YOU SOON AS I
POSSIBLY CAN OR EVEN SOONER ALL MY
LOVE MY LITTLE CABBAGE

                                              TEDDY

~~~~~~~~~~~~~~~~~~

(From the Daily Mail Continental Edition)

The Kit Kat Club is a popular place these days, partly because of the sensational vogue of Le Megot, the fiery little apache, and her partner Marcel, but also because one may get a glimpse here of an unusual number of Indian princes who always bring a certain amount of Oriental brilliance to our somber London scene. The Maharajah of Rajpipla and the Tika-Rajah of Kapurthala are constant visitors as well as Prince Damrong of Siam and the lovely little Princess Takamatsu who has won everyone's heart. The last two or three nights have been enlivened by the effervescent eccentricities of one of America's most colorful playboys, young Teddy Page, only son and heir of W. K. Page, international industrialist and banker.

~~~~~~~~~~~~~~~~~~

Hotel Ritz, Paris

Nita darling,

Teddy is still over in London on some important business his father cabled him about so I've had to go ahead with my shopping but fortunately the Prince has been so charming and helpful that I have been getting along just wonderful. He seems to know everybody and every place in Paris and I've been letting him take me around because I certainly can't go around by myself and besides he can just walk right into those big dress houses where the average person needs a card of introduction or a letter from your ambassador or something.

Teddy was going to take me over to Mary Novitsky who makes the smartest pyjamas in the world but he had to go to London so I went with the Prince who sent me flowers and an invitation to lunch the same day. Well, Nita, you'll curl right up in a tight ball when you see the beach costume I got, solid cork shoes and hat and suit and everything to match.

I sat in the little showroom on the second floor while mannequins paraded by in pyjamas for beach and street and formal pyjamas for dining believe it or not.

One ensemble I couldn't resist. It has blue chiffon velvet trousers and jacket. The tuck-in blouse is of two shades of blue, the yoke midnight and the bottom French blue. The trousers start at the cuff with a four inch band of midnight blue followed by one of royal, followed by lighter bands grading up to pale blue. The same idea is carried out in the jacket, only the light blue starts at the bottom and keeps getting darker until the yoke which is of midnight blue. The collar is of the lightest blue, very soft and crushed, and tied at the neck with a velvet bow. The trousers are very long and wide.

Also I bought a yellow bathing suit with a blue geometric design in front and blue linen pyjamas to go with it with trousers fitting tight around the hips and bell shaped at the ankles and on the trousers is a design with various shades of yellow and the sleeves of the coat have the same design on them, a blue and yellow hat and the blue and yellow cork shoes and a yellow leather container for beach oil with a strap going over your shoulder just like field glasses.

And she had some of the cutest separate trunks to wear over your one-piece bathing suit although I hear some places you don't have to wear anything but the trunks. I wanted to start with just a beach ensemble but the Prince made me go ahead and buy some pyjamas for afternoon wear and evening too saying that girls went to formal dinners and casino dances in the Riviera in pyjamas and Novitsky said it was true and she was beginning to regret that she started the pyjamas vogue because women were wearing them everywhere now even to the theatre and the Opera although you really wouldn't know some of them were pyjamas, Nita, the trousers are so full they look more like divided skirts.

Well, I finally relaxed and went crazy and when I got back to the hotel and totaled it all up I found I had spent nearly two thousand dollars of Teddy's money and had six ensembles and a big cork ball with a cocktail set in it the idea being the more you roll the ball on the beach the better the cocktail gets and when you open it up there is a tightly corked thermos in it wiih four silver cups. Just too bad. Imagine it on Long Beach. Or even at Southampton. I'll slay 'em when I get back to the States.

Novitsky is very nice and very clever and was dying to hear all about Hollywood. So was the Prince. So I told them all about what a delightful madhouse it is and she invited the Prince and I to lunch with her the following day at a little restaurant where we sat and ate 78 kinds of hors d'œuvre both hot and cold and finished lunch at four o'clock with a special brandy served in huge goblets, called balloons.

I started to swizzle it right off but the Prince says but no my little barbarian, you must do it this way so he warmed the glass with his hands then he swished the brandy around and around and then leaned over it and said now inhale it and then think about it a while and then sip it and then take a little black coffee and then a sip of brandy. Feature that, Nita, you'd think the way these foreigners drink that they were christening a baby or something but I'm beginning to learn and like it too. I can see myself back in the States swishing cut Scotch around and inhaling it and falling over backwards in a dead faint.

Tonight the Prince is taking me to hear Raquel Meller at the Palace. I've always been dying to hear her but not for twenty-five bucks a seat which they charged for her when she came to New York. After the theatre the Prince is going to take me to Brick Top's up in Montmartre, a colored night club in the rue Pigalle. Must hurry and dress. Just got another radio from Teddy in London, says he loves me but can't get back to Paris for a day or two.

Well I'm glad to see he's really getting interested in business. Maybe if he pleases his father on this job it will be the beginning of something really worth while for him when we get back to New York this fall.

Meanwhile he doesn't seem to lack for money. And credit! All you have to say here at the Ritz or at any of the shops is "Page" and they open right up like morning glories and nothing is too good for you. Or too dear either. It would salivate you if you knew how much our three room suite here costs.

The Prince is horrified at my extravagance. It seems he comes from a very noble family in Rome but they haven't much money. I can't get much out of him about what he was doing in America but he was entertained all over the place and quite a Park Avenue pet and lived at the Savoy-Plaza and came back on the boat as a guest of Larry and Peggy Thaw.

Well I will say he's a fascinating critter and going around Paris with him is an education. Certainly Teddy doesn't begin to know what he knows about food and wine and little out of the way restaurants and shops and clothes and cabarets and whatnots. Just the same I wish Teddy would come back. I can think of several nicer ways of spending a honeymoon than spending it by yourself.

DIXIE.

(From Variety)

EUROPEAN CHATTER

By Mike Toohey

What does a Variety mug know about society says you—Well, there was a time when he couldn't know anything about it except what he read in the society column. And anyone who thinks that's the real McCoy believes Al Capone is Santa Claus. I hear tell that when Ward McAllister was top-sarge of the old 400, newspaper reporters sneaked in the service entrance and were thrown out with the garbage. The big wigs stayed at home—and try to get in. But now they go out nights like the Joneses and you don't have to move out of your ringside at Tex Guinan's or your banquette at Brick Top's over here at the rue Pigalle to see the crème de la crème, which, when slightly soured, becomes the big cheeses of the upper classes.

Ever since Cole Porter, who doesn't have to write music for a living, threw a party at Brick Top's for the haut-monde of Paris and gorged a flock of caviar-bored counts and princesses and marquises with corned beef hash and chicken à la Maryland washed down with champagne, it is quite de rigueur—look it up, I did—to pass up the scented sensuousness of Le Boeuf Sur Le Toit and Le Grand Ecart for the low-down hot cha-cha of Brick Top's little bit of Harlem on the hill.

The other night, for example, Bonnie Brae, society's pet party-thrower, had 20 or 30 titles, most of them guaranteed not to rub off or turn green, all gathered around the festive board, at some one's expense—not Bonnie's, you may be sure, putting away ham and eggs country style, and deep dish apple pies, while Brick Top strolled around, patting blue-bloods on the back, and singing her own New York-to-Paris version of "Mean to Me," which fills the Americans with wonder and convulses the French. Give it a look, but don't tell 'em about it up at 135 Street. Here it is, as near as I could get it down:

"Vous êtes méchant avec moi,

Pourquoi chéri,
Vous êtes pas gentil,
Dites-moi, ma coco, oui, oui, oui.

Vous désirez, je pleure tous le jourai
J'ai resté toute seule dans ma maison,
Parceque vous avez dit vous telephone, but jamais,
And je reste all alone, chanting the blues and sighing.

Pourquoi vous êtes très froid, ma chérie,
Vous avez raison, parceque tous monde regardez
Vous désirez pour boxez avec moi
Oh, mais non, parceque ça c'est pas un gentilhomme.

Not it must be
Beaucoup plaisir pour vous
To be méchant avec moi—but you shouldn't
Comme vous avez pas vue
Vous êtes tous le quelque chose pour moi!"

At another table looking on with round-eyed wonder was Dixie Dugan, who has just got over here but wasn't with her husband already. Don't they learn fast? Her new husband, Teddy Page, is burning up London, so my spies report, so why shouldn't Dixie have a little Prince show her the town?

Can't expect her to sit all alone in the Ritz, which is used principally by Americans, who go there to be awed by other Americans, who in turn think that the previously mentioned Americans are European nobility, and so in consequence are even more in awe of them. The result being they spend their whole stay there in a state of chills and fevers wondering whether they are really on the Cambon side or the Vendôme side—it makes such a difference!—and having the jitters because Olivier the head-waiter won't speak to them.

It would probably salivate the mugs at home to know that the bulk of so-called American society comes over here each summer to visit the head-waiters and the bartenders—those being the only Europeans whom they really know by name and who seem at all glad to see them again.

Oh, I forgot the orchestra leaders. Billy Arnold at Deauville makes many an American's stay there a complete success by smiling at him from the rostrum, or occasionally playing a special number for him and his sweetie—or her and her gig, as the case may be.

So you needn't be surprised to learn that a hearty greeting from Brick Top can make you quite a social success in Paris and the envy of the upper classes, which is as it should be, for anyone who can come up out of the chorus of "Shuffle Along" and tell a Vanderbilt she has to sit next to the drums and like it, has got That Thing.

Had quite a chat with Dixie and her Prince Pio Pochito, which sounds like something by Cecil de Mille, but is real wops, my dear, only Mussolini doesn't like him which gives him the same in and around Rome that Al Smith has in Georgia.

Dixie got along so well with Brick Top that before the evening was over she was out on the floor with her doing a duet for the party, which immediately fell for her. The last I saw of her Bonnie had adopted her and the Prince, and Dixie was wise-cracking all the assorted titles with great success.

Well, I never saw it to fail—any gal who can smack Broadway and lick Hollywood can make the average society dame look like the Kenosha stock company lead playing "The First Mrs. Fraser."

~~~~~~~~~~~~

*Sir Charles et Lady Mendl
prient Mlle. Dixie Dugan
de leur faire l'honneur de venir dîner
chez eux le Jeudi, à 8 hrs. 30.
Villa Trianon
57 Boul'd St. Antoine
Versailles (S. et O.)*

Pour Mémoire

~~~~~~~~~~~~

RITZ HOTEL
PARIS

DEAR NITA,

I don't know whether I shall ever speak to you again. I'm really getting too swell. Just a moment while I go and chase a few Barons out of the backyard. They call it a garden here at the Ritz, but after the place I had dinner at last night, it's just a backyard to me.

And where do you suppose I had dinner last night? You'd better hold on to your B.M.T. strap, because you will positively fall down in a fit and get highsterical with envy. At the Villa Trianon, Versailles, no less, as the guest of Lady Mendl and Sir Charles Mendl, and sitting right between Sir Charles and the Duke of Alba and right across the table from a Baron Ginsberg, believe it or not—tell Ripley to tie that!

Also at the table was the Spanish Ambassador to France and some French nobility I never did get clear about, and last but not least, Bonnie Brae, *The* Bonnie Brae, who throws those big society parties in New York and Paris and Venice, like that big one at the Ritz last fall where everybody came as somebody else.

Molyneux was there too, you know the famous dress designer, and young and good-looking. Said he'd like to dress me. I told him I'd never heard it put that way before.

Lady Mendl was darling to me. I'm finding out already that the big shots are the nicest. Take the Duke of Alba for instance, one of the oldest titles in Europe. When I asked him if he'd ever been to Palm Beach, he said he'd heard of it, wasn't it the name of that new Casino down near Cannes. Did he know the Pages? Never heard of the Pages. But he had seen me in "Loving Sinners" in Madrid so I was all right, but who are the Pages?

I told him Mrs. W. K. was my mother-in-law, and she wore pearl collars and carried Pekes and ruled Newport with an iron hand. Newport, he says, how droll. Isn't that the place where they do all this cod-fishing? No, I says, that's Gloucester. But that's in England, he says. It's in America too, says I.

They seem to have everything there, says he. I was there once. I had to make a lot of speeches, and I went to a lot of dinners, but I can't remember now where they were or who gave them. I really wanted to go see Hollywood, but nobody would tell me where it was. So I told him all about Hollywood and we got along famously.

After dinner we all walked around the garden, acres of trees and paths and fountains, all flooded with hidden lights, until Sir Charles insisted I must see his vegetables. This stuff is all right for Elsie, he says to me, but give me a lot of good honest vegetables, growing slowly but earnestly until the great day comes when they fulfill their destiny either in a luscious bowl of soup or a piquant dish of salad.

And so we walked around the garden, and he pointed out his pet radishes and his favorite artichokes and wondered aloud what Louis XIV would have thought if he had known that part of his Versailles park would be devoted to raising vegetables for the British Embassy, which Sir Charles has something to do with, what I don't know, because instead of business or society he'd rather talk about vegetables and love.

After Sir Charles showed me the garden Lady Mendl took me through some of the rooms in the house which is very old but which she has filled with priceless furniture, rugs and tapestries. Of course by this time I'd learned that she was also Elsie de Wolfe so I was prepared to be astonished and I got more than I bargained for.

Lady Mendl herself is a knock-out, beautiful grey hair, very bright eyes that see everything, listens with her head on one side like a bird and misses nothing. And her mind works like a trap. Snap, and she's got it. I guess you don't always have to have something to get to the top, but you sure must have plenty to stay there.

Bonnie Brae was nice to me too. Met her at Brick Top's a couple of nights before. Last night she said I ought to come to the Lido in Venice this summer and if I did to let her know that she would throw a big party for me. I guess that'll be just too bad for little Dixie because when this Bonnie baby throws a party it stays thrown.

Lady Mendl is going to give me some letters too. There's one person you must meet on the Lido says she and when you know her you'll know everybody. Dear old Jane says she you must meet dear old Jane. Never heard of her I says. Oh, you will says she—the Princess Jane di San Faustino. I won't try to describe her to you—you've never met anyone like her before and you never will again. I asked the Prince about her and he said well, besides being the First Lady in Rome she has the kindest face and the wickedest tongue in all Europe. You'll love her, says he, she's a devil.

So that's what I've been up to, Nita. Meanwhile I don't know what Teddy's been up to. Toohey, the Variety reporter I met at Brick Top's the other night, told me I'd better keep him on a shorter chain if I wanted to hold him. And I said, well he's over in London on business and Toohey said that's all right with me—this is no Sunday School over here—and I'm just warning a nice little American gal and she can take it or leave it. After that he closed up like Trenton on a Sunday night.

Maybe I'd better do something about this London stuff. It's beginning to look a little cock-eyed to me. He wouldn't have gone over there to see that dancer, would he Nita? Or would he? Maybe he would. Maybe he did. I'm going to find out about it. And pronto.

DIXIE.

VII

Le Fétiche, rue Fontaine.

Une Boîte de Nuit—or a Night-Box as the Parisians quite aptly call their night-clubs. Two little boys from Harvard are doing post-graduate field work in abnormal psychology, but they don't know it.

FIRST LITTLE BOY FROM HARVARD: Say, this is kinda hot, huh?

SECOND LITTLE BOY FROM HARVARD: It's the nuts.

FIRST: I don't get it, do you?

SECOND: Sure. A votre santé.

FIRST: Well, what is it then, huh?

SECOND: Search me.

FIRST: Which one is Riki?

SECOND: The one that looks like a good-looking boy, dancing with the girl in green.

FIRST: Girl gigolos! That would make 'em sit up in New York, huh?

SECOND: It's the nuts.

FIRST: They say this isn't anything to what goes on in Berlin night life.

SECOND: Our bicycles will never hold out that far.

FIRST: Paris suits me—huh?

SECOND: It's the nuts. A votre santé!

FIRST: I hear everybody's going down to Juan-les-Pins this summer.

SECOND: It's the nuts.

FIRST: Look over there. There's a hot number. I've seen her before some place. Who is it?

SECOND: Over where?

FIRST: In the corner, with the young fellow in tails.

SECOND: Say, she's the nuts.

FIRST: She's in the movies. I remember now.

SECOND: Well, it isn't Clara Bow.

FIRST: Clara Bow! Don't be a sap. It isn't Louis Wolheim either.

SECOND (*brightly*): Nancy Carroll, maybe?

FIRST: I got it. Did you see *Loving Sinners*?

SECOND: Sure.

FIRST: Well, that's her—Dixie Dugan!

SECOND (*sincerely*): She sure is the nuts.

FIRST: That must be Teddy Page with her. Imagine having all the dough that guy's got and then getting her in the bargain?

SECOND: Them that has—gits.

FIRST (*indignantly*): It isn't fair. It isn't right. Say, what do you call the waiters here? You can't call them garçon and they aren't mademoiselles.

SECOND: Just say whiskey and soda.

FIRST: Duh whiskey and soda. That's right! Say, my French is getting pretty good. She understood right away.

SECOND: Look! They're arguing over there. Wow! Dixie is sure getting him told.

FIRST: We are privileged to see an historic moment, mon vieux.

SECOND: A votre santé!

FIRST: The end of the honeymoon!

SECOND: It's the nuts.

* * *

DIXIE (*furiously*): Then you did see the magot—or whatever you call her—in London.

TEDDY: It's not the magot. Her name is Le Megot.

DIXIE: Same thing. And taking care of business for your father—that was a lot of hooey, too.

TEDDY: Say, you didn't sit in a corner with your hands folded while I was gone, did you?

DIXIE : Why should I?

TEDDY: Who is this Prince Punko you're running around with?

DIXIE: Prince Pio Pochito.

TEDDY: Big spaghetti-bender!

DIXIE: He's a gentleman and a real aristocrat.

TEDDY: He's a big gig.

DIXIE: He's not a gig—he's an Italian nobleman. Besides, we're not discussing him.

TEDDY: *I* am.

DIXIE: We're discussing the magot.

TEDDY: You are—I'm not.

DIXIE: So you did go to London to see her.

TEDDY: Certainly. She's a great artist.

DIXIE: She's a rat.

(*Half an hour of this, washed down with a quart of champagne. A rosy-cheeked, bright-eyed contralto in tweeds sings through the din.*)

> "Bugs do it—
> Slugs do it—
> Evil-looking thugs in jugs do it—
> Let's do it—
> Let's fall in love.
>
> In holes the nice little mice do it—
> Tho they are pariahs—lice do it—
> Let's do it—
> Let's fall in love."

Dixie (*moodily*): Lice do it is good. All right, then, I'll take your word for it.

TEDDY: I don't see why you always doubt me.

DIXIE: Honestly, you're miscast, Teddy. You're really a great comedian.

TEDDY: Why? What's funny about that?

DIXIE: Have you ever done anything but give me reasons for doubting you?

TEDDY: I don't know what you're talking about.

DIXIE: When people are stalling for an answer they usually say that.

TEDDY: Look here, just because I'm married, I'm not in jail, you know.

DIXIE: I'll say you're not.

TEDDY: How about this Prince you've been chasing all around Paris with—and on the boat, too?

DIXIE: Well, my God, Teddy, I had to have someone to take me places so long as you ran out on me. I can't go around Paris like two schoolteachers.

TEDDY: I had to go to London on business. I told you that.

DIXIE: Business is another name for it.

TEDDY: I did, too.

DIXIE: You went to see that magot. Well, take her.

TEDDY: I told you a thousand times it isn't magot—it's Le Megot.

DIXIE: Same thing. It means something you pick up out of the gutter—that's where she came from.

TEDDY: People can't help where they come from. You came from Brooklyn.

DIXIE Look here—another crack like that and I'll go back to Brooklyn. You know I didn't send for you, baby, you came out to Hollywood and chased me.

TEDDY: Yes—and if you went back I'd go out there and chase you again—what do you think of that?

DIXIE: Oh yeah?

TEDDY: Yeah. The trouble with you is you're crazy with jealousy.

DIXIE: I'm crazy, all right—but not with jealousy.

TEDDY: All right, then, you're crazy.

DIXIE: Yeah, I'm crazy, but not about the way you're treating me.

TEDDY: What have I done?

DIXIE: What have you done? Say, what have we been talking about all night? What *haven't* you done?

TEDDY: Well, what have I done?

DIXIE : You tell me.

TEDDY: Nothing. I haven't done anything.

DIXIE: I suppose you and that magot were playing backgammon, over in London every night, huh?

TEDDY: Sure, that's what we were playing.

DIXIE: Backgammon's still another name for it.

TEDDY: She's a great artist.

DIXIE: She's a little gutter-snipe. Take her, if that's what you want.

TEDDY: All right. Have a drink on it. Hey you—another bottle—la même chose.

DIXIE: You're a dog.

TEDDY: I'm a dog. A votre santé!

DIXIE (*crying in spite of herself*): Honest to God, Teddy, you're the meanest man that ever lived.

* * *

FIRST LITTLE BOY FROM HARVARD: She's crying. I'll go over there an' punch his nose. I'll punch his nose—right in th' nose.

SECOND LITTLE BOY FROM HARVARD: I'm goin'. I shaw him firsht.

FIRST: Shay, don't shtart pushin' me.

SECOND: Shure I'll push you—push you—push an'body.

FIRST (*bitterly*): Drunk again.

SECOND (*proudly*): So'm I.

(*Both rise—table goes over—they fall into each others' arms.*)

SECOND (*on the floor—dreamily*): 'Sa-nuts!

* * *

TEDDY: Dixie, honey, don't cry. Don't cry like that.

DIXIE: What do you care?

TEDDY: I do care. You know I care. I don't care for anybody but you—you know that.

DIXIE: Well, why do you chase so then?

TEDDY: I don't know—I'm crazy I guess. Always been crazy. Don't mean to be.

DIXIE (*sobbing*): We could be so happy together. Why aren't we?

TEDDY: It's my fault. 'Sall my fault.

DIXIE: Maybe it's my fault, too.

TEDDY: No, it's my fault. But I'm going to stop it. There's nothing in it.

DIXIE: You do love me, don't you, Teddy? Say so if you don't. I just couldn't bear it if you didn't and were just making believe. You don't have to do that with me.

TEDDY: Oh, Dixie! The first time I ever saw you, I fell so hard for you, it wasn't even funny. You know that, don't you?

DIXIE: So you told me.

TEDDY: But don't you know it? Didn't you feel it?

DIXIE: I—I guess so.

TEDDY: And after we had that fight on the ranch—that was my fault too—and you left me—and I came running right down to Hollywood after you—Didn't I come running?

DIXIE: Y—e—e—s.

TEDDY: And about London and Le Megot, I'm sorry about that, Dixie, I really don't care for her. You know that. She just fascinated me, I guess. But I'll not see her any more. I'll not see anybody but you. I'll quit all this helling around and it'll be just you and me from now on—everywhere—all the time.

DIXIE: Oh, Teddy—if I could only believe it. Is it true? Do you mean it? Can't we just go somewhere together—all by ourselves—take a little house—and just be us—you and me? All the time—just be us—you and me? I just want you, Teddy—you know that—and I don't want you to be such a bad boy. You are a bad boy—don't you know that?

TEDDY: I won't be bad any more. Let 'em look. Who the hell cares!

* * *

FIRST LITTLE BOY FROM HARVARD: They're kissin'. I'd like to kiss her. Wouldn't you like to kiss her? I would—wouldn't you?

SECOND LITTLE BOY FROM HARVARD (*straining to see*): Who? Who? Whash happened?

FIRST: Over there—shee—over there. Dixshie an' Dixshie an' Dixshie.

SECOND: Can't shee. Who turned out lights? Where'm I?

FIRST: How can you shee if you don't openya eyes, huh? You ashleep?

SECOND: 'Sgood idear—shleep. Gonna shleep. Call me—nine.

FIRST: Me too. Nine o'clock. Move over.

SECOND (*smiling happily*): S'nuts.

* * *

DIXIE: You look so funny, darling—you've got lipstick all over your face.

TEDDY: And your mascara has run all over yours.

DIXIE: That makes us a couple of Elks.

TEDDY: God—you're sweet!

DIXIE: Teddy-honey . . . Let's make a night of it. Whoops!

TEDDY: What'll we do?

DIXIE: Let's go crazy together. Let's get drunk as a coot.

TEDDY: Two coots.

DIXIE: All right. Two coots. And then we'll climb on the wagon.

TEDDY: What's that? Never heard of him.

DIXIE: You will, baby, you're gonna climb right up and sit with me in the rumble seat.

TEDDY: Never heard of him. Hey, garkon: La memy chosey, tooty sweety.

CONTRALTO IN TWEEDS:
"The Infusoria in Peoria do it—
And the better classes in Emporia do it—
Let's do it—
Let's fall in love."

~~~~~~~~~~~~~~~~~~~~~

AMERICAN PLAYBOY AND SHOW GIRL IN BAD WITH PARIS POLICE

Teddy Page, Park Avenue's pet cut-up, and his young bride, Dixie Dugan, who learned her stuff in Hollywood, threw a party in and around, under and over, behind and in front of the staid old Ritz Hotel last night, which ended in a free-for-all-fight, a mob scene, a police raid and the flight of Teddy and Dixie for parts unknown.

They were asked by the Ritz to go. They were asked by the police to stay. But whatever they have decided to do, they have the satisfaction of knowing that the rue Pigalle will miss them, and the Place Vendôme will never look the same.

Piecing together the stories told by various dizzy participants, it seems Teddy Page of the Page millions had just returned from London, where rumor had it he was more than benevolently interested in a certain or rather uncertain nightclub dancer there. Followed one of those lover's quarrels, which the newlyweds decided to patch up with a celebration which took the shape of a mad canvass of Montmartre night clubs, starting with Le Fétiche and Chez Florence and coming to full flower with a taxicab parade to the Ritz of guests, invited and otherwise, headed by the band from Brick Top's.

You can imagine the exclusive surprise of the Ritz's exclusive clientele when, at three o'clock in the morning, they heard Brick Top's band blasting away in the sacred foyer. But their surprise was nothing compared to that of the management dashing to the scene in nightshirts, only to discover that Teddy had hired the entire troupe of Can-Can girls from the Bal Tabarin, and they were doing their stuff all over the lobby while Teddy directed them and the band from his perch on the porter's desk.

The whole place seethed with a crowd, variously estimated from 200 to 500, and composed of some of the snootiest social register names on both sides of the water. To the bewildered police, however, summoned to the scene by the hysterical management, one and all gave the name of Smith.

Two college boys who had lost their papers are being held for identification. One couldn't answer any questions, and the other, when pumped for information, could only reply, "It's the nuts." The French police are baffled.

~~~~~~~~~~~~~~~~

Darling Nita,

Teddy and I are on the famous Blue Train headed for the Riviera, and I have a new Reboux hat made on my head by Madame Lucienne herself while the Paris police were hunting for us, and Teddy's crazy about me, and I've decided to have a baby, a real 100% cooperative baby, and the whole thing is going to belong to Teddy and me and it's going to be a boy with blue eyes and play fullback for Notre Dame and Teddy and I are going to sit in the Yale Bowl and cheer while he plows through the team for fourteen touchdowns and after the game we're both going to snake dance on the field and I'm going to throw my new Reboux hat over the goal-post.

If this sounds a little bit woozy blame the party, the hat, my sweet man and this Riviera sunshine streaming through the windows here in Toulon just a few hours from Cannes, Juan-les-Pins, Nice, Monte Carlo and what am I offered.

The party was a couple of nights ago. I'm sending you a clipping. It was a wow and we had to hide for a couple of days before we could get reservations to go south. While we hid in a cute duplex studio with a private bar in the Rovaro on rue Brunel we lived entirely on caviar, champagne and love and decided after many long discussions that we were going to play only a little while more and then we were going to settle down and raise little Teddys and Dixies, two or three or five or eleven, and Teddy was going to work hard and I was going to stay home and knit spats for our brood and when he trudged home in his Rolls from Wall Street evenings with a big bond on his shoulder for me and some little stocks in his pockets for the babies we would all jump off our Park Avenue penthouse terrace with parachutes to greet him.

Maybe I'll have a little girl first. But a boy's better, isn't it? When he's older he can take her places and dig up boy friends for her. I'd better hurry up or I'll be forty before she's sixteen and that would never do. Teddy thinks I'm crazy to want a baby and be tied down to it but I certainly don't want to bat around and make society whoopee all my life. If I never make any more I'll have had my quota. Me too, says Teddy, but nobody has babies if they can help it, do they, and I says I want one. And I do, Nita, and I bet Teddy and I would have a little heller.

Hoping you are the same. Next stop—Juan-les-Pins.

DIXIE.

VIII

Variety

15 Blvd. des Italiens
Paris

Dear Dixie Dugan Teddy Page,

So you're going to the Cote D'Azur and Juan-les-Pants and don't ask me how I know because Variety mugs know everything. They get it only half-right if they're lucky, but who does better? My spies followed you to the Rovaro after the Ritz kicked you and Teddy out for profaning their sacred foyer with jazz bands and Can-Can girls, although I've seen much worse in their foyers paying space rates and so have you and you, and even you cowering over there in your corner.

And now you're asking is he just a smarty writing to gloat or is there some hidden significance in this? The answer's simple. Your old uncle mug wishes to tip you off to the sights, sounds and scents of the world's playground (trade-mark registered by the Riviera, Atlantic City, Long Beach, Finger Lakes and The Dells, Wisconsin). You will take Le Train Bleu, of course, which leaves an hour later than a train just as good and costs more and doesn't get you there any sooner, and you will sit around for half the trip wondering what P.L.M. means and why they have those silly doilies on the backs of the seats. And the answer is that one means as much as the other. When you wake up in the morning, you'll see cactus, jackpine, vineyards, a lot of trees that look like they need dusting—those will be olives, oodles of flowers, names sent on request, and one beach after another from Marseilles to Mentone. You'll probably go to Cannes but there are a lot of better places which you won't hear about until you're ready to leave. San Rafael is one, and Toulon is two, and there's a little hideaway tucked between the two, entirely populated by the most delightful pixies, male and female, but you'll never find it unless you meet one of three people, names enclosed here in sealed envelope. They'll take you there if they like you.

Otherwise you'll go to Cannes and stop at the Miramar or you'll go to Juan-les-Pins and stop at le Provernçal, or to Cap D'Antibes and stop at the Hotel Du Cap, or if you want to have lots of fun you'll go to Cagnes-sur-Mer and stop at the Hotel Colonies, or if you want to see a lot of Mr. Cook's friends you'll go to Monte Carlo, or if you want to see a lot of Mr. Mussolini's, you'll go to Mentone. These places are all strung along the Riviera like those red peppers you see hanging up outside of the pueblos in New Mexico. And each has a different kind of crowd on the same kind of beach, though each crowd will tell you the other beach is lousy and they will all tell you that the Normandy coast is a bum, and if you go to the Lido you're crazy.

But now that you are in society you will go to all of these places and in their proper seasons which is usually the worst time of the year, and instead of switching around to dodge the people who bore you you'll make it a point to go where you know they are going, hoping against hope that they won't bore you this time but knowing in your heart that they will. You are getting down there about the right time to meet all the American bores and if you stay a little longer you'll meet all the English ones who are now up in Le Touquet amusing each other no end but boring everybody else stiff, everybody else being Americans, Argentines and Greeks, all of whom know it is very top-hole and spiffy to be seen with the English but can't bear 'em which makes it mutual. Being your mentor, self-appointed, you should do the Riviera now and dash over to the Lido for not more than a week, then get back to Deauville for Grand Prix week. When the last race is run you should be on your way to Paris or you will be ostracized forever, unless of course you belong to an old Scotch family who can do what they please and make the English like it, and if it's good enough for the English it's good enough for you, you outlandish Colonial.

And now for the Riviera and the Promenade des Goddam Anglais, as the French call it privately. Go to the Palm Beach Casino at Cannes if you want to die of lonesomeness, but elegantly, and go to the Casino in Juan-les-Pins if you want to see the cream and the scum of all the world mix every night in hilarious bacchanalia. Go to the Chateau Madrid on fight-nights where you can dance in the ring after they've swept up the fighters, who, being French, are handicapped by not being able to use their feet. After you've been poured out of there, you'll trickle naturally to Le Boeuf sur le Toit, very elegant in crystals and mirrors and onyx like a Frankl interior. There will be a jazz band of those darling negroes and they will be playing *I'm crying for the Carolines*. It will look like the Band from Brick Top's or Florence's band or Fess Williams from the Savoy (Harlem, not London). And there will be one epileptic dancer, male, and one swell-looking café-au-lait moaner doing torch songs like *Go back where you stayed last night*, which the French think is one of our national anthems, and wouldn't it be a good one?

You must get up early because only the poule ordnaire sleeps late and you play tennis until noon and swim until one and lunch until three thirty and you swim off Eden Roe and lunch on the balcony where they serve hors d'œuvre cafeteria style and the brandy comes in demi-johns, but being a lady you pass it, the first time, anyway. After you've passed it the second or third time you take it and you will find it's the old old fine maison but makes the Mediterranean look bluer than ever and you are quite sure that all the surfboard riders being pulled around behind motor boats are not really falling off the boards, but you're wrong because they really are. You will have had cocktails while you reclined on the rocks, or if not cocktails what they call Champagne quelque-chose, which gives you the effect of aqua-planing but still keeps you with both feet on the ground figuratively speaking. You will have wine with your lunch and *fine* with your coffee and then you will go to a cocktail party and after that to another one and then you will have cocktails while you dress for dinner and cocktails after you're dressed, and you will dine at the Casino at Juan-les-Pins if you want fun, at the Hotel Du Cap if you want good music, at Le Tête if you want good bouillabaise, at du Logis-du-Loup if you want the best food on the Riviera now that the Caramello on Cap Ferrat is closed for the summer.

You will find out about Maxim's when you get there and Chez Frederick's on the Island of St. Honorat and Joseph's Duck Bar on the beach and aperitif dancing from eleven to thirteen and a half, and what I haven't told you about you'll see, and what you don't see ask for. And you'll get it. That's where you're going. Too bad, isn't it?

And now a little soupçon of news. Guess who I met last night over at Dagorno's wrapping himself around one of those big steaks for which the place is famous? A New York newspaperman and ex-playwright over here in Europe, at great expense for the Colossal Films Corp. and charged with the responsibility of gathering material for a high society movie. Someone was talking about your farewell party at the Ritz and I happened to mention that I knew you, whereat this lad jumped clear out of his chair and landed around my neck. Dixie—Dixie. Do you know Dixie, says he? And I says sure.

And he says where is she, what's she doing, and I says who might you be stranger? Me, he says, I'm Jimmy Doyle. And I says not Jimmy Doyle who wrote and produced "Get Your Girl" starring said Dixie Dugan? And he says, the same, where is she, what is she doing, how is she getting along? And I says Whoa and I tells him as near as I can, and then he tells me he's got to make the rounds of all the play-places in Europe like Deauville and Biarritz and the Riviera for a movie he's writing and I says you may run into her because that's just where she is at this moment, arranged tastefully along the Mediterranean, getting a load of that famous infra-red, for which the sun in them parts is justly noted.

And he says hopefully maybe I'll run into her down there, and I says anybody who's anybody from H. G. Wells to Peggy Joyce, from Stravinsky to the Dolly Sisters, and Frank Harris to Nigger Nate Raymond, will be, have been, or are infesting said coast of pleasure. Not to mention hordes of dukes and shoals of counts and a wilderness of millionaires, dowagers, gigolos, poules de luxe, demi-luxe and ordinaire, movie stars, mannequins, women kept or keeping, German tourists with cameras, American schoolteachers with repressions, croupiers, blackmailers, a few Frenchmen, a lot of artists, and too many American authors spending American money and giving America hell. So of course you'll be there too and you can't help but meet Dixie.

And with that I send you a parting benediction and the assurance that no matter what you do down there—and you will—you have a plenary indulgence and full absolution in advance.

Ever thine,
MIKE TOOHEY.

~~~~~~~~~~~~~~~~

PARIS FRANCE

```
    SOL NEBBICK
    COLFILMCORP
    HOLLYWOOD
    CALIFORNIA
    U S A
```

CLEANED UP PARIS FOR FILM STOP TOO
COLD AND EARLY FOR NORMANDY COAST
RESORTS RIVIERA NOW HOT WHOOPEE
SUMMER SPOT FOR SOCIETY STOP LEARNED
TODAY DIXIE DUGAN OVER HERE AND
TALKED WITH BOB KANE JOINVILLE
STUDIOS ABOUT POSSIBILITY OF
SHOOTING HER HERE IN LOCAL COLOR IF
SHE COULD BE PERSUADED TO COME BACK
TO MOVIES STOP SHALL I PROPOSITION
HER COULD COMBINE EUROPEAN ANGLE
SOCIETY AND DIXIES POPULARITY CABLE
                                  DOYLE

CHATEAU MADRID
CANNES
GALA SAUVAGE

Conférencier:

M. "TEDDY" PAGE

Diner de gala

100 francs

au profit des pauvres de Cannes

THE DAILY MAIL

Paris Notes & News and Gossip from the Summer Resorts

(From our Riveria Correspondent)

The Riviera demand for novelty is resulting in a crop of amazing settings for gala dinners, and in this respect the Chateau Madrid at Cannes is living up to its reputation for originality.

Last night the famous roof garden was transformed into an immense training-quarters for fighters, wrestlers, etc. and most of the reservations were for guests of Mr. Teddy Page, the young American sportsman, who originated the idea of the gala and the costumes for himself, his beautiful bride, Dixie Dugan, the cinema star, and his guests, all of whom came dressed as prizefighters or wrestlers. One of the original notes was that each guest, as well as the host, should come decorated with one large beautiful black eye apiece.

The origin of the idea for the party was even more droll than the party itself.

According to Mr. Teddy Page's explanation to your correspondent, he had had a minor domestic altercation with his young bride a few nights previous and she, with that impetuous vivacity for which she is internationally famous, threw a complete set of Victor Hugo at him, all of which he managed to dodge with the exception of Volume II of "Les Miserables." Feeling that he could not venture forth into elegant society with what in the American idiom is referred to as a "shiner" he decided to solve the dilemma by giving a party in honor of his decoration and advising all his friends of the cause thereof and his desire that they come in a similar guise. It was the merriest party of the season. Dancing continued into the small hours, and many magnums of champagne were drunk in gay toasts and tributes to Dixie Dugan's marksmanship.

~~~~~~~~~~~~~~~~~~

<div style="text-align:right">

LE PROVENÇAL
JUAN-LES-PINS

</div>

DARLING NITA,

Well, let us see what has happened since I wrote to you last. I have a tan from the nape of my neck to all points south, Teddy has a mouse on his eye which we celebrated with a party—clipping enclosed—only I followed up "Les Miserables" with "A Wanderer in Venice," and "France on 10 Words a Day." My Novitsky pyjamas are the cats. I've never seen so many parties or had so much fun or went so many places or met so many different kinds of people or ate so much or drank so much or danced so much, etc. And when I say etcetera I mean and so forth—and so on—and how!

But this is the real news. Hold your hat. Guess who's in Europe? In Paris? Maybe down here by this time for all I know. JIMMY! Tie that. Got a letter from a friend in Paris who had seen him and told him I was down here and Jimmy was all questions and goose-flesh. And me too. Gee I'd love to see him. Gee I hope I do. And don't think I won't if he's over here. I don't think Teddy will care and even if he does, what of it? After all he hasn't been behaving himself so well either, not even after all his promises in Paris. That's why I crowned him. Got tired of talking to him. All worn out.

Can you imagine, Nita, he's been carrying on a correspondence all the time with Le Megot—that Apache dancer he met on the boat and followed to London. I found a note from her saying if you don't come to see me I'll kill myself. Fat chance. No such luck. More likely to stick a knife in Teddy. Well, he's asking for it. I can't police him all the time. He went out on a yacht for tea with some playboys and a bunch of girls the other afternoon and stayed for breakfast. That's how he got the mouse on the glim. Next time, says I to him as he came out of the gauze, it will be a palm and I won't stop to take it out of the pot either.

Gee I'm glad Jimmy's back with Colossal. He's doing a story for them about society in Europe. I certainly could tell him more about a few sections of it now than when I was sitting around in Brooklyn reading the society column hooey. I've met plenty of them here. More than I'd ever meet in the same time in America and certainly under better conditions for learning the truth about them. There's nothing that will flatten a flock of broad A's or dynamite that old golden-horseshoe reserve like a warm summer night and a champagne party on a moonlit terrace overlooking the Mediterranean. Then you really hear how the de Puyster Sniffle-Snoofles crashed the Social Register and under yonder palm you find the haughty dowager holding the young Baron in what you could hardly call an aristocratic embrace, and who is the blonde beauty wading around in the goldfish pond with her evening gown tucked up under her arms? Well, it isn't a Follies girl, Nita, and if I told you who it was you'd never read Cholly Knickerbocker again.

I heard one cute story the other day which will give you an idea of one section of this dizzy Cannes crowd. Oh, said someone the other day, so you know the Prince Pio Pochito, and I said well I met him on the boat. Coming from America they ask and I say yes. Do you know why he left? I certainly would like to know why he went, why he stayed and why he left, says I.

Oh, says they, why he went is simple—to get a rich American bride and why he stayed is the same reason, but why he left is because he was too gallant and it happened as follows. It seems that the daughter of one of America's magnates had become enamored of him and he seeing she was the daughter of an American magnate became enamored of her. And she had been out for two or three years without causing any great stir in the matrimonial market and since he's a real prince and looks good Mama was very pleased and Papa said all right and so Papa and Mama and the daughter and the prince were on their way to Havana for a little trip. Papa and Mama and daughter for the air and the prince for the outing.

But it seems Papa and Mama and daughter were bridge fiends and the prince doesn't care about it and it seems that one day the prince spied a beautiful red-headed girl on the boat and conversing with her learned that she was an excellent bridge player. Hoping to keep in touch with her and not incur the displeasure of his hosts he introduced the red-headed girl to the host and when they learned she was a good player they were very much pleased and so it went for the rest of the trip. But the prince became more and more interested in the red-headed girl and she in the prince and they arranged to meet after the boat docked and have what is the princely and red-headed equivalent of a good time. And so it was done. And then the prince discovered that Mr. and Mrs. Magnate had become very cool toward him which he naturally attributed to his interest in the red-head and subsequent neglect of the daughter. So he stopped seeing the red-head, that is he didn't see her so much.

But still the trip was unaccountably shortened and Papa and Mama and daughter and prince went back to New York where the prince was given to understand that everything was off. Being quite puzzled by this sudden turn of affairs he talked it over with some of his boy friends along Park Avenue and when he told them the story they laughed uproariously and he didn't know why. And they said you mean to say that you brought this red-head over and introduced her to the parents of this girl? Surely, he says, she was a nice girl and played good bridge. And then you went out with her in Havana? Surely, he says, why not? But you big sap, says they, don't you know who the little red-head is? And he says no and they says she was Papa's girl friend.

Wonder how Jimmy looks Nita. Gee, when I think of seeing Jimmy again, Nita, my heart stops. I'll never get over him. Why Dixie! Is that any way for a bride on her honeymoon to talk? Oh, shut up.

Your loving sis,
Dixie.

                                                            PARIS
LE PROVENCAL
JUAN LES PINS
A M
PLEASE RESERVE ROOM BATH TOP FLOOR
AND WITH SEA VIEW IF POSSIBLE
ARRIVING TOMORROW
                                                    JAMES DOYLE

IX

Jimmy: *Entrez!* Oh, there you are. Where did you have to go for that champagne? Back to Paris?

Waiter: Pleez?

Jimmy: I think I'll have it out on the balcony.

Waiter: Comment?

Jimmy: The balcony. Dehors, s'il vous plaît.

Waiter: Pleez?

Jimmy: Oh, nuts! Give it to me. Here, take this and go buy yourself a French dictionary.

Waiter: Merci. (*In the hall—to femme de chambre*): Mon Dieu, qui'ils sont bêtes, ces Américains!

~~~~~~~~~~~~~~~~~~~~~~

<div style="text-align: right">

le Provençal
Juan-les-Pins

</div>

Darling Nita,

I'm sitting up here in my room with nothing much to do except wait for Teddy to come home. He went to a dinner party Capt. White is giving Mary Garden at Eden Roe and promised faithfully he would be home early. I haven't been feeling so peppy all day—too many parties I guess—so I thought I'd lie around up here and listen to the music on the terrace down below. There's a balcony just outside the window and I can sit out there and watch them dance seven stories down on a marble terrace with strings of colored electric lights over them, a French jazz band singing *Zank Your F adder* and a full moon hanging so low over the Mediterranean you can almost reach it with your hand.

Now they're playing *I'm Crying for the Carolines*. Imagine being in a spot like this and crying for the Carolines or any other place. I've heard more Frenchmen crying for the Carolines this summer. People ought to get what they cry for once in a while. Teach them a lesson. I think I'll go out and sit on the balcony and look at the moon. I may finish this and I may not. It's twelve o'clock and Teddy isn't home yet. Well they dine late here. Sit down at ten. Fall down at twelve. Eighteen course dinner and it all might just as well be fish. What a moon I It's just coming up over the tops of the pines. Wait a minute, Nita—I'll go out and slice off a piece for you to put under your pillow to sleep on....

* * *

JOAN: You'd better go home, Teddy, it's one o'clock.

TEDDY: Who?

JOAN: You're ory-eyed. Go home and paw your wife.

TEDDY: Nice lil' wife.

JOAN: Why aren't you home with her? I guess you're afraid to go home. She'll give you another black eye.

TEDDY: Mind your own business.

JOAN: Glad you didn't bring her to this party. Little Brooklyn hoodlum.

TEDDY: Hoodlum yourself.

JOAN: How did you ever come to marry her? How? That's what I could never figure out. None of us can.

TEDDY: How you come marry anybody? Wan to.

JOAN: You were a damned fool getting yourself tied up to a little nobody. You could get that kind without marrying them.

TEDDY: Not Dixie.

JOAN: Pushover.

TEDDY: Pushover yourself.

JOAN: Little Broadway tart. Hollywood bum. Didn't I see her out at the Ranch when you first married her? I could see it then. I know the kind. Out for all they can get.

TEDDY: So are you. So'm I. So's everybody. Sure—why not?

JOAN: You could have had your pick—and what have you got? We only tolerate her for your sake.

TEDDY: S'kind of you. Wanta 'nother drink.

JOAN: Here—take mine.

TEDDY: Good. Twenty-five bucks a bottle in New York. Sink of it. (*Thinks of it*) T'hell with New York!

* * *

JIMMY: But I can't get over it, Dixie darling.

DIXIE: You mustn't say darling.

JIMMY: But I can't help it. Believe it or not, I was sitting out here drinking all alone for hours thinking about you.

DIXIE: No fooling!

JIMMY: And out you come on that balcony right beside me—like a—like a—well, like a vision.

DIXIE: You're tired, Jimmy. You can do better than "vision."

JIMMY: Tired! I'm dizzy. You see, darling.

DIXIE: Don't say darling, Jimmy—

JIMMY: All right. You see, darling, I knew you were in the South of France but I had no idea you were in Juan-les-Pins, let alone in the next room to me.

DIXIE: Well, I was.

JIMMY: If a fellow wrote that in a book they'd say he certainly had to reach for that one.

DIXIE (*softly*): Never mind. My, you look just the same, Jimmy. Gee, it's good to see you. How long since I've seen you? It seems ages.

JIMMY: Just about a year.

DIXIE: Ah, go on. Year. Century. Don't you think I've changed a lot?

JIMMY: You're beautiful.

DIXIE: I like that! So that's how I've changed! I thought I was pretty good-looking before.

JIMMY: I don't know. You're changed. Lovelier—I don't know. More serious, I guess.

Dixie: I am more serious.

JIMMY: Happy?

DIXIE: Oh sure.

JIMMY: Sure?

DIXIE: Sure, I'm sure. Why not?

JIMMY (*bitterly*): Of course—why not.

DIXIE: Aren't you? What have you been doing?

JIMMY: Batting around.

DIXIE: In love?

JIMMY: You know that's all over for me.

DIXIE: Now Jimmy, you talk like an old man. All over! Bet you've been in love forty times since I saw you last.

JIMMY: Nope.

DIXIE: Well, twenty then.

JIMMY: Not even once. I can't see anybody but you—you know that.

DIXIE: You mustn't talk that way to me, Jimmy. I'm married.

JIMMY: Don't I know it!

DIXIE: Well, then—

JIMMY: Where's your husband tonight?

DIXIE: Out on a party.

JIMMY: Doesn't he take you?

DIXIE: Not always. I didn't want to go tonight any way. Didn't feel like yipping around till dawn again tonight. Felt funny all day—low—blue—I don't know.

JIMMY: Me, too. Thinking of you all day—hoping I'd see you—

hoping I wouldn't—all mixed up—so instead of going out tonight I just ordered champagne up here and looked at the moon and listened to the music and wished you were here—and sure enough you came. Who said there wasn't any magic anymore?

Dixie: Jimmy!

Jimmy: Dixie!

* * *

Man: Where is she tonight?

Woman: He left her at home.

Man: I don't see him around anywhere. Has he gone?

Woman: Disappeared. With Joan, I suppose. She's been hanging around him all evening.

Man: All evening? For years. She thought she had him once—

Woman: And along came Dixie.

Man: It won't last.

Woman: Who wants anything to last?

Man: He couldn't stick to anybody.

Woman: I wouldn't mind him sticking to me for a little while.

Man: She's a nice kid, I like her. Natural—that's what I like about her.

Woman: Can't say Teddy isn't natural!

Man: He's a bum.

Woman: But good-looking.

Man: Yes.

Woman: And filthy with it. They say his old man was one of the few who was on the right side of the market last fall.

Man: He would be.

Woman: I wouldn't say Teddy inherited much of his brains.

Man: He'll get the money, which is just as good.

Woman: You can't blame Joan for trying then, can you?

Man: I don't blame her.

Woman: I'd try myself if I thought there was any chance. But he's too crazy about Dixie.

MAN: Looks like it, doesn't it?

WOMAN: Oh, he's just playing. Dixie's smart. Let him play.

MAN: He's always playing.

WOMAN: Sure, and he always will. You can't keep a squirrel on the ground.

* * *

DIXIE: The music's stopped, Jimmy. It must be late.

JIMMY: It's been stopped for an hour.

DIXIE: Good grief, what time is it?

JIMMY: No idea. Who cares anyway?

DIXIE: The music stops at three, I think. We couldn't have been talking for three hours, could we?

JIMMY: Sure. We've talked longer than that lots of times, haven't we? Remember how we used to sit around in Jimmy Durante's Club and talk until they tried to stack us up on the tables with the chairs.

DIXIE: Oh, Jimmy, that was fun!

JIMMY: And in the Brown Derby in Hollywood—and that little German restaurant behind the Ritz in Atlantic City when we were trying out—"Get Your Girl"—

DIXIE: Oh, Jimmy—and the Rocking Stone Restaurant up at the Zoo—

JIMMY: And Moneta's on Mulberry—the Santa Marghareta—and Zabaglione—

DIXIE: And Louis and Martin's—the corner table near the bar—writing our names on the little lamp and shade—

JIMMY: And the Willard out on Pico in Hollywood where we had our last dinner together before I went back East a bum and you stayed in Hollywood and became a star and—

DIXIE: Let's not go all over everything again Jimmy. We've had sweet, sweet times, but that's all over now, isn't it? We have to grow up some time, don't we?

JIMMY: Why?

DIXIE: Because we must. Anyway, I'm married. I shouldn't be sitting out here all hours talking to you like this!

JIMMY (*bitterly*): I know you're married. But are you happy though? No!

DIXIE: Of course I am. And even if I wasn't—just being happy isn't everything. Who is happy all the time anyway?

JIMMY: I don't know.

DIXIE: I know—nobody. I certainly wasn't happy when I was single.

JIMMY (*jealously*): I thought we were happy.

DIXIE: Happy! Who ever said being in love was being happy. It's the most miserable feeling in the world most of the time. (*wistfully*) But I loved it.

JIMMY: Then why did you ever marry this guy Teddy anyway?

DIXIE: Oh, let's not talk about me any more. Let's talk about you. What are you writing now? A book? A play?

JIMMY: Just a movie.—All about you.

DIXIE: About me?

JIMMY: You and your society friends, and what you do at home and abroad—that's what I'm here for. Going to all the play places, Deauville—Le Touquet—Biarritz—La Baule—the Riviera—the Lido—St. Moritz—Aix-les-Bains—everywhere—for material.

DIXIE: Is it fun?

JIMMY: I don't know yet. I don't think so.

DIXIE: I don't either. It's fun in a way. But it's no pleasure—if you know what I mean. We're all so bored—Teddy's friends and their friends—and they work so hard to be amused—and nothing makes 'em really laugh—only when they're full of champagne and are their real selves but don't know it.

* * *

(*A fumbling at the lock of Dixie's door and Teddy's voice singing gaily off key.*)

TEDDY: *Happy days here again. Happy days here again. Happy days here again.* (*As the door opens suddenly and he lurches in*) *Happy days here again!* 'Lo, Dixie, m'love. *Happy days here again. Happy days here again.* Where's the light? Why don't they put lights where lights are? Where's light? Aw, you don't have to answer. Don't have to answer. Be sore. I can be sore too. Sore as you. Sorer. But I won't. No. No sir. Firm control. Gonna sing instead. *Happy days here again. Happy days*—nev'mind light. Keep your old light. Got all light I need. Got a nice moon. *And high above moon was new—so was love—Lover, come back to me-e-e-e!* Pretty. Lover come back to *me-e-e-e-e!* Where're you? Sleep? Sore? Why doncha talk? I can see you. I can see you—lying over there. Peek-a-boo! Here, catch this. Don't drop it, s'good watch. Catch it. Aw, you missed it. Now poppa's gotta buy new watch. One shoe off and one shoe on. Hi-diddle-diddle-my son John! Goddam these studs—who the hell invented studs? T'hell with 'em. *Oh, the moon is fair t'night 'long Whabash.* Isn't that a love-aly moon, darling? Love-a-ly love-a-ly moon. Gee, I'm tired. Why don't you say something? Why don't you talk to me? Sore? Don't be sore. Jus' in'cen'lil' dinner party—jus' lilicen'—dinnercen'—lilicen'—nev'min'. *Here am I. Here I'll stay, till you notice me.* Home with my sweet lil' wife. Where's p'jamas? Can' find p'jamas. Can't find bed—can' find nothin'. Oh, dear, oh dear, oh dear, back in a minute. Back for a sweet kiss from darlin' lil' wifie darlin'. Where's the hell light in bathroom? Hey, can' find light in bathroom. Oh—there you are. Hidin' from me, you lil' basket. *Happy days here again. Happy days*—(*Slam.*)

* * *

DIXIE: I better duck in there now while I have a chance.
JIMMY: Oh, Dixie, I can't let you go.
DIXIE: Don't do that.... Are you crazy? ... Goodnight.

JIMMY: I can't bear it . . . Dixie . . . that drunken—
DIXIE: Sh-h-h. . . . Goodbye, Jimmy.
JIMMY: Not goodbye—just goodnight. I'll see you tomorrow.
DIXIE: No, I better not see you any more.
JIMMY: Why?
DIXIE: Why? Why? My God, do you think I'm made of wood? Dammit, I can't stand everything—
JIMMY: Dixie . . . I can't bear it not to see you any more. I just can't—
DIXIE: You'll have to, Jimmy. Goodnight. Goodbye—
JIMMY: One minute—one tiny minute . . . one kiss. . . .
DIXIE: Don't . . . are you crazy?
JIMMY: Yes I am. . . . I don't care.
DIXIE: You see . . . I can't see you any more . . . mustn't . . . nowhere . . . Goodbye. . . .
JIMMY: Oh, Dixie . . . Dixie. . . .
TEDDY: *Happy days here again—here again—here again—*'Lo sweetheart—'lo lil' darling—you've been out there lookin' at the moon—lookin' at the moon. I can tell. Give Teddy sweet sweet kiss—sweet—sweet kiss. Whassa matter, huh? Mad, huh? Sit down here on bed with Teddy. One lil' sweet sweet kiss. Oh yes you will, you lil' devil—yes you will—Now, for Chrissake what's the matter? What are you crying about? What t'hell have you got to cry about? Come to bed—come on. . . .

X

Introducing Mrs. Teddy (Dixie Dugan) Page

Princess Jane di San Faustino
Excelsior Palace Hotel
The Lido
Venice.

LA VILLA TRAINON,
BLVD. SAINT ANTOINE
VERSAILLES,
SEINE ET OISE

Dear Jane,
  This will introduce to you the delightful Dixie Dugan, of whom I have written you. I am sure the acquaintance will be mutually agreeable.
  Affectionately,
  Elsie Mendl.

(From the Daily Mail Continental Edition)

REVUE FOR SUN CURE HOME IS GREAT SUCCESS AT LIDO

Princess Jane di San Faustino's Entertainment Draws High Society

(Special Correspondence)

VENICE—The spectacular revue which Princess Jane di San Faustino gives each year at the Lido for the benefit of the sun cure home for children in Rome was this season called "A Great Day" and, as usual, proved a great success. Professional and amateur talent are so cleverly combined in these entertainments that a crowd is always assured and 500 was the estimated number enjoying the fantastic, beautiful and amusing fantasy of an opium-smoker's dream.

"The Great Day" began with the entrance of Count Pollastrella, a handsome slave, leading the Marchioness Sommi Picenardi di Calvatone to a divan, where she reclines on a leopard skin as he presents her with the wonderworking drug. The marchioness, with her ivory skin and black-circled eyes, in a gorgeous Oriental costume of silver, was very picturesque. Then followed the Duke of Verdura and Miss Dixie Dugan, the American cinematique star, in an amusing burlesque of a Greek dance, and the Marquess di Calvatone, Princess Pignatelli, Countess Zogheb, in a colorful trio, "The Flame and the Butterflies."

Followed an amusing performance by a troupe of acrobats, featuring the Princesse Faucigny-Lucinge Mme. Ralli, the Countess di Buccino, the Duke de la Verdura, Count Rocca, Count Balbi Valier and Carlos Bestegui, all in green satin tights, and the men with decorative moustaches of startling ups and downs.

Among distinguished Americans present were Mr. and Mrs. Whitney Warren and Miss Bonnie Brae who came with a party from the Grand. Also present were: Countess Morosini, Baroness d'Erlanger, M. and Mme. Lucien Lelong, the French artist, Sem, several officers from the American cruiser Northampton and from the Italian fleet in St. Mark's basin, Alice Nikitina of the Russian Ballet, Baron and Baroness Empain of Brussels, Don Guido and Donna Irene Brance of Rome, (formerly Irene Flannery of New York), Prince and Princess Cito Filomarino di Bitetto . . .

(THE LIDO—*The sea flat and warm and shallow, the beach long and wide, fringed with gaily painted cabins, and looming in the background a huge hotel with iron grilled balconies, inquisitive windows and a constant murmur of music, fountains and international gossip.*)

(*The Princess Jane di San Faustino—snow white hair, snow white dress, snow white sandals—sits in the shade of a painted sail and holds court through the heat of the day.*)

PRINCESS: You were sweet, my child. Didn't you think the party was nice? Principessa' parties are proverbially dull, you know.

DIXIE: It was lovely.

PRINCESS: It was all right. I didn't make the lire I hoped for. Do you see any rich Americans on the beach who could help me with my children? I don't see as well as I used to. What I haven't seen on this beach—every summer for twenty-five years I've been sitting right here on this beach, in front of my cabane, and what I have not seen! And behind the cabanes too! When I fell down and broke my hip I used to sit up there near that window, and what I didn't see going on. The world's a funny place, my child. Don't you think so?

DIXIE: Sure.

PRINCESS: You don't know anything about it. You are too young. How old do you think I am? Do not tell me. But I am older than that. And I am tired. Parties tire me now. I suppose I am tired of parties. More than fifty years of parties. And such parties. Well, I have done everything. If I died tomorrow I would not feel I have been cheated. Do you know what I was doing when I called you over to talk to me? I was sitting here planning a beautiful death. Like to die nicely. What would you suggest?

DIXIE: You don't want to die now, do you?

PRINCESS: I think so. If I don't, I will have to have some more parties. I thought Chez Vous with the costumes and fountains and that big artificial moon hanging over the cypresses was rather lovely last night, didn't you? But I was very angry at Pio. You must go to bed, he said. You're staying up too late, he said. You'll be dead tomorrow, go to bed now. The nerve of him, sending me off to bed. Go to bed, mind you. To be sent to bed, that was the blow. Not taken, not followed, but—sent. Such a thing could not happen to you, my child. So I think I will plan a beautiful death. Something not too noisy or too tiring. Did you have a good time? And you must thank your nice husband for me for his generous contribution. He is very nice. You should be very happy, I suppose, but you are not.

DIXIE: What makes you think so?

PRINCESS: Children show their feelings. It is so easy to know when they are happy. And when they are not, their faces crinkle all up like little monkeys. Maybe you are not in love with your husband. That has happened. I have heard of it. So much the worse for him. But you are in love with someone. I can see that too. You would not have been so unhappy last night when everyone else was gay. I can remember all the times I was in love, but I don't. There is no pleasure in memories. Only repetitions. Just now I am too tired to do anything except plan a beautiful death. Here comes that portrait painter who has been working on me. I promised to let him paint me if it does him any good. But he is making me too beautiful. Thinks he is flattering me by not painting the wrinkles. And that is what gives my face character. All these little wrinkles around the eyes—this big deep one around the mouth—what would I do without it? I have earned them too. Entertaining people, trying to make them happy for over fifty years. Why, it is a wonder there is anything left of me.

DIXIE: Fifty years!

PRINCESS: Oh, more. I forget how much more. And don't let anyone tell you that fifty years of society does not wear you down. You will see.

DIXIE: I don't expect to be in it fifty years.

PRINCESS: I hope not, for your sake. It is quite stupid. If it was not for my Sun Cure Home for Children, I would feel I was wasting my life. I wasted years of it. Do you know what changed me? One remark. Did you ever hear of Dr. Munthe?

DIXIE: Didn't he write that book, "The Story of San Michele"?

PRINCESS: The same. Axel Munthe. Do you know what he said to me one day—years and years ago? "Look here, Jane, are you going to spend all your life looking for a fourth for bridge?" Well, it stunned me. It was so true. I hadn't realized that was what I was doing. But I was having such a good time. You do, you know, when you are entertaining and being entertained. You have a lot of fun. You give a lot of pleasure. But that isn't happiness. I suppose I have had more pleasure and less happiness than anyone else in the world.

DIXIE: I don't know much about society. I don't know anything about it. You see, I just married Teddy a few months ago, and that was my first glimpse of it. Before, that, all I knew about it was what I read in the society columns.

PRINCESS: Well, that would not tell you much.

DIXIE: Every Sunday morning I used to sit around the house in Brooklyn and read all about the parties in Newport and Southampton and Palm Beach, and look at the pictures of society brides and debutantes and counts and countesses and dukes and whatnot. But I never thought I'd actually be sitting on The Lido some day and talking to a real live Princess. You know, I thought they all wore crowns.

PRINCESS: I don't wear mine any more than I can help.

DIXIE: I used to think a lot of things about society that I won't think any more. I used to think the real society people were the ones who were very haughty and hard to approach and looked down their noses at you. But that isn't true.

PRINCESS: No, those are the ones who feel they must pretend to be more important than they know they really are. By pretending not to care what you think of them, they show they really do or they would not think of pretending. I am not sure that I have said that just right, but you know what I mean.

DIXIE: I know. Even just a few weeks over here I've met lots of them. And I've met some of the real ones too. And they've always been the nicest.

PRINCESS: My child, I suppose there is more nonsense talked and written about society than anything else in the world. That is because so few people know anything about it. Even those who are right in the middle of it all the time. All they know usually is just what their little set is doing, and that is composed for the most part of a few bright souls and a lot of bores. Each set thinks its set is the best. But none of them are really much use in the world, except that they buy nice things and wear nice clothes and give nice parties and help to circulate a lot of money. They don't even set the styles, much less create them. They make things fashionable, but by that time something better has already been thought of, so they are always a few jumps behind the creators, and a few jumps ahead of the mob. It is not enough to be somebody—you must do something. Almost anything, so long as it is not just looking for a fourth for bridge . . .

~~~~~~~~~~~~~~~~~~~~~~~~

<div style="text-align: right">LE PROVENÇAL
JUAN-LES-PINS</div>

DEAR DIXIE,

You left Juan-les-Pins so suddenly I had no chance to tell you what I really wanted to say. One night you were here—the next morning gone. Why? Was that fair? Anyway, here's what is on my mind—among other things. You know I'm over here in Europe gathering material for Colossal Films for a movie about high society and I cabled Nebbick about an idea which I had and which he thought was good, to wit, that if you could be persuaded to do one picture,

Colossal would take most of it over here on this side, star you and shoot the scenes with you in real localities, such as Deauville, Biarritz, etc. Would you be interested in making this picture? I know the money wouldn't be any inducement, but maybe you are tired of just playing and this would be a chance to play and work at the same time. You can reach me here for the next few days. After that you'd better write me care of the Chase Bank, Paris, because I don't know what my route will be.

Did you ever think I could write such a businesslike letter? Nor I. Why did you run away like that?

Jimmy.

Excelsior-Palace Hotel
Lido-Venise

Dear Jimmy,

Now how can you be so dumb as to ask me why I ran away after what happened that night on the balcony?

And how could you possibly think that Teddy or his family will let me work in the movies as long as I'm married to him?

And why don't you let me alone when you know I'm trying as hard as I can to forget all about you?

Be reasonable.

Dixie.

PRINCESS: I hear you are going away, my dear.

DIXIE: Why how did you know?

PRINCESS: I hear everything, my dear. I sit right in this chair and it all comes to me. For twenty-five summers I have been sitting right here on the Lido, and what I have not seen I have heard, and what I have not heard I can imagine. Did I tell you what I heard in the next cabane yesterday? A man's voice saying, "How beautiful you are, my darling. How I should like to see you with your clothes on." And the lady's reply was even better. "How dare you," she cried, "I shall tell my husband." Ah, what this bewitching Lido does to people, otherwise sane and settled—especially the fog-cursed English. They go quite mad down here in the sun. Did you have a nice time at Bonnie's party last night?

DIXIE: Oh, such fun.

PRINCESS: Bonnie gives good parties. Where she gets the money is a mystery. That is her business, and it is quite a business, I assure you. She reminds me of, I forget his name, who, they used to say, had no enemies but his friends did not like him. Did she ever tell you about the Treasure Hunt party she gave here one season? They all met on a dance boat on the Grand Canal. A couple of hundred of them, and the first clue was in the pocket of a man wearing glasses and drinking coffee on the Piazza San Marco. Oh, that was all right, except that it was Band Night and everybody in Venice was there, all sitting around or walking around, listening to the band and having a nice quiet time, when all of a sudden 200 crazy people dashed in and ran all around the tables, diving into people's pockets and yelling and whooping like Indians. My dear, it almost started a war. The Venetians rose as one man and yelled throw those crazy Americans into the Canal. Police came from everywhere and soldiers and Bonnie's guests barely escaped with their lives. They never did get the first clue because the man with the glasses got so frightened when the riot started that he disappeared and hasn't been heard of since. What was the party like last night?

DIXIE: Well, each guest was supposed to come made up to represent his or her favorite dream or nightmare. Teddy's is walking into a crowded parlor in his underwear so that's how he came. It seems he wasn't the only one.

PRINCESS: What did you go as?

DIXIE: I made up as nearly as possible like somebody I know, because he's my favorite dream.

PRINCESS: Is he the one who makes you look sad?

DIXIE: Perhaps. Wouldn't that be telling? Anyway, I had lots of fun last night, and after the party was over Bonnie let Teddy and I have her gondola and arranged for another gondola with singers in it to go ahead of us, and we rode all around Venice through the Grand Canal and all the little canals. My, it was beautiful, except for one thing.

PRINCESS: You were with your husband?

DIXIE: Oh, no, that wasn't it. But I was all set to hear some beautiful Italian songs. And what do you suppose they serenaded us with all through Venice? *I'm Crying for the Carolines!* Fancy!

PRINCESS: You hear nothing but American jazz in Europe nowadays. I can't say I don't like it, because I do. Sometimes I wish I had a jazz band of my own, and a club like the Chez Vous with a nice team of dancers to dance for me when I feel depressed. It was almost like that last summer. There was a wonderful team here and they danced for me whenever I asked them. You must have heard of them. They are famous all over Europe. Le Megot and Marcel?

DIXIE: Do you know them? They were on the boat coming over with us.

PRINCESS: Of course I know them. Marcel used to sit by the hour—right there where you are—and tell me his troubles. And he had plenty of them too, poor boy.

DIXIE: I can imagine.

Princess: He used to think I could do something about it. Wanted me to talk to her and get her to stop running around with other men. I used to tell him he ought not to pay any attention to her. Let her run around all she wanted to and run around himself. But he used to cry and say he could not. He was so crazy about her and it killed him to see her with anyone else and she used to flaunt every new admirer in front of him and laugh at him when he said anything. Hard as nails, but—isn't she wonderful? Why the men followed her up and down this beach in droves and you could hear them pant clear over to Venice.

Dixie: It was like that on the boat, too.

Princess: It has been like that everywhere, and it has been hell for poor little Marcel. Some day he will do something about it, you will see. When those quiet little fellows do explode somebody always gets hurt.

Dixie (*fervently*): I hope she'll be the one . . .

```
                              LIDO-VENEZIA
LE MEGOT
KIT KAT CLUB
LONDON
JUST READ IN DAILY MAIL YOU ARE
DANCING AT AMBASSADEURS DEAUVILLE
GRAND PRIX WEEK STOP CANT GET AWAY
FROM THIS AWFUL PLACE SOON ENOUGH TO
SEE YOU STOP MISS YOU TERRIBLY STOP
LEAVING HERE TODAY FOR PARIS
                                    TEDDY
```

XI

Hotel Chatham
Rue Daunau
Paris

Darling Nita,

Back in Paris. Already the Lido is like a dream and the Riviera a beautiful story half remembered. I wrote to you about meeting Jimmy in Juan-les-Pins—meeting him on the balcony of his room alongside of mine. It was very sweet and dizzy and sad seeing him again but I couldn't stand the thought of running into him any more, so I made Teddy take me right off the next day to Venice. We had had enough dinner parties in pyjamas and cocktail dances at Maxim's and tanned men bathers without tops, and as Teddy said, if we never see another back or leg we'll be way ahead of our quota. We didn't stay in Venice long. It's a drowsy dreamy place, where you lunch on aquatic bicycles, sleep on couches in front of your bathing cabins or on inflated mattresses floating in the sea. The bathing isn't so hot, if you ask me. The sea is so shallow you walk half way across the Adriatic before it's deep enough to swim and the water is like very blue milk. So the life guards lie around in their boats fully dressed and roast coffee on the prows while they sleep peacefully and dream of whatever Venetian life guards dream about.

I met shoals of Italian nobility and American visiting society, and learned among other things that the way to insure privacy on a European train is to put up a sign saying "Reserved for Mr. Cook." Also whenever you hear Americans giving Mr. Smith hell for this that or the other, you can be sure they are talking about Mussolini because it seems every other Italian is a soldier and the other one is a spy and all you have to do to go to jail is to criticize the Duce. So he's Mr. Smith one week and Mr. Jones the next, and so on. And with that simple little process you can say anything you want—and don't you though.

Well, anyway, here I am back in Paris and thrilled to pieces because all the new collections are opening up and Teddy wants me to get my winter clothes for New York now. I wish you were here to help me. Wouldn't we have fun! But I suppose I'll get along, what with the Page name and Teddy's money and my entree through Novitsky and Lady Mendl. One week of running around looking at collections, ordering, getting measured and then Teddy and I rush to Deauville, take in Grand-Prix week, come back for my fittings, and then off to Biarritz. Does that sound thrilling? Well the clothes part of it is, but the rest I can assure you is a damn bore. I know perfectly well that whoever I meet in Deauville, I'll meet later on in Biarritz and won't like them any better. How blasé the gal's getting! No, just beginning to be fed up with this senseless chasing from one beach to another, one Casino to another, one night club to another, trying to keep track of Teddy, pretending to his friends that it doesn't matter, sometimes pretending to myself that it does, tired of Americans trying to speak French and Frenchmen trying to speak American, and all of 'em trying to sing *Body and Soul* and *Crying for the Carolines*. Oh, so damn tired! Maybe there is something wrong with me. I don't seem to have the bounce I used to have. Feel heavy and sleepy and don't-carish. It isn't old age and it can't be love—so maybe it's a baby. Wouldn't that be the pay-off!

DIXIE.

MADELEINE VIONNET

50 Avenue Montaigne

WINTER COLLECTION

Madame VIONNET will show her new Collection as follows:

To Buyers: Today, at 2:30 p.m. and afterwards every morning at 10:30 a.m. and every afternoon at 2:30 p.m.

AMERICAN LADIES will be received on and from today

THE NEW YORK HERALD, PARIS, MONDAY, AUGUST 16
Notes From Resorts In France
GAY WEEK END AT DEAUVILLE FOR PRINCES AND MILLIONAIRES
(From Our Own Correspondent)

Deauville.

The famous Plage Fleurie was never more animated than during last week-end. The Route de Quarante Sous from Paris was crowded with motor cars bringing their contingent of visitors while extra trains were depositing many others at frequent intervals.

Tout Paris was well represented while the host of foreign personalities were unusual even for Deauville. There were two sultans, princes, American millionaires, noted international bankers and society leaders, not to mention the crowds of other smart people who add to the animation of the resort.

The festivities opened with the gala dinner at the Restaurant des Ambassadeurs. Billy Arnold's orchestra being supplemented by the Orquesta Tipica Ingles with the singers Sanchez, Ferraro and Aquitira, and the sensational Le Megot with her partner Marcel, fresh from their London triumphs.

```
                                        PARIS
       LE MEGOT
       LES AMBASSADEURS
       DEAUVILLE
       CANT WAIT DRIVING FROM PARIS
       ARRIVING TONIGHT
                                        TEDDY
```

~~~~~~~~~~~~~~~~~~~~~~~~~

Dear Nita,

Whoops what a day! This morning Reboux, early this afternoon Vionnet, later Mauboussin, or you might say—hats, gowns and jewels, in the order named. You should see Mlle. Lucienne, who designs all the Reboux models, make a hat on your head while you wait. Takes a big piece of felt that looks like a large stovepipe without the brim, a scissors, a handful of pins and she's off. I sat in front of a triple mirror ankle deep in scraps of felt, snips of ribbon, and pieces of feathers all over the floor, and the first thing she did was to feel my head all over for bumps, and then brush my bangs back, and pull this piece of felt down over my ears. Then she started to slash and pin and take it off and jerk at it and stretch it and jam it back on my head again and slash and pin some more, and all the time a running conversation with her helper who stood by and handed her pins. Well, it was magic. Almost as quickly as it takes me to tell it to you she had the hat all cut, designed and pinned on me as close as my scalp, and a much better fit. Then she shook me out of it, handed it to her helper to be sewed, smiled, said au revoir, it is ready tomorrow, and went out of the room like a rocket. Immediately the place all quieted down even though it was full of people, and it seemed empty like a stage when Al Jolson has just finished singing and walked off. Personality! Pep! You don't wonder any more that every year she tells the women of the world whether they're going to wear their hats down over their eyes or on the backs of their heads and make them like it.

Mme. Vionnet is just the opposite—calm, poised, silvery white, but just as sure, in a different way. Makes all her designs—about three collections—eight hundred a year—first on little dolls about thirty inches high and then drapes the mannequins and cuts the material on them. She showed me just how she does it and I was taken all through the establishment, including backstage among the mannequins. Each mannequin has her own collection, ranging from four to as high as twenty "pieces," as the gowns and cloaks are called, which she "passes," as they call parading them, twice a day once in the morning and once in the afternoon. You never saw such tall, thin babies in your life. If they ate a grape, it would show, Nita, and when they started to parade through the salon in white chiffon velvet evening gowns with no foundations, several nice old greyhaired ladies, who were sitting facing the windows practically fainted. But not so the nice old gentlemen with them. Even Teddy began to sit up and take notice. Up to that time he complained there were too many sharp hip bones to suit him. But the mannequins don't seem to mind anybody. They stare off over your head into the distance, announce the numbers in a bored far-away voice, and exit haughtily dragging behind them on the floor the most gorgeous cloaks, as though they were so many rags.

Your vendeuse, or sales-lady, sits beside you, translates the numbers and helps you get your selection. You start off by checking everything and then you realize that if you took all you wanted, you'd have eight suits and a dozen evening gowns. I'm going back tomorrow, take another look, make my final selections, and I'll tell you all about them later.

After we left Vionnet's, Teddy says, I'm going to take you to a place where they throw half a million dollar ruby necklaces around on kitchen tables, and let you play catch with diamonds as big as walnuts. Where is that, I says. Not very far, he say. We go up a little side street, climb three flights of rickety stairs because the elevator is temporarily out of order and has been since the Revolution and when we get up there it will be a little room with wooden tables and show cases around the wall, and if you like to see some pearls Papa Mauboussin will fish into his pocket and pull out a handful of matched ones as big as bird eggs and drop them in your lap.

Well, Nita, it was just like that—only more so. Just for fun I said, I don't suppose you have a blue diamond, have you, and Papa Mauboussin, the proprietor, said, oh yes, a few, and put down a handful of emeralds on the window-sill and opened a little desk drawer and pulled out a diamond—eleven carats and blue as a sapphire. There's a couple more somewhere here, he says, feeling around among the old papers and he came up with a handful of something, took one look, shook his head sadly and said, no, just rubies. When I came to, I was half way back to the hotel. Where was that place, Teddy, I says. I'm going back there some time. The name is Mauboussin, says Teddy, but I'll never tell you where it is, and you're going back there over my dead body.

And I will, too.

DIXIE.

HOTEL CHATHAM
RUE DAUNAU
PARIS

DIXIE, MY LOVE,

Running up to Deauville while you do your pesky shopping. Sick of collections. Come on up when you're finished. Have reservations for us at the Normandy. Hope you don't mind note. Can't stand discussions.

Love,

TEDDY.

MYSTERIOUS GREEK PLUNGER, SADDENS CASINOS AS HE QUITS

Gambling for big stakes at the leading resorts of France will be lessened necessarily by the withdrawal of the Greek syndicate and plungers who find the 25 percent government tax on winnings to be too exorbitant. Over last weekend at Deauvllle, one individual lost more than $350,000. That individual took over the bank in the private baccarat room where Zographos, head of the Greek syndicate, had held forth for long. His reputatlon as a heavy player attracted scores of gamblers. Luck was against him though and in one hour of play he lost 1,000,000 fr. After several long sessions with fortune still against him he packed up and left, his opponents being richer by nearly 10,000,000 francs.

The Zographos group won a great battle of baccarat at Deauville when the challenging Italian syndicate was vanquished. The threat was the most serious the Greeks have had to face, but six nights of play completely emptied the Italian moneybags of the 18,000,000 francs fortune they contained.

Among those seen in the salle privé last night were Grand Duke Dimitri, Lord Michelham, the Duke de Santa Christina, M. and Mme. Phillippe Berthelot, the Marquess of Villaviciosa, the Aga Khan, Maurice Rostand, M. Andre Citroën, Prince Aage of Denmark, and numerous Americans including the effervescent Mr. "Teddy" Page and his bride, the famous cinema star, Dixie Dugan, who are stopping at the Normandy.

DEAUVILLE AUJOURD'HUI

THE NEW GOLF et GOLF de Deauville }	Tous le Jours	8h à 19h.
TENNIS	Sur les Courts de Club	9h à 19h.
BAR DU SOLEIL BAR de la PLAGE NOUVELLE PLAGE }	Au Plein Air	9h à 24h.
CONCOURS HIPPIQUE		

	(Saluts d'Obstacles)	14h. —
	Officiers	
	(Presentation de Hacks)	
TIR aux PIGEONS		
	Prix d'Italie (20,000 fr)	14h. —
POLO	Match	16h 30
CINEMA	Le Danseur Inconnu	
	Tout Deauville à l'Ecron	20h 45
THEATRE	Mireille	21h —

LES AMBASSADEURS: Thé Dansant

Au Diner
Attractions
BILLY ARNOLD et son Orchestre
Orquetra Tipica INGLES
Avec les danseurs Le MEGOT et MARCEL

"CHEZ BRUMMELL"   Soupers

FIRE BALLOONS IN DEAUVILLE SKY

    Fire balloons floated slowly over Deauville on Sunday evening, when the sky was ablaze with rockets, fire stars and golden rain, a fitting climax to a glorious day.

    Powerful searchlights displayed to the night the beauties of the casino gardens, the multitude of flowers glowing richly in the brilliant light.

Chez Brummell

Billy Arnold's Orchestra (*singing*)

Deauville, Deauville,
Plage de luxe et de beauté, plage de fleurs....

Dixie: How much did you lose tonight?
Teddy: I don't know. What does it matter, anyway?
Dixie: You haven't a chance against a gambler like Zographos. You get too excited. What a cool oyster he is.
Teddy: I'll get it back tomorrow night.

Deauville, Deauville,
Sur ta rive enchantée on criot au bonheur.

Dixie: What are they singing about?
Teddy: Deauville.
Dixie: My God, I can hear that.
Teddy: Oh, there goes Le Megot. Let's ask her over.
Dixie: Don't you see enough of her when I'm not along?
Teddy: Don't be like that.
Dixie: Don't *you* be like that.

Deauville, plage d' amour
Deauville, divin séjour ...

Dixie: It made me sick to my stomach to see them shooting those live pigeons today. They haven't a Chinaman's chance.
Teddy: Everything makes you sick to your stomach these days.
Dixie: That's kidding on the square, too.
Teddy: Who's kidding? Oh, hello there!
Le Megot (*softly brushing by*): Ça va, mon chou-chou?

DIXIE: What's that?
TEDDY: What's what?
DIXIE: What she just said as she went by. Shoo-shoo.
TEDDY: How do I know?
DIXIE: Why don't you ask her sometime?
TEDDY: Lay off me.
DIXIE: You better lay off her. Her partner will put a knife between your ribs some day.
TEDDY: That would please you.
DIXIE: Immensely.

Deauville, Deauville,
Plage de luxe et de beauté, plage de fleurs.

~~~~~~~~~~~~~~~~

DEAUVILLE GRAND PRIX PAGEANTRY

Rieur (93 to 2 against).................... 1
Motrico (20-1)................................ 2
LeChatelet (8-1)............................. 3
L'Abbesse de Menin (60-1)............. 4

The Grand Prix de Deauville and 560,000 frs. were won today by M. Georges Wildenstein, with his 41 to 1 outsider, Rieur.

The Grand Prix marks the end of the "Grande Semaine", and the scene on the famous and pretty racecourse was a fitting climax. It was a great scene, the stands seething with animation; the most famous names in France, America and Britain chatting, and all equally excited; the gay silks of the jockeys; the beautifully garbed women moving across the lawns; and from the stands could be seen the great yachts in the new basin, with thousands of flags and pennants flying from their masts in honor of the day. It was an immense garden party.

~~~~~~~~~~~~~~~~

Hotel George V
Paris

Nita, old socks!

In Paris again, believe it or not. After one mad week in Deauville—a movie director's dream of black princes and white shoulders and red tennis courts and pink geraniums against a blue sea. Teddy wouldn't leave the Bar Du Soleil where you can dive from under a striped umbrella into the ocean and back to your cocktail without losing a drop. That is if you can get through the Maharajahs, African diamond merchants, American brokers and the cocottes de luxe, each a Baroness, no less, to hear her tell it.

Says Teddy, pushing me on the train, why should I leave here to look at a lot of skinny mannequins with clothes on? Get over your fittings or whatever you call it, and I'll come back to Paris and take you to Biarritz. O.K. says I, only on the condition that you stay away from the baccarat. So here am I and tonight I'm going to L'Escargot with Toohey, the Variety mug, and taste my first snails—fooey!

How are those dear Etats Unis? I found a month old Sunday paper in the lobby today and forgot all about a luncheon date at Armenonville in the Bois reading the funnies and what's even funnier the society news from poor old Newport where it seems my dear mother-in-law, Mrs. W. K., is doing herself proud these days giving stuffy parties for Teddy's deb sister Serena who will be brought out in November and I'll have to be there, worse luck. Teddy's father, it seems, is in London doing something about a new British oil company. I wish he'd come over to Paris and visit us. He's a swell guy, Nita, simple as an old shoe, for all his millions. I'm crazy about him, and he likes me too.

Nita, I don't know what to think. Maybe I'm just imagining things, but you remember I wrote to you just before I went to Deauville and said I was feeling funny. Well, it isn't so funny any more, and

I don't know what to do. I haven't said anything to Teddy—there'd be no sense in that anyway unless I was sure. Maybe I ought to go to a doctor and find out. I'm going to ask Toohey tonight how I can go about finding a good American doctor, although I suppose a French doctor could tell you just as well if you're going to have a baby or not. But they have such funny whiskers—French doctors, I mean, not French babies. Maybe it's twins— God's teeth! But wouldn't Teddy jump clear out of the ocean if he got a wire from me tomorrow saying you're going to be a father, poor boy. Telephone! Toohey downstairs, my guess, and I'm only half dressed.

S'long,
Dixie.

~~~~~~~~~~~~~~~~~~~~~~

```
                          DEAUVILLE
WEBBPAT
NEW YORK
IMPERATIVE YOU COMMUNICATE WITH MY
FATHER IMMEDIATELY STOP IN TERRIBLE
TROUBLE HERE WITH FRENCH AUTHORITIES
AS RESULT OF SUICIDE OF MARCEL A
DANCER WHO LEFT LETTER TO POLICE
CLAIMING MY INTIMACY WITH HIS
PARTNER LE MEGOT CAUSE OF HIS DEATH
STOP AM INNOCENT BUT BEING HELD HERE
PENDING INVESTIGATION CABLE ANSWER
HOTEL NORMANDY
                                PAGE
```

~~~~~~~~~~~~~~~~~~~~~~

                                    NEW YORK
PAGE
HOTEL NORMANDY
DEAUVILLE
FRANCE
ON RECEIPT YOUR CABLE LOCATED YOUR
FATHER IN LONDON AND TELEPHONED
HIM STOP HE IS FLYING TO DEAUVILLE
IMMEDIATELY KEEP ADVISED
                                    WEBBPAT

~~~~~~~~~~~~~~~~~~~~~

                                    PARIS
TEDDY PAGE
HOTEL NORMANDY
DEAUVILLE
JUST CAME FROM SEEING DOCTOR AT
AMERICAN HOSPITAL AND HE SAYS
CONGRATULATIONS LITTLE GIRL YOU ARE
GOING TO BE A MOTHER STOP ARE YOU
HAPPY TEDDY DARLING
                                    DIXIE

XII

						NEW YORK

W K PAGE
NORMANDY HOTEL
DEAUVILLE
FRANCE
HAPPY TO INFORM YOU WE HAVE MADE
ALL RESERVATIONS ACCORDING TO
INSTRUCTIONS FROM YOUR OFFICE HERE
FOR ILE DE FRANCE SAILING LE HAVRE
SATURDAY STOP VILLAR PURSER WILL
SUPPRESS NAMES OF YOUR PARTY FROM
PASSENGER-LIST AND FROM SHIP CABLES
OF PORT ARRIVALS AND TAKE EVERY CARE
OF YOU KINDEST REGARDS
					TILLIER
					FRENCH LINE

(From The Tatler)

    Many a night club owner in the Febrile Fifties is rubbing his hands with glee over the news that Playboy Teddy Page is back In town from Europe. He might be across the water yet if it hadn't been for the potent ministrations of his father who got him out of the Deauville police clutches and smuggled him and his show-girl bride, Dixie Dugan, back on the Ile de France under assumed names.

THE MEMOIRS OF PATRICIA PAGE

by

PATRICIA PAGE

(*To Be Opened Fifty Years After Her Decease*)

CHAPTER FOUR

I am sure the interested readers who will pour over these Memoirs fifty years from hence will be startled at the lack of interest in life by one so young as I, specially since apparently I seem to have everything to live for and am blessed with the advantages of wealth and social position. But the more discerning of these readers will see at a glance that when one's first young love is blighted then what price the world and its pleasures, specially when most of these pleasures are denied one because you are still considered a child although you have twice the brains of your sister who just because she is a couple of years older and is coming out gets all the cake while you must be content with the crumbs that fall from the table like Lazarus of old.

I had every intention of not going on with these Memoirs and letting them fall by the wayside but now that I am back in school again thanks to pressure from my family because the school wasn't so keen to have me after my escapade where I escaped from tirany and started off for Hollywood there to win fame and fortune but paused in Chicago long enough to meet my fate. Ah, Dimi, Dimi! When will these straining eyes see your beloved form again? So here I am once more interested in literary matters and determined to put down a faithful record of Memoirs so that many years from now these poor words of mine will faithfully mirror the morals and manners of my epoch.

First I will pass over lightly the usual summer anticks of my family in Newport where Mother gave a lot of stupid parties for sister

Serena leaving me out in the cold as usual. Nothing too good for her—but for me—only rags and ashes. So we will dismiss the summer as of no importance and Newport too which is a place where nothing much happens except the people eat off each other all summer and pass on to the present which is one continual uproar around the place. Pins everywhere you sit and pieces of this and snips of that and lists and fittings and piles of engraved invitations and secrateries addressing envelopes in a neat but not classy hand writing and telephones ringing all the time all over the place and Serena dashing off to the Junior League for lectures and field trips for provisional members as if a dumbell like Serena could ever make the grade and Mother saying get out of here and go to your room. Why you'd think I was a leper just because I tried on a few of Serena's dresses and if I do say so they looked better then than they'll ever look again. She could learn a lot about human desensy and the simple art of being just a regular person from Dixie my sister in law who is back from Paris with the spiffiest bunch of clothes you ever saw all of which she lets me try on and parade around the house in to my heart's content, proving once again that old adage kind hearts are more than cornets, etc.

Maybe I'll fall heir to some of these swell models even though Dixie hasn't said anything to me about it but I overheard Mother and Father discussing it when they thought I wasn't around but they promptly shut up and changed the subject when I hove into site because I'm still supposed to be an infant and believe in storks I presume or cabbages like that French song I used to learn in the nursery, which I call pretty hard luck getting a lot of lovely clothes from Vionnet and places like that and then find you can't wear them because you're going to have a baby with the possible exception of Reboux hats which look simply ducky on me when I push my hair back making me look at least 18 years old if not older. And don't I wish I was (were?)

The house seems to be full of secrets these days which I can get only snatches of by appearing unexpectedly where I'm not wanted so I still don't know just how father got Teddy out of that scrape in Deauville where somebody comited suicide just because he was jealous of Teddy which would puzzle an older head than mine but he did and I suppose Father bought off the French government which he has enough money to do because money is power as Dimi used to say.

Dear, Dear Dimi—where are you now? I see your somber black eyes and your pale studious face rise before me in stern accusation like Banquo's ghost which we are having in school these days worse luck. Out, Out, Dam spot, but I don't mean you Dimi Darling. Are you still working in that dark gloomy shipping room of the True Faith Book Concern sending out tracks to the heathens? Are you still toiling secretly and with dire determination to overthrow the capitalistical system of which I alas, am a useless member but lucky for me you don't know it. Will these tear dimed eyes ever feast themselves on your beloved face once more. I fear not, alas, and so ending on this despairing note I close the fourth chapter of my Memoirs.

~~~~~~~~~~~~~~~~

Hotel Scribe
Paris

Dixie darling,
Everything over here pretty much as you left it. Paris still buzzing over Marcel's suicide. You and Teddy pretty lucky to get out of the mess so easily. Ran into Jimmy the other night. He told me about meeting you down at Juan-les-Pins. Had just come back from Biarritz and is still gathering material for his society movie for Colossal your old outfit. Wanted to know if I would ask you to get together

some authentic inside dope on debutantes and what it costs to bring them out and how it's done, etc., and I told him it just happened there'd be one coming out in your family this fall and you'd be in a good spot to tell him all about it. Do you want to send it to me over here or to him direct care of New York office Colossal Films?

I had to get away in such a hurry to cover the collections over here while they were still fresh I didn't have a chance to talk to you as much as I wanted. Of course the family's thrilled about you going to have a baby. Now as to helping you to get your layette over here. It seems that's a foolish extravagance. There's a 90% duty on handwork and you can get practically the same thing for much less in New York at Kargère or Grande Maison de Blanc, etc. which specialize in that sort of thing. Write me care of the Chase Bank if there's anything else you want.

Love,
Nita.

~~~~~~~~~~~~~~~~~~~

<div style="text-align:right">New York City</div>

Nita darling,

You should see me in my new role of young society matron. I always associated that word with a generous waistline. Reminds me of that song "Careless Love." Where am I? Just now I'm in a new six room duplex on Park Avenue which the family has furnished for Teddy and me and the baby makes three. I'm sitting very pretty with the family these days. The old girl isn't so happy that I'm going to make her a grandmother but old W. K. is very pleased and is going to settle a lot of money on the little stranger which will probably ruin him twenty years from now just the way his father was spoiled. Nobody ever learns. Meanwhile I'm in a welter of new glassware, new linen, initials and servants and Teddy's mother who keeps coming up and rearranging the furniture and Teddy staggering home around four o'clock all tired out from a big day down on the Street. It seems he is a customer's man whatever that is. Something to do with digging up new accounts for one of the brokers who handled a lot of his father's business. Everyone is very thrilled over Teddy actually being at work. The family can hardly believe it. Teddy seems in a daze himself especially after we've been out on a late party and he has to be dragged out of bed in order to be at his office by nine-thirty. But I haven't much time to console him 'cause I have not only my own house to put in order which is lots of fun but I'm helping with teas for Serena who is coming out this month—that's going to be a real riot. Ever since we came home it's been one shindig after another, beginning with a party at Teddy's mother's place for the polo players out at Westbury last September. And what a party that was!

It was held one night on the grounds of the Page estate, an orchestra behind every tree and a tub of champagne in every bush and Teddy suggested pepping it up for the polo boys and the other guests by getting the Vanities troupe out there to do the fan dance number the way they did it in the show before the police objected. It seems the darlings wear nothing but the fans which they wave in an absentminded manner so Mrs. W. K. hired the whole troupe to come out after the show and at the very height of the festivities they danced out on the lawn in their birthday clothes and waved their fans. From that point on the party got completely out of control so much so that Mrs. Page hunted up the manager of the troupe and begged him frantically to take the girls away. He said he was sorry but he couldn't. And she says why not I'd like to know. And he says because the guests won't let them go. And that was only one incident of the party which seemed to scatter over a good part of Long Island until it finally wound up around eight o'clock in the morning.

The Tuxedo Autumn Ball was very tame in comparison, but very utterly ut and hoity-toity and of course Serena being a new deb she had to make her appearance at this or she simply wouldn't count. Even at that she barely got under the wire because while her mother is all right W. K. rates only because he has money. The next big spree was the opening of the Opera which really starts the season and gave me a chance to knock the other young matrons for loops with my new outfit from Paris. Well, I'd better wear the darling things while I can still get into them. Isn't that just my luck the first time I had a real wardrobe?

The Horse Show gave us another excuse to have flocks of dinners, before, during and after. It was loads of fun, and some of the riders, especially the foreign teams, were cute stuff. I was wishing you could meet them but I suppose you do pretty well yourself over in Paris. What else is there to report? I can't think of anything except to answer Jimmy's query about debutantes. As I told you before Teddy's family is bringing their daughter Serena out this month, just before Thanksgiving and since I'm right in the middle of the campaign I'm in a good spot to gather all the data Jimmy could ever hope for. Suppose I wait until after the big ball which is only a couple of weeks away and then I can either send you the whole thing or jot it all down and ship it direct to Jimmy. Judging from the elaborate preparations it looks like something for Cecil de Mille. Joseph Urban who does the Ziegfeld scenery is going to redecorate the Crystal Room of the Ritz. The ceiling will be covered with orchids, the walls and stairways lined with silver trees on which individual rosebuds—real ones—will be fastened, and 3000 engraved invitations are going out for the ball and supper to follow. You should have what it'll cost to wet down this mob with champagne.

DIXIE.

556 SOCIETY

JUNIOR LEAGUE OF THE CITY OF NEW YORK, INC.
221 EAST 71 STREET
NEW YORK CITY

Miss Serena Page
1053 Fifth Avenue
New York City.

Dear Miss Page:

Enclosed you will find an abridged summary of the current work for provisional members showing the time and place of the next two field trips. Please note the girls leave the Junior League promptly at ten o'clock sharp, so it would be well to get here about nine-thirty.

As you know, original papers are to be written by the provisionals on each field trip and will not be graded unless they are turned in on the days due.

Sincerely,
Margaret Sparrow.

BEHIND CITY SKYSCRAPERS

An Introductory Survey of Social Work
Offered by
The Provisional Members Comniittee
of the New York Junior League

(*The satisfactory completion of the course is necessary to qualify for membership in the Junior League. Any girl failing to pass the course will be dropped from Provisional Membership next October.*)

Thursday.

10:00 A. M. Trip to the House of Refuge Reformatory. The Committee will leave the Junior League promptly at 10:00 o'clock.

Tuesday.

10:00 A. M. Trip to an Industrial Plant (The National Biscuit Co.)

~~~~~~~~~~~~~~~~~~~~~~~~

Grande Maison de Blanc, Inc.
The Trousseau House of America

New York   Palm Beach   Paris

Mrs. Theodore Page
895 Park Avenue
New York City

18	plain slips and 18 dresses @ 7.50	$270.00
18	embroidered and lace trimmed @ 38.	686.00
2	Christening robes @ 300	600.00
24	long white skirts @ 16.50	396.00
2	Christening skirts @ 75	150.00
24	flannel skirts @ 9.50	228.00
24	silk and wool shirts at 1.50	36.00
24	plain flannel binders @ .65	15.60
1	Christening coat -	150.00
10	Silk bonnets @ 22.50	225.00
12	Lingerie bonnets @ 26.50	318.00
9	crepe de chine wrappers @ 21.50	193.50
6	Cashmere silk lined wrappers @ 17.50	105.00
18	Crepe de chine short sacques @ 12.50	225.00
20	Baby sweaters @ 5.75	115.00
12	Crepe de chine wrappers padded @ 22.50	270.00
12	Crepe de chine afghans to match @ 22.50	270.00

4	Crepe de chine carriage covers @ 110.	440.00
4	Pillow covers to match @ 42.50	170.00
10	Lingerie covers for basinette @ 58.50	585.00
24	Lingerie pillow slips @ 28.50	684.00
24	Plain hand hemstitched sheets @ 2.	48.00
12	Embroidered and lace trimmed blankets @ 12.50	150.00
18	Wrapping blankets @ 16.50 pair	148.50
18	Knitted afghans @ 10.50	94.50
12	Lace trimmed @ 20.	240.00
9	dozen diapers 18 x 36 @ 2. per dozen	18.00
9	dozen diapers 22 x 44 @ 3. per dozen	27.00
36	crib pads 17 x 8 @ .35	12.60
36	crib pads 27 x 40 @ .95	33.30
18	rubber sheets @ 1.65	29.70
18	Arnold knit night gowns @ 1.10	19.80
12	Arnold bath aprons @ 3.	36.00
	Total	$6,989.50

~~~~~~~~~~~~~~~~

Hello—hello—I want to speak to Mrs. Page. Hurry up.

This is Mrs. Page.

Oh, hello Dixie. Is this you Dixie? Hello.

Hello. Yes, who is it? What's the matter?

This is Pat.

Who?

Pat. Patricia. I'm Patricia. I'm so excited. I had to call you. Guess what's happened?

How can I guess?

You'd never guess. The family would kill me. Right on the corner. Right near the school. Isn't it thrilling?

What are you talking about?

Selling apples. I was going out for lunch with Theodora and I heard a voice say "Buy an apple for the unemployed" and even before I had time to look I knew that voice. Isn't it exciting? I nearly died. Well—Goodbye.

Wait a minute. What are you talking about? Don't you feel well?

Well? Wonderful! I'm so happy I can't stand it. Aren't you happy? Don't you think it's wonderful? Did you ever hear anything so thrilling?

No. Never.

I knew you'd think so. I knew you'd understand. I had to tell somebody. If the family ever knew they'd kill me.

Knew what?

What I've been telling you. Haven't you been listening?

Sure I've been listening. Every word.

Did you ever hear anything so romantic? Selling apples right near the school. Big red ones—five cents "Hey, little girl, buy an apple for the unemployed," he said, and then I turned and there he was.

Who?

Who? I've told you a dozen times. Dimi.

Oh, Dimi. What's he doing here?

Good grief. Didn't I tell you? Selling apples on the corner near the school.

I thought he lived in Chicago.

He's in New York now. Couldn't get any work in Chicago so he came here.

That was original.

Well, he had to do something. Now he makes two or three dollars a day and I'm going to get all the girls in school to buy their apples from him. Or maybe I'd better not. What do you think? He doesn't know who I am, you know.

Who does he think you are?

Just a little school girl.

Well, aren't you?

Well, he doesn't know I'm W. K. Page's daughter. He hates my father. He hates the whole capitalistical system. He'd hate me too. I'll have to be careful, won't I? Theodora promised not to give me away. She's just as thrilled as I am. Just to think that you know a real radical, she said, a real red. Isn't that just too wonderful.

Pat darling, do you think you should be talking to strange men on street corners?

Strange men? Dimi? Why, Dixie, how could you say a thing like that?

I'm sorry.

Poor Dimi. He's so unhappy and yet he's so fierce. We're going to arrange some way to have some more nice long talks together like we did in Chicago. We can't talk on the street corner—can we—and besides if they ever found out in school! I told Theodora if they said anything about me talking to Dimi we'd tell them I was getting material for a class theme on the problem of the unemployed. Isn't that a neat idea?

Listen, Pat—why don't you ask your mother to let you come and have tea with me some day after school and we'll talk it all over. Maybe I can suggest something. What do you think of that?

Oh, Dixie, that'll be just divine. We could talk about him for hours, couldn't we?

Sure.

He looks just the same, only thinner and paler and his eyes are bigger and blacker and he's still working for the Revolution and he says thousands of his comrades are going to march on City Hall and Wall Street carrying banners and demanding jobs and if the police cossacks interfere they'll kill 'em with their bare hands. Could I carry a banner, do you think? Wouldn't that be gorgeous? I'm so excited. I've got to go back to school now. I'm calling from the corner drug store. Maybe I should have bought an apple with this nickel but I had to tell you about Dimi. Did you ever hear anything so romantic?

Isn't it marvellous? What? Why I wasn't talking more than a minute. What? I haven't any more nickels. You're a mean woman and you'll never have any luck. Goodbye, Dixie, can't talk to you anymore. Haven't any more nickels. Goodbye!

XIII

Eight of the season's debutantes are pictured on this page. Immediately above is a photograph of Miss Serena Page, daughter of Mr. and Mrs. W. K. Page, of 1053 Fifth Avenue, who will be introduced on Thanksgiving Eve....

Miss Serena Page, daughter of Mr. and Mrs. W. K. Page, who will be a fashion model at the supper dance at Pierre's next Thursday for the Henry Street Visiting Nurse Service....

Miss Serena Page is a member of the Debutante Committee of the Victory Ball to take place Monday, November 10, at the Astor Hotel....

A special Debutante Committee selected to assist the Spinsters is composed of the Misses Mary Kelley, Louise Leeds and Serena Page....

Mrs. Lawrence Copley Thaw has asked Miss Serena Page to sell programmes at her Spence Musicale for the benefit of...

Among the provisional members of the Junior League this year are a number of the season's prettiest debs, including Miss Serena Page....

A TRIP THROUGH A BISCUIT FACTORY

by

SERENA PAGE

A biscuit factory is a place where crackers which ordinarily would be made by hands are made by machines, but in much bigger quantities than you can imagine would be possible to consume. This factory is only one of more than fifty scattered throughout the length and breadth of the land and makes dozens of different kinds of biscuits ranging from soda crackers up to the kind that have marshmallow fillings and covered up with chocolate. The girls are all dressed in aprons and the men in white jackets and present a pleasing appearance.

It requires many hundreds of men and women to make the crackers or biscuits as they are more commonly known in England, and the workers are allowed to eat as much as they please, which is quite humane when one considers the constant temptation of toothsome tidbits passing constantly in tempting array. It is quite a satisfactory feeling also to know that all these people are employed when otherwise they might be out of work like thousands that one reads about in the papers.

One is taken through the factory by a soft-voiced, well-mannered attendant in groups of fifteen or twenty beginning with the mixing rooms where all the dough is mixed and from there into the various rooms where automatic machinery rolls the dough and cuts it up into individual crackers or biscuits, as the case may be. These are put into the oven and baked and afterwards are assembled by deft-fingered girls with wide faces and high cheek bones who look as though they might be foreigners. They pack the biscuits into various sizes and shapes of boxes although the automatic machinery which seems almost human does most of the work.

Having tea can never be quite the same to one who has been through a biscuit factory because one will not only see the plate of tempting delicacies but will also remember all the processes which it takes to make these in tremendous quantities, which it is apparently necessary to bake in order to fulfill the desire of all those who would have cakes with their tea.

Serena Page,
Provisional Member,
Junior League.

---

895 Park Avenue
New York City

Dear Jimmy,

What would you like to know about debutantes? There isn't much to know. The annual crop in New York seems to be around two hundred. They average eighteen years old, but they seem much younger. They go to each other's teas and dinners given by their mothers and their mothers' friends, at Sherry's, or the Ritz or Pierre's or the Colony Club. They come out either at a tea, at a dinner dance or at a ball. This year it's mostly teas and dinner dances because a ball costs more and all the papas are down to their last three Rolls-Royces, and walk around talking to themselves about the market. The family usually turns over the details of bringing out the deb to a professional social secretary who has lists of all the so-called eligible young men, very few of whom are, and manages the whole affair for a fee plus what she can chisel from the florist, the hotel, the orchestra, etc. For this sum she makes out the list, sends out the invitations, advises the family when is the best time and what is the best place.

She sends out 3000 invitations to get 1000 attendance of which the deb and her family know less than a third. In addition there are a lot of crashers from Yale, Harvard, Princeton and Broadway. The biggest deb parties are during the Thanksgiving and Christmas holidays because a long collegiate stag line is assured.

What does an average debutante ball cost? From twelve to fifteen thousand dollars. That will get you the ball room at the Ritz for the evening, a Meyer Davis orchestra, supper for eight hundred at five smacks a head, champagne, flowers, tips, invitations, entertainment—not much, to be sure, and not very much champagne either. Of course the Ritz doesn't furnish the drinks and would be filled with well-bred amazement to hear about them. Sometimes when Mother is feeling ambitious she goes out and hires Moss and Fontana or Bill Robinson, or if she feels five thousand bucks worth of ambition she gets Chevalier who sings delightful dirty songs in a French that the debbies never learned in Finch or Miss Chapin's.

However, a real big riot like the one old W. K. is giving Serena Thanksgiving Eve will set him back that much for floral decorations alone. There are going to be electric fountains, two dance orchestras, a gypsy band, the ceiling will be covered with orchids, and the party won't cost less than fifty thousand bucks. Put that in your movie.

A typical day for a typical debutante, taking Serena Page for example, starts about ten thirty or eleven in the morning with breakfast in bed, toast in one hand and telephone in the other. She calls all her friends, asks each one how they liked the party last night, what are they going to do all day, and to which of the half dozen teas, luncheons and dinners they have been invited to their particular crowd is going. There are about twenty in a crowd and when one has been invited the trick is to get the rest of your crowd wangled in so you can have a good time. After breakfast she walks down Fifth or Madison with her chum, goes into all the shops, prices everything, buys nothing and then goes to lunch at whatever is the most fashionable place of the moment. After luncheon they go to the movies since they can't shop all the time, and always pick the balcony of a house where they can smoke. Here dozens of them collect every afternoon and they yell at each other all through the performance to which they pay no attention. They tell me all the little debbies used to pile into the Plaza Theatre on Fifty-Eighth Street but now they go to the balcony of Loew's Lexington. After the movies they scatter for the various teas. After the teas they rush home and dress for the various dinners. After the dinners they rush to the various supper dances, sometimes taking in two or three a night and meeting each other all over again. They dance literally from tea-time until dawn, and after a breakfast of bacon and eggs eaten either at the party or at Childs afterwards (and they would all much rather go to Childs just as they would rather go to Loew's Lexington), they go home, roll in, grab a few hours sleep before the telephone starts ringing, which will start them all over again for another day.

This goes on all through November and December, and by the time the Christmas holidays, which is no name for them, are finished, the little deb is too. So if she's real swank, she must go to Placid to rest, and then to Palm Beach soon after the first of the year to do it all over again, until it's time to come back to New York to do it all over again, until it's time to go to Southampton or Newport to do it all over again, until it's time to come into New York to do it all over again, and so on and so on and so on, until either she's married or goes in for a "career."

Does that help you? How does it fit in with the material you're gathering in Europe? Are you having fun over there? Did you get a lot of stuff? When is Colossal going to make the picture? Where? When are you coming back to New York? And if there is any more information you want about the social racket, ask dat ole dowager.

DIXIE.

Attention
Mr. James Doyle
Colossal Film Corp.
New York City.

(From The News)

TURKEY WEEK! DEBS SHOW FINE FEATHERS

Every train that puffs into town during the next few days will be crowded with collegians coming home to fill the stag lines and gladden the hearts of the debbies. Wise parents always have chosen the Thanksgiving and Christmas holidays as the ideal time to present a deb datter.

. . . On Thanksgiving eve, the whoopee begins in earnest with three large dances. Mr. and Mrs. W. K. Page will introduce their Serena at a supper dance at the Ritz-

> Turn bum times
> to boom times—
> BUY NOW.

Carlton that night; and Mr. and Mrs. . . .

~~~~~~~~~~~~~~~~~~~~~~

Dear Comrade Dimi,

My chum Theodora will give you this note because I am being watched in school on account of talking to you so much on the corner at lunch time, although I pretended I was trying to get material for a class theme on the unemployment situation and how many apples a day they sell. I am so thrilled you are going to make your big speech tonight at the big Red meeting at Bryant Park and this is to tell you that I am going to try and sneak out of the house and come to hear you because the family is going to a big party for my sister tonight at the Ritz. But even if I could go to the old party I would rather come and hear you make your big speech and be the first to ring your hand and congratulate you on your Noble work for the Cause, and maybe after the meeting we can go to a cafeteria and eat together and discuss Life the way we did in those "olden golden days" in dear old Chicago.

Your Comrade,
Pat.

~~~~~~~~~~~~~~~~~~

(From The Times)

REDS MARCH ON RITZ
POLICE HOLD SIXTEEN IN UNEMPLOYMENT CLASH
Many are injured in pitched battle.

(From The Daily Worker)

TAMMANY COSSACKS DEFENDS SACRED RITZ
FROM CONTAMINATION BY STARVING WORKERS
THOUSANDS OF DOLLARS FOR ORCHIDS
WHILE MILLIONS CRY FOR BREAD.

Jazz and Jeers Drown out Screams
of Trampled Women and Children.

(From The Evening Graphic)

PAGE SUB-DEB JAILED
AS REDS RIOT AT RITZ

(Story on Page Two)

(1) Start of march on Ritz by unemployed after fiery speeches in Bryant Park.
(2) Crowd outside Ritz watching three cops rush young Radical speaker into wagon.
(3) Patricia Page, sixteen-year-old daughter of W. K. Page, international banker, who joined Red march on Ritz debut party for her sister Serena.
(4) The Grand Ballroom of the Ritz which was decorated with thousands

of orchids for Serena Page's debut party, which is said to have had 3000 guests and cost over one hundred thousand dollars (as conceived by our staff artist).
(5) High hats and White Shoulders scurrying for safety in their limousines as cordons of police hold back milling mob.

~~~~~~~~~~~~~~~~~~~~~~~~

Dearest Dixie,

Many thanks for the darling Chanel necklace which helped to brighten my gloomy Christmas day far from home although I would hardly say loved ones. The necklace is just too divine and I appreciate it more than anything I got from my heartless parents who think they can buy me like Greeks bearing gifts. What did I do that was so terrible I should be banished from my home even on Christmas Day when all should be peace and good will? Sent away to this living death of a boarding school. What? Echo replies— What indeed?! But alas, such is the case. So there is nothing to do but suffer in silence beneath these slings and arrows of outrageous fortune and await the day when I will become of age to do with my life as I see fit.

There are a lot of poor wretches here who cannot get home for the holidays, but that is only because of geographical distance. They cannot understand why I must stay here and they glote over me because they are secretly envious of my stirring crusade against capitalistical tirany. Also they are green with envy over Dimi who alas is still in durance vile for all I know, after having been trodden by the hoofs of the Cossacks police because he had the courage to raise his voice against the wrongs of the working classes.

And what an eloquent voice my Dimi had as he stood up there in Bryant Park and urged his comrades to demonstrate against the bloted aristocrats who are grinding all of us into the dust of oppression. After he made his first speech I rushed up and rung his hand and as we stood and talked while another speaker leaped on the rostrom of empty apple boxes I told him how I had sneaked out of the house while my family was disporting themselves among the orchids of my sister's party at the Ritz. His eyes flashed fire and his white teeth snapped like a wolf. Orchids, he cried, orchids at the Ritz while we starve here behind the Public Library, so leaping again on the rostrom of empty apple boxes he pushed the other speaker away and cried Comrades do you realize while we are talking idly here thousands of the bloted oppressor class are reveling in orchids and swimming in champagne at the Ritz Hotel in this very city beneath our very eyes while we howl like hungry dogs outside the walls. Come, Comrades, let us not waste any more time in idle marches on the City Hall. Let us go and face the foe face to face. ON TO THE RITZ!

Well, Dixie, it was electrical the way that whole seething hord took up that cry, ON TO THE RITZ, and on they marched with Dimi and I being pushed and shoved along raising our voices together and screaming ON TO THE RITZ! Oh, it was thrilling! And then came the police on horses, and plain clothes detecktives and cops with clubs and armored motorcycles and there I was screaming outside the Ritz while inside Serena revelled in champagne and danced from the arms of one stag to another to the swooning strains of *Go Home and Tell Your Mother*.

Well, Dixie, that is the real truth how the whole thing started and how I found myself locked up in a jail cell next to Dimi, who was bleeding at every pore, when newspaper photographers found me and took flashlights until my father rushed lawyers to get me out and take me home to face a hysterical family, Serena screaming that she would scratch my eyes out for spoiling her debut, and Mother fainting all over the parlor from one chair to another, and Father saying sternly young lady this is too much, tomorrow you go away to boarding school. First it was Teddy, and now that he's settled down, it's you. The injustice of it all! The next day Serena's party was on the front page of every newspaper and everybody in her crowd said it was the hit of the year and accused my father's press agent of thinking the whole thing out to put her over in a big way! My Dimi should bleed and suffer to put her over! But that is the cruel injustice of this world. So Dixie I've made up my mind this fight will go on to the finish though they shut me up in a dozen boarding schools, for stone walls do not a prison make nor iron bars a cage. (Longfellow—I think.)

When the excitement around the house calms down enough will you please like the darling you are, go over and see if you can find my Memoirs if they haven't been destroyed and send them to me secretly so that I can work on them here during my inkarseration. Please do try to do that before you and Teddy leave for Palm Beach. Please. A Merry Xmas and a Happy New Year, and I hope you'll feel lots better when you get South.

From your unhappy little

PAT.

XIV

(From the New York Tab)

Jimmy Doyle, playwright, author of "Get Your Girl," returned from Europe last night on the S. S. "France," with the completed manuscript of a new picture for Colossal Films Corp. "The picture will be based on how society amuses itself here and abroad," said Mr. Doyle. It was also his opinion that France and Italy are arming for a new conflict and that the Russian Five Year Plan will fail.

SNAPPED IN THE SUNNY SOUTHLAND

(right)

BEAUTY: Mrs. Teddy (Dixie Dugan) Page on the sands of Palm Beach, enjoying . . .

(left)

BEAST: Alligator Joe—Barehanded he wrestles the grim saurians, prying open their dripping jaws and . . .

~~~~~~~~~~~~~~~~

DIMI ? ? ?
℅ THE TOMBS
NEW YORK CITY.

DEAR COMRADE IN ARMS,

You are languishing in durance vile and so am I, but where are our enemies? Ah! They are sunning their fat capitalistical selves on the shining sands of Palm Beach, little recking or caring that you are suffering for the Cause or that they have locked me up in this grusome boarding school, far from life and love and laughter, while they flit like butterflies in the sun, but we will not forget. I won't especially I can promise you, with Serena's scornful laugh still ringing in my ears as I was loaded on the train like a lot of cattle and shipped away, while she tripped off to Milgrim's with mother for her spiffy Palm Beach clothes, as if that could help her from being a total flop, in spite of Papa launching her in the matrimonial market with showers of orchids and torrents of gold.

But I know that you will be glad to hear that I am reaping a subtile revenge because I am sowing the seeds of social unrest and discontent among all the girls in the school each of which will be a sore spot in her home and a thorn in the circle in which she moves. And in this way I will continue to work for the Cause and you, Dimi dear as well as continuing my diary which I have decided not to keep secret for fifty years but have published right away so that it will be an inspiration to all other young butterflies who like me were fluttering vainly and foolishly in society's gilded net. For a time I thought it had perished and was forever lost to posterity. That was when all my effects were seized, but Dixie, my sister-in-law who is a darling, scrummaged through the house for me and found it about to be thrown away with a lot of old papers. Horrors! When she wrote and told me this, I nearly swooned. But that was nothing to the ecstasy with which I viewed my long lost child and poured once more over its pages. How are you? Do you have anything else to eat but bread and water? Would you be allowed to receive a box? The girls are all dying to help me fix one up for you with sandwiches and apples and fudge and whatever we can smuggle away from the table. I promise faithfully not to hide any knives or saws or ropes, although I read once about a girl who saved her inkarserated lover by baking a rope in a pie and smuggling it into him. Isn't that keen?

Your devoted Comrade,

Pat.

ROYAL POINCIANA HOTEL

Mr. Sol Nebbick
Colossal Films Corp.
Hollywood, Cal.

Dear Mr. Nebbick,

How about Palm Beach? I think we ought to have it in the movie. Combining business and pleasure this week by coming down here with the Artists and Writers and picking up material as well as looking over likely locales for good society whoopee shots. Some of them of course have been pretty well done, such as Cocoanut Grove and the beach shots, but there are some marvellous villas and private hideaways. Also we certainly should have shots of the Bath and Tennis Club, Bradley's, the Patio Lamaze and the Everglades Club.

Important! Dixie Dugan is down here. Ran into her at the Cocoanut Grove. She's with her husband and family. Had short talk with her and think there is still a chance of getting her for the lead if we're not in any rush, even though she turned us down cold in Europe. Have a hunch she is pretty well bored with this society racket. Will have a talk with her again and let you know.

Heard a swell story last night. Something that is supposed to have happened here last season or the season before. One of those grim bits of gossip that everyone swears is true but never gets into the papers. We might work it into the movie. It would be a sock!

It seems there was a party going on in one of the swank hotels in a corner suite some eight or ten stories up. The usual Palm Beach mixture of society, show folks, champion swimmers and divers, cabaret dancers from ritzy night clubs, everybody having fun and getting beautifully oiled. Long about two or three in the morning the party was zig-zag and gay and the boys and girls started to play children's games, "Ring-around-a-rosie," "Post Office," etc. Someone suggested

"London Bridge." Two well-known society men made the "bridge." A young Baron, handsome and penniless, but popular as only young Barons can be in Palm Beach, was "caught." The party danced round them in a circle singing. *"Take the key and lock him up—lock him up—lock him up,"* everyone shouting and laughing uproariously. They continued the song. *"Out the window you must go—you must go—you must go—out the window you must go,"* and the two men still laughing, picked the Baron up and swung him two or three times and then tossed him out through the open window. The party went right on, a few people wondering why the Baron didn't come back, but no one was sober enough to remember that it was a ten story drop to the sidewalk, until the house detectives and the police broke in. Next day the papers carried the story that Baron so-and-so had accidentally fallen to his death from the open window of his apartment in a local hotel.

Wouldn't that film like a million? No use trying to invent fiction when facts are better.

Sincerely,
JIMMY DOYLE.

THE BREAKERS
PALM BEACH

DARLING NITA,

The doctor just left. Had terrible cramps. I did—not the doctor. Gave me hell. Said I had to be home early every night and go to bed. Stop drinking. Stop running around. Or he wouldn't be responsible. Told him had to run around to keep track of Teddy and even then I could barely keep him in sight. If I don't go out with him, he goes out anyway. But you don't have to drink so much, says the wise old medico. And I says, who could sit through these dumb parties without drinking. Well then, you'd better stay home, says he. And I says, and be alone all the time? Teddy won't stay home. Teddy isn't going to have a baby, says the doctor. No, says I, he's up in the stands cheering while I carry the ball. I don't care where he is, says the doctor, I'm not worried about him. I'm worried about you. And then I says to him, honest, doctor, I don't enjoy running around to all these parties, but if I don't go, Teddy'll go with somebody else. Let him go, says he. All right, then says I, you're the doctor. I'll stay home and knit two purl two while Teddy goes out nights on the yachts in the harbor and rolls back mornings with the skinful of Bimini rum. That's a good girl, says he. Be good and you'll be happy, says he. Lonesome, says I.

So that's that. Meanwhile who should I meet the other day in the Cocoanut Grove but Jimmy. What are you doing here, says I. Same as you, says he. Having fun. Who told you I was having fun, says I. It said so in the papers, says he. I read it only this morning. "Among those who enjoyed themselves last night at the Hutton party were Mr. and Mrs. Teddy Page." I'm surprised at you, says I. In the newspaper racket yourself and still believing what you read. When are you going to grow up?

I tried being grown up once, says he, and it wasn't any fun, so I've gone back to my childhood. I'm down here playing in the sun just like you. I thought you were in Europe working, says I, getting material for a society movie. Oh, that's all finished, says he, and now I'm down here with the Artists and Writers. Golf tournament.

But you don't play golf, says I. Well, I lie in bed in the hotel mornings and read about it, says he, and then I go out and lie around on the beach and then I come back and lie around the Cocoanut Grove and then we all go out nights and lie around first one place and then another. We artists and writers come down here and do that once a year, by way of a change. We get tired lying around New York.

So does New York, says I. Funny, I haven't run into you at a party down here before. You will, says he.

I thought for a minute I'd tell him about the doctor and then I thought how silly it would sound with the orchestra playing *I Got Rhythm* and everybody dancing under the palms.

Oh, I'm so mixed up, Nita. One minute I'm glad I'm going to have a baby—the next I'm so tired of this silly empty life and realize the baby is going to tie me down to it tighter than ever, and then Jimmy comes along and all the old thrills come back and then I realize I'm married to somebody else, somebody who cares for me only as an amusing toy, and not so amusing now that I can't bounce around like mad the way I used to. And then I get mad and the madder I get the sicker I get, and the sicker I get the more hopeless everything seems, and then I cry my eyes out and come to after a while asking myself what the hell I'm crying about—married to a million dollars, living the life of Reilly, going to have a baby by a cute man who isn't mean—just crazy—and aren't we all?

So that's the way it goes, Nita, round and round—the same people—the same gossip—the same kind of dinners and teas and luncheons and parties and balls here or New York—New York or Paris—Paris or the Riviera—the Riviera or the Lido—and back to Paris and New York and Palm Beach—and round and round until—oh, damn everything! What's it all about, anyway? What the hell does it all mean? God, but I'm sick of it all—everything—everybody.

DIXIE.

THREE DROWN, TEN FEARED DEAD
IN BLAST ON PALM BEACH YACHT,
THIRTY RESCUED FROM WATER.

PALM BEACH, Fla. Thursday. (A.P.)—Death crashed a merry party given tonight by society folks to visiting artists and writers on the "Albatross", anchored in Palm Beach's gay harbor. Death drank and danced with the doomed—then flicked a lighted cigarette. A sheet of flame swept the deck, an explosive roar shook the harbor, and three lives were snuffed out, as women in evening dress and men in gay flannels leaped or were thrown into the water in a mad panic of fear.

THE DEAD

NIXON, MRS. T. JUDSON
    Prominent in New York and Boston society.
DOOLEY, DOLORES
    Dancer in a Palm Beach Night Club.
LARSEN
    Sailor.

    Almost before the echoes of the explosion died away, boats were put out from neighboring yachts at anchor, and as searchlights picked out the struggling survivors they were taken out of the water. Those suffering from burns and shock were rushed to the West Palm Beach Hospital.
    The others, grateful to be alive, hurried home, chilled with horror, to talk over their miraculous escape from one of the most shocking tragedies that has ever saddened this coast of pleasure.
    Mrs. Teddy Page, better known on Broadway and in Hollywood, as Dixie Dugan, is one of the most serious sufferers from shock in the West Palm Beach Hospital. Her condition is described as critical. . . .

~~~~~~~~~~~~~~~~~~~

NURSE: More flowers for 11! Get me a vase, handsome.

INTERNE: Get it yourself, beautiful. I've got to take the temperature in 24.

NURSE (*sweetly*): Well, I haven't any, big boy. Hands off!

INTERNE: Just washed them and can't do a thing with them.

NURSE (*reading*): "Please get well. Stop your fooling. Jimmy." I thought she was Mrs. Teddy,

INTERNE: Two-timing is not exclusively a plebeian pastime, my love.

NURSE: Don't be an ass. You don't hop around two-timing when you're seven months.

INTERNE (*airily*): Well, she won't have to worry about that any more.

NURSE: Poor kid.

INTERNE: Lucky, I'd say.

NURSE: Say, I suppose you think it's a lark for a girl to carry a baby seven months and then lose it.

INTERNE: She's damned lucky these ain't lilies. And she's not out of the woods yet. Are you off tonight?

NURSE: Yes. Off you. My God, there's 14 ringing again, the old witch.

~~~~~~~~~~~~~~~~

```
                            NEW YORK CITY
    MRS TEDDY PAGE
    WEST PALM BEACH HOSPITAL
    WEST PALM BEACH
    FLA
    JUST READ DREADFUL NEWS IN PAPER
    FAMILY WORRIED SICK PLEASE IF YOU
    CAN HAVE SOMEONE WIRE MOTHER HOW YOU
    ARE I AM CATCHING NEXT TRAIN LOVE
                                     NITA
```

~~~~~~~~~~~~~~~~

```
                            WEST PALM BEACH
        MRS DUGAN
        439 FLATBUSH AVENUE
        BROOKLYN NEW YORK
        DIXIE GETTING ALONG AS WELL COULD BE
        EXPECTED AFTER FRIGHTFUL SHOCK AND
        DEATH OF BABY STOP TEDDY'S FATHER
        AND MOTHER HERE DOING EVERYTHING
        POSSIBLE FOR HER STOP I SEE HER
        EVERY DAY AND SHE ASKED ME TO BE
        SURE AND TELL YOU NOT TO BE WORRIED
                                    JIMMY DOYLE
```

~~~~~~~~~~~~~~~~~~~~

Nurse: Right in there, Miss Dugan. But you mustn't let her talk too much.

Nita (*tiptoeing in softly*): Dixie. Dixie, honey.

Dixie: Nita! (*starting to cry*) Nita . . .

Nita (*kissing her*): There, there. I thought you were glad to see me. You mustn't cry or I'll go right away.

Dixie: Don't go. I'm not crying. Oh, Nita, I'm so glad to see you. Did Mother come too?

Nita: No. I jumped on the first train. Jimmy told me he wired her you were getting along all right.

Dixie: Jimmy—I wouldn't have been here if it weren't for Jimmy—he was the one who jumped in after me and held me up until a boat came along and then the next thing I woke up here and they told me my baby . . .

Nita: Dixie . . . sweet . . . you mustn't cry any more . . . don't cry . . .

Dixie: I can't help it. I didn't want to go on that party but Teddy said he was going anyway and he kept on drinking all night and

I wanted to go home and then all of a sudden there was an awful explosion and it looked like everything was on fire all at once and ...

Nita: You mustn't talk any more, Dixie. Just rest. Everything's going to be all right. Teddy wasn't hurt, was he?

Dixie: No—just scorched a little. Scared mostly. The water sobered him up. Somebody fished him out and put him to bed. He was here next morning. Been here most of the time ever since. His father, too. And mother. And Jimmy. Those flowers are from him.

Nita: Teddy?

Dixie: Jimmy. I don't want to ever see him again!

Nita: Who? Jimmy?

Dixie: No, Teddy. I'm through. I told him so too. And his father. I told him I only stuck to him this long on account of the baby but now that the baby is ... that I'm not going to have ... Oh, Nita, I did want it so. I was willing to stand almost anything—I wanted my baby so—Teddy drinking and running after other women—even in Europe after he had been Le Megot's lover I took him back only because of the baby, and I told him so, too, after his father begged me over there to stick to him and try to make a man of him and I did stick and his father said only this morning he was grateful to me and sorry for me, too, and he'd see that everything came out all right, but how is he going to make everything all right now? It's all ruined and I'm ruined and what have I got to live for—I don't want to live—why couldn't I have died too?

Nita: Sis, darling, don't! Everything's going to be all right. You'll see.

Dixie (*sobbing*): All right! How? How can anything be all right again? Ever?

Nurse (*at door*): I'm sorry, but I'm afraid you'll have to go now, Miss Dugan.

XV

                              HAVANA CUBA
MURFITZBERG
NEW YORK
MY SON AND DAUGHTERINLAW WISH TO
OBTAIN DIVORCE QUIETLY AND QUICKLY
AS POSSIBLE STOP COMPLETE AGREEMENT
NO CONTEST STOP RENO OUT OF QUESTION
ACCOUNT UNPLEASANT PUBLICITY STOP
PLEASE ADVISE SEVILLA BILTMORE
HAVANA
                                  W K PAGE

MURPHY, FITZGIBBONS AND BERGMAN

1 WALL STREET
NEW YORK

Mr. W. K. Page
Sevilla-Biltmore
Havana
Cuba

Dear Mr. Page:
   Following receipt of your cable we communicated immediately with the office of Roberto Haberman, who specializes in obtaining

divorces in Mexico. Where there is no contest and both partes submit to the jurisdiction of the Mexican Court either in person or by Power of Attorney, these divorces are valid in the United States. Incompatibility is sufficient ground and no proof is necessary, the Mexican Courts holding with commendable sagacity that incompatibility cannot be proved. You will receive direct from his office the necessary papers to be executed and his representative in Havana will call on you and assist you.

Awaiting further instructions, we remain

Very truly yours,
MURPHY FITZGIBBONS AND BERGMAN.

Special Power of Attorney

KNOW ALL MEN BY THESE PRESENTS that I, THEODORE PAGE, 31 years of age, by occupation a broker, a resident of the City of New York, State of New York, U. S. A., and with full capacity to enter into contractual and other legal obligations, have made and appointed, and by these presents do make and appoint Licenciado IGNACIO LOPEZ my true and lawful attorney in fact, for me and in my name to appear for and represent me before the Courts of Justice of the State of Morelos, Republic of Mexico, in a certain action for absolute divorce instituted against me by my wife, DIXIE DUGAN, giving and granting unto my said attorney full power and authority to submit me expressly to the jurisdictiom of the said Courts of the State of Morelos and to that of all the authorities in the Republic of Mexico, clearly and conclusively waiving the jurisdiction of the laws and authorities of my domicile in the terms and articles 150 and 152 of the Code of Civil Procedure of the State of Morelos; to file the necessary appearances in my behalf; to sign and present any petition, motion or other papers relating to this action; to present witnesses and to challenge those of the opposing party; to be present at any hearing or meeting of conciliation and to state my irrevocable determination to prosecute this action to its conclusion; to examine and absolve the opposing party with respect to interrogatories; to accept service of all papers in said action; to interpose all classes of remedies, including that of the writ of guarantees (amparo de garantias) and to abandon them; to request the issuance of all copies of motions or other papers and to make publication of same in the Official Bulletin; to solicit the legalization of the signatures of any of the authorities, be they judicial, consular or administrative; and generally to act or accomplish any matters whatsoever as I might or could if personally present; with full powers of substitution; hereby ratifying and confirming and holding valid all that my said attorney shall lawfully do or cause to be done by virtue of these presents.

GIVEN AND SIGNED in the City of Havana, this — day of March, 1931.

10 WEST 10 STREET
NEW YORK CITY

Mr. W. K. Page
Sevilla-Biltmore
Havana
Cuba

Dear Sir:

Acting on the advice of your attorneys Murphy, Fitzgibbons and Bergman, am enclosing two copies of Power of Attorney, one for your son and one for your daughter-in-law, to sign and authenticate before the Mexican Consulate in Havana.

These are to be mailed to Roberto Haberman, Cuernavacca, Morelos, Mexico. Any time after the receipt of these papers, your daughter-in-law, Mrs. Page, or Dixie Dugan as she will be known in the action, can come to Cuernavaca, where Mr. Haberman will meet her and will expedite her divorce. By appearing personally, Mr. Haberman will take her to the Presidente Municipal where for a payment of 18 pesos poll tax she will be enrolled on the list of the residents of the town, and immediately after file complaint for her, following which she can return at once to Havana. No other appearance will be necessary and the Decree will be granted within ten days and forwarded to Mexico City to be authenticated by the Consulate of the United States and which will be mailed direct to you in Havana or New York as you wish.

We understand of course that there are no children, no distribution of real property involved and the grounds for the action will be incompatibility and there will be no contest.

With renewed assurance of our esteem, we remain

      Faithfully yours,
      Roberto Haberman
       by
        Milton E. Friedland.

COPIA CERTIFICADA DE LA SENTENCIA DEFINITIVA DICTADA EN EL JUDICIO DE DIVORCIO NECESARIO PROMOVIDO POR LA SENORA DIXIE DUGAN EN CONTRA DEL SENOR THEODORE PAGE.

Cuernavaca, Mor. March 12, 1931.

(TRANSLATION)

CITIZENS LICENCIADO SALVADOR ALVAREZ AND EZQUIEL SALCEDO, JUDGE AND SECRETARY RESPECTIVELY OF THE COURT OF THE FIRST INSTANCE OF THE CIVIL BRANCH OF THE FIRST JUDICIAL DISTRICT OF THE STATE OF MORELOS WITH RESIDENCE IN CUERNAVACA,

CERTIFY: That in the records of the action for absolute divorce instituted in this Court by Licenciado Roberto Haberman, as the duly appointed legal representative of Mrs. Dixie Dugan Page, against Mr. Theodore Page, there is a judgment which, with the order which makes it final, is as follows:

That this action for absolute divorce has proceeded regularly and Mrs. DIXIE DUGAN PAGE has proven her case, and the defendant, Mr. THEODORE PAGE, did not oppose nor prove any exceptions. . . . SECOND. The marriage contracted between Mrs. DIXIE DUGAN and Mr. THEODORE PAGE, in the City of Las Vegas, State of Nevada, United States of North America, on the 23 day of April in the year nineteen hundred and thirty, is hereby declared conclusively dissolved. THIRD. The wife recovers her full legal rights and both parties are free to contract new marriages when this decree becomes final. . . . FOURTH. Make this known, and as soon as this decree becomes final, let certified copies be issued at the expense of the interested parties so that they may be recorded in the Civil Register. . . . Thus at a final hearing Licenciado Salvador Alvarez, Judge of the

First Instance of the Civil Branch of the First Judicial District of the State of Morelos conclusively adjudged and signed this decree. . . . Attest: S. Alvarez. E. Salcedo, Sec'y. . . . Signatures . . . Cuernavaca, Morelos, the eighteenth day of March, in the year nineteen hundred and thirty-one.—Upon the submission of a written petition by Licenciado Roberto Haberman, legal representative of Mrs. DIXIE DUGAN, soliciting that the decree of absolute divorce made on the 12 day of the current month be declared final, there having been no appeal therefrom within the time allowed by law; and it appearing from the records that no appeal has been taken from such decree, under the provisions of article 21 (twenty-one) of the Constitutional Law of Divorce of the State, let it be adjudged, and it is so adjudged:—

FIRST. The decree rendered on the twelfth day of March, in the year nineteen hundred and thirty-one, in the action for absolute divorce brought by Licenciado Roberto Haberman in the name of Mrs. DIXIE DUGAN against Mr. THEODORE PAGE, is hereby declared final. Make this known and issue the certified copies referred to in the fourth paragraph of the judgment herein, and let this order making this decree final, be added to the record.—Thus Citizen Licenciado Salvador Alvarez, Judge of the First Instance of the Civil Branch of the First Judicial District of the State of Morelos, adjudged and signed this final decree. . . . Attest: S. Alvarez.—E. Salcedo, Sec'y. Signatures. . . .

UNITED MEXICAN STATES, FEDERAL DISTRICT: CONSULATE GENERAL OF THE UNITED STATES IN MEXICO CITY.

I, William J. Brown, Vice-Consul of the United States of America at Mexico City, Mexico, duly commissioned and qualified, do hereby certify that Jose Santos, whose signature and official seal are respectively subscribed and affixed to the document hereto annexed, was on the 19 day of March, 1931, the day and date thereof, Secretary of

Interior, United Mexican States, to whose official acts faith and credit are due.

IN WITNESS WHEREOF, I have hereunto set my hand and affixed the seal of this Consulate General at Mexico City, Mexico, on this 20 day of March, 1931.

(SEAL)   WILLIAM J. BROWN
Vice-Consul of the United States of America at Mexico City, Mexico
Service No. 9893, Fee No. 68, two dollars, equal to 4.76 pesos.
                                             (STAMP)

SEVILLA-BILTMORE
HABANA

DEAR DIXIE,

My attorneys in New York inform me that the final decree has arrived from Mexico and I have instructed them to deliver it to you. As I told you during our long talks together in the hospital, and afterwards here in Havana, I have been touched beyond words by your fairness toward my son and all of us, and always you will have a place in our hearts even though we have lost you. My son is heart-broken that I insisted upon upholding you in your desire for freedom and assisted you to obtain it, but then he has only himself to blame, as he well knows and would be the first to admit. You did everything you could to make this marriage a success, and you will always have our gratitude, his mother's and mine, but you are still a young girl with all your life before you, and surely will find the happiness you so richly deserve.

And now I have one last request which you must not refuse. While I admire your spirit and independence in refusing any alimony or settlement, I cannot allow you to be a victim unnecessarily of your own generous nature, so I have arranged to put in trust for you a sum sufficient to guarantee you a life income of approximately $10,000 a year. When my attorneys deliver the decree to you they will ask you to sign the papers relative to this financial arrangement, and I know you will do me this last favor and sign them.

One thing more. If ever there is anything I can do for you, do not hesitate to call on me, as though you were my own daughter—which I sincerely wish you were.

Good luck!
W. K. PAGE.

```
                              HOLLYWOOD CAL
MORRIS NEBBICK
COLOSSAL FILMS CORP
PARAMOUNT BUILDING
NEW YORK CITY
SEE BY PAPERS DIXIE DUGAN HAS
DIVORCED PAGE STOP THIS MAY MEAN
OPPORTUNITY FOR US TO GET HER FOR
STAR ROLE IN SOCIETY PICTURE BY
DOYLE STOP WOULD BE DOUBLY VALUABLE
TO US NOW ON ACCOUNT PUBLICITY STOP
SEE HER AT ONCE OR BETTER YET SEND
DOYLE TO PUT PROPOSITION UP TO HER
STOP HOLDING UP PRODUCTION PLANS
HERE PENDING REPLY ADVISE PROMPTLY
                              SOL NEBBICK
```

                                    NEW YORK CITY
SOL NEBBICK
COLOSSAL FILMS CORP
HOLLYWOOD CAL
HAVE SEEN DIXIE WHO AGREES TO PLAY
LEAD IN SOCIETY PICTURE PROVIDED
TERMS ARE AGREEABLE AND SHE CAN HAVE
THREE MONTHS REST TO RECOVER FROM
ILLNESS BEFORE STARTING STOP WILL
REPORT HOLLYWOOD FOR PRODUCTION IN
JULY STOP WIRE ME IF THIS MEETS WITH
YOUR APPROVAL AND I WILL COMMUNICATE
WITH HER
                                    JAMES DOYLE

(From The New York Times)
SERENA PAGE
ENGAGED TO WED.

Mr. and Mrs. William K. Page of 1053 Fifth Avenue and The Oaks, Westbury, L. I., have announced the engagement of their oldest daughter, Miss Serena, to Godfrey Scroggins Ross, youngest son of Mr. and Mrs. Charles Graham Ross of this city and Southampton, L. I. Miss Page was graduated from the Chapwell School, is a member of the Junior League and a debutante of last season. Mr. Ross was graduated from Harvard and the Columbia School of Architecture. He is a member of the Harvard, Knickerbocker and Racquet & Tennis Clubs.

SOCIETY

Miss Georgiana Totten
478 Madison Avenue
New York City

May 16, 1931.

Mr. W. M. Willy,
Maître d'Hôtel,
Ritz-Carlton Hotel,
New York City.

Dear Mr. Willy:
Miss Totten has asked me to confirm the reservation of the Main Ball Room for a coming out supper-dance, to be given by Mrs. William K. Page for her daughter, Patricia, on Thanksgiving Eve, November 26.

Very truly yours,
Agnes Adams,
Secretary to Miss Totten

(From The Herald-Tribune)
**NEWPORT SEASON
TO BE BRILLIANT**
**Mrs. W. K. Page Among Early
Arrivals—Plans Parties for
Deb Daughter Patricia . . .**

(From Walter Winchell's Column)

. . . the dirt in Dixie Dugan's new society picture opening Monday night is the real McCoy . . . . the third gel from the left In Earl Carroll's Fannyties is Teddy Page's new heart . . .

SMASHING HIT!
DIXIE DUGAN
in
Society Girl

A Sensational Expose of the Haut Monde At Play.

ASTOR THEATRE
CRITERION THEATRE

Ex-Society girl scores stunning triumph in double gala opening last night ... A Colossal Picture ... a Sol Nebbick Production ...

A new Dixie Dugan ... the little show girl grows older ... mature, wise, touching ... (*RICHARD WATTS, JR.—HERALD TRIBUNE*).

Dixie Dugan, after last night's astonishing performance, rightfully takes her place among the great actresses of the screen ... (*MORDUANT HALL—TIMES*).

Dixie Dugan has lived since her last performance on the screen. Of that you may be sure, for only suffering could ripen a young fresh talent to produce the genius that glowed on the screen last night ... (*IRENE THIRER—NEWS*).

(From The New York Tab)
SUCCESS!

Dixie Dugan, surrounded by flowers and admirers, on the French Line pier last night. "I have no plans," said the young star, "I am going to travel and rest." Meanwhile, her picture "Society Girl" is crowding two houses on Broadway ... also sailing last night was James Doyle, playwright and happy author of Dixie's successful vehicle. ...

~~~~~~~~~~~~~~~~~~~~~~~

```
                                        S/S PARIS

NITA DUGAN
439 FLATBUSH AVENUE
BROOKLYN NY
                         WHEEEEEEEE
                            DIXIE AND JIMMY.
```

~~~~~~~~~~~~~~~~~~~~~~~

ACKNOWLEDGMENTS

The publisher extends his profuse thanks to the following individuals for their generous financial support which helped to defray some of the cost involved in the production of *The Dixie Dugan Trilogy*:

Edward Abbott, Alan J Abrams, Samuel T. Adams,
Stephanie Alsworth, Kristen Altmann, Kate Alyssa, Tom Aston,
Thomas Young Barmore Jr, Nick Barry, Barry Bedrick,
Ron Beiswanger, Traci Belanger, Kian S. Bergstrom, Sam Bertram,
Brad Bigelow (The Neglected Books Page), Gavin Bloch,
Gina Boiardi, Brian R. Boisvert, David Brownless, Matt Bucher,
Elaine M. Cassell, Rod Chen, Scott Chiddister, Greg Cobb,
Eric L. Collette, J Conlon, Jeff Conner, S Costa, James Crossley,
Malcolm & Parker Curtis, Edward De Vere, Travis DeSilva,
Craig Duckett, Curtis B. Edmundson, Isaac Ehrlich, Myrhat Eliot,
Lauren Fairbanks, Dr Michael A Feldman, William D Ferry,
Randy Fields, Frederick Filios, Zack Fissel, Jean Fischer,
Brennan FitzRoy, Nathan Friedman, Nathan "N.R." Gaddis,
Beth Ann Gallagher, E Gaustad, David George, Joe Gillis,
Thomas Gladysz, Damian Gordon, Jason Gray, David Greenberg,
Everett Haagsma, Ryan Ronald Hertel, Aric Herzog,
Tom Hochman, Dave Holets, Conor Hultman, Christopher Hyde,
Mike Hynek, GMarkC, Sahil Jain, Peter J. Jansen, Greg Jarrett,
Erik T Johnson, Fred W Johnson, Jacob H Joseph, Andrew Kaplan,
Jennifer Keenan, Keric, Jimmy LaPointe, The Great Brian Last,
J. A. Lee, Frederic Lepage, Gardner Linn, JacqueLyn Lobelle,
Paul & Eileen Lutz, Elizabeth Lynch, Peter MacDougall,

ACKNOWLEDGMENTS

Erin Maher, Keith and Cheri Martin, Jim McElroy, Ms. McKayla McHugh, Kelly McMahon, BT McMenomy, Jack Mearns, Dr. Melvin "Steve" Mesophagus, Artie Miller, Jason H Miller, Jody Mock, Spencer F Montgomery, Geoffrey Moses, Gregory Moses, Luke Douglas Mosher, Scott Murphy, Colin Myers, Naticia, David Neel, Paul Nightingale, Mr. Noodle, Richard Novak, mr.chrisvia@gmail.com, Michael O'Shaughnessy, Joseph P. Ohlenbusch, Matt Patrick, Andrew Pearson, Travis Pelkie, Andrew Pepoy, Micheal Jeramy Lee Perez, Peter Rockwell Petto, PhantomOfTheKnight, Robert Pirkola, zasu pitts, Pedro Ponce, Michael Pritchard, Ned Raggett, Myles R. Reagan, Judith Redding, Kevin Rollason, Blair Roberts, Roxanne, Steve Ruffin, julius ruskin, Kian Ryan, Dave Samuelson, Diane Sanders, David W. Sanderson, Suzanne Scherrer, Jason Seaver, K. Seifried, Bill Shute, Jonathan Sieders, Alexander Silva-Sadder, Robert E. Slaven, Kelly Snyder, Yvonne Solomon, Elijah Kinch Spector, K. L. Stokes, David Streitfeld, Michelle and Perry Swenson, Stephen Tabler, Zachary Tanner, Jacob Tashoff, Steve Tomasula, Elisa Townshend, Zachary Clemmitt Tredwell, William True, Tim Tucker, Rob Turner, Sydney Umaña, Edmund Vosik, George Watt, Elizabeth Weitzman, Christopher Wheeling, Leanne Whelan, Isaiah Whisner, Trainor Houghton Whyte, Charles Wilkins, Jeffrey R. Williams, Jeff Wilson, Lance Wilson, Nicholas Wolf, T.R. Wolfe, Sara Zeglin, The Zemenides Family, and Anonymous